Fabulous
8

Fabulous 8

BUDDY ATKINSON

Copyright © 2021 by Buddy Atkinson

All rights reserved. No part of this publication may be reproduced, distributed, or transmitted in any form or by any means, including photocopying, recording, or other electronic or mechanical methods, without the prior written permission of the copyright owner and the publisher, except in the case of brief quotations embodied in critical reviews and certain other noncommercial uses permitted by copyright law. For permission requests, write to the publisher, addressed "Attention: Permissions Coordinator," at the address below.

ARPress
45 Dan Road Suite 5
Canton MA 02021

Hotline: 1(800) 220-7660
Fax: 1(855) 752-6001

Ordering Information:
Quantity sales. Special discounts are available on quantity purchases by corporations, associations, and others. For details, contact the publisher at the address above.

Printed in the United States of America.

ISBN-13:   Paperback   979-8-89389-477-6
               eBook   979-8-89389-481-3

Library of Congress Control Number: 2024918470

Table of Contents

Chapter 1

There was a brother and a sister.

Jenny and I were in the same class together in the ninth grade. Both of us were on the honor roll with As and Bs. Jenny's friends were Bella, Tammy, and Angie. They had been best friends ever since they were little. All four of them were cheerleaders for the football and basketball teams. They also played softball, basketball, tennis, gymnastics, and hockey. Jenny was a brunette with blue eyes, Bella was blonde with blue eyes, Tammy had auburn red hair with green eyes, and Angie had reddish-blonde hair with green eyes. We also had another sister.

My name is Buddy. I had three friends; two of them were my cousins, James and Clay, and the other friend was Shon. We played football, basketball, baseball, and hockey for Drysdale High School. It was about five miles from Chicago. I had black hair with brown eyes, James had blond hair with green eyes, Shon had brown hair with brown eyes, and Clay had blond hair with blue eyes.

Shon and I played hockey together. I had twenty-five goals and fifty assists this season. Shon had twelve goals and thirty assists. I had three goals and two assists when I was kicked out of the game for hitting a defenseman so hard that they had to put him in a hospital. The official said to the commissioner of the hockey league that they had to suspend me for three games, but instead they suspended me for six games. Jenny and her friends were upset; Shon told them I had to pay for that hit! I saw the game; I was the defenseman on our team, and the referee had already put the penalty on me when I hit him; it took the penalty off me. We lost the game that night, six to five in the overtime.

We wanted to date other people during high school because we saw each other every day. James started to date a girl name Rosie; she was blonde with green eyes. He liked her very much and was dating her on and off. Jenny was dating a guy named Jack while Tammy was dating Kevin and Clay at same time. We didn't know they were dating; they hid it from us for three months. Angie was dating a guy named Billy before he moved to Washington, DC.

We won the state championship in football, basketball, baseball, and hockey in the first year of high school. We won the state championship in football with ten to zero. Then we won the state championship. It was Drysdale's first state championship in thirty years for football.

I told my sister that her friends were hot! Shon and my sister had been dating for a long time, since she'd broken up with Jack, and they were still dating. They weren't the only ones. Clay had been dating Angie for six months. Bella asked my sister about me dating anybody. She told Bella that her cousin Lauren always said that she and Tammy didn't want to date me. She never asked me, until I heard her and my sister talking in her bedroom. I wanted to kiss her, but then she was dating Becky and the summer was about over.

We were fixing to go into the tenth grade, and getting ready to win another state championship for our second year. Our parents always took a week off to go to the beach, so we decided to go to Myrtle Beach and enjoy ourselves. Meanwhile, we were talking about what college we were planning to attend. We decided to go to Florida State, but some of our friends wanted to go to other colleges. Jenny, Bella, Tammy, and Angie went on to the beach without us. They were lying out in the sun while we rode on jet skis. Our parents, Judy and Steve, went, too, and were walking on the beach, holding hands and talking.

James and I approached the girls and we talked about Clay and Angie. We already knew about Shon and Jenny. We should have known this would happen. Jenny said to Bella, "You've liked Buddy since second grade, and now it's tenth grade." Bella didn't respond.

Bella and I decided to go to Florida State. Tammy, Jenny, James, and Clay said they wanted to go to Clemson. Shon wanted to go to South Carolina, and Angie wanted to go to Miami. Our second choice was Hawaii. Everybody decided to go to Hawaii.

School was starting back and we had a game on Friday. James and I were partners on a project. It was the first day of the school year, and we had until October to finish it. We asked Mrs. Beltzur if we could make it a group project with teams of four, and she said, "That sounds like a good idea." James and I were thinking about asking Bella and Tammy to be partners with us, but Steve and Kevin asked them before we could. Clay and Shon got Angie and Jenny with them. So we asked some other girls, Brittney and Lauren, to be our partners, and they agreed. They were gorgeous, and we eventually asked them out on a date. We wanted to make Bella and Tammy jealous. We knew they were upset. I knew Bella was in love with me. She didn't know we would ask Brittney and Lauren out. That's why they said yes to Steve and Kevin.

Well, Friday was here, and we had been practicing. Everybody asked if we would be champions again, and our coach said, "We will!" We started our season with a bang! Our first game was against the team we'd played in the state championship, and we won thirty-seven to twenty-four. Our quarterback had his best game that night. He threw thirty-four/forty-five for four hundred and eight yards and three touchdowns. Then he had twelve carries for a hundred and twenty-five yards and two touchdowns. Our punt returner had a good night, and our defense had seven sacks and three interceptions. Our special teams were playing really well. We played every Friday night and won every game.

As our projects were due, I was dating Lauren, who had red hair with green eyes, and James was dating Brittney, who had blonde hair with bluish-green eyes. We dated them almost the whole school year. I saw Bella and Tammy every day; they come to my house a lot. Bella and Tammy looked just alike, but they were cousins to Angie and Shon.

James and I were thinking about getting a band together. I played the drums and James had played the electric guitar for five years in church. We asked Bella and Tammy if they wanted to be in our band and they said yes. We needed more people, so Shon, Clay, Angie, and my sister Jenny joined as well. Shon played the bass. Clay played the electric guitar, James played the lead guitar, and the girls sang. We called ourselves Fabulous 8! We played in clubs, bars, any place that would have us to play for them.

We played at a club in Chicago called Bobby O'Hare's. He was a famous producer. He signed us up for a talent show and I told the band we needed new outfits so we could perform better. Bobby told me we needed to be there by 8:00 p.m. and we would play at 8:25 p.m. Shon told me he'd written a song and wanted us to sing it that night. I told everyone to meet at the garage at the house. We had a lot of practicing to do. We went to the garage and set our equipment up, then practiced for six hours.

Bella, Tammy, and Angie spent the night with Jenny. The guys went home, except for me. Dad told me I had to stay home and help him. We woke up the next morning and got ready to go to school. The girls were in the bathroom getting ready and I was downstairs eating breakfast when I heard Mom talking on the phone with Aunt Susan. She'd heard about the talent show. At the club, there would be music producers. I heard that whoever won the talent show would get a recording contract and a record deal. I went upstairs, walked by Jenny's room, and saw Bella getting ready. She saw me go by. I called James and told him I'd heard that our moms were talking about the talent show, that whoever won got a record deal and a recording contract. James told me he'd heard it, too.

I wondered who was going to win the talent show. I left my room and went to the bathroom to brush my teeth. Bella went and smiled at me. "Everybody's waiting on you, Buddy," she said. I told her I was coming. Later I put my arms around Bella and Tammy after they got in the car. Mom told Jenny to get in the driver's seat. When we got to school, Lauren was waiting for me. Brittney was already with James, and all three were standing together. I was getting out of the car, and Lauren saw me getting out with Bella, Tammy, and Angie. She didn't like me talking to Bella. I walked toward her. The first thing she asked me was, "Do you like Bella?"

I told her that I did. Then she slapped my face, said, "It's over," and walked off. Brittney saw her walking by herself crying and ran to her ask her what had happened.

Lauren told her I liked somebody else and that she was no competition for her. Then Brittney asked her, "Who is it?"

"Bella!"

"No, not her!"

"Yes, her! I saw him getting out the car with her. He was talking to her and hugging her. She saw me and grabbed him, making me so jealous that I wanted to kill her."

We walked to the classroom. Lauren sat behind Angie and kept pulling Angie's hair. I told her to stop. She looked at me, stood up, and slapped Angie. Mr. Byler told her to go to the principal's office.

It was 3:00 p.m. and school was out. We went home and did our homework, then our chores. Then we went to the garage. I told everybody that all we had to do was win the talent show. We needed to practice the new song Shon had written, and we had Tammy as the lead singer. Bella, Angie, and Jenny were the backup singers.

We had three hours before we would perform, and were wearing new outfits because a lot of big music producers were going to be there. We could get a record deal and a recording contract. After practicing for an hour and a half, we got ready. Clay told me that our agent had said good luck with the show and not to embarrass him in front of thousands of people. Then we arrived, and there were a lot of people watching the show. Before we knew it, it was our turn to play. We were nervous. When everybody was done playing, they announced the winner.

We won!

We couldn't believe it, and everyone congratulated us.

It was Friday, and we had a couple of games left before the championship game. We wore our jerseys at the pep rally. Our quarterback was the player of the year, and our defensemen of the year was our linebacker. He had seventy-eight tackles (with a tackle of loss sixty-five) with twelve sacks, five forced fumbles, three recovery of fumbles, and two interceptions. We were playing in the playoff as the number one seed.

Shon and I had a game that night. We needed to win to stay in the playoffs. At the start of the third period, the lights went out, and when they finally got them back on one of the officials had been killed. He'd been stabbed to death! Nobody knew who had done it or why.

Our next game was Monday. We left with our families, and Brittney and Lauren followed us. When we got to my house, I talked to James about Brittney and he told me he was still in love with her! They'd broken up after Lauren and I had.

I asked, "How can you still be in love with her?" He told me that was what he felt in his heart. "I'm not in love with Lauren. I'm fallen in love with three girls: Bella, Tammy, and Angie, though Angie is taken. I don't know which one I like the most yet. The girls are spending the night with my sister. Do you think they ever found out who killed the referee? I betcha I can solve that case before the cops do."

"You're on. How much?"

"One hundred dollars."

"Okay."

We shook on it. About that time, I heard some bikers go by our house. There must have been at least thirty of them. Then I remembered there were a few bikers at the game. They'd argued with the referee, and one of them had had a knife on him.

There was a knock on my bedroom door, and I found Bella, Tammy, and Angie standing there with their nightclothes on. It was midnight. I asked them why they were standing at the door. They told me they were waiting for me to decide which one of them I was asking out, because we were leaving in the first week of June to go to New York to sign that contract. I told them I wouldn't let them know until the next week. Right then, I liked it the way it was. Angie left first, then Tammy. Bella took her time. Before leaving, she grabbed me and kissed me. As she left, she looked back and threw another kiss at me.

We won the state championship again in football and lost four games to three in the state championship for hockey. Our basketball team was on a winning streak. We won ten in a row against teams that were ranked. It was the middle of January, and our basketball team was ranked number three in the state.

If we won this game, we could take first place. We'd lost only seven games, so if we could win this, it would boost our players up to win another championship. Monday night would be the game. Hopefully, we could take first place. I was the only one home when Bella came over. James was over at Brittney's house and Clay was at Angie's. Shon had left with my sister and our mom and dad. After Bella arrived, I closed the door and she grabbed my hand. We sat down on the couch. She asked, "When are you going to ask me out?"

I told her, "When you stop asking me." She pushed me down on the couch and took my clothes off. Later, she asked if we'd be in first place if we won Monday night.

I told her yes, then heard a car door close. I went to the door. "It looks like your dad." We went upstairs and took a shower together, then went to my room. I closed the door. "We can keep your thong and bra here and Mom can wash it. Don't you have some clothes here from when you stay the night?"

Bella and I finally got together. Time passed and summer vacation arrived again, and we did things together. She came over every day and went swimming. Then there was the trip to New York we had to take. Our parents made reservations for us to go together.

One day I asked James if he'd had sex with Brittney. He told me she was going to wait until she got married. "What should I do, Buddy?"

"Do you love her?"

"I don't know anymore."

"Well, you better find out. There are girls waiting on you to let her go so you can go out with them. I think Lauren is making girls afraid to go out with me. There's one I know of who isn't afraid of her, and maybe one more. I can go out with her, and you can go out with Bella or Tammy."

"I can't do this!" he said.

"What are you going to do, stay with her? There are a lot of girls waiting on you. They ask me about you and I tell them you have someone. What are you going to do about that?"

He sighed. "Okay, let's do this." He called Brittney and heard another guy in the background. It wasn't her brother or her dad.

He hung up and went to her house. Her brother opened the door for him and he went upstairs to Brittney's room. She was in bed with Kevin and was buck naked. James grabbed Kevin and beat him, then asked her, "How long you been doing this?"

"About a month."

Then he said, "It's over between you and me."

He left and came to my house, telling me it was over and he was ready to move on. Then he asked who wanted him and I named about twelve girls. I said, "Tammy really wants to go out with you. She told me just the other day."

We were getting ready to go to New York to sign the contract and would leave the next morning. I told the band that a limousine would be there at 8:00 a.m. to take us to the airport. We looked at each another and I said, "I can't believe this is happening to us."

James grabbed Tammy by the hand as they were leaving. They talked to each other. He told her that he would like to date her, but she wanted to date others. They went back to my house. Our parents were trying to get everything ready to go. James asked my dad what time they should come over. My dad said to tell everyone to be there around 7:00 a.m.

Chapter 2

We needed to be ready to go. I asked James how his dating was going. "Have you decided to date Tammy yet? There's Kim. She been waiting on you to ask her out, too."

Angie asked if she could spend the night with Jenny. Her parents told her yes, if it was all right with our parents. "We don't mind," they said. "Are y'all going with us?"

"No, we can't get off work."

Everyone else's parents were going with us.

It was about 9:00 p.m. and we needed to go to bed. At about 12:00 a.m. somebody walked into my room. I pretended that I was asleep, then felt their cold feet on my leg, then their hand on my body. When I opened my eyes, it was Angie. She was sleepwalking, and her hands were all over me. Then she went back to Jenny's room. We got up at 6:30 a.m. and they took a shower. When I passed the bathroom, Angie had a towel around her.

She went back to Jenny's room to put her clothes on and I winked at her, then went in the bathroom to brush my teeth. She joined me to brush her own teeth, then kissed me.

The limousine finally arrived and we went to the airport. Once we arrived in New York, another limousine took us to the hotel.

After checking in, we went to the studio. The producer was there waiting for us. We read over the contract, then signed it. A few pop stars and R&B stars were there listening to our music, and they all wanted us to play their type of music, telling us to think about it. We went back to the hotel and changed clothes, then went walking downtown, looking in shops and putting our money in the bank. People stopped and talked to us, asking us questions about one another. All of us were asked out by all kinds of people. We told them we were already dating other people. Our fans had started to grow in New York. They'd seen us playing on television.

Shon told me, "I've got another song that I've been working on. I want it to be a special song for our record."

We saw a lot of stars at the hotel, then went out to eat at a fancy restaurant after practicing Shon's new song for a while. There were a lot of stars at the restaurant, too, preparing to go to an award ceremony. We were invited to it, but we didn't know that they wanted us to sing. After we ate, a limousine picked us up and took us to the award ceremony. We started to sit down, but people ushered us backstage. We told them it was a mistake.

"Are y'all Fabulous 8?"

"Yes."

"Then we didn't make a mistake."

We looked at one another while the host of the show announced us. "The next hottest group to come out here in person is Fabulous 8." We came out and the people went crazy. I told Shon we'd sing his new song. He said, "Let's do this!" Tammy sang the lead, and she was nervous at first, but she got over it as we played Shon's new song.

The audience loved it. People stood up for us as we sang our hearts out for them. They wanted an encore, so we came back onstage and sang another song. It was awesome playing and singing in front of billions of people.

We left and went back to the hotel to get some sleep. We were going to be a busy the next day until 4:00 p.m., then we'd go to the Statue of Liberty. We got up at seven o'clock and took showers, then got ready to go to the studio. Once there we grabbed our instruments and played our songs. The producer said we'd have to go to Tennessee in January and finish our recording.

At twelve o'clock we stopped and ate lunch with our parents. When we got back to the hotel, Brittney and Lauren were standing there waiting on us. Brittney went to James, but Lauren stayed by herself. I called the security guard to escort Lauren out the building. She had a bomb strapped to her. I told everybody to get out, that I would take care of it, so everybody left except Lauren and me. I tried to explain that it was over between us, but she kept on saying that she was still in love with me. The producer called the cops and the bomb squad, then called me.

"How big is the bomb?" I told them how big it was. They said, "What color are the wires?"

"Blue, white, and black."

They told me I had to cut the white wire. "But before you do that, you've got to open the box that contains the wires. The code is four numbers, and you've got to get the numbers one by one. How much time do you have?"

"An hour. I need to start and keep Lauren calm. She's panicking, plus it's getting hot in here. Can you get them to turn on the air?"

"Sure. How many numbers have you figured out?"

"Three, but I can't figure out the fourth. I'm going to attempt to open it by breaking it, unless you can figure out the other number."

"Well, try your best to get it open."

I worked on it for a while, making little progress. When next I glanced down, I saw we had only twelve minutes left. I told Lauren, "If you sweat it might trigger the bomb."

Eight minutes remaining. There was one number I hadn't tried yet: zero. I put it in and the door on the box opened. I cut the white wire and it stopped. I took the bomb off her and threw it in the trash can, then grabbed her. But then I heard another noise, like something ticking. I looked in the trash can.

I picked the bomb up, and another self-destruct device had gone off when I'd thrown it in the trash can. We had twelve minutes to clear the building, but she didn't want to leave. I told her we had to leave now, but she refused. I picked her up and ran out the door. While I was running, I hollered, "Get out of the building! Get out of the building!" Everybody ran. I told Brittney to take her cousin and run, then told James, Clay, and Shon to go to every floor and tell everyone to get out.

Someone called the fire department and we heard a girl scream. One of us had to find her. A lady said, "I can't find my daughter." We asked her what floor she was on. "The sixth." I'd thought everybody had gotten out. We all went upstairs to the sixth floor to rescue the little girl, getting there just in time. We turned a corner and there she was. James grabbed her and ran downstairs, then we all ran out the building. It blew up as we came out, knocking us down. As the windows shattered all over the pavement, some people got cut from falling glass. We were lucky. We could've gotten killed, all because of a girl who was still in love. *Where is she now?* I thought. She'd been outside with Brittney. "There she is! Brittney, where is Lauren?"

"She went back in the building after she found out y'all four were still in there."

"She shouldn't have gone back in. You were supposed to watch her."

After the fire was out, we asked a fireman if they'd found her body. They said no, they'd found no one.

"Wait a minute. You're saying you didn't find a girl in that fire?" We looked at Brittney. "Thought that you said she went in the building. The fireman said they didn't find a body in the building. We'll ask you one more time: where is your cousin?"

"She went in the building. I saw her go in. That's the truth. I saw her go in the front door, and I didn't see her come out."

We walked to the police department and told them we wanted to file a missing person's report. The police officer asked how long she had been missing. "Only six hours." He told us she had to be missing over twenty-four hours before they would look into her disappearance.

My dad gave them his phone number. "If y'all find any information, call me at this number." We left the police station and found a new hotel, then went to a Broadway show. During the middle of the show my dad's phone vibrated. He went outside to answer. It was the police department.

The police officer said they'd found a girl. She wasn't dead; she was in the hospital with smoke in her lungs. My dad said that he would be there in twenty minutes. They told him what hospital she was in. My dad came back in and told all the men to go with him. He told Mom what was going on, saying to tell everybody else after the show and to go back to the hotel room afterwards. James, Clay, Shon, and I asked if we could go with them. "Only one of you needs to go." So I went. He didn't tell me about her until we got there. We went up to the third floor to room 333. There were three police officers watching over her.

I called her name. "Lauren? Lauren, what happened to you?"

"I still love you," she answered.

"It's over between you and me, and has been for a long time."

My dad told her that he'd called her mom and dad. "They will be here tomorrow to get you. You have to stay in the hospital for now."

I hoped the next time I broke up with someone I wouldn't have to worry about this.

We left the hospital and went back to the hotel. When we got there something was happening across the street in a bar. It sounded like gunshots. My dad and my uncles went across the street. Bella's, Tammy's, and Shon's dads stayed back with me. Then we heard a gunshot. We ran over to see what had happened. My uncle Roy was on the ground; he'd been shot in the back. I ran to my dad. He had two stab wounds. One of the other dads called 911; my other uncle was wounded, and my uncle Roy died as we sat there.

I asked my dad, "Who did this?"

"Two guys were beating a girl and trying to rape her. When we got here, we stopped them. Roy was running to help his brother when he was shot in the back."

I moved aside to talk with the guys. "We've got to pay those two guys back before we leave."

James asked, "Do you know where they are?"

"No, but we can find them. All we've got to do is find out who they are, and we can pay them a visit."

Jerry, one of the dads, overheard us and told my dad. He told Jerry to take us back home. "All of you, go with Jerry. Your mom and I will be home soon. Y'all will stay with Jerry until we get home."

The next morning, we all got up and got ready to go to the airport. The only ones who stayed were my mom and Aunt Susan; they stayed to be with their husbands. The limousine picked us up and took us to the airport. I sat between Bella and Tammy on the plane. James sat beside Angie, and Clay sat on the other side of her. Shon sat beside Jenny and tried to comfort her, but the ones who really needed comfort were Aunt Karen and Clay. They'd lost a husband and a father.

Clay was torn up inside. He didn't want anyone to get close to him. Later, he said to me, "Can I talk to you for a few minutes, you and James?"

"Yes, of course."

He told us that when we get home he was staying on the plane and going back to New York to find those guys and make them pay. "Are y'all with me?!" I told him no, that it was wrong. Clay asked James, "Are you with me?" I told him to say no. Clay got mad at us and stormed off, sitting by himself.

I told Aunt Karen what Clay had said. She got Jerry to talk to Clay instead of David, because David was the pastor of a church. Jerry sat beside him and talked to him, telling him that the same thing had happened to him.

Clay asked, "What did you do?"

"I was mad, just like you. I wanted to find the people who'd done it. They were on their way home when three guys in a truck saw their limousine and rammed them. They took everything, raped my mother and killed her, then shot my dad three times in the head."

"Did the police find them?"

"Yes, after three months. My uncle Jason, he sold the company to the highest bidder after that: Buddy's and Jenny's daddy."

"Why didn't you ask Uncle Steve about that business?"

"He asked me to be a partner. I told him it was my dad's business he wanted me to go in, but I was already a cop and was working to be a chief of police. That way I could get the bad guys off the street, so it won't happen to anybody else. My family didn't want me to get the business. That's why I chose to be a cop. Bella can have a good life, and a safe one, knowing her daddy is out there protecting her from harm. But there's a chance I'll hurt her one day."

"What do you mean?"

"Oh, Mr. Klein, one day you'll find out about it. It will affect all of y'all."

"We want you tell Bella now. That way she won't find out later and get mad at you."

"You might be right. I need to tell her. Let me get David. Shon needs to find out the truth, too. He's old enough to know about his parents."

"What do you mean? Are his parents not his real parents?"

"No. They're his aunt and his uncle, his real mom's sister."

We went to Jerry's house, Jenny and I, until our parents got back. Jerry called everybody in the living room and said, "This going to affect a lot of y'all, so everybody sit down."

"What's wrong?"

"Something we should've told y'all sooner."

"Tell us now."

"All right, here it goes: Bella, you and Tammy are sisters. Your mother's name was Mary. She was our sister. Your father's name was Kevin. He was a famous stunt person. Your mother was a famous movie star. Before she died, she asked each of her brothers to adopt her two daughters. Your father didn't want y'all with him. He went back to show business, until last year. He died from a stunt when a cable broke. He fell twenty-five feet and was killed instantly. We just found out last week about his death."

Bella and Tammy looked at each other and said, "That's why lot of people thought that we were sisters. Y'all are just now telling us this? Who else knows about this?"

"All the grown-ups know."

Tammy looked at David and Marie, her adopted parents, and said, "Y'all weren't going let me know I was adopted and that Bella is really my sister."

"We were going to tell you after you came back from college."

"Know what? I'm glad you told me. I always wondered why I'm different from y'all, and why everybody says that Bella and I look like sisters."

"Shon, your mom is Angie's mom. Angie is your sister."

"Her dad is my dad?"

"No, he's your stepfather. Your real dad is a leader of a mafia in Las Vegas."

"Well, Mom is that true?"

"Yes, it's true. Your dad is the leader of a mafia."

"Does he know about me?"

"No. If he did, he'd tried to get you to go into his business and I don't want that. Well, I didn't have anyone at that time, and your sister was born. It took her daddy a long time to decide to marry to me, and now we're a happy family. You can join us, if you like. Or you can stay with my sister. She is moving to New York."

"I was thinking about finding my dad in Las Vegas."

"He is nothing but trouble, and we don't need that."

"I'll stay with y'all, my sister and my parents."

"You want to stay with us?"

"Yes, I'll staying with my real family. John, do you mind me calling you Dad?"

John said, "I'd be proud to call you my son."

The day was Saturday, and our parents were coming home from New York. When I spoke to my mom on the phone, I said, "Mom, how long did you know that Bella and Tammy were sisters? And how about Shon?"

"How long did everybody else knows? That's how long."

"You didn't tell us, your son and daughter?"

"Nope. We figured y'all shouldn't know because you might accidentally tell them."

We had two weeks left before school started back. Like every summer, our family took a week to go to the beach in Florida. Before I asked if the boys could go, my sister asked first about her friends. My parents told me I couldn't have anybody with me because she'd asked first.

Mom and dad said, "The girls are going this time."

Then we packed our bags and went on our trip to Florida. I sat in the back and Bella sat beside me. Most of the time we flew, but this time we drove. On the way, Mom told us she was having another baby.

We were driving to Florida to spend quality time together. When we got to the hotel, we had to make sleeping arrangements. We only had two rooms because it was packed there, with bikers staying at the hotel. I told Mom and Dad I would sleep on the couch in the room with the girls. There are two beds in that room. I put my stuff in the closet. Tammy and Bella were changing their clothes, putting on their bikinis.

Tammy was wearing a lime green one and Bella was wearing a hot pink one. Angie and Jenny went to the bathroom to put theirs on. I changed my clothes in the room, but not in front of my sister. She was looking the other way.

They said to me, "We're waiting on you!"

"I'm ready."

I told Mom and Dad what we were planning to do. We rented three jet skis, and Tammy got on the jet ski with me.

Angie and Jenny got on one, and Bella got on the other. We rode around for a while. I rode with Angie next while Tammy got on by herself, and Jenny and Bella rode on the other. I turned around and Angie kissed me on the lips.

"What that for?"

She smiled and said, "I just wanted to kiss you, hopefully get somebody jealous."

Bella got on with me next. Before we left, I asked my sister, "What are y'all doing?" She said that she, Tammy, and Angie were going to walk down the beach.

"Don't go far. We have to be back at the hotel soon. It's already 4:00 p.m., and these jet skis have to be back at 5:15 p.m."

Bella and I rode for a while, then we talked and she asked me if I'd get mad if she went out with Bobby Friskburger.

"No, I won't get mad."

We'd always be friends, and one day I hoped we'd get married. When I turned around to say something to her, she kissed me on the lips. We kissed for a while, then we left and went back to shore. The others were waiting on us.

After turning in the jet skis, we walked back to the hotel. Mom and Dad were waiting on us. They told us they'd rented a sailboat for us to go on a little tour. We asked what time we were supposed to be there.

"We've got to be there at 8:30 p.m., no later than 8:40 p.m. Y'all go take a shower and be ready in thirty minutes."

Mom and Dad didn't think of the fact that I was the only boy with four girls. They'd locked their room and we couldn't get in there to take a shower, so how could I do this? I couldn't take a shower with my sister.

While the girls were showering, Mom and Dad came back and told me to go in their room to shower. The girls were in the bathroom when I came returned. Mom and Dad had gone downstairs. I had to brush my teeth, and some of the girls weren't ready.

I said, "Let me pick out what y'all should wear."

Chapter 3

I picked out dresses for them, except Jenny. They were gorgeous, low-cut at the neck and short up to their thighs.

Tammy was wearing purple, Angie was wearing black silk, and Bella was wearing turquoise, with matching high heels that made them about six feet five inches tall. We left the hotel and went to a nice restaurant to eat. People stared at us, and some said things about the girls. I told them that if they didn't like what they saw they could close their eyes. The people stopped talking about them when they overheard who we were.

"Can y'all sing a song for us?" they asked.

"We can try." I got on an electric keyboard someone loaned me and Tammy got up as the lead singer, the other girls backing her up. We sang four songs.

School finally started back. We were juniors. Could we win three championships in a row? For the first game of the season, we had to play a team that had been the weakest last year. They'd only won three games, and we needed to watch out for teams like that. They could get better. We had schoolwork to do, but some of us thought we could get by because we were the best players. We had seven good players who would fail without help. They paid other classmates to do their homework. I told them if they didn't do their own papers or homework, one day a teacher was going to ask them to explain how they'd got an answer, and they wouldn't be able to explain.

Lauren made it to school. She was in therapy, but she was still in love with me. I was sitting behind Angie and was talking to her when Lauren dropped her books in Angie's lap, then grabbed Angie up out of her seat.

Angie was furious. She grabbed Lauren and threw her to the other side of the room. Lauren got up and ran toward Angie with her head down. I grabbed Angie by the hand and pulled her toward me, and Lauren tripped and fell to the floor. As everybody laughed at her, she walked out of the classroom. The teacher asked her to come back. She cursed at the teacher with bad language. The teacher got the principal. By the time they returned, Lauren had stabbed Pete and cut Angie's arm. Pete had tried to grab her, but she had turned around and stabbed him. Pete was taken to the hospital, where he died the next morning. They could not stop the bleeding. He was our kicker and goalie for our hockey team. He was the best goalie we'd had.

The cops put Lauren in prison at first, to get help, but then sent her to the crazy house. We had the funeral on Thursday, and Friday was our first game. After football practice, we all got together and went out to Bernie's Palace, where the cheerleaders and football players went to eat burgers and make a toast in memory of Pete Kalong, our kicker and goalie. On Friday we played our first game.

That was when I saw Stacie. She was hot! She had blonde hair and green eyes. She was about a nine point seven on the scale, and was there with her cousin, Cam Baker. He had black hair and blue eyes; they'd just moved to town and lived together. I asked Cam if Stacie was dating anyone.

"No."

"Can I ask her out?" He told me to go ahead, and then I asked him if he played football. He told me yes, that he played linebacker. I said, "Come and join our football team."

He told me he'd already joined. "My cousin is a cheerleader."

"Okay, I'll ask her out now."

We were having a fall dance, and I wondered if she'd go to the dance with me. It was the next night after the game. When I asked her, she said, "Well, I'm new around here." I told her I'd like to show her around. She said, "Bella and Tammy told me you would ask me out. I told them if you did, I would say yes. They told me to be careful, and if someone named Lauren found out, I might be in trouble."

"I've got a Harley Davidson fat boy."

"That's cool! I like guys on a motorcycle."

I always let Bella ride because the rest of the girls rode with the other guys. I asked Stacie if she wanted to ride.

Later, I asked Cam who he liked since he'd been here. "Angie or Tammy." I asked him who he wanted to ask out. "Tammy."

"It doesn't matter. Both girls are great kissers."

"How do you know?"

"I've kissed both."

"Who have you not dated or kissed?"

" Stacie, and that's it."

"How about Kathy?"

"Yep. I've kissed her five times. I've kissed Bella plenty of times when she comes to my house. Now I'm dating your cousin. You and Bella can date if you want to. I give you my permission."

"Do you kiss her if you're dating somebody?"

"No, that would be wrong! I think if you date someone, you should kiss that person, not anyone else."

Later, I asked Stacie again, "Do you want to ride with me?" She looked at Bella and Tammy. They told her to go ahead with me. "We can do this Thursday."

On Thursday, she got on the motorcycle with me and put her arms around me. I told her to hold on tight. We stopped at a red light and a chopper came besides us. The guy driving winked at her and said he wanted to get in her pants. The light turned green and we took off with the chopper behind us. He tried to stop us. She asked, "Can you go any faster? He's gaining on us."

"Let him gain. He doesn't know any of these roads like I do. Let him come."

"Do you see that bridge is out?"

"I have jumped that bridge plenty of times. Watch this." I gave it some gas and we made it over.

The guy on the chopper stopped. We looked back and heard him say, "It not over. I will get both of y'all." We laughed and drove off. It was getting late, and I still had to get Stacie home. We took a shortcut, but my motorcycle started to have problems. Then Stacie started to get scared.

"Don't worry. I will get us home," I said. I knew there was a little white house around there somewhere. It was only the fourth day of school, and we had a big game the next night. The fall dance we had every year for juniors and seniors was coming up, and now we could finally go to that dance. I asked Stacie to the dance, Cam asked Tammy, Bella was asked by Bobby, James asked Brittney, Clay asked Angie, and Shon asked Jenny.

Stacie and I made it to the old white house, which was about one mile from Bella and Tammy's. I called Bella and asked her if she could come and pick us up. She asked her parents and said she was on her way.

Meanwhile, we found the old house and went inside because it looked like it was going to rain. Stacie and said it was cold, so I gave her my jacket.

She said, "Buddy, I'm still cold!"

Bella called us. "I'll be there in thirty minutes." That gave us plenty time to get to know each other.

She kept on getting scared. I put my arm around her and said, "Don't be scared! I will protect you." We kissed for a long time. It was better than kissing Lauren. Hopefully, she was getting the help she needed.

By that time Bella and Tammy had arrived. We got in the car and I told Bella to take Stacie home. She told me Stacie was staying at her house. We all went to her house and my dad was there. He took me to pick up my motorcycle and we dropped it off at Phil's. Then we went home. I took a shower and put my nightclothes on, then went to bed.

The next day, I got up and got ready to go to school. We took the Hummer and I went around and picked up the girls.

We all met in the parking lot at school. While the girls walked to class, the guys carried the girls' books. Most of the guys were polite; the cheerleaders were dating most of the football players and wore their jackets.

During the pep rally, all the football players had to wear the cheerleaders' outfits, and the cheerleaders had to wear the football players' uniforms. We wore our jerseys to class. Bella was dating James now, I was dating Stacie, Cam was dating Tammy, Clay was dating Angie, Shon was dating Jenny, and Lauren was going to the crazy house. Brittney had to give up cheerleading because she was moving to another school.

We put on a little show, all the football players coming out in their cheerleader outfits; the girls had their football uniforms on. It was a good show for our classmates.

Our coach said, "Come out and support our players. They need to win this first game of the season. Come tonight and support the bulldogs."

The teacher in charge of the cheerleaders, Mrs. Hines, said, "Girls, we've got ourselves a new captain and co-captain, Bella Klein and Tammy Klein!"

Once school was out, we went home to get our stuff done. Coaches wanted us to get to the field early. I asked the other guys what they were wearing to the dance after the game. They told me they were wearing black tuxedos. I told them we were riding in different cars. James was driving Bella in a Porsche, I was driving Stacie in a Lamborghini, Cam was driving Tammy in a Ferrari, Clay was driving Angie in a Corvette, and Shon was driving Jenny in a Porsche. We took our clothes to the game, planning to change in the gym.

The game was starting, and we got the ball first. By halftime we were winning twenty-eight to three. Second half was starting. By end of the third quarter, it was forty-five to ten. During the fourth quarter we put in our second string. We had one minute left in the game, and they scored a touchdown with forty seconds left. We held the ball until the final seconds. We won, and fifty-two to thirty-five. Afterwards, the guys and the cheerleaders went to the locker rooms, taking showers and putting on their tuxedos and evening gowns. Then we got in our cars and took off.

We made it to the country club, and there were a lot of people there. They already had a band playing, so we started to dance, then took picture after picture. We were dancing when one of the band members got sick. The leader of the band told the principal they couldn't sing or play music.

The principal said, "Can we get anybody to sing and play?"

A couple of people said, "How about Fabulous 8? They're here."

"Fabulous 8 is here? Where?"

"Those four couples. They have the most gorgeous lead and backup singers."

I told the principal, "*No*, we wanted to dance."

The other band said, "Let the five girls come up. We'll play music for them."

But I told them no, that we would play. The first song we performed was a love song Shon wrote for Jenny. He should've sung it with Jenny, but he refused.

Tammy and I sang it instead, then sang six more. We were getting ready to leave when Clay said, "Let's go eat at Bernie's Palace." Once there, we talked about going to college and what everybody's plans were in the future.

I told Bella I hoped my future was with her, and she said, "I hope that's true."

Then James said, "It's getting late. We'd better go."

In the car, Jenny called Jerry and asked him if Bella could stay with her. He told her he didn't care, but she needed to be home early in the morning to help her mother. Bella got the phone from Jenny and told her dad that she would be home on time.

"Okay, honey, y'all just be careful when y'all get there. Call us when you get to Steve's house."

We made it home and I told her to call her dad. She called as we went inside. Our mom was up. As we walked in, she said, "Look at what time it is. Everyone was worried about you. Y'all should been home an hour ago. What have you been doing this late?"

"Everybody was hungry, so we went to Bernie's Palace. We talked about college and decided to go to Hawaii."

"It's time to go to bed now. Please don't wake your dad and little sister up. Your sister is sick." Jenny and Bella had already gone upstairs while Mom was talking to me. As I came up the stairs, Bella grabbed me and kissed me while Jenny went to her room.

Bella went to my room and shut the door. I changed in front of her, putting on my shorts while we kissed. I had my arm around her and she stripped down to her bra and panties. I was back down to my boxers. She crawled into my bed and pulled the covers over her, falling asleep quickly. I turned the lights out and crawled into bed.

She slept until the alarm went off, then got up and got ready to go home. I drove her there, and her dad had already gone to work. Mrs. Klein was up and fixing breakfast. She asked me if I wanted some and I told her yes, if she didn't mind.

She said, "No trouble at all. We like you more than some of Bella's boyfriends, like that Kevin. He acts like he knows everything. He doesn't. Sometimes he acts stupid. I think he tries too hard to impress the girls."

"That's what I said."

"Do you know Kevin?"

"I do. He's one of our receivers. He's also our center in hockey. We are in Mrs. Diary's English literature class, all ten of us, and have tons of homework. We just won the state championship in football and hockey and are now starting to enter our baseball season."

We had more project to do for our two classes. They were due in April and May. For one of the projects we had only five people, and for the other project we had ten people. We worked hard on them. The one due in April was about life in science, and the other due in May was about drama. Stacie and I were getting serious. We weren't thinking about marriage yet! We broke up on and off. I dated Tammy, Angie, and Bella when Stacie and I broke up. We talked about what we were going to do when we finished college. James, Clay, and Cam all were in the same predicament; the girls said they wanted to date somebody else.

The first game of our baseball season started and we won fifteen to ten in extra innings. Our project was coming up. It was March 7, 2033, on a Tuesday. We had baseball practice and also prom coming up. Bella, Stacie, a girl named Tiffney, another named Sabrina, and I had to do our project on life. We interviewed different couples and had different views on life from other cultures. I was the leader in the group; it took us ten days to finish our project. We did it and had another project to do, but we did it in a song.

I asked James who was he taking to the prom. There was a new girl who was a transfer from a school in Chicago. Her name was Cheryl. She drove a gold car with purple stripes down the middle, a Corvette. I told him I was thinking of asking her to the prom. He looked at me and said, "I thought you going to ask Bella. Everybody said you are, but Bella said she's hoping I'll ask her out."

"Well, are you going to ask the new girl out instead?"

"Yes. You know Bella and you are the only ones going out to the prom together. Tammy was asked by Jackson, the backup quarterback. Cam asked Sabrina. Clay asked Catherina, and you know Shon will ask Jenny."

"Yep, he's asking her."

"Angie's going to the prom with Casey, and Stacie's going with Bobby, our center in basketball."

Everybody gathered around. I asked, "Well, are you going to ask the new girl out or not?"

"Yes, right now." He went over to her car and said, "Nice wheels."

"Thank you." She didn't give him a chance to say who he was. She said, "I know who you are. You're Buddy Smithson."

"No. I'm James Smithson."

"I thought you were Buddy."

Then he said, "Do you want to go to prom with me?"

"Sure."

He told her he'd pick her up on his Harley at 7:00 p.m. and they'd go out to eat.

She kissed him, then popped him on the butt in front of the school. He grabbed her and kissed her back for a long time, then popped her on the butt. She told him that when she'd seen me last week she wanted to ask me out, but everybody told her that Bella and I were dating each other. We left school and went home.

When we got there the first thing Jenny said, "Why did you and James argue about that new girl?"

"I wanted to ask her out, but James said that wanted to, so we argued about her."

"Well, Bella was happy when you asked her to the prom. I don't want you to hurt her feelings because you and James want to fight for the new girl."

"Let's drop this, sis. I know it will hurt her, but we've talked about seeing other people. Let me go and work on my Harley."

"Buddy, you need to do your chores!" Mom called.

"Okay, Mom." I did them in a few minutes, then worked on my Harley. James, Clay, Cam, and Shon all came over and talked to me. Shon told me that Cheryl had wanted to go out with me since the day she arrived, because she was kin to Brittney. Cheryl was Brittney's cousin from England. She'd heard a lot about James, Clay, Cam, Buddy, and me, but there were two guys she wanted to go out with: James and me.

James said, "I'm taking her out tonight to Bernie's Palace to eat. I'm supposed to pick her up at 7:00 p.m. I have to go home and get ready yet."

"Well, call us when you get back home."

"Okay."

The guys left and went home.

Angie asked, "Is James taking Cheryl to the prom?"

"Yes," Shon said.

"I heard that Bella wanted to go out with James."

"Who is taking you to the prom?"

"Casey. He's in our English class. He's is a good artist, and he's smart. He was picked on by Kevin and George every day, even when he helped them in Spanish. Y'all just laugh at him."

"He asked you to the prom and you told him yes?"

"I sure did."

"How about Cam? Didn't you want to go to the prom with him?"

"Yes."

"Do you still want to go to the prom with him?"

"Yes, but I can't break a promise to Casey after I told him I'd go to the prom with him."

"What if I can get him another date? Will you try to tell Cam how you feel?"

"Yes, I will if you can give me a chance."

"Just leave it to me, okay?"

"How are you going get Bella to come over?"

"I'm just going to ask her over here to talk. That way I can find out what's going on and why they wanted to go out with other people."

I got dressed and went to the garage to get on my Harley. Then I stopped by Brittney's house. Brittney came out to talk to me. I said, "I'm glad you decided to stay and finish high school here with us. Who are you going to the prom with?"

"I don't know."

"I heard Jack wanted to ask you to the prom."

"Well, I don't know yet. Here comes Cheryl."

Cheryl called, "Tell her mom I'll be home later!"

Brittney said, "Okay. Where is James? I thought he was coming to take you out."

I told Brittney he wasn't coming, then told Cheryl to get on. She got on the back of my Harley and we drove off. I blew my horn at Clay as I went by.

Clay called James and said, "Our cousin just drove by with your prom date on the back of his Harley. Do you still want to go with Bella?"

"Go pick her up. We know where they're going. We'll meet you there."

"I thought you wanted to take Tammy to the prom."

"I'm planning to take Stacie out."

"You always said that you and Tammy were going to the prom."

"All of us need to get together to discuss who we're actually taking to the prom."

Cheryl and I parked at Bernie's Palace and went in to eat a steak dinner. It was a Texas-style steak with a baked potato and curly fries. We also shared a large soft drink together.

Then we saw Stacie, Tammy, and Angie. We moved to the back booth. They didn't find us for a little while until the guys came. They sat with the girls. They asked where Buddy and Cheryl were, then Tammy said, "I knew that Harley was familiar. That's Buddy. Hey, there they are in the last booth."

"We're here," I said. "Let's discuss who we're taking to the prom. Wait a minute, we're missing two people."

James and Bella pulled up at that moment. "Why are you with Cheryl?" someone asked. "I thought James was taking her out."

"I stopped at Brittney's house and told her I was glad she was staying and finishing school with us and ran into Cheryl there. Okay, here they are now. We can discuss who's taking who. Wait a minute, we aren't discussing prom right now. I thought everybody was going with somebody different to the prom. I'm on a date right now, not with my friends, but with Cheryl. That's right, she's here with me. Goodbye. Talk to y'all later."

Cheryl and I got up and left on the Harley. We went to Pigeon Point and parked out there. We started to kiss when she saw her old flame from the other school. He was in his Jaguar with a girl he'd just met. She told me the kiss was nice.

She wanted to go over to him and talk. He'd picked up Karen Hagur, who was the cheerleaders' dance teacher and our world history teacher. Her husband was overseas for military purposes. Karen asked me to take her home. She was a gorgeous young woman. I left Cheryl there and Karen got on the motorcycle with me. She had her arms around me as I took her home. When we arrived, she asked me to come in and gave me some money for taking her home. Her next-door neighbor, Mrs. Givens, had never liked her. She tried anything to get her in trouble. I was in her house for about thirty minutes, then left.

When I got home and was heading upstairs, my sister stopped me and asked, "How was your date?"

"Well, you know about up until we left Bernie's Palace."

"Yeah. How about after that?"

"I took her to Pigeon Point."

"You did what?"

"I took her to Pigeon Point."

"What happened then?"

"We got there and I stopped the motorcycle."

"I knew you weren't going to try to have sex with her on the motorcycle."

"That's where you're wrong. I *was* planning on having sex on the motorcycle, but she saw her old boyfriend. Guess who I saw with him? Our world history teacher. I took her home, and her neighbor was giving her a hard time. When I left, I told the neighbor that if she says anything to upset her, I will personally tell her children what she did. Then I left and came home. I didn't get to have sex with her. Well, that's all right. Mrs. Bryant told me that I'd better stick with the ones I love in the beginning."

"We think you and Bella should be together. That's all I heard, that y'all are going to the prom together."

"I also heard that Stacie wanted to go to the prom with me."

"Well, I'm going to bed."

"Good night, sis."

I went upstairs to my room, took off my clothes, and crawled in bed.

The next morning, I got up, went downstairs to eat breakfast, then back upstairs to take a shower, but my sister was still in there, so I had to wait on her. After I took a shower, I got ready in my room. Everybody was hollering, saying, "Buddy, let's go! We're waiting on you. Everybody else is ready."

"I'm coming!"

"Let's go! We're going to be late."

" I'm coming!"

"Are you riding with Bella?" they asked when I came downstairs.

"She's driving to school today."

"She's been waiting on you."

"Okay."

Bella was waiting outside in the Porsche. I got in and she took off as I was shutting the door. It was just Bella and me in the car. I asked her if she was still going to the prom with James.

She said yes. I said, "Why isn't he in the car with you? Why are you driving and not me?"

"You were late coming out, so I jumped in the driver's seat. So, what happened on your date last night?"

"Well, it didn't turn out like I wanted it to. We went to Pigeon Point."

"You what?"

"I took her to Pigeon Point on my motorcycle."

"Y'all must not have planned to have sex."

"I had planned to have sex on my motorcycle, actually, but she saw her old flame from her old school. Then I saw our world history teacher, Mrs. Hagur."

"Oh, no. Why was she there?"

"She was with Cheryl's old flame."

"You've got to be kidding."

"I took her home and Cheryl stayed with Kevin. I went in Mrs. Hagur's house. She needed help moving stuff in her bedroom, but her neighbor thinks she's having sex with us. I told the neighbor last night that if she tells Mrs. Hagur's husband that she's been cheating on him, I was going tell her children what she did. Mrs. Hagur hasn't had sex with any of us."

"Okay." Bella leaned over and kissed me. When we finally got out, I carried her books to class. I went to my seat, but first I put her books on her desk. She was coming in while everybody was asking me why I'd dumped Cheryl after the first date. All her friends and her cousins believed that I'd dumped her.

Kevin, Tyler, and Jackson asked me, "Why did you dump Cheryl? She has a perfect ten body."

I told them, "You rate her a ten. I rate her a nine point five. Bella is perfect ten. She has a perfect body that you can love forever." Bella sat down at her seat. Cheryl was going around saying that I'd dumped her.

But I found out it wasn't Cheryl saying that; there were some girls trying to get even with me. I hadn't asked them out. Cheryl approached me.

"Is it true that Buddy dumped you last night?" someone asked.

She looked at me and said, "No, that's not true. I don't know who came up with that idea, but it's wrong. I went back to my ex-boyfriend from my old school. You can say that I dumped Buddy to go back my old boyfriend."

It was April of 2033, and we had to practice. We had a game the next day, a doubleheader, plus we had to turn in our project for science.

I was glad Shon and Clay passed their exam. That way we could beat our rivalry. We could make it three in a row, which our school had never done against our rivalry. We could do this! It was 6:00 p.m., and we were in the locker room getting ready to take a shower when we heard the fire alarm. Half of us were naked when it went off. We came out with just a towel around us. Lots of people were laughing. I told them if they didn't shut up that I'd show them something to laugh at. A couple of people were still laughing. I took my towel off. They stopped laughing. All the girls smiled and whistled at me. I put my towel back around me before the teachers and coaches saw me. Some of the girls had towels around them. They'd also been in the shower.

I snatched towels off some of the girls and went around popping them on their butts. Everybody was laughing. The coaches told us to go back in and finish what we were doing, so we did. As we were waiting for the girls, one of our teachers asked, "Am I attractive?" We told her yes.

She was one of the hottest teachers we had besides Karen Hagur. We told her we only considered four of our teachers hot because most of them were males. Then she said, "Okay, name the four and what rank they are."

"Well, our number four is Mrs. Lisa Gallery. We rate her about nine point five. The third one is Mrs. Nicole Twain. We rate her at nine point seven. The second one is you, Mrs. Swanson. We rate you a nine point nine. The number one is our world history teacher, Mrs. Karen Hagur. We rate her a perfect ten. Y'all four are the only lady teachers we have." The girls came out just as Clay said, "I would like to see Mrs. Hagur naked."

Angie said, "Why would you want to do that? You don't want to see us naked?"

I said, "I'd like to see you naked. I'd like to have sex with any one of you, except my sister."

"Come on, then," Angie said, grabbing me. She took me to her car and we had sex, staying in there for an hour. Cam was waiting on her, then we were done and I climbed out of the car. She kissed me before I got out. I then got in the car with Stacie. Next month was our prom night, and I was still taking Stacie. I put my hands on her boobs and squeezed them as she was driving. She popped me on the hand. I told her to just keep on driving, let me do other things while she was driving. I was messing with her, then all of a sudden we stopped and were in the back seat having sex.

Once we got done, she took me home. It was about 8:00 p.m. when I walked in the house, and everybody asked me, "What are you doing home so early?" I told Mom we'd just left the school and the fire alarm had gone off while half of us were naked, just a towel around us. Then we'd all gone home. Jenny and Bella approached then, and Jenny asked Mom if Bella could stay with her. Mom told her that she didn't care as long her dad said it was okay. Bella called him at work. Mom asked, "What did your dad say?"

"He said he don't care." Bella went home, got her clothes, and told her mom and dad goodbye and that she loved them. She went over to Tammy's house, but she wasn't home.

"She was over at Clay's house," her uncle said to her. Bella made it back to our house.

I tried to call James and Clay, but no one answered their phone. I told Mom I was going to Bernie's Palace. I asked Jenny and Bella if they wanted to come. "Yes," Bella said.

"How about you, sis? I'm buying."

"No, you and Bella go on. Bella, you're company. She asked me to spend the night so she could be with you."

"Do you want to go in your car or mine?"

Bella said, "We'll just go in yours."

"Okay." I grabbed my keys and told Mom we'd be home at about 11:00 p.m.

"Okay. But no later than eleven."

Bella and I left the house and went to Bernie's Palace. When we got there, John and Jenifer were there, so we sat at the booth in the back. I ordered us a double cheeseburger with curly fries and a large Coke to share. There was one straw in the drink. We ate, then ordered a banana split. We had one spoon to eat with. I gave her some, and she put some in my mouth. We ate all the banana split, then talked for a while. Then we left

Bernie's Palace and went to Pigeon Point. We talked some more and had sex. I rated it a ten. Then we left Pigeon Point and went home. As we were getting out of the car, I kissed her and went in the house.

We were home before 11:00 p.m. When we went upstairs Mom and Dad were downstairs. Bella tried to enter Jenny's room, but couldn't go in. Jenny was fast asleep. So Bella came in my room. She shut the door and we sat and talked for hours. We watched television until she fell asleep in my arms, so I set the timer on the television to go off as I took her shoes and socks off, then unbuttoned her pants and took them off. She was wearing a thong, and I took her shirt and bra off, then put the covers over her. Then I took my clothes off, leaving only my boxers, and crawled in bed with her. I cut off the lights and was asleep in ten minutes. I woke up at 5:30 a.m., and Bella was still in bed with me. I eased toward her and put my arm around her.

She woke up at 5:45 a.m., went to the bathroom, and jumped in the shower. I got in when she got out. Mom came up and saw Bella in the room with Jenny and told her she needs to shut the door when she's putting her clothes on because I could pass by.

She told my mom, "It's all right if he sees me. I want him to."

My mother said, "I thought you were dating James."

"I am, but I also like Buddy."

"You want both of them is what you're telling me. Does James know about this?"

"He knows that the more I'm with Buddy, the more he can mess with my sister, Tammy. Stacie and Angie said that Tammy was with him last night. She was supposed to be at Clay's last night watching a movie with them, but instead she went to James's house."

I hadn't known that my mom, sister, and Bella were standing in the hallway. I hadn't brought any clothes and was naked. "Can somebody bring my clothes to me?" Bella said she would.

"We've got a guest, even though she doesn't mind you be naked," Mom said. "Put some clothes on and come downstairs to eat breakfast. You two, finish getting ready and come downstairs." They said okay as she went downstairs to finish getting our sister Elizabeth ready, telling my dad it was time to get up. Later she asked me about Bella. "I thought she was dating James. She told me she's dating both of y'all."

"Well, she's dating James. I'm dating Stacie."

"Why did she say she was dating both of y'all?"

"Don't ask me, ask her."

"They're coming down the stairs now."

"So ask her."

"Bella, Buddy told me you're James and he's dating Stacie. Is that true?"

Bella looked at me and said, "Yes, it's true."

"Well, do you think James will care if Buddy sees your body?"

She looked at me again and said, "I don't know if he will or not. He probably doesn't care that I heard what he did. It's time for us go to school."

"Buddy, you take Elizabeth to school. I'm not ready yet," Jenny said.

"Okay, sis." Elizabeth got in the car with Bella and me.

I was going to pick up Stacie, but Bella told me to drop her off at school first. She was supposed to wait on James. He was bringing Tammy to school. She got out of the car and stood across from the school while Cam and Angie walked right by her. I left and went to Stacie's house. She was coming out when I drove up in the car. She said, "I thought Bella was in the car with you. I didn't know you were in Bella's car."

"I drove her car because my dad needed mine. Plus, she spent the night with Jenny last night. She's at school waiting on James."

"Well, I heard Tammy was supposed to go to Clay's to watch a movie. Instead, she was at James's house. I heard she was in James's room, and you know what they probably were doing."

"We don't know. Don't assume we know what they did."

Stacie got in and asked again, "Why are you in Bella's car? Why didn't you ride your motorcycle?"

I looked at her and said, "Are you jealous because I'm driving Bella's car and not mine? Or is it that Bella and I spent some time together? Looks like you're jealous that you don't come over and spend the night with Jenny like Bella does. She comes over to the house just about every day. A lot of times she spends the night. Only time we ever doing anything is after school. You don't come to the house, and my mom always asks me if we're still together, and I tell her yes. Then she asks why you don't come to the house."

Stacie asked, "Do you love Bella?"

I said, "In a way I do, but I'm going out with you. I love you, Stacie. We're going to the prom. I just found out that they got somebody else to play at the prom, so we can dance all night. Unless you're still jealous of Bella. How about her sister, Tammy? Are you jealous of her if I dance with her or Angie? I don't understand. Why you so jealous? You spend more of your time at Clay's house than mine, and you're jealous because I drove Bella's car?"

We got to school and she got out of the car, then went to Clay. He asked me, "What did you do to Stacie?"

I told him, "Nothing. I just went and pick her up, then she got mad at me. She asked me why I was driving Bella's car."

"Why *are* you driving Bella's car?"

"My dad needed mine."

"Why didn't he drive Jenny's car?"

"It needs to be repaired. He needs another vehicle while Jenny's car is in the shop."

"Oh, okay."

"I told Stacie to stop being jealous. Have y'all heard that we don't have to play at our prom? Now they've got somebody else."

"Yes, we heard just a while ago. But back to Stacie. Let me talk to her."

I told him to go right ahead, that we were all going to dance with each other, so I went to class and sat down. James and Tammy approached me and asked, "What the matter?"

"Stacie got upset because I picked her up in Bella's car. I was going to take my car, but my dad asked me and Elizabeth to ride with Bella. We did. I drove because Stacie wanted me to pick her up. I took Elizabeth and Bella to school so she could meet y'all, then I picked Stacie up. When she got in the car, first thing she said to me was, why are you driving Bella's car? I told her, then she asked if I loved Bella. I told her that in a way I do, but I'm with her, not Bella. If she acts like this, she might need to go with somebody else. I was thinking about asking Jenifer out."

"So you're going to ask Jenifer instead of Bella?"

"Yes. I think all of us should ask somebody out else instead of the same ones we've been dating, because you are always going to dance with that person anyway. Plus you're still going to date that person. I figure I'll take somebody else to the prom instead of the ones I'm around day and night."

I asked Jenifer, but she was already going to the prom with somebody else.

I told James, "I'll go with Bella to the prom."

"That what I'm talking about! You're supposed to go out with Bella."

"Have you seen her?"

"No, I haven't seen her all day."

"I'm going to the office to see if they've seen her."

I walked to the office and overheard one of the teachers saying, "That guy grabbed one of our students. He had a gun at her back just a while ago."

Another teacher asked, "Which student?"

"Bella Klein."

"What are you going to do about this?" I asked. When none of them answered, I headed for the door.

"Buddy, come back here!"

"Tell me what vehicle he was in. Y'all didn't call the cops."

"No, he said if we did he'd kill her."

"Just tell me what color truck he was driving."

"It was blue with four doors. An F-150. He went toward Spark Drive."

"I'll be back with Bella. Don't tell anyone where I've gone, none of my closest friends. I'll do this alone."

I took James's sniper rifle out of his car, got in Bella's car, and drove off.

The principal started to call the cops, but Mrs. Helen said, "Don't call the cops. He will kill her. She's one of the best students we have, and you're trying to get her killed. Let Buddy do what he's going to do. If he isn't back to school in one hour, we'll call her dad."

"We need to tell her family. Her sister needs to know."

Her cousin went by the office and overheard them. He ran back to the classroom and told James that Buddy wasn't there. James said, "What do you mean, he isn't there?"

"He wasn't in the office. Bella's car is gone."

"Okay, everybody, let's go to the office."

They all went to the office, and all the teachers, coaches, and the principal were worried. James asked them what was wrong.

They said, "One of our students was taken. Bella. The guy told us not to call the cops. If we did, he would kill her." Tammy burst out crying, and some of the other girls did, too.

"Did anyone go after her?"

Mrs. Helen said, "Buddy left here about twenty minutes ago. We're giving him an hour."

James, Clay, Shon, and Cam looked at one another.

James said, "Let's go help Buddy and Bella."

The football players and cheerleaders left school. Mrs. Helen and Mrs. Hagur told Mrs. Angel to call the cops and their parents. Everybody left, and about five minutes later Bella and Buddy pulled up. Mrs. Angel said, "Everybody's gone to find you two."

Then the cops pulled up. The first person to arrive was Bella's dad, who was the chief of police. He said, "Where is my daughter?" She ran to him and he asked, "Are you all right?"

"Yes, he didn't harm me."

"How did you get away?"

"I didn't."

"He let you go?"

"No, he wasn't going to let me go."

"Then what happened?"

"It was Buddy. He shot the man twice, then untied me. Then he grabbed the guy, tied him up, and dressed his wounds. All y'all have got to do is pick him up."

The chief sent two patrol cars, but by the time they got there the man was gone.

"I want you to put a bulletin on the suspect: a male Caucasian, about six foot five inches, brown hair with a gray beard, blue eyes. He is armed and dangerous. Be very cautious. Do not shoot unless you're shot at. I repeat, do not shoot unless you're being shot at. Be careful. Okay, everybody, go home. School is out for the rest of the day. Buddy, take my little girl home."

"Yes, sir."

We got in her car and I took her home. Before I left, she told me to come in. She grabbed me by the hand and we went upstairs. Nobody was there, so we went to her room. She took her clothes off then came toward me. We kissed, then she ripped my shirt off and we had passionate sex.

We heard a vehicle; it was her dad. Her mom pulled up as her dad came to the door. She had her robe on and a towel around her head. Her dad came to Bella's room and said, "Thank you, Buddy, for saving my daughter."

"You're welcome. How did you know I was still here?"

"There's a ripped shirt on the floor. Plus, I know you better. You wouldn't leave unless one of us was here. Plus, I know my little girl. She wouldn't let you leave until we get home. I'm saying it again, thank you for saving my daughter."

He left the room. Bella was in the bathroom. When her mom came to the room, she didn't know I had just put on my boxers. "Buddy, put your clothes on!"

"Sorry, Mrs. Klein. I didn't know you were there."

"By the way, you've got a good-looking body. But you need to put some clothes on."

Bella came out the bathroom with no clothes on. She said, "Mom, what are you doing up here?"

"You just got kidnapped and I come to check on you."

"I'm all right. I was in the middle of doing something."

Her mom walked to her bedroom, where her husband Jerry was. Bella walked to her door, shut it, and locked it.

I told her that I had to leave soon. "I've still got chores to do."

She left the room to talk to her mom and dad about going to our house. I called Mom to see if Bella could come to the house.

It was May and getting closer to the prom, plus our state championship in baseball. We won most of our games, except ten games. We were twenty-five and ten. Now if we won that night, we'd go to the state championship for the third time. Our prom was two weeks away!

Today our project for our drama class with Mrs. Heather Walker was due. I'd forgotten about her. She was about a nine point eight on the scale She wore the shortest dress that she had. She liked to show everything. A lot of times, some of the guys popped her on the butt. There was a time when one of the guys accidentally dropped something on the floor, just to watch her pick it up. I left something in her classroom one day. When I went back, I heard someone moaning. She and Mr. Brook, the PE teacher, were having sex when I went in. She screamed at me to get out. I grabbed my notebook, but before I left the classroom, I took pictures of her naked.

They locked the door behind me and pulled the shades down. I walked around the corner as one of the coaches went towards her classroom, then I met up with Bella. We walked to her car and I opened the door for her, then went around to the other side and got in. We went to Bernie's Palace to hang out. We ate some hot wings and sat at our usual table. Some guys came over and said it was their table. They both were six foot five inches, and were about two hundred and thirty-eight pounds.

We said, "What? I don't think so. This has been our table as long we've been coming here. Y'all think you can just grab our table?"

"Who's going to stop us? I can beat y'all."

The guys laughed as they backed up. I stood and told the first boy, "Bring it."

The boy came toward me. I chopped him across his chest with a thrust that knocked him down. The other boy saw what I did and ran out the door. That was the last time we saw them.

We sat down again as the rest of the gang arrived. James asked me, "Where have you been?"

"We've been together."

"No you haven't."

"Yes, we have."

He said, "The only person I saw earlier was Bella."

I looked at Bella.

She said, "When you left something in Mrs. Walker's classroom."

"Yeah, I went back in to get it."

"Did you get it?"

"Yes. I've got to talk to you later about a situation I heard about someone in our class."

I turn around and Stacie kissed me. Bella saw her do that, so she grabbed me and kissed me.

Clay got back from ordering their food. Stacie got up and went to the restroom. As she was coming back, we saw Lauren at the window. I got up and went outside.

Lauren asked, "Why are you with that girl?"

"You are crazy. How did you get out?"

She told me some of the guards helped her. She'd even had sex with two of them, and she'd drugged another. "I came straight here to get you back."

I told her, "We've already call the cops."

Suddenly Bella came out. Lauren called Bella names, then ran toward her. Something knocked me out from behind. By the time everyone else came outside, Lauren had taken Bella. They were gone. James helped me up.

"What happened? Where is Bella?"

They were gone. Somebody had helped her escape. "I tell you what. Let's split up and look for them. If you think you spot them, call us and we'll meet up."

We searched different places, finally meeting up by an old church. James said he'd seen Lauren there talking to some guy who was dressed like her. I told everybody we needed to surround the church. I went in the front and James went in the back.

"When I get Lauren away from Bella, I want you to untie her," I said.

I went in the church and got Lauren's attention. She had a gun and shot at me. Two of the bullets hit my leg. I fell to the floor and she came at me. Tammy jumped on her, wrestled the gun away, and shot her in the head, killing her. My sister called 911, then Bella's parents.

James, Shon, Clay, and Cam approached me and James said, "Well, you don't have to worry about her anymore."

"I know who I'm taking to the prom," I said. "Tammy! She saved my butt."

After the paramedics put me on the stretcher, Tammy came over to me. They were going to take me to the hospital. I asked her, "Do you want to go to the prom with me?"

She told me yes, she did! Then she kissed me as they loaded me into the ambulance. My parents and everyone else met me at the hospital.

I was stronger by the time the prom arrived. The girls wore red velvet evening gowns and the guys wore black tuxedos. James rode in Bella's Porsche, Tammy and I rode in a Ferrari, Clay and Stacie rode in a Lamborghini, Cam and Angie rode in a Viper, and Shon and Jenny rode in a Corvette. Mrs. Westco had asked my parents if they wanted to be chaperones for the prom, and they'd told her they would be proud to do it.

We all went in together and started to dance. We were the only ones on the dance floor when our parents showed up. Then the DJ got sick and left. The principal asked us to play instead. Luckily our parents had some of our instruments with them, so we played for about an hour. We took turns dancing after that. I danced with Tammy mostly, but I did dance with Bella, Stacie, and Angie as well. Our prom lasted until 1:00 a.m. There was a girl who didn't get to dance, so Tammy told her that I would dance with her. Nobody knew her. We found out that her mom was our principal. Her name was Jenifer and she went to a private school in Chicago.

She'd come with her mom to our prom. They'd had their prom last week, but she'd came with her mom to keep her company while her dad was in Russia. I grabbed her by the hand and asked her if she wanted to dance. Shon and Jenny were singing that song that Stacie and I had sung before. They sang to each other as James and the rest played and sang with them. I danced with Jenifer, then afterwards I grabbed Tammy by the hand and we all got in our cars and went to Bernie's Palace, staying there until 4:00 a.m.

Then we packed up and went to Pigeon Point, staying up there until 6:30 a.m. After we got there, everybody switched cars. I jumped in Bella's car at first and James jumped in Tammy's car, then Clay jumped in Stacie's. Then I got in the car with Stacie and we got in the back seat. We kissed and made passionate love.

The windows fogged up. I finally got out of Stacie's car with no shirt or boxers on, just my pants and shoes. Then I got in the car with Bella. She took off her dress while I cranked the car. We arrived at my house and went upstairs to take a shower, then I went to bed. She crawled in my bed and went to sleep. I slept on the couch. We slept until 2:00 p.m., then I got up. Bella went home, then I went to my cousin's house. We had a lot of things to do. We went to the coach's house to get ready for next season. He grilled out for all the players and the cheerleaders. Mrs. Hagur came and brought her husband and kids. The coach cooked steaks, baked potatoes, and French fries.

Summer was here, and we were going to be seniors. We were getting ready to go to Tennessee for our recording, and had to leave the next morning. Bella came to the house with Tammy and Stacie. All of them went into Jenny's room, trying on clothes for the trip. I didn't know they were in Jenny's room because she wasn't home. She was out with Shon. When I walked by, I saw them changing. All three were in their bra and thongs, putting on different clothes. Tammy and Bella didn't see me. They were bent over to get some clothes. Stacie was too busy to see me coming in the room with them.

"These are the clothes we're are going to wear for our recording," Bella said.

"The producers are going to take our picture and put it on our album cover. The Fabulous 8."

The girls followed me to my room and I shut the door.

I kissed all three of them, then I grabbed one by the hand and started to dance. My mother came and knocked on the door. I said, "I'll be down in few minutes."

"Okay. If you see the girls, tell them to come down, too."

"Okay."

We got dressed and went to the living room where everybody at. Everybody who was making that trip was at our house.

Bella was sitting in my lap. There weren't enough chairs, so several of the girls were sitting on the boys' laps. I had my hand in my lap and she sat down on it while my parents were talking. She was laughing at Cam. We talked about who was staying with us and who was staying with Jerry Klein. Half stayed at our house, and the other half stayed at Jerry's. All the girls stayed at my house, and it was getting late. I stayed with the guys at Jerry's house. I didn't know the girls had come back to Bella's house. I was walking around with nothing on. Stacie came out of Bella's room while I walked toward the bathroom. She entered the bathroom, where I was putting on my clothes, and shut the door. Then she pulled her pants down and peed. I was brushing my teeth and shaving.

When Stacie finished, I messed with her before she walked out. She left and the girls went back to my house. As I went to Bella's room, I tried to call James, but I had trouble getting in touch with him.

The next morning we ate a good breakfast, then jumped in the car. Our parents rode in one vehicle and everyone else got in the Hummer. As only six of us could ride in the Hummer, I drove Bella's Porsche 911. James drove Tammy's Ferrari. It took us six hours to get to Nashville. Clay and Shon took turns driving. When we got to Nashville, our parents met us at the hotel. We went to our room and my dad called the producer and told him we were in town. The producer wanted us to eat lunch with him at a restaurant.

"A lot of stars have eaten there!"

We drove all four vehicles to the restaurant. The record producer was there waiting for us. The name of the place was Elvis Presley Diner.

Later we had steak and lobster for supper. It was getting late, and we had to get up early in the morning. Everybody was eating when Bella hollered that she had seen a ghost. There was a girl who looked like Lauren, but she was twenty-one years old, with black hair and bluish green eyes. She was a lot taller than Lauren. We got back to the hotel and made sleeping arrangements. The guys were in one room and the girls were in the other. Our parents all shared a room together.

The next morning at the studio, the girl was there. We signed the new contract.

Before we left, Clay asked her name. She told him it was Jenifer. He said, "You're gorgeous."

"Thank you."

"See that girl over there beside that boy?"

"Yeah, what about her?"

"She thought you were somebody else, someone who tried to kill her. Can I get your phone number?"

She said she'd given her number to Shon. He was the who one wrote our songs.

Chapter 4

We were finally seniors in our last year of high school. We'd had a wonderful summer vacation. We'd gotten our record deal and signed our contract. I went out with a twenty-one-year-old woman during our summer. I drove my Harley Davidson to Nashville every weekend, and at one point I stayed up there for three weeks. After everybody went back home, I stayed with Jenifer in her apartment while she went to work every day. When she came home, I had her supper fixed and her apartment cleaned up.

Now I was a senior. We were going to have the best year ever. We'd all decided to go to Florida State to college. Some of our teachers were beautiful women. They were from twenty-four to twenty-eight years old. We had four female teachers and two male teachers. One teacher wore tight dresses or skirts that went up to her thigh. Her name was Mrs. Kerrie Strajax. She was about a nine point seven. She wore thongs and a see-through bra.

We had a project to do for English and had to get in a group of four this time. I was in a group with three girls. Two of them I went out with, and the third I wanted to know better. They'd just moved to our school this year. Their names were Kelly, Stephanie, and Donna. Donna's brother was our safety. His name was Fritz. She was the one I wanted to go out with and was a nine point eight. Bella wanted to go out with Fritz. James, Bella, Tammy, and Fritz were in a group together. Clay, Cam, Stacie, and Angie were in another group together, and in the final group were Shon, Jenny, Kevin, and Derek. We left one class and went to the next, which was drama class with Mrs. Walker. She was different that year. She usually wore a miniskirt or tight dresses that went up to her upper thighs. When she bent over you could see everything. But now she wore pantsuits to school, and she behaved more like a teacher.

She'd almost gotten caught with another teacher, or so we'd heard. We didn't know who it was yet. She'd almost gotten fired, but no one had confessed who the other teacher was.

"We heard you were in Mrs. Walker's classroom when it was locked," Jackson, a classmate, said.

"You heard wrong," I said. "I was there, but I got what I needed, then left. She shut the door behind me. She must have locked it after I left." All of a sudden she hollered at us and told us to get in our seats. This was our first day of school. She was mad when I went up there and asked her what we'd done to deserve this. She told me to get back in my seat!

"Everybody's getting homework today, so shut up and listen when I call your name. The names I call out will be your partners on this project, which is due in January. Go sit with your group when I call your name. Donna, Bella, Tammy, Shon, Kevin, and Fritz in the first group. The second group is Sabrina, Kelly, Stephanie, Clay, James, and Chavez. The third group is Angie, Amy, Stacie, Buddy, Cam, and Vincent. The fourth group is Jenny, Lori, Becky, Bobby, Leroy, and Jacob. The final group is Serene, Brittney, Renee, Jackson, Carl, and Derek. You will sit with your partners in my classroom. I've got five tables, one for each group."

"We know why you're mad. You almost got fired!" someone said.

"I'm not mad at y'all. I'm mad at myself. I should've known better."

"Some of us heard it was Buddy in the classroom with you. We heard you got caught playing with yourself."

She looked at me and said, "I was not caught playing with myself, so let's drop this subject. This is your homework, which is due Friday. Think about who your favorite actor or actress is then write a report on how they started acting. I want ten pages. Friday, you will give your report in front of the class."

It was time for us to go to our last class, which was gym. We all went to our locker rooms and changed into our shorts. For twenty minutes we exercised, then for the last twenty-five minutes we played basketball. The girls played basketball on the other half of the court. Then the school bell rang. It was 3:00 p.m., so we went to the locker room and showered, then put on our clothes and went outside to the parking lot. We sat in the parking lot for a while, waiting on everybody to get there. Fritz was the last guy to get to the parking lot and Jenny and Angie were the last girls. I got in Donna's car, which was a BMW Mercedes Benz. It had a 440 engine in it and was built differently. It could outrun a Lamborghini or a cop car. The windows were tinted. It was two-toned, green with red. Everybody followed Donna and me to Bernie's Palace, and I asked her to go out with me. She said yes! We celebrated at Bernie's Palace.

I told Jo Ann, the waitress, we wanted our usual table, but she told me there were two guys sitting there. I told her we'd take care of it. Clay and Fritz asked the guys nicely to move. They were seven feet two inches tall and were about three hundred pounds, but Clay and Fritz asked them again to move. They stood up and said, "Who going to move us?"

"They are," I said, then I nodded to Clay.

The guys laughed at them and said, "Come on, let's see what you've got."

Clay did a flip in the air and kicked one of the guys. Fritz kicked the other in the thigh and made him fall. When they finally got up they couldn't walk, but they managed to hobble off.

We all gathered at the table and were talking about what we were going to do after we graduated high school. Ten of us were going to Florida State, then Donna said she and Fritz were going to Florida. "We'll probably see ya'll during the summer."

"Okay."

"Hey, Buddy, those guys are back with reinforcements," Clay said.

"Okay, let's go outside, guys."

We met the guys outside.

"Hey, punks, we want to see what y'all have got!" one of them said. "We don't want to fight y'all. We might hurt y'all really bad in front all your friends."

"Well, I don't think that's going to happen."

"Why you say that?"

"Because look, your friends are running."

The guy turned and saw his friends fleeing. "Come back here, cowards!"

"We aren't cowards!" one called. "Did you see what one of those boys did?"

"No. What did he do?"

"One of the boys was holding a board. He turned a flip and broke the board with his foot!"

The final guy ran to his friends and we went back inside and ordered food. After we finished, we jumped in our cars and went. I drove Donna to her house and then went to my own. Mrs. Walker was talking to my mom and dad in the living room. I said, "Why are you here?"

"I need to talk to you about some things. Can we go somewhere to be alone?"

"Yeah, follow me." I took her to my room. As I closed the door and locked it, Jenny came upstairs and went to her room. Bella went in with her. They saw my door close.

Mrs. Walker sat on my bed. She said, "No one knows about what happened last year. We need to keep it quiet. No one needs to know. Come here." I walked toward her. She grabbed me by the arm and whispered stuff in my ear. While she whispered, she unbuttoned my pants and kissed me. I pulled away from her.

"I thought you would go along with this," she said.

"I've already been accused of it."

I told her to lie back and then pulled her pants off. She took her panties off, then I took all my clothes off and we had sex, just like she wanted.

My mom knocked on my door. I told her that I'd be down in twenty minutes. We put our clothes back on and she went down the stairs, told my mom and dad thank you and goodbye, then walked out the door. I went downstairs and sat at the table right beside Bella. After we ate, I went upstairs and took a shower. Jenny went outside and Bella went upstairs to Jenny's room. She got her pocketbook and was leaving Jenny's room when I came out of the bathroom. I was still naked. She followed me to my room and told me she would always love me. I told her I would always love her, too, even when we weren't officially dating. She headed for the stairs and I followed her. When she turned around, I was right there behind her and we kissed.

The kiss lasted for ten minutes, then she went downstairs and outside, getting in the car with Jenny. I put my clothes on and went outside, got on my Harley, and rode to James's house. We rode to Bernie's Palace and met up with Clay, Shon, and Cam. Jenny and Bella had gone to Stacie's house. Tammy and Angie were already there. We discussed what we were going to do over the Christmas holiday. We were thinking about going to Daytona Beach. Our parents were going out of town during our holiday.

When I got home I talked my parents and told them everybody else was going to talk to their parents.

They were going on a trip for business, so I asked them if we could go to Daytona for our Christmas holiday. Afterwards we decided to go to Stacie's house. That was where the girls were, so we left on our motorcycles. When we arrived we talked to the girls to see if they wanted to go to Daytona for our Christmas holiday. They said yes, so I got on the computer and reserved a hotel. I paid for the rooms for everybody, and we let the girls draw to see who would ride with whom. Bella would ride with me, James and Tammy would ride together, Clay and Stacie together, Cam and Angie together, and Shon and Jenny together.

We would leave on the twenty-first of December at 7:00 a.m., and hoped we'd get down there at 4:00 p.m. That way we could get on the nude beach. It was the eighteenth of December and we had three more days before we'd leave. I went to Donna's house and she was the only one home. I asked her where everybody was and she told me they were gone. I asked her if she wanted to go to Bernie's Palace. She told me no!

Then she asked if I wanted to stay. I told her okay, I'd stay with her. "You sure you and your brother don't want to go with us to the Daytona Beach?"

"Yes, we're sure. We've got to go to New York with our parents to see our family."

I asked her again if she wanted to go to Bernie's Palace, then she told me yes. On the way, there were cops everywhere. I asked, "What happened here?"

They told me to keep going, there was nothing to see or do there. I said, "Okay, you don't have to get an attitude with me. I'm going." Donna and I went on to Bernie's Palace. When we got there the girls were there. I asked where the guys were. They said they were at the mall getting things for the beach.

I trusted Bella enough to know what to get for me and her. I gave her my credit card, then Donna and I left Bernie's Palace and headed back to Donna's house. There was a guy in a gray car following us. I'd noticed him when we left Bernie's Palace. I told Donna to hang on. We hit a hundred and twenty miles per hour, but the guy was still back there. We hid behind a house as the guy sped by and a cop pulled up behind him with their lights flashing. He pulled over, so we left and passed right by him. I looked in my mirror and saw the guy shoot the police officer.

He took off after us again, but we were faster than him. We stopped somewhere and hid and I got off the motorcycle. When he went by, I threw two knives at his tires. It stopped him! He got out and ran toward us then, but we got back on the motorcycle and I took off.

We finally made it to Donna's house. We went in and told Donna's parents what happened. I ask them if they were in trouble. They told me no. I said, "Okay, I'm going home."

"Okay, be careful."

When I arrived home my family and friends were there to greet me. They were happy to see me and couldn't wait to hear everything that had happened. Bella, Jenny, and Elizabeth began to question me about the trip. They knew something was wrong.

I was not myself. I finally told them what had happened. They immediately told me to call the police. I disagreed and told them I was not calling the cops, that I would take care of the problem. Soon after, Bella talked to me alone. She convinced me calling the cops was the best option. A few minutes later the cops showed up to our house, asking questions left and right. Sergeant Boyd asked me what the guy looked like. After several hours of questioning, Sergeant Boyd said he had enough information, that he was getting right to work on the case.

Relieved, the girls and I began to get excited about our trip. Sitting around the dinner table, the only thing Bella, Jenny, and I could talk about was the trip to Daytona Beach. Elizabeth was upset that she couldn't go to the beach. She was still excited about going on the trip with our parents, though. After dinner everyone helped clean the kitchen, then we packed our bags and went to bed. We got up at 5:30 a.m. and some of us had to take a shower.

Everyone gathered their things and began to head out. Bella, Jenny, and I waited on the gang to arrive at the house. I told everybody bye, then went outside and put everything in the saddles. Bella got on the motorcycle with me and we left round 7:00 a.m.

We made it to Daytona Beach at 4:00 p.m. First thing we did was go to the hotel to put our bags up. We put our stuff in the room, then went looking for a nude beach. The staff told us to go two blocks down. We did and there was the beach on the next right. We parked our motorcycles and walked about a half mile before we saw people naked on the beach. Some started to run and took their clothes off. Before we got to the beach, we put our clothes in a locker. There were beautiful naked girls. We were walking down the beach when a girl ran into me and fell. Her sisters came running toward us and one said, "Look where you're going!" to her sister.

"It isn't her fault," I said. "It's my fault, too. What's your name?"

"Lynn. These are my sisters, Missy, Tammy, and Shannon."

I was falling in love with her. I helped her up and brushed the sand off her. She had a nice body. Then we turned and walked one way and they walked the other way. We went to a restaurant to eat and sat there naked. I saw some people teasing Tammy and Lynn. They wanted to have sex with them. Cam and I went to their rescue. while James and Clay stayed with the girls. There were six guys messing with them. I told Cam to take three and I would take three. We fought them and beat them up. Lynn and Tammy ran toward us and said, "Our heroes." They hugged our necks and said thank you.

They told us they didn't have any clothes or jobs, and wondered if we had any clothes for them. I told them I'd ask the girls. The girls told me no, that we weren't helping them, that we were leaving to go to the hotel. I told the guys to give those girls some money to buy clothes. We told the girls we were leaving, and that we left some money for the other girls to buy clothes, food, and a ride. We started to leave when the cops showed up and arrested the girls for getting the money. The mayor had told them that we gave the money to him and those filthy girls had taken it.

Bella, Tammy, and Stacie told the cops the girls had been on the beach for a year. Jenny said I had given the money to those girls so they could buy clothes, and the other boys had done the same.

"You're saying the mayor is the thief? How about I put all you girls in jail for slurring the mayor?" the officer said.

Tammy and Stacie said, "We didn't know he was the mayor. All we know is that he said those girls were thieves, that they were trying to get out of here, but somebody kept them from getting their clothes. We tried to give them money so they could get clothes, food, and a ride."

We grabbed the cops and the mayor and held them as our girls got the other girls on the motorcycles and took off. James and I were shot at by the cops as we ran and hid. We found a place on the beach to hide until the cops and the mayor left, then they went further down the beach. We spent the night at one of the lifeguard shacks. We texted the girls and told them, "Don't come back until early in the morning. We'll just spend the night in the lifeguard shack. Come back in the morning and pick us up." We tried to make ourselves comfortable.

We took turns staying up and watching to make sure no one found us. It was 6:00 a.m. when the girls came back to pick us up. We went back to the hotel and showered. Bella was the only one in the room when I got out. "Where did the other girls go?" I asked.

"They bought some clothes and left early this morning for Las Vegas for a job your dad got them."

"Okay, that's good. That's all we wanted." I was putting on my clothes when I asked her, "What do y'all want to do today?"

"Let's go to the beach!"

"Okay, we'll go."

We let the others know the plan and Clay said, "What about the cops and the mayor? The chief of police is going to have every officer looking for us."

"That's okay. We can get out of it, just as we got out of that predicament in New York. Don't y'all remember?"

"Yes, we remember. But the building still blew up."

"I didn't know it was going to do that. What about the other times when Bella got kidnapped twice and we got out of that?"

"You're right. We'll get out of this. There are cops all over this hotel looking for us, and I heard somebody talking to the clerk about what room we're in. We came in here to find out how we're getting out."

I went to the window and saw all the cops outside. I thought about how we could escape, then saw the vent and said, "Let's get in the vent."

"We might not all fit in there!" Clay said.

"We have to try!"

We tried and all of us fit. James and Clay went in first, then Jenny, Angie, Shon, Tammy, Stacie, Cam, Bella, and finally me. We heard voices. It was the chief of police telling his guys to go in. They called out, "This is the police. Open up! Y'all are under arrest." They didn't get an answer, so they busted down the door and came in. They searched everywhere and couldn't find anybody in the room. The chief of police told his guys to look in the other rooms on the floor. Everybody left except two guys.

They went in another room. I got out of the vent and went to check on where those two cops were. I looked down the hall, then told Bella to tell everyone else to stay there, that we would find a way out of there. Bella passed the message on.

"When you see the cops leave, then come out of the vent. We'll come and get y'all when coast is clear."

Bella and I left the room and the cops returned shortly afterwards.

We went down the stairs to the third floor and found an empty room whose door had been left ajar. It was under our room. We called our room and Shon answered the phone. "Where are y'all?" he asked.

"In room 325. Be careful, there are still cops around. Y'all might need to have a disguise to get where we are."

"No, we've found something that will help us lower ourselves to the third floor!"

The idea was that they would tie sheets together, secure them to the rail, and then they'd slide down to the third floor. The girls went first and did not look down.

"Bella and I will help y'all while you're coming down."

All the girls made it. James and Shon went next, then Cam and Clay.

Then we heard the chief of police. "They're on the third floor! I want them arrested!"

We got on the elevator and went up to the roof instead of going downstairs to the lobby. When we got to the roof, there was a wire that went from our building to the next building. All the guys took their belts off. I said, "Okay, who wants to go first?" Shon said he would. He put his belt over the wire and told Jenny to hold on to him. They slid to the other building. The next two were Cam and Angie. They slid to the other building, then the next two, and so forth until everybody was on the other building. We went in and used the elevator to the lobby. James and I looked out and saw four cops! I told him I would distract them while they got on the motorcycles. I went to the closest cop car and hot-wired it. Then I took off with the sirens on. All the cops came after me while everyone else got on the motorcycles. They rode by the hotel and the police chief saw them through the windows. He told the rest of the cops to go after them.

I did a three-sixty and headed back toward the hotel. There was a cell phone in the seat and I called Tammy, telling her to tell Bella to turn off Minesfield and 12th Street. I'd be waiting in the parking garage on top of the building. Bella did so and I was waiting there to jump on the back of the Harley. We took off. When I told her to go to the right, she went right and we met with the others.

They asked, "Where are we going?"

"Let's ride to Miami."

"What about our clothes?"

I told them we'd get new ones when we got to Miami. We rode for miles and everybody was getting hungry.

We stopped at a restaurant and my cellphone rang. I answered it. A guy said he knew who we were, that he was the most powerful man in Florida. His family was Derek Coley, and he was the leader of the biggest mafia family in Florida.

"If y'all don't want to worry about any cops, I can help you. I've got a proposition for you. I know you're heading to Miami. When you get there, go to the Crab House. That's where you'll find me."

We hung up at the same time.

James asked, "Who was that on the phone?"

I told them, "I'll tell y'all when we get a seat."

We went in and asked for a big table. I told them when we got to Miami we'd go to the Crab House. "There's a guy, Derek Coley. He said he's got a proposition for us."

"Did you say Derek Coley?"

"Yes."

"He's the most dangerous mafia leader in Florida. He's nothing but trouble."

Then we noticed there were two people there who had followed us from Chicago. We found out they were FBI agents. We went up to them and said, "We know y'all are FBI agents. Why are y'all following us?"

"Did we hear you right, that Derek Coley called you?"

"Yes. He said he's got a job for us when we get to Miami."

After we ate steak and baked potatoes we got back on our Harleys. Then we went to Miami where we stopped at the Crab House.

We parked and went in the restaurant. I told the guy Mr. Derek Coley was expecting us. He told him we had arrived. The guy came back and told us to come inside. We followed him to a room and he told us to sit down.

Mr. Coley said, "I've got a proposition for y'all. I heard you wanted to go to Hawaii for college. I tell you what. You'll do me favors, and I will pay for y'all to go to Hawaii. If all fails? You'll be on your own and I will make your lives a living hell. Then I will hunt your families down and kill them. Not you guys, but your families. This not a threat, but a promise. I will split y'all up. All the girls and Shon will stay with me. He will join my men as one of the executioners. Stinger, take the girls to join the others. Tell our girls to help the new ones out. After lunch, bring them to my room. Disel, take Shon and show him where he's staying. Well, guys, that leaves only you four. You can come back tomorrow. I'll tell you then what your job is. Steve will show you what hotel you're staying in."

After checking in to the hotel, we went to a restaurant to eat. I gave them my plan. I told them what we would do was try to get our families out. I knew Bella and the girls were already thinking of how to escape. I told them, "We will come up with a plan when we find out what our job is tomorrow. Right now, we'll eat." Clay went to the bar and asked for a pitcher of beer. He overheard some guys talking about Shon and how Derek Coley knew Shon's father. That was why he'd wanted Shon with him. We knew Shon could get out of this.

Clay came back to the table and we asked him why it had taken so long. He said he'd had to wait on the beer! We drank and played pool as we waited on our food. We ate, then we went back to the hotel. We each had our own room.

Then we went down to a bar, where dancers were on the stage dancing. Their names were Kaylin, Layne, Chelsea, Rhealynne, and Savage. Some of us stayed and watched them dance. Then we returned to our hotel and went to bed. Suddenly it was 8:00 a.m. Coley's henchman came around and told us we had one hour to be ready to go to his boss's office. We showered, then went downstairs to eat breakfast. Afterwards we went to the Crab House to meet with Coley.

"I hope y'all are enjoying the hotel and slept well." We told him we'd enjoyed it. "Here's the job: I want y'all to steal a rare diamond in the

National Bank of Miami, along with fifty million dollars. Just you four. If anything goes wrong, the five girls and your friend Shon will die."

"We want to see the girls."

"Bring the girls here." They brought them out.

I asked, "Why are they dresses like hookers?!" They hardly had any clothes on. "We want to see Shon." They brought Shon out with a bomb strapped to him. "We'll do it! Just don't harm them."

"Tonight. I want you to use your skills to get it done. Bring the diamond and money to me and I will do what I promised. Do I make myself clear?"

"Yes." We left and went back to the hotel.

"Buddy, what is the plan?"

"The plan is we're going to steal the money and the diamond. Then we're going to use it as leverage."

"Why do you say that?"

"Bella and the girls are going to help Shon get out. They're going to use the bomb to get away. Bella's going call me to let me know they've escaped. Then we're going to meet them in Texas. Let's go to the bar before we go to the hotel."

We went to the bar, and those same dancers were there. We talked to them. They were twenty to twenty-two years old. Layne was the youngest. We drank and danced with them. I was dancing with Kaylin, who said, "Let's go to your room."

We went to the room and I shut the door. She sat on the couch and I asked her if she wanted something to drink. "Water and scotch!" I told her to get comfortable.

She took off her shoes and coat. She had on a see-through bra and thong. I fixed her drink and gave it to her. She drank four glasses. Then I carried her to my bed and wrapped her up. I put fifty thousand dollars on the dresser for her and left a note. It was time to go to the bank.

We arrived at the building next to the bank. Cam shot a harpoon spear to the other building. We slid to the roof and Clay put his device to the roof, which shut down all the alarms. Then I cut a hole and opened the glass window. We slid down to the vault and James cracked the safe.

He opened it and there was the biggest diamond we'd ever seen and fifty million dollars. We got all of it and closed the door. James went up first and I went last. We resecured the window and Clay turned the alarm back on. Cam shot the spear again to the other building. We slid to the roof of the building, then went to the airport and stole a plane. I got a call from Bella. I told her I missed her and loved her. She told me they had escaped and hot-wired a boat. "We'll meet y'all in Texas." They'd found some ballroom dancers on the boat, Brent and Chance. They'd told Bella they'd give her and the others money if they didn't hurt them.

Cam got us off the ground. I found a missile on board. I told the others about it and that we needed to be careful. We got to Texas and saw people fighting below. Some were Americans and some were Mexicans. They saw us land, then got in their trucks and headed towards us.

We pushed the missile off the plane and it landed between two cars and blew up.

We met up with the others and they got on board. "Hawaii, here we come! Who is this young lady?" I asked when I noticed a girl I didn't recognize.

"This is Heather, Mr. Coley's sister," Bella said. "She wanted to come with us. Brent and Chance wanted to come as well, but I told them just keep on going."

Derek Coley knew about our escape now! He said, "Curses, those kids have escaped! They've got my sister, the diamond, and fifty million dollars."

He knew we were headed to Hawaii, so he made a phone call. "Hello, Samon. This is Derek Coley."

"Coley, how may I help you?"

"There's a plane heading your way with a bunch of kids on it. They stole a diamond and fifty million dollars. I want you to apprehend them until my guys get there. Bring them back to Florida."

"Buddy?" Cam said.

"Yes, Cam?"

"We've got trouble ahead. There are cops everywhere."

"Just fly by them and try to land on one of those islands." We flew right by them.

Shon asked Heather, "Who are you?"

She repeated that she was Derek's sister and she wanted to get away from her brother. "My brother killed my boyfriend, just shot him in front of me. I still haven't forgiven him. I've been planning on leaving. Just waiting on somebody willing to leave. That why I got close to y'all, so I could get my shot at leaving."

Cam said, "Get your seat belts on and prepare for a rough landing!" We landed and he asked, "Is everybody all right?"

We said yes. I told everybody to stay in the plane, except James, Clay, and me. We went out and looked around. We found wood for a fire, then hunted some wild hogs and killed them.

James said, "There's a snake behind you."

I killed the snake, the girls cooked it, and we ate it. We were on the island for two months before we finally saw a ship going by. It was heading to Hawaii. They picked us up and dropped us off in Hawaii. We went to a bank and split the fifty million dollars between five couples. Then we walked on the beach. We needed to find a place to stay. Our clothes were ragged by that point. Heather went her own way, and before we knew it, it was April 12. We only had a month and a few weeks before we would graduate. We were staying at a hotel.

Bella and I got a room together. We took a hot shower together, then relaxed until I received a phone call. It was a Mr. Yang, a millionaire and art collector. He wanted a painting that was worth over five hundred million dollars. He said he'd pay us one hundred million dollars each to steal it! I told him we would do it and he gave me the address to the owner's house. I called James to get all the guys together, telling them to meet me in the lobby in an hour. Then I went to Bella and put my arms around her. She hugged me and I kissed her.

She asked, "What's wrong?"

"We're going to do a job that's considered dangerous."

I kissed her and we had sex in the living room. Then I put my clothes on and met up with the guys in the lobby. James asked me what was going on.

"We've got a job that will pay us one hundred million dollars apiece."

"What's the job?"

"We've got to steal a painting that's worth five hundred million dollars. We'll get the painting. Then we're going to try to get five hundred million dollars. The guy is a millionaire; he's got a lot of money."

We went to the address the guy had given me. Clay cut all the alarms and I picked the lock on the front door. Cam and James grabbed the painting. After I locked the door again, Clay turned the alarm back on. It went off. We jumped in the jeep and Shon, who was driving, took off. We stopped about three miles away.

I called the millionaire and told him our price had gone up to five hundred million each. He told me he wouldn't give us any more money. I said, "If you don't give us the money, we'll take the painting back to the owner."

"All right, I'll pay it. Meet me at the Milo Bar."

When we got there, he pulled a gun on us and said that he wasn't paying a dime.

Cam punched him and took the gun from him. He gave each of us a check for three hundred and fifty million dollars. We gave him the painting. Then he said, "I've got another job, if y'all want it. Just give me a call if you do."

We went back to the hotel and talked to the girls about our plans. They talked it over. Two didn't like it and two did. One didn't vote. Then they decided together that it was dangerous, but fun and exciting. "Let's go out and eat at a nice restaurant tonight. What time is it?"

"About six o'clock."

"We'll meet y'all downstairs. Plan to leave at seven."

Bella and I got in the shower, did a little hanky-panky, then got out and got ready. There was a restaurant about two blocks from the hotel, so we met up with the others and walked there. While we were waiting on our food, we talked what we were going to do. I said, "The guy said he's got another job for us."

"What is the job?"

"I didn't ask. He just told me if we decide we want it to let him know. We just made three hundred and sixty million dollars each."

"You know y'all could got killed?"

"It was exciting and adventurous! It gives you have a rush and gets your adrenaline pumping!"

"I don't know if I want y'all to do it. That's how we feel," Bella said. The girls agreed.

"How about we do one more job? We'll see what he's got for us. I'll call him when we get back to the hotel."

When we got back and I called him, he told us to come tomorrow morning at eight o'clock. We would see then what our job would be.

Bella said, "I still don't like it."

At the hotel, we were back in our room. Bella and I were having sex. We got up at seven o'clock and got ready.

"You know, next year we're going to start college," she said. "Some of us are fixing to have real jobs to pay for it. Tammy, Stacie, and I are going to work at a bank, and Jenny got a part-time job as a secretary at a law firm. Angie will be working at the hospital. I'll see you later, honey."

Then we kissed and the guys went to Mr. Yang's house. He greeted us and said, "Here's the job. I've got two packages that need to be in California by tomorrow morning at nine o'clock. You'll leave tonight at 9:00 p.m. and arrive in California at 12:00 a.m. Then you'll take taxis to 1334 Hickory Street. Don't be late and don't open the packages. Come back here at 8:30 p.m. tonight to pick the packages up. It pays one hundred and fifty thousand dollars a package."

We went back to the hotel. I told Bella to pack all our stuff, that we were going to our new home.

She said, "It's not the glass house like I wanted!"

"Yes, it is."

So she packed all our stuff and got in the jeep.

Just before we got there, I told her to close her eyes. She did. "You can open them now. We're here." She was amazed at how big it was. On the computer, it hadn't looked that big. Of course, that was the computer. I asked her if she wanted to look inside and she jumped on my lap and said, "Yes, let's go in!"

When we went in the kitchen the light came on automatically. We walked out again. The light went off in every room. We went in, the light came on, and when we left the room, the light went off. When a person stayed in the room, the light stayed on.

"How about it?" I asked.

"It's nice, but we can't afford to stay in here."

"Why not? It's paid for."

"Who paid for the house?"

"I did! It was fifteen million dollars, and we've got over three hundred and sixty-five million dollars in the bank. We've got to leave tonight at 9:00 p.m. to go to California for that job."

It was 8:30 p.m. and I kissed Bella goodbye. The guys were waiting for me. When I got to the jeep, the girls were on the porch waiting for Bella to open the door. We went to the airport and one of Mr. Yang's men was there waiting for us.

"Here are the packages," he said. "Remember, do not open them, and good luck."

We got on the plane and it took off. We got to Sacramento at 2:00 a.m. and a limousine driver hollered at us. He asked if my name was Buddy and told us to get in the car. When we got to a big mansion, we couldn't believe our eyes at how beautiful it was. A butler came to the door and let us in. He told us to wait in the study and that Mr. Yang would be ready for us soon. We waited in the study for about ten minutes before the butler came and got us. The butler showed us to an office and Mr. Yang was behind the desk. He was in a wheelchair and had no legs.

"You're probably wondering how I got like this?"

One of his big men was called Dewayne the Slasher. He was his right-hand man, along with his two assassins, Andy "Hitman" Jackson and Larry "Broken Bones" Wyatt.

He told them, "Tomorrow, make sure these guys are taken care of and with the cars and the big packages."

Turning to us, he said, "Three of you will ride in one car and the other two will be in the other. One will go to Florida and the other to Chicago. You'll meet Big Joe in Chicago and Derek in Florida, then both cars will drive to New York. The last drop will be to Big Boss Daniel. He owns five nightclubs and has the two best assassins, Bailey and Thomas. The cops have been trying to get them, but somehow they have always escaped from their crimes. Big Joe has three assassins also. Their names are Daredevil Bailey, Finger-Biting Brantley, and Gunslinging Dusty. They are the most wanted hitmen in the United States. Then there's Derek's group of assassins, Big Man Philip, Strongman Douglas, Mastermind Bo, and Sharpshooter Michael. They are the roughest redneck assassins you'll ever face. They have killed two hundred law enforcement officers and will kill anybody who stands in their way. You don't want to give any of these people any trouble."

"Thanks for telling us this. Good night." We walked to our rooms, and I told Shon, Clay, and Cam they could ride together. James and I would ride together, and I told them to pick which state they wanted to go to.

They picked Chicago, so we took Florida. "We'll meet y'all in New York on Friday."

We went to bed because we had to get up early in the morning.

"Good night, y'all," they said. "James, do you want to go with us to the bar?"

"No, I'm not going."

"You don't want to go, or did Buddy say you can't go?"

I asked Clay, "Why are y'all going to the bar when we've got to get up at five in the morning?"

"Since you put it that way, good night."

We went to bed. It was 4:30 a.m. when we got up. We took showers, then ate a good breakfast. Mr. Yang came in. "Well, guys, y'all ready to go on the trip?" We were ready to go. James and I got in the Charger, and Clay and the others got in the Lamborghini. We took off at the same time. I called Bella and she said she missed me. All the girls said they missed us.

"We miss y'all, too. I'll call you Wednesday when we're in Florida. I love you, and see we'll see y'all Saturday. Goodbye, sweetheart."

We left California and headed to New Mexico while Clay and the others headed for Las Vegas. We would arrive in Texas that night, then we'd stop and spend the night in Dallas. We needed to be in Florida by Wednesday.

We went by a cop going over a hundred miles per hour. The cop moved right behind us, then we did a three-sixty and went straight for him. We waited a few seconds and the cop turned off the road. James did a three-sixty again and we were trucking to Arizona. We had three different cops chasing us from New Mexico to Texas. Clay called us and said they were between the Utah and Colorado line. Clay and the others were running from the cops, too.

We found a nice hotel to spend the night in. We took the packages inside with us and paid for two separate rooms. The hotel had rooms available on the third floor and the fifth floor. I took the fifth floor and took one of the packages with me, and James took the other packages with him. We decided to go out to a nice restaurant.

When we came back to the hotel, somebody was messing with the car. We had locked the doors. Now they were unlocked, and somebody was inside looking for something. We went up to our rooms and found the packages safe. I went downstairs and asked where the nearest bar was. They told me to go one block and look for the Pony Express.. I did and showed my fake ID to get in. I sat at a table close to the girls on the stage. One was staring at me.

One of the waitresses brought me a pitcher of Bud Light and a glass. I watched the girls dance while I drank. Then I got a call from Mr. Yang. "How is your trip?" I told him we were doing good. He asked, "Why are you at the Pony Express?"

"How do you know where I am?"

"You don't think I'm going let you go without knowing what's going on, do you? I'm having you followed by two of my hitmen." I looked around and saw both of them walking out of the door.

I stayed a couple more hours. The girl on the stage came to my table and sat down for thirty minutes. Her name was Claire, and she asked me where I was staying and said she'd never seen me before. I told her, "We're just here for tonight. We're leaving early in the morning to head to Florida."

I asked if she wanted to come to my room at the hotel and she said yes. We left the club around 2:00 a.m. and went to my room. I went to the kitchen and poured her some shots of whiskey, then told her to sit down and get comfortable. I sat on the couch next to her and we drank. I kissed her, then we took our clothes off and made passionate love to each other. We had sex until 6:00 a.m. I was in the shower when James came to my room.

Claire opened the door and James asked, "Have you see my cousin, Buddy?"

"He's in the shower."

He said we should leave in one hour, that he would have everything ready to go. She came into the bathroom and got in the shower before I got out, asking me to wash her body. I did and we had some more sex before I got out and got dressed. I told her to turn in the room key when she left.

When I saw James coming out of the dining room, we went to the car and I asked him about the packages.

"I thought you got them?"

I went back inside to the room. Claire was still there. I went to my hiding place and grabbed the packages. She asked, "What do you have there?"

"Nothing."

I left the room and went downstairs to the lobby. I knew she would probably call her friends and tell them about the packages, which was why I took the stairs. The desk clerk was arguing with some guys when I came down. One guy grabbed the clerk and threw him into the wall.

I ran toward the car. James saw me and headed toward me. I jumped through the window and we left Dallas heading to Louisiana. We were going seventy-five miles per hour in a fifty-five mile per hour zone when we heard another cop. I called Clay when we were in Mississippi. They were almost to North Dakota. We'd just escaped another cop. In Alabama we drove about a hundred miles per hour in a fifty-five mile per hour zone. At the Alabama and Georgia line, we were heading straight for the bridge, but it was out. "We've got a car with a lot of power. What do you think we should do?"

James said, "Well, we could turn around, go straight for the cops!"

"We can take a chance jumping the bridge to get where we need to be. Well?"

"Hold on. We're about to attempt the jump!" James put the car in reverse to get a lot of speed. "Okay, here we go!" James gave it a lot of gas. We were going about a hundred miles per hour when he made the leap.

It took us over the roadblock and we made the jump. We were gone. The cops didn't try to chase us. We turned off unto another road and went down about two miles. We waited to see if the cops were coming. There were none, so we got back on the main road. All of a sudden, we heard a siren go off. The cops were right behind us again and gaining. We tried to shake them off, but it wasn't working. They were still right behind us. I told James we needed to get rid of them. "Let's do a three-sixty and go toward them." We kept going until we were out of Georgia and were on the Florida and Georgia line going to Tallahassee. We stopped there. It was Tuesday afternoon at 6:00 p.m., and we stopped at a nice hotel.

We ate at a restaurant called Smokey's. It was good. Then we went to a bar and drank, but we only had one drink.

In Kansas, Clay, Shon, and Cam were in trouble with the locals. Clay said to one of them, "You don't want to fight one of us."

The local said, "Five of us will fight one of y'all. Who do y'all want?"

They picked Clay to fight.

We'd just left Tallahassee and were headed to Miami. Derek found out that it was James and me that were heading his way. He told his guys, "When they bring me my packages, I want two of y'all to follow them and kill them. I want both of their heads on a platter for what they did to me."

We would arrive at Derek's lair the next afternoon at 12:00 p.m.

"Just let them go about twelve miles away from here, then run them off the road. Shoot them and cut their heads off. Tell Big Man Philip and Strongman Douglas that's what I want."

Meanwhile at the Kansas and Missouri state line, Clay, Shon, and Cam had just escaped the cops. Clay had killed one of the locals. He'd stabbed Clay in the arm. Instinctively, Clay had pulled the knife out of his arm and stabbed the guy in the neck. All his friends had rushed toward Clay to kill him. Cam, who was already in the car, saw everybody rushing toward Clay and Shon. Cam hit a few of them and Clay and Shon jumped in the car. Cam was heading in the Missouri state line. They were twenty miles away.

Meanwhile in Miami, James and I were two hours away from Derek's lair. We stopped and ate at one of the nicest restaurants we'd ever been to. Then we saw two of Derek's guys. They approached us and said, "Y'all got something for Derek!" James told them we'd give it to Derek tomorrow at 12:00 p.m. They said they could give it to him.

Meanwhile in Missouri, Cam found a hideout until the cops left. They had fifteen hours left to get to Big Joe to give him the packages.

In Miami, Derek's guys ran toward us. I kicked one, then hit him with an uppercut. We managed to get away and found a place to spend the night.

In Missouri, Cam, Clay, and Shon found a place to spend the night. They had to leave at 5:00 a.m. to get to Big Joe. On the way, they made a detour. They stopped for gas and a car tried to run them off the road. The driver of the other car wanted the Lamborghini, but he didn't get it.

Clay got it back on the road and made it to Big Joe's mansion. Big Joe got his package, then gave them another package to give to Big Boss Daniel.

In Miami, James and I arrived at Derek's lair. He was there waiting for his packages, and we got out of the car. We opened the trunk and handed the packages to him. Then I asked, "Did you send two guys to get the packages from us? We beat them up if you did." We got the new package from Derek and put it in the trunk. Then we got back in the car and took off. He waited a few minutes and told two of his guys to run us off the road. "I want you two to kill them and bring me their heads."

We expected him to send somebody to kill us. We went down a dirt road and sat there until we saw the guys go by. Later we saw a car just like ours on the side of the road. We stopped and saw two bodies with their heads cut off. We called 911 and stayed until the cops got there. They asked if we knew who did it, and We told them no. I asked if we could leave and they told us yes. We got in the car and drove off, heading to New York. We went through South and North Carolina, stopping in Virginia to spend the night.

Clay, Cam, and Shon were heading toward Pennsylvania. They were in between the Indiana and Ohio state line and were hoping to be in Pennsylvania by 6:00 p.m.

We got to Norfolk, Virginia and found a nice hotel. Then we went out to a nice restaurant to eat steak and shrimp. We were talking about going home tomorrow after meeting up with the others. "We can take these packages with us."

James said, "That sound like a good plan."

When we got to Manhattan, we'd take a plane back to Hawaii and surprise the girls. We went back to the hotel and stayed there the rest of time. I fell asleep at 9:00 p.m. and got up at 6:00 a.m. I took a shower and met James down at the lobby. We ate breakfast on our way to the car and drove toward New York. When we got to the state line it was about 9:40 a.m. and we went to the Manhattan Hotel. We met up with Clay, Cam, and Shon there and ate lunch at Manhattan Manor.

I said to everybody, "How about we go home today?"

"What are we going to do when we get done eating?"

"Shon, can you get tickets online while we finish eating? That way we can shop for a couple hours."

Clay said, "That's what we were thinking, too!"

"Since all of us agree, let's order our food. Shon, find tickets for Hawaii and get the earliest you can. I would like to leave today soon as possible." He checked online and found the earliest flight was in a couple of hours. I gave him my credit card to get the tickets and Clay paid for our food. We ate, then left the restaurant and went shopping for our girls. I bought Bella three bikinis, thongs, bras, and nice dresses. James bought for Tammy a diamond necklace. Clay bought the most expensive watch for Stacie. I also bought Bella three diamond rings with matching earrings, necklaces, and bracelets. Cam bought a pocketbook that was worth six thousand dollars, and Shon bought Jenny a diamond bracelet and matching necklace. We left and went to the airport.

While waiting for our flight, we went to the bar and had a drink. Finally we boarded and the plane took off. We slept off and on during the flight. Hours later the captain came over the loudspeaker and said, "We are about twenty-five miles from Hawaii. Please get back in your seats and buckle up. We will land in ten minutes."

Something was wrong with the wheels. They didn't want to come out. I unbuckled my seat belt and went to the captain's cabin.

I asked, "What wrong?"

"We fixing to crash!"

I told him try to keep the plane in the air for about twenty minutes. I got the guys and we went down where the landing gear was stowed.

We worked on the gear, which was bent. We beat it out until it was straight. Then we came up and told the captain that he could land the plane. He waited until we were seated and buckled. Finally the wheels touched the ground.

"It was a good landing, and we'd like to thank those five guys for fixing our wheels."

James said, "It was no problem, but he does need to fix those wheels!"

We got off the plane, grabbed our bags, and headed out of the airport. We set our bags down as we called home. Nobody answered the phone!

We called a friend and told him to go get the Hummer. He went to the house and asked for the keys.

Bella asked him, "Why do you need the keys to the Hummer?"

"It's a surprise for Buddy!"

"All right. Here are the keys."

He opened the garage door and drove the Hummer out, then went to the airport to pick us up. We saw him outside the building and grabbed our bags, storing them in the back. He told us he had to make one stop before taking us home.

"Okay, what do you need to do?"

"I had to tell Bella that I was going to do something to the Hummer so she'd give me the keys. I can't go back without having some work done on it, can I?"

"No. Do anything you can, that way it gives us time to get our stuff ready. Call Bella and tell her to get the girls together. Say we're coming home and they can throw us a party." He called her and told her what I said, and that we should be home in three hours and that he would pick us up at the airport.

She said she would. That was about 6:00 p.m., and we would get there about 9:25 p.m. At 9:00 p.m. everybody was in the back of the house having a good time. We got there and nobody was in the house. The back door was open, so we went upstairs.

I put all my stuff up and left Bella's presents on the bed. Then I went downstairs and met the guys in the den. I turned on the television as the girls came back in. We stayed in the den, and Bella told everybody she was going to take a shower. She went upstairs to the room and found two bikinis, four thongs, four bras, and a set of earrings. They had real diamonds in them and were worth fifteen thousand dollars. She hollered and came running down the stairs saying, "Where are they?"

The other girls said, "What are you talking about?"

Bella showed them the earrings and repeated, "Where are they?!" They looked everywhere except the den, and then they went outside and saw the Hummer in the garage.

We followed them and asked, "Who are y'all looking for!"

"For the guys!" They stopped and turned around, seeing us standing right in front of them. They jumped in our arms and Bella said, "Thank you for all the gifts!" She kissed me. "When did y'all get home?"

"A few minutes ago."

"What's in those bags?"

"Stuff that we took from some people."

"Cocaine?"

"We think so. We were in New York and decided to come home."

"You know they're going wonder what happened to their drugs."

"We know! They're going to wonder why we delivered to two of the mafia bosses and not to the main one. Hopefully they'll blame each other."

"What are we going to do now?"

"I've got a buyer for the cocaine and that will pay for our college. I talk to the dean and we can start this fall. For now, I've booked us a cruise for the next three weeks. We'll leave next Thursday and go to Miami."

We would get on the cruise Saturday morning, and we had a week and a half before we left to go to Miami. We went surfing every day and were on the beach either swimming or lying out.

We went to several movies during the week and a half, and enjoyed ourselves the whole week. We had three more days before we'd leave for Miami when Bella got sick. I stayed in with her and took care of her until Stacie and Tammy came over. They told me to go out, that they would take care of Bella. "You've been taking care of her for the last two days. Just go out and surf for a while with James and Clay."

I changed clothes and put on my bathing suit, then grabbed my surfboard. I walked a little way down the beach until I saw the boys. James asked, "How is Bella doing?"

"She's getting better! I think she needs to stay in bed another day and she'll be all right. I think she'll be better before we go to Miami."

I surfed for about three hours, then went back to the house. Stacie was fixing lunch when I came in, and I told her it looked good. She said mine was in the microwave. I told her thank you and got it out. She fixed me some tea and I ate. All of a sudden Tammy came down saying that something had happened to Bella! We ran upstairs and she was on the floor. She was burning up with a fever. I picked her up.

Chapter 5

I carried her to the Hummer and took her to the hospital. Once there I put her in a wheelchair and ran to find a doctor. A nurse tried to stop me, but she couldn't. I found a doctor and told him Bella had fallen on the floor. She'd been sick. Tammy had told me she'd gotten up and was going to the bathroom when she's fainted. She was burning up when I'd picked her up. The doctor told the nurse to take Bella to a room, that he would be there in a few minutes.

One of the nurses asked, "Do you have insurance?"

"No, I will have to give y'all some money! If you need more, I'll have to bring you the rest."

I went to Bella's room and sat in there until the doctor came in. I stayed there as the doctor checked her.

"Let's step out of the room," he said.

"What wrong?"

"She's got the flu, and a disease that is curable. It will keep her from walking and talking, but we caught it in time. You need to keep her in bed for three days and give her this medicine. Hopefully, in three days, she'll be back to normal."

"Will she be able to travel a long way?"

"Yes, if the medicine works like it's supposed to."

"Thank you, doctor."

"Just take care of her. You can take her home." I picked her up and put her in a wheelchair, then pushed her to the Hummer. I returned the wheelchair and signed some papers, then took Bella home. When we got there, I took her upstairs to bed. Everybody was downstairs in the kitchen. Tammy came up and asked if Bella had said a word.

"No, she's been like this for a while now, and the doctor told me she's got the flu. He also said she's got a disease that affects your brain and keeps you from talking and walking. The doctor caught it before it got bad and in three days it's supposed to clear up. We might have to leave Friday instead. See if we can change our departure to Friday. I need to go get her medicine. Can y'all stay here until I get back?"

As I went downstairs, everybody else was starting to go upstairs.

I told them I'd be right back, then drove to the drugstore. There were a lot of cars there. I went in and gave them the prescription to get Bella's medicine. I paid for it all and went home. When I got there, everybody was gone except Tammy and Stacie. I parked the car in the garage and went inside, then fixed some orange juice and took it to Bella. She was up, and I told her to take the medicine. She took it all, and I told her to get some sleep. It was 8:00 p.m. and I wrapped her up. About ten minutes later, she was asleep.

I went back downstairs and Tammy and Stacie were washing the dishes. I told them they didn't have to do that and asked when the guys were picking them up.

"Right now!"

"See y'all tomorrow."

"Take good care of her."

"I will."

I walked them to the door and waited until they were gone before locking it. Then I went back upstairs and took a shower. As I was getting out I heard a noise. I put my shorts on and grabbed my 9mm. Then I went downstairs and saw someone in the kitchen. It sounded like somebody was looking for something in a drawer, but I couldn't see their face because they had a mask on. I heard someone else going upstairs. I sneaked around and saw their feet. I followed and eased toward our bedroom. Once there, I got behind the door. One of them came in our room.

I hit the guy's nerve, putting him to sleep, then tied his hands and feet. I put him in the closet and heard another guy telling a third that he couldn't find his brother. The leader of the guys came in the room. I stood behind him and put him in a choke hold. Once he was out, I tied his hands and feet. Then I put him in the closet and came out of the room. There was one guy still left, so I threw my shoe downstairs.

The third guy called for his friends, but they didn't answer, so he came upstairs. When he got there his buddies were tied up in two chairs in the middle of the hallway. The third guy saw that and said, "Who's here?"

I got on a microphone and said, "You have woken Pele, the goddess of the volcano! Pay the consequences!" I fixed Bella up like a volcano goddess and had her flying around. The medicine had knocked her out, and I fixed to where it looked like her touch turned things to ashes.

It had the guys scared! She flew back into the room and landed on the bed. I climbed down and took everything off her. I put her nightclothes back on and washed her face. When I opened the door, the three guys were gone. I went downstairs and looked out the door. They were still in the yard.

I grabbed the shotgun and shot in the air. They got in their car and left. I closed the door and locked it. After turning everything off, I went upstairs. It was 2:00 a.m. when I went to bed.

Tammy and Stacie woke me up. After we went downstairs, Stacie said, "What time did you go to bed? Why are there two chairs in the hallway and rope on the floor?"

"We had three burglars, but they didn't take anything. I scared them. You ever heard of Pele, the goddess of the volcano? I took Bella while she was knock out, dressed her like Pele, and had her floating in the air. Everything she touched turned to ashes. The guys left, but were still in the yard. I took the shotgun and shot it in the air. They got in their car and took off. It was about 2:00 a.m. before I was in the bed."

Suddenly, we heard Bella calling me. I went back upstairs and she was sitting on the bed.

"What are you doing?" I asked.

"I'm coming downstairs."

"No, you're not coming down. You're staying in bed and getting plenty of rest. You can come downstairs tomorrow. I'm going to try to have everything done before we leave Thursday evening. Tammy and Stacie are staying with you while I go and get everything done."

I got our plane tickets to Miami, got our stuff for all three cruises ready, and made phone calls. I asked our parents if they could come tend to our homes until we got back from our cruises. They told me they'd be glad to come and stay for three weeks. They'd be here the next day at 12:00

p.m. I told them we'd pick them up at the airport. After I hung up, I went in the kitchen. Tammy and Stacie had already fixed lunch.

I told them our parents would be there tomorrow at 12:00 p.m., and all the guys needed to be there at 11:00 p.m. The guys were at the beach surfing. I told them I was going to set up the grill and we were going to grill out tonight. Then I went down to the beach and got on a big wave and turned a flip. I told the guys, "Come to the house. We're grilling out, and I've got to talk to y'all about tomorrow."

Cam said, "You just did one flip. Watch this!" He did two flips, but when he came down the waves carried the surfboard further down and he landed in the water. We ran into the water as he was coming up. Luckily he was all right.

I came out of the water and walked back to the house. Everything was ready for grilling out. I heard Bella in the kitchen and walked in there. She was trying to help them get the stuff ready. She looked at me and told me not to say anything, that she was going to do it anyway. I grabbed the food, put it on the grill, and heard Tammy holler. "Are you all right?" she said. Bella didn't say anything. I went back in and she was on the floor. I used some smelling salts and she woke up.

I told her to sit and not to get up. Then I finished getting the stuff to cook and kissed her. She stayed there until we got the table set up. Finally the guys showed up.

"Go get yourself a steak, baked potato, and fries," I said.

I fixed Bella a plate and the girls' food as they sat at the table with her. Then I fixed my own plate and went to the living room. Everyone sat except for me. I told the boys that the next day at 11:00 a.m. we needed to be at the airport.

"Why?"

"Our parents are going to be at the airport by 12:00 p.m., so we need to be there no later than 11:50. We'll take them to a restaurant to eat lunch, then decide will who stay where."

After we ate, everybody went home.

I checked everything and locked the door, front to the back, then I turned off the lights and went upstairs. I took Bella's clothes off, helped her in the shower, then took off my clothes and got in with her. I washed her body and her hair, then washed my own and helped her out. I dried her off first, then myself while she sat her in a chair. She was still naked while I brushed her hair and blow-dried it. I put her panties on, then her nightshirt, and picked her up. Then I put her in bed, gave her her medicine, and went back in the bathroom.

I got my shorts on, then brushed my teeth and turned the light off.

I woke up at 7:00 a.m. Instead of waking her up, I went downstairs and cooked breakfast. I wanted her to sleep as much she could. After breakfast I went upstairs to get dressed. Tammy and Stacie arrived and I told them, "At 12:00 p.m., be at that restaurant called Aloa Mount. That is where we're bringing our parents. Be there, and call my sister and Angie. Make sure they know where to go." Some of the guys were at the beach surfing, so I joined them and did tricks. At 11:00 a.m. I told them, "We've got fifty minutes to get to the airport. I will meet y'all there. I've got to get a shirt."

"You don't have a shirt in the Hummer?"

"No! I've got to go to the house to get one." I got in the Hummer and saw a shirt. Stacie called me.

"Bella said you needed a shirt, so I left one in the Hummer."

"Thank you." I was on my way to the airport and told her to bring Bella with her. "She can ride back with me." Then we hung up.

It didn't take long to get to the airport. It was about 11:45 a.m. We only had to wait fifteen minutes until the plane landed. When it arrived, the landing gears were stuck. They had to land the plane without tires. Ambulances and fire trucks arrived and waited until they landed. The plane was finally coming down, but it was coming too fast.

It crashed and we ran to the crash site and helped people out of the wreckage. All our parents were all right except Angie's and Shon's dad. He'd suffered a broken foot. They took him to the hospital, but everybody else was all right.

I told Dad and Mom to go to the Hummer and then found Jerry and Kathy. My sister Elizabeth was crying. I helped everybody else get out, the stewardesses and the pilot, and they were all good. I shook the captain's hand for landing the plane, then joined my family in the Hummer. On the way to the restaurant I called Shon and asked about his dad.

"He's doing fine. He's got to stay in the hospital for a couple days. Mom's going to stay with him."

"Are y'all coming to the restaurant?"

"No, we're staying up here."

"How about Cam and my sister?"

"They said no, they're staying here."

I relayed the news to everybody else as we arrived and found Bella, Tammy, and Stacie.

Tammy asked, "Where's everyone else?"

"Shon and Angie are at the hospital with their father and the others decided to stay with them. He's the only one who was hurt. I think he'll be all right. He has to stay in the hospital for a couple days."

We ordered steaks, baked potatoes, and a bottle of wine, except Bella. She had to drink water because of the medicine she was taking. We finished our food and drank one glass of wine, then I paid for it. Everybody was waiting to leave. We got a taxi for our parents and told it where to drop them off and that I would pay for them when they arrived.

Then I helped Bella get in the Hummer. Elizabeth rode with us. The taxi arrived and I paid the fare, then unlocked the door.

I showed everybody the whole house. Afterwards, we went in the game room and played pool before bed. I gave Bella her medicine and told Mom and Dad they could stay up. We were the ones who had to go to bed. Jerry and my dad played pool. My mom and Kathy were in the den drinking coffee. They were watching television while my sister was in the bed sleeping.

At 7:00 a.m. Bella and I took a shower, then got ready and went downstairs. Mom and Kathy had breakfast for us. We sat at the table and ate, then heard a noise in the game room. Jerry and my father were still playing pool. I told them, "Don't tear anything up." Then I gave them a hug and told them we were fixing to leave in a little while.

They said they would be up there before we left. I went back to the kitchen and heard two car doors slam. It was the rest of the gang, except Angie and Shon. I asked, "Where are Shon and Angie?"

Jenny said, "They're not going. They're staying here."

"Why?"

The idea was that all ten of us would go on these cruises, and we might be playing on some of them. We had to leave in thirty minutes. Everybody was ready to go, so we hugged our parents and told them we would be back in three weeks. They told us to have a good time, and we told them same thing. Then they drove us to the airport.

After boarding, we realized we had company. It was three of Derek's guys. They'd arrived the day before They didn't have first class passes and were sitting in the regular coach. The plane took off and the captain announced everybody could move around the cabin. I walked back to the coach and saw the three guys, thinking they looked familiar.

I got James. We both went back to coach and those three guys were still sitting there. They were following us. I called Big Ben and told him that three of Derek's guys were following us. I asked if there was any way we could get off without them knowing. He told me there was a place down with the luggage, and that the door to the luggage compartment was in the lavatory. "You have to go one at time. That way they won't get suspicious."

I hung the phone up and returned to the others. I told everybody to get up one at a time and go to the back. "I will show y'all where to go." James went first. Cam went next, then Bella, Tammy, Stacie, Jenny, Clay, then me. The guys finally wondered where we went because we didn't come back to our seats.

I had just closed the top as they came in the lavatory, but they couldn't find us. As soon we landed, we'd open that door and go out. Meanwhile, one of the guys called Derek and told him they'd lost us. "Where are you landing?"

"Miami."

"I will have the cops on my payroll search the plane. I can convince security to help out. I run this city, and we will find them. Search everywhere in the plane when it lands."

We stayed put until we landed. When we heard the landing gear come out, we opened the trap door and watched as we landed. Then one by one we went down to the wheels and ran toward the fence. We went over the fence and into the parking lot. We saw a bus and ran toward it. I hot-wired it, then we took off.

Back at the plane they were still looking for us. They looked everywhere, and one of the airport staff asked them who they were looking for.

"For some kids."

"I saw eight of them in the parking lot. They stole a bus."

"Why didn't you tell me? Boys, go get the car and pick me up." He told the chief of police to put an app on us. "Find that bus!"

The chief of police said, "Why is everyone standing around? Go find them! Go to every hotel there is until you find where those eight people are. They've got to be at one of these hotels."

We left the bus at a hotel, then took a taxi to another hotel, the same one we'd stayed at before. Then we went to eat and passed a tattoo parlor.

Bella said, "Let's get a tattoo!"

"I was thinking same thing," James said. "We just passed a tattoo parlor."

A meeting was called between the big wigs of each mafia group from New York to California, and they all met in Texas. They all were furious because of five guys and five girls.

We got done eating and returned to the tattoo parlor. Bella got a rose on her boobs, and Tammy and Stacie got tattoos on their bosoms too. Tammy got a dolphin, Stacie got an angel, and Jenny got a bee around her navel. James, Clay, and Cam got barbed wire, and I got a pirate on my shoulder. We paid for our tattoos, then went back to the hotel.

Mr. Yang told the mafia men, "When they get back, we need to call our hit men. We need to take these ten people out and get what belongs to us."

Big Joe said, "They didn't take anything of mine! I will send Bailey with the other hit men. When are they going? Let's wait until they get back to Hawaii."

"We'll wait until they start school. That way we can get our hit men prepared and ready. I want all of their heads."

We went to the beach and surfed the rest of the day. Then we went back to our rooms. Some of us went to the movies and some had sex. Nobody wanted to wear condoms, but we weren't ready to be fathers yet. First, we wanted to finish college, then we'd have sex without protection.

We had sex all night, and it was 3:00 a.m. when we finally went to sleep. We got up at 8:00 a.m. and took showers, then got dressed. All of us went down to the café and ate breakfast, then got in a taxi and went to the beach and swam for a while. Then we went to the mall and got stuff to go on our cruise.

We talked about wanting to date other people, then went back to the hotel. We sat around, then I left to see a girl in room 320. Her name was Jenifer Lowly and she was a model for Victoria's Secret. She opened the door, wearing only a bra and thong. We shut the door and it was all over. I kissed her. Then we were in her bed having sex.

I got up, sneaked out of her room, and went to my own. Bella was gone. She'd gone with Tammy, Stacie, and my sister. James was in his room. I told the guys, "I know where we can get fifty million dollars in diamonds. There's a Victoria's Secret model in room 320 named Jenifer Lowly. The girls can take her out for a late movie and we'll go to her room from the balcony. When the girls come back, we'll talk to them and see if they can take her to a late movie. Here they come."

"What are you guys doing?" they asked.

"There's a girl in room 320. We want y'all to take her out to a movie."

"Why?"

"She's got five necklaces worth ten million dollars each. They have diamonds in them. We can get necklaces for all of ya'll!"

"You're saying they're worth ten million apiece?"

"Yep."

"Buddy, how do you know?"

"She showed me. She thought I was security."

"We'll do it!"

"Don't go until 8:00 p.m. Go and ask her." The girls went to Jenifer's room. They knocked on her door, but no one answered. They spoke to security and he got the desk clerk to let him in.

As he went in, the girls returned and told us what had happened. We went down to the room. It was mess, like somebody had been looking for something. They found Jenifer facedown with two gunshot wounds, one in the head and the other in her shoulder. She was soaked, like she'd just gotten out of the shower when the person surprised her. She must have tried to run from him. I went to her safe. It was empty. Then one of the detectives told the captain to come and look at the video.

"Can we leave?" I asked.

"Everybody can leave except you."

"Why me?"

"I'll tell you later after everybody leaves."

"We're leaving tomorrow to go on a cruise."

"Well, if we don't solve this, you won't be going anywhere. The rest of y'all can go. Sergeant, take Mr. Smithisom to office. Do not do anything until I get there." They put handcuffs on me, then put me in the police car. Once there, he told me to sit down. Two hours passed before the captain arrived and told me to follow him. In his office he showed me a video of Jenifer and me making love. Then it showed me leaving. Jenifer was alive.

"My question is, where did you go?"

"To my room! You can ask any of my group."

"I will!" He called Clay. "Mr. Smithisom, was Buddy there with y'all at 3:00 p.m.?"

"He was in the shower with Bella."

"How do you know?"

"That's what Bella told Stacie."

"And where are the girls?"

"They should be with James and the guys."

"The girls did not come up to the room."

When we realized the girls were missing, James called 911 and told one of the police officers that they had been kidnapped. Then he found a ransom note. "See what happened to the model?! If we don't give him five million dollars, they will all die!"

I asked, "Am I free?"

"Go ahead," the captain said.

I left the police station and called James, asking him to get the guys together and meet me at a little restaurant about two blocks from the hotel. I got there in ten minutes and saw Donna and Fritz. Donna saw me, came up to me, and slapped my face.

I asked her why she'd done that.

"For leaving us to finish school on our own!"

Fritz shook my hand and asked, "Where is everybody?"

I told them the guys were supposed to meet me here and that the girls had been kidnapped. I asked, "What y'all doing here?"

"We decided to go to Miami for college."

I grabbed Donna and kissed her, and we were still kissing when the guys arrived. They shook Fritz's hand and hugged Donna.

Inside at a table I asked, "What you think we should do?"

Clay and Cam said, "Let's just pay the guy! We can get the girls back."

"How about you, James?"

"Well, in a way I'm with Clay, but we know that's not what you want to do, Buddy."

"That right. I say let's find him and get the girls without paying him."

"Buddy, we'll do what you want, but how are we going to find him?"

"This is what we're going to do." Then suddenly I got a phone call. It was Shon and Angie. They were at the hotel, and I told them to come to the restaurant. We waited on them before continuing. When they arrived, I told them what had happened. "This is what we're going to do. When he calls, we're going to tell him we've got the money. That way he can tell us where to go. James is going to take the money to the meeting place. I'm going to follow. Angie will stay with y'all until everything is over." The phone rang. "That must be the call. Answer it, James."

The kidnapper said, "Do you have the money? Well, change of plans. I want a jet plane and five million dollars to go to Mexico. I prefer an experienced pilot to fly me. Doesn't matter, as long as I get to Mexico."

"Tell him we'll have it ready in twenty minutes."

"Have it ready tomorrow."

They hung up.

"We just missed the ship," James said. "But the girls are more important! What we going to do?"

"Cam's going to fly me and Clay," I said. "Angie and you are going to get the plane ready for us, then we're going to parachute out of the plane. Once we're above the ship then the fireworks should be shot up in the sky. We'll make our entrance with the fireworks. We will be in the back. Once we're up in the air, we will come out, and then you can turn the plane around. Then we'll fly back to Miami airport and the cops should be there waiting. We should go find the girls."

We went back to the hotel. I invited Donna up to my room and asked what she wanted to drink. "Do you have some wine?" she asked.

"Yes."

I poured her some wine. We drank about four glasses, then I told her everything we'd done while we were gone. She said she was getting hot, so I told her to take some of her clothes off. She stripped to her bra and thong.

We sat down and watched television, and she sat close to me. I put my arm around her and she lay her head on my lap. I put my fingers through her hair, then she looked at me and I looked down at her.

We started kissing. One thing led to another and we had sex in the living room. We took it to the bedroom and made passionate love until 8:00 a.m. Then we got up. I was in the kitchen cooking breakfast and had to be at the airport by 9:00 a.m. We ate breakfast, then we took a shower, and she took me to the airport in her Dodge Charger. We kissed before I got out.

James asked, "Does Bella know about you and other girls?!"

"She does. Fritz wants her to go out with him. Everything's ready. Let's go, Clay, and get in the back."

We got in the back of the plane. The kidnapper arrived our girls. He got out and James asked, "Where are the girls?"

"In the car."

James looked, but the girls weren't in there, only a bomb. The guy was getting on the plane when he pushed a remote button and the car blew up. James got on the walkie-talkie and told me that he'd blown up the car and the girls weren't in there.

"We don't know where they are. We'll go after the guy, but y'all need to go find them. We can get this guy."

I told Cam to turn the plane around and head back to Miami. Later I called James and asked if they'd found the girls. He said no. I called the guy and asked, "Where is my sister and our friends? If anyone harms them you won't make it to prison; you'll be under the ground. You call your buddies and tell them to turn them loose, or I will put a bullet between your eyes." He relented. James, Angie, and Shon headed to the pick-up point. Then the kidnapper changed his mind and ordered his lackeys to kill them.

One of the lackeys was about to shoot Stacie. Shon jumped in front of the bullet and took it in the chest. James shot the guy in the arm. He dropped the gun, then fifteen more guys came running. One of them shot Bella in the leg. James said, "Everybody, get some cover!"

Angie retrieved Bella and Jenny got Shon. James slid some guns to Tammy, Jenny, and Stacie, then James moved to where Tammy was. She kissed and hugged James's neck. "We've got to try to get out of here." James called me and said, "Shon and Bella got shot and we can't get out. We are in an old abandoned warehouse."

"Get us close, Cam. We're going to jump on top of the building."

He got us real close. We got on top of the building and made it to the window.

We saw all of them inside, so we started to shoot, then I jumped from the window and climbed down. I picked up Bella and carried her outside. We managed to kill all of his guys.

An ambulance arrived and we went to the hospital. Shon had surgery when we got there. He'd lost a lot of blood. Angie gave some of her own blood to help him out. Those of us who were compatible gave some, too. I went in the room with Bella and she said, "I heard Fritz wanted to date me. How do you feel about that?"

I told her it was up to her. "He's outside."

"Let him in."

I went out of the room and told Fritz he could go see her. Then I found Donna and said, "Let's go somewhere."

We went outside and were walking to the parking lot when Donna said I needed to tie my shoe. I bent down and a bullet flew by where my head had been. I pulled Donna down by the car. "We need to get back inside the hospital! Do not stop until you're inside." We ran back inside the hospital and I told James, "We're in trouble."

"What wrong?"

I told him there were guys shooting at us.

Cam said, "I heard the mafia came together in Texas! They're after us for what we did."

We had to get Shon and Bella out of the hospital. The doctor told us, "You can't move him. He'll die if you do."

"If he stays, all of y'all will die," I said. "What if we him get to another hospital? Do you think he can make the trip to Daytona or Tampa Bay?"

"Possibly."

"We can take an ambulance, but we need someone to drive it. How about you, Fritz? I've seen you drive. Jenny can ride with y'all."

"We have two nurses who can go with them," the doctor said. "Nurse Tharus, Nurse Halfway, I need you to go with them and make sure the patient is comfortable. Let's go."

"Doc, when they come in and ask where we are, tell them."

There was a noise in the hall and we hid. Several guys came through the door. "Where are they? We know they're here."

"That way," the doctor said, pointing.

"Thank you." Then he shot the doctor in the leg. They came down the hall and we waited until they passed by. We eased out and shot them in the leg, then grabbed the girls and ran out of the hospital.

Cam said that he'd take Clay, Angie, and Tammy with him. I'd take James and Stacie with me. We took off and headed for the Tampa Bay hospital.

When we arrived hours later, we got out of the cars and slammed the doors. The cars blew up and we were knocked unconscious. When we opened our eyes, we were at a hospital. I asked, "What happened?"

"Your car blew up," a nurse told me.

The mafia must have planted bombs on them.

"How are the others? Can I see Shon and Bella? Did my sister survive?"

"She's here in this hospital."

"And the others?"

"They're here. In time you will get see all of them. Your friends Bella and Shon had it the worst. Their vehicle flipped over three times and they both died, but we brought them back from the dead. Your friend Shon will be different. Come with me."

She took me out of the room and through a tunnel. We were at a different hospital.

"Wait a minute," I said. "One of the nurses with the ambulance. She was a double agent, wasn't she?"

"She wasn't with the others."

"What do you mean, she wasn't with them? I saw her go with them."

<h1 style="text-align:center;">Chapter 6</h1>

"You are now in Alaska in a special hospital."

"What do you mean, a special hospital?"

"You're fixing to find out. What is your name?"

I told her, then she left. Someone threw something at me and I caught it. I sat there. The woman came back in the room. "I want you to hold this eight ball and put pressure on it."

I did and it busted.

"When the car blew up, you lost your left hand. You have a bionic hand now."

"How about everybody else?"

"They are good, except Cam. He lost one eye. Now he's got a bionic eye."

"And my legs?"

"Let's check them out. Everyone thinks y'all are dead, which you technically are. Here, get on this machine."

I got on the machine, and she put it on the highest it could go. I ran like it was nothing.

"Does anybody know about me?"

"Just your friends. Something different happened to all of you. Let's go to the hangar."

We went to the hangar, and I ran from one end of the building to the other five times in thirty seconds. Our next test was how high I could jump. "We'll first try five feet, then ten feet."

"How tall is this hangar?"

"About forty feet. The chief wants to see you and your group. Go right through that hall, and it's the door on your left."

I went down the hall until I came to the door on my left and knocked. A woman told me to come in.

"Let's wait on the others," she said. "How is everything?"

"It was good, until we got blown up."

"Buddy!" Bella arrived and hugged me. "Everybody all right?"

"We're all right." I kissed her while the others arrived.

"Everybody sit down now," the woman said. "We can get down to business. My name is Cynthia Rider. I am your new boss. All of y'all are now double agents."

"Madam, we were hoping we go to college in Hawaii."

"You don't have the same life anymore. The Fabulous 10 is no more. Now you've got a new life and new names: Buddy and Bella Warren, James and Stacie Bell, Clay and Tammy Jackson, Cam and Angie Stryker, and Shon and Jenny Watson. You have a month to get married. No more Fabulous 10. Now your group is called Nobody. It consists of eight who plays instruments and sing. The other two are the group manager and coproducer. Everything changes. You'll have different phones when you get back to Hawaii. You'll have new looks, too. Not all of you have power. We had no choice with some of y'all. One more thing: you all have news code name. Buddy is Lone Wolf, Angie is Little Eagle, James is Hitman, Stacie is Butterfly, Clay is Hammer, Tammy is Tinkerbell, Cam is Papa Bear, Bella is Mama Bear, Shon is Total Package, and Jenny is Wild Thing."

"What about our friends, Donna and her brother Fritz?"

"They know all about this. They've got jobs when they get out of college as CIA agents. You've got a job when you get back. You will go on a cruise as a group playing for the president and prime minister of Ireland. Big John will be on the ship, and he's after the president and prime minister. While you're playing Angie and Stacie will work as the hostesses. Y'all keep Big John from getting the president and prime minister." The nurses from the Miami hospital entered the room. "Hey there, Peyton, Megan," Cynthia said. "How do y'all like our facility?"

"It's good. Where is our headquarters?"

"A little town in Alaska. You haven't met some of the other double agents. Here they are: Ashley, Edie, and Becky."

Three more people entered the room.

"Ashley's mother is the president and her husband is her secret agent."

Another agent named Cameron had left that morning to go to France for an undercover operation. There was a young lady named Fryretta, or Fran in English, and he was supposed to meet her in Paris. He was out in the ocean when a couple of Russian ships took his boat. Nobody had heard from him since. Becky and Edie volunteered to go look for him.

We were still in training when we had a visitor: the president of the United States. She came to check on everything. She had her son-in-law with her, as well as her grandsons and granddaughter. They had taken a vacation. When they arrived, Ashley was in New York on an undercover case that dealt with the mafia leader Derek Marsh and one of the congressmen, Daniel Terrie. She was supposed to discover if Derek had given Daniel illegal money for his campaign, but Derek was two steps ahead of Ashley. He had her followed. They tried to kill her by running her off the road, and she tried to follow them. The congressman had her arrested for possession of illegal substances. The New York Police Department arrested her and the news got to the president. She was furious. She ordered Cynthia to get her daughter out, but she told her she couldn't without blowing her cover. Ashley went to court and the judge sentenced her to twenty-five years in a women's prison. The congressman and Marsh had a lot of evidence on her.

The president and Ashley's husband, Duck, talked to Cynthia. She had no choice but to send out ten new recruits without the proper training, so she called us to her office. We were supposed to leave the next day to go to our new home in Texas, but it was postponed until next week.

"I need four of you to go to New York, two to Miami, and two to France. Okay, Drake, Brittney, Billy and Jenifer, y'all go to New York and take care of the congressman. Get him to change his mind and help Ashley get out of prison."

"You want us to break her out?"

"No, make sure he does what's right. Do not let him know she's the president's daughter, okay? Now, which two are going to Miami? Daniel, you and Carolina need to keep an eye on Big John. He is up to something. Keep your distance. Do not let him know you're watching him. If he makes a move, call the headquarters. We'll send help. Cameron is still missing. You'll go and meet Fran at the Eiffel Tower. She is your contact. If you need something, she can get it for you. Be careful."

Jill and I packed a bag and they flew us to Seattle, then we took a flight to Paris, France.

Meanwhile Steven and Tiffney were in the communication room. They were in charge of making sure we had contact when we got to France. I hoped we could find Becky and Edie so we could look for Cameron.

Meanwhile back in New York, Brittney and Jenifer became the congressman's secretaries. They got close to him as Drake and Billy pretended they were with the phone company. They tapped his phone and then went to his house. They told his wife they were told their phone was messing up and were there to fix it. She confirmed the phone was making a weird noise.

In Miami, Daniel and Carolina opened a little coffee shop across from Big John's building, where he lived and work.

"I'm going outside to sweep the sidewalk," Daniel said. "I saw somebody go in the building who looked like Derek's guys. They came out with a bag of something."

"Use your bionic eye."

He watched them. They had a 9mm on them with a ten-round clip. "It was four guys. They have about twenty million dollars' worth of cocaine in a bag."

He told Carolina he was going to the store and asked if she needed anything. She told him no. He got on his motorcycle and followed Derek's guys.

Back at the coffee shop, Carolina saw Big John leave, so she closed up and followed him. She finally got in touch with Daniel and told him that Big John was on the move and that she was following him.

In New York, Jenifer became the congressman's personal secretary. She went to his penthouse with him.

Billy and Drake had given her a microphone so they could hear everything. They left just as Drake and Brittney went to his office. Brittney kept a lookout while Drake unlocked the door to the office. They went in just before the security guard came back through the area.

They looked for any evidence they could find, then heard footsteps coming down the hall, like somebody was heading that way. It was a young woman. Billy called and said they were on their way back, to get out now.

The young woman entered the room.

Drake asked, "Who are you?"

"My name is Jessica Wright. The congressman owes me twenty-five thousand dollars."

In France, Jill and I arrived in Paris. We took a taxi to the Eiffel Tower to meet Fran. When we got there, the police were there. Jill asked them what had happened. They spoke to her in French.

"It was Fran," she translated to me. "Somebody threw her off the Eiffel Tower."

Somebody knew she was our contact. The chief of police told us we must leave or we'd die.

I said we wouldn't go and Jill translated.

"Okay," he said, "I warned you. You saw what happened to the other young woman."

"Where is the nicest hotel around here?"

"Come with me. I'll show you."

We went with him and he put us in jail. "You leave tomorrow morning for the airport."

"No, we aren't. We were sent here to gather information."

Back in Miami, Daniel left Derek's lair and was going back to Big John's hideout while Carolina was still following the car to a dock where a ship had just arrived. It was called *The Big Whale*, and it belonged to Mr. Yang. It must have had the big cargo Big John was waiting on. Carolina listened with her bionic ear and heard the captain of *The Big Whale* tell Big John they had the packages for him.

She called Daniel and told him he needed to come to the dock. "We have a lot of activity and it's Mr. Yang's ship. The package contains 1.7 million dollars' worth of diamonds, so we need to move fast. They're unloading the ship now."

Back in New York, Drake and Brittney got Jessica out of the office before the congressman and Jenifer came in. Billy asked Drake, "Did y'all find anything?"

"No. Maybe he has it at his penthouse. After we take care of Jessica, we'll go there."

"Okay, just be careful."

"We will. What is he saying now?"

"He's telling Jenifer he loves her. I think he kissed her because I heard her holler and slap him. He said, 'I will kill you,' then the microphone cut off. We need to get to her."

"No, you need to stay where you are. We will go." They got there and Brittney used her bionic ear to hear where they were, then they ran up the stairs to the top of the building. He was about to push Jenifer over the edge when Drake pulled his gun out and told him he was under arrest.

The congressman said, "If you don't put that gun down, I will push her."

"Okay. I'll put it down. Just don't push her."

"Come and take her from me. I'll give you two minutes if you think you can save her." Drake moved toward him. "Which one will you save?" Drake ran, then flipped, picked up his gun, and shot the congressman. As he fell backwards he grabbed Jenifer.

They were going over the edge, but Drake grabbed Jenifer by the hand and pulled her up to safety. They were hugging when Brittney came toward them. "We haven't found any more information."

In Paris, Jill and I were in jail. "We need to get out and find out why Fran was killed. Somebody has to know she was our contact. Stand back, Jill." I grabbed the bars and bent them so we could get out, then bent them back to their normal shape.

We left and went between the two buildings, then jumped to the top of the building and sat there. We heard one guy tell the chief of police that we'd escaped. I told Jill to listen and find out what was going on, so she went close to the edge and heard a guy talking to another guy about what had happened to Fran. One of the Russians had grabbed her and gone to the Eiffel Tower. We went across the building, then jumped down and ran to the Eiffel Tower.

Back in Miami, Daniel arrived on the dock and saw Carolina standing beside some crates, so he went to where she was. She told him to look and pointed. Some people were moving stuff, so he used his bionic eye and saw submachine guns and about five grenade launchers. Carolina said, "What's going on? It's like they're preparing for a war. We need to get closer."

"We need more guys. They've got too much firepower." Daniel called headquarters and got in touch with Steven.

"Go ahead, Daniel. This is Steven."

"You know we've got our code names."

"Okay. Go ahead, Papa Bear. This is Total Package."

"We need more guys. This just got bigger."

"How many do you need?"

"At least four."

"Let me talk to Cynthia."

Back in New York, Drake, Billy, Brittney, and Jenifer were at the hotel when headquarters called them.

"Total Package, this is Hitman. Go ahead."

"The boss is wondering how long you'll be in New York."

"If everything goes well tomorrow, we should be on a plane tomorrow night and will head back to headquarters."

"When you get on the plane tomorrow night, go to Miami and meet up with Papa Bear and Mama Bear."

"Okay, over and out."

In Paris, Jill and I were going to the top of the Eiffel Tower. Jill looked down with her bionic eye and saw something nobody else had seen. "There. Looks like blood."

"Why would there be blood up here if she was killed when she fell? She must've been killed up here."

Jill saw the police coming from about two miles away. We ran and leaped to the top of a building, then stayed there until the phone rang. It was headquarters.

"This is Lone Wolf."

Total Package said, "How is everything?"

"Right now, we're hiding from the cops. Our contact is dead. A Russian threw her off the Eiffel Tower. I think she was killed with an object Little Eagle found. She's got it with her. I wonder if you can tell us whose blood and fingerprints are on it. Ask Kevin in the lab to use the device. I'm sending you a picture. Ask him if that device works. If you put the picture under the device, it should transfer the real thing there. Okay?"

"I'm at the lab now."

"Okay, Jill, put the object down."

He told Kevin what I wanted. "Is the picture okay? I don't know if it's going to work well."

"Tell him try it anyway."

"Try it anyway."

"Okay, here goes. Now put the picture under the zapper and cross your fingers." *Zap.* Jill and I watched the object disappear. "It worked! I want him to see whose blood that is and check for fingerprints, okay? Call us back."

"Honey, what are we going to do?"

"We're going to get a hotel, Le Mans, about fifty miles away. Maybe we'll find Cameron, Becky, and Edie there. Those Russian guys might have all three of them."

Back in New York, they were at the police station getting everything done. They hadn't found Ashley. She was supposed to be in New York for the case, but they hadn't seen her, so Drake called the president and asked, "Have you seen your daughter?"

"No, I haven't seen her in a month. Her three children miss her, so y'all need to find her."

"We will try."

In Chicago, Big Joe had his guys kidnap Ashley. She was in a building that was highly guarded, Drake called headquarters. Big Joe called Mr. Yang and told him he had a big surprise, so Mr. Yang told him to call all the big bosses and tell them they'd have a meeting next Tuesday in their usual spot in Texas. Big Joe called everybody and relayed the message. He told all three hitmen to come, also.

"We need to double up on our guards."

Headquarters told Drake to go to Miami and help Daniel and Carolina. "We will send a couple of agents to search for Ashley."

Drake told headquarters, "Okay, we on our way there now." Back in a little city called Le Mans, Jill and I were getting a room. Then we got a phone call from headquarters. It was Kevin.

"The blood is Fran's and the fingerprints belong to Jock Lacrosse, a Russian KGB. She must have had something on them if the KGB wanted her dead. We must find that guy. The girl was a spy for France as well as our contact. We work for the United Nations, you know. You no longer answer to your boss."

"What are you talking about?"

"I already called your boss and told her we need you guys to work on this case with us and that you'll report to us."

"We want to hear it for ourselves," Jill said.

So I called headquarters and talked to our boss, and she said, "Yes, it's true. Whatever you find, you will report it to the United Nations. That's why we need to find Cameron, Becky, and Edie. They are still missing. Ashley is, too."

"Wait a minute. She went to New York for that case."

"It's over, and I sent a couple of double agents to New York."

Meanwhile on the cruise, Brent and Chance were on board teaching dancing. The four sisters were in a strip poker tournament on the second deck of the ship. Both Jenifers were there in the tournament, but they did not inspect the ship, which was fixing to be taken over by Derek and the Italian mob.

The president called headquarters.

"Have you seen the news?"

Cynthia said no. She told her to turn it on. It showed the cruise line being overtaken by the Italian mob. The leader's name was Lorenzo Bernardello, from Campobasso, Italy. His father was the richest man in Italy. The Bernardello family made the sweetest beer in the whole country. It made you drunk slower than any beer, but that wasn't what made them the richest family in Italy. The drugs they made and sold were the most powerful. They also made you feel good. The family was trying to expand it into America, and the KGB had found out the family had stolen from them. They'd also expanded their business to France.

Cynthia called the United Nations and said, "We need our two agents back. The cruise ship has been taken by Derek, the mafia in Miami, and one of the Bernadello family, the son Lorenzo. They've got hostages, and he will kill one hostage every hour if we don't accept their commands."

"How about I send two others in their place?"

"Like who?"

"Steven and Tiffney. They are in my communications center, but they've got better power."

"Send them to the UN headquarters."

Jill and I went back to the headquarters. "We here, boss."

"You guys need to get on the ship. We don't know how many mafia men are there."

We went to the gym to get some things, then went to a boat cruiser. I tried to get close without getting seen or heard, then Jill used her bionic ear. She heard Derek talking to the Italian mafia leader.

We swam to the ship and climbed on board. "I see four guys," I said and ran inside. I knocked them out and tied them up. I went down the stairs and Jill went up, and she heard someone coming. She kicked him as he walked by. He went flying against the wall. She ran circles around two guys, she stopped and punched them in their throats.

Then she clotheslined them and they went flying. Another guy came up behind her and grabbed her. She tried to use her legs but couldn't. They took her to Derek, and he recognized her.

"Oh my god. It can't be," he said. "I thought you were dead. You're Bella. You're part of Fabulous 8."

"My name is Jill Warren," she said. "I'm married to John Warren. We live in Texas on a ranch and have two companies. One deals with oil and the other cosmetics. You are wrong about who I am."

Downstairs, I found the hostages. They were in a room with one guard. I moved behind the guy and broke his neck, then used my bionic hand and ripped the door off the hinges. Brent, Chance and both Jenifers were there. Then I saw the five girls we'd met in Miami: Rhealyane, Chelsea, Kaylin, Savage, and Layne.

I asked all of them if they were all right, then I heard someone coming. Four guys opened the door. A couple of them came at me. I grabbed one and slung him at the other guy, then kicked the gun up and caught it. Then I broke it in half. I bent the nozzle like a bow. Another guy ran toward the door, but he didn't make it. I grabbed him and hung him up where no one could get him down.

Back upstairs, Derek had two of his guys hold Jill down. He pulled out a sword and was fixing to chop off her head, but she ducked and jumped the highest she could and grabbed their arms, pulling them up in the air. The two guys hit their heads on the ceiling and broke their necks, Others shot at her as she jumped and kicked the guns out of their hands.

She grabbed one gun and bent the barrel down, then jumped, flipped, and kicked two guys to the wall. After that, she ran out of the room. Two guys ran and shot at her as the Italian mafia leader and Derek escaped.

Their guys were either dead or tied up for the authorities. All the hostages were free, and the captain took the ship back over.

"Did you get the leaders?"

"No, they escaped. But we know one of the leaders. It's Derek, the mafia leader in Miami."

Then some of the girls said to me and Jill, "We know y'all part of Fabulous 8."

We said to them, "No, we are John and Jill Warren. We lived in Texas and own two big companies. We also have a big ranch in Austin."

Back in Miami, Daniel and Carolina met Drake, Billy, Brittney, and Jenifer as they got close to Mr. Yang's ship. There was another ship right beside.

They asked a worker whose ship it was, then a huge guy walked toward them and said, "This is my ship. Who wants to know?"

They showed him their badges.

He asked, "What are y'all going to do about my ship?"

"We'll take it for evidence unless you let us borrow it."

"Just don't mess it up, okay?"

They went on board and now Drake climbed to the top and used his bionic eye. They were moving a big container. It had to contain drugs and guns. There were twelve guys guarding it, so it had to be important.

Meanwhile in the United Nations, Steven and Tiffney were waiting on Mr. Jacob Reed, the American representative.

"Sorry for keeping y'all waiting," he said. "Come this way and we show you what's going on. There was a Russian KGB who killed one of our own, Fran, at the Eiffel Tower. She was the contact for our agent. Your job is to find out why Fran was killed and who did it and report all the information to us at UN. Here are your plane tickets to France. You'll stay in the hotel next to the Eiffel Tower and are posing as a married couple on a honeymoon. Find out as much information you can. If you need anything, just call this number. Be careful."

In Chicago, Ashley was trying to get untied, but Big Joe kept appearing and trying to persuade her to be his woman, even though he was married to his high school sweetheart. Her name was Hilary Cooper nee Ranes. He'd always wanted Ashley, but she'd never given him the time of day.

She'd fallen in love with a secret agent when he became the president's bodyguard.

He was part of the Secret Service and his name was Duck Torre. He was from Hawaii. He had a brother named Russell Torre, and their parents were descended from kings and queens of South Kona. They also had a sister named Wendy, a teacher who'd married a surfer. He was the famous Jimmy Wayne Cha Cha, the most famous surfer. He was from Maui. Duck was still in New York and thought Daniel had gotten Ashley.

In Mexico the cruise ship dropped us off. We called headquarters and asked where they wanted us to go next. They told us to come back, so we left returned to Alaska. First thing they told us to do was take a shower.

Cynthia came to us as soon as everybody got back. "You guys are going to different states. Then you'll do normal stuff. Do not let anybody see you do anything you shouldn't be able to do, like jump higher than a normal person. Don't do anything that shows you have more strength than a strong man, unless it means life or death. You'll leave tomorrow. Steven and Tiffney are on their way back from France. Four FBI agents just arrived recently in Miami and already got the information from our people. They are on the plane to headquarters right now. They should be here in thirty minutes."

Jill and I went to our room, then I went to the gym and pumped irons.

I had a problem with my right arm. It was weaker than my left. I went and talked to the doctor and asked him what I could do to get my right arm as strong as my left. He told me to come with him. I followed him to the lab and he shut the door.

"What's going on?" I asked.

"I figured you'd come to me about your right arm. I made you another right arm, but I will have to cut your real arm off. The new one looks and feels like a real arm. You'll have to exercise it every day to keep it from cramping up."

"Do it now."

"I can't do it now. You'll have to have your arm off for one day."

"Do it now."

"I don't have time."

"Do it!"

"We have never done this in the same day. Harry, come hold John here. You might want to bite on this because I can't put you to sleep. When I put the other arm on, you must be awake. Are you ready?"

"Yes, I'm ready."

He put my arm through a sling and tied it, then took a saw, sterilized the blade, and moved it across the my arm above the elbow. One clean hit it and it was chopped off. They took the bionic arm and hooked everything together, getting the blood flowing in my arm again about two hours after the switch.

The doctor said, "It's time to test your new arm." He lifted the skin and tinkered with the wires, then hit a nerve and it made my fingers tingle. He said, "That is a good sign. Now the test of strength."

He brought me a cue ball and put it in my right hand. I crushed it, shattering it to dust.

"We're going to try one more thing," he said. "Lifting weights. Let's go to the gym." We did and he said, "Lie right here. We're going to put a hundred and fifty pounds on the bar. Lift it ten times."

I did.

"Okay, now it will be three hundred and fifty pounds. Lift it five times."

"Okay." I did.

"Now we're putting a thousand pounds on there. Lift it one time."

I did.

"How is your arm?"

"It feels good."

"You might have some soreness in it, but you'll be okay. Be careful about what you hold for two weeks. If you can avoid holding something, I would advise you do it."

"Okay." After I left the gym, I returned to the room where Jill was watching our family get off the plane.

Meanwhile, in the office, Cynthia had a phone call from the president. She cried and said, "I want my daughter back. I sent her husband out looking for her, and he's still in New York. We usually stop at Miami before we get to New York."

"Wait a minute. Steven, get on the computer and find the flight. Then find out what airport they stopped at. See if she got on the next plane."

Steven found out she'd booked the flight and had a layover in Chicago, but they didn't find a person who could describe her on the plane to New York. We needed to go to Chicago. We would leave tomorrow. Cynthia called the president and told her we might find her because the flight had a layover in Chicago. We'd been born and raised there, so we told her to call her son-in-law back home. "She's going to be okay."

"Y'all be careful. You don't know who has her."

"John?"

"What?"

"First thing we're going to do is go home and check some places there, like our favorite spots, plus some typical places that people go if they kidnap somebody."

"We'll check everywhere. First we'll go home to get our vehicles, like Jill's Dodge Charger. Just don't let anybody know we're there. At some places we might have to say we were friends with Fabulous 8 before they died, and they told us about these places. We'll tell them we're looking for our friend. Do not tell anyone she's the president's daughter. Well, guys, see y'all in the morning. Jill and I are going to bed. We've got to get up early."

Suddenly my arm started hurting and I cried out.

Jill said, "Do you want me to get the doctor?"

"No, he said it's going be like this for a little while."

"How bad is it?"

"I'll get through it."

We went to bed. I woke up in the middle of the night hollering in pain, and Jill got up and fetched the doctor.

"What's wrong?" he said.

"It's John," she answered. "He's punching through things."

They came to my room and my arm was big, so he told her to hold me. "I can open the skin to check the wires." Then he grabbed my arm and opened the skin, cutting the wires. Then he took me to his lab.

Jill held my hand. She turned my head toward her and said, "Everything's going to be all right." Then she kissed me. Afterwards, they helped me back to the room and she stripped me to my boxers. Then she got in bed and put her arm over me and we fell asleep.

Meanwhile in Chicago, Big Joe checked on Ashley. Before he arrived, the three guys were talking about the other hitmen and how they could run the business. They had more weapons than any guy in the family. "Wait a minute. Big Joe is outside. We'll talk about it when he leaves."

He knocked three times. "Open the door, Dusty."

The door opened and Big Joe came in. "Well, how is our visitor?"

"She won't eat a thing."

"I brought her something to eat. Open the door." Dusty opened the door and Big Joe went in and gave her some food. Then he said, "You might as well join me. Then you can go free."

He told Brantley to get everything ready, and Brantley got the machine running. Then Big Joe told Bailey to put the helmet on her head. He strapped it on. Then they hooked the wire to the system, put it on full power, and turned it on.

Meanwhile, back at the headquarters, we were getting ready to go. We got on a plane and flew from Alaska to Seattle, Washington, then got on another plane that took us to Chicago. We took a taxi to our houses. Tiffney and I walked in the house. All our stuff was still in our rooms.

I told everybody we would meet at our old place. Tiffney took me to Jill's house, and I drove Jill's Porsche as Tiffney went to Steven's house and Brittney picked up Drake at his house. Then Jenifer got in her Corvette and went to Billy's house while Carolina got in her Ferrari and went to Daniel's house. We all went to Bernie's Palace. It was still open, but there was a new owner and management. We all got there and went in. The people looked at us with weird expressions. We went to the back tables and saw a couple of people we knew, but we couldn't speak to them. The new owner was our principal at Drysdale High School. I wondered what had happened, so I went up and talked to her. There was a photo of us on the wall, so I asked her who the people were. She told me they were her pupils. She used to be a principal at a school.

"Can I get y'all something to eat?" the waitress asked.

"We'll have whatever this group used to have."

"Okay. Mike, we want the ten entrées that our Fabulous 8 used to have."

"Okay, it'll be right up."

They still had the jukebox, so I played our songs. People watched as we danced. A man approached and told us to stop, then unplugged the jukebox.

"I don't want y'all to say anything or dance to anything that deals with Fabulous 8. They are history. I told Darlene to get rid of those songs and bring in some country artists, but she didn't do it. Mike, you're making regular orders. There's nothing special about the orders. Bella and Tammy made me mad for getting themselves killed. I was their uncle on their mom's side. She was my sister. I was in Portugal at the time. My two brothers didn't call me or write to me when our sister died. Her two daughters are now dead, along with my cousins, Shon and Angie."

"Have you seen this person?" I asked, showing a picture. "Her name is Ashley. She's our friend and we need to find her."

We couldn't get anyone's attention.

"Let me call the sheriff. Who is the sheriff here?"

"Billy Fangs. Here he comes now."

"Hey, John, Darlene, Mike, I'll have the usual. Who are y'all?"

"We're looking for our friend. Her name is Ashley." I showed him a picture of her.

"Sorry. I haven't seen her before."

Jill and Jenifer heard two guys talking about Ashley. They were around the corner and were talking softly.

"Well, good luck. I hope you find her. I'll take that to go, Darlene."

"That's unusual for you."

Tiffney heard the guys say where Ashley was, a warehouse about ten miles away. Actually, everybody knew where was. They just couldn't fight the ones who had her. He owned part of Chicago.

"Why are y'all afraid of him?" I asked. " I didn't mention his name was Big Joe."

Everybody stopped talking.

The two whispering guys called Big Joe, then came toward us.

"Y'all ask too many questions and now we're going to hurt you."

Then Big Joe arrived with his guys and said, "Why are y'all looking for somebody who isn't here?"

"Oh, she's here. You either bring her here or we're going to get her."

Big Joe told his guys to get us. One guy had a pipe. He hit my arm and the pipe bent. He threw the pipe at me and ran. By that point most of the guys were on the ground or running.

I picked one guy up by his throat. He was lifted off the ground at least two feet, then I let him go and he ran. "Now you either let her go, or you will be next," I said to Big Joe.

He called his men and said, "Let her go, but follow her. She'll probably lead you to the agency."

"Do you think it will work?"

"We'll find out in twenty-four hours. That's how long the agency has before we take over, and with Ashley on our side, we'll have her mother, the president. Then, the United Nations. Our work is done."

"Call Cynthia and tell her we found Ashley and that she will be on her way back to headquarters," I said.

Jill called and relayed the message.

"Good job, you guys. The president will be pleased and happy. Now go home. We'll see you back here within a year."

Chapter 7

Before we went to Hawaii for our four years of college, Jill and I watched Daniel and Carolina leave to go to Hawaii. That was where they lived. Then we got in her Porsche and went to Austin, Texas. We made it at 10:00 p.m. and drove until we asked somebody where Warren Dew Ranch was.

"Go straight on this road until you get to a stop sign, then take a left and go three miles. The ranch is on your right."

We followed the instructions and there was the ranch. I turned down the road until we got to the house. As we stopped, people came out of the house with rifles pointed at us. One guy came toward the car and told us to slowly come out.

The guy in charge of the place asked, "Who are y'all?"

"My name is John Warren, and this is my wife, Jill."

"Wait a minute. Did you say your name was John Warren?"

"Yes, I did."

"Is your father's name Big John, of the oil company?"

"Yes, it is."

"And you said this is your wife?"

"Yes."

"Y'all must be tired. John died two years ago from a heart attack. My uncle was going to give me the ranch, and I was going to get rid of it."

"My father gave it to me before he died. Who's in charge of this place?"

"My name is Kevin Tilman. Just call me Kevin."

"Kevin, is there anywhere private that we can talk?"

"Sure, come this way."

"Okay, this is the deal," I said once we were alone. "Big John told me before he died that Jill and I can come here just like we are and be part his family."

"Now tell me who you really are."

"I told you who we are. My name is John Warren, and this is my wife."

"Big John didn't tell me about this."

"Well, here is everything you need: the tape and the paperwork."

I gave them to him and he pressed play on the tape.

"Okay, Kevin, here is everything you need to know: this guy is my son. His name is John Warren, and he is with his wife, Jill. Everything is legal. Show them everything they need to know about the business. You are still in charge, but let them go to meetings. They might surprise everybody. Oh, my nephew? Fire him. He killed my son. That's all. Goodbye."

"Okay, John," Kevin said, "y'all need to get to bed. I will show you everything tomorrow. Herod, take John's car to the garage. Now, Jamison, show our couple to their room."

We went in the house. It was a big two-story house. "Ma'am, sir, come this way. Here is your room." The bathroom was down the hall to the left. Jill got her laptop out. We needed to find out about Rodney, Big John's nephew.

She put in "Rodney Warren" and the information came up. He had been in prison for ten years for theft. He came from a troubled family. His father was killed in a plane crash, and he'd blamed his uncle. He needed to fire him now instead of waiting until in the morning. "Call Drake and Brittney." We did and they answered. "How is everything in New York?"

"We just got to our room and jumped up to the top of our building. It nice up here. Wait a minute, I hear somebody fussing at another person. It's a man and a woman. Here, Brittney, talk to Jill while I jump down there. Oh my god, he just pushed the girl off the edge!"

Drake caught her, put her down, and walked around the corner, then jumped up to the top where Brittney was. They jumped to the ground and walked around to the front of the building as the guy was coming out. He looked shocked. Drake said, "Are you all right?"

"Yes, I'm fine."

"You're acting like you're looking for something. Or someone."

"No, I'm all right."

"Are you sure?"

"Yes. Stay out of my business."

Back in Austin, Jill and I were in bed making love. Then it was 5:00 a.m. Time to rise and shine. Everybody else was geting up, so we did as well. Jill went to the bathroom and shut the door. One of the guys told her, "Don't shut the door. We have to prevent it from locking on its own."

"Honey, come here!" she called. I arrived and she said, "Stand there. Don't let anybody come in."

"Why don't you just shut the door?"

"That guy said not to."

"I shut it early this morning."

"You did? And the door didn't lock on its own?"

"Nope. Honey, who asked you not to close the door?"

"Those two guys right there."

"I'm going have a talk with them. They are not going to make us leave. That what they want, for us to leave here. We just need to adapt to the ranch life. We need to do things better. We need to wake up before anybody else, then we need to take the ranch over. Before we leave here, we need to give the ranch to Big John's family. They'll keep it going. Let's go downstairs and make the best of it."

We both went downstairs.

"Good morning. How did y'all sleep last night?" Kevin asked.

"We slept good."

"Here's breakfast."

We ate and then went to the office to check on the workers.

"How is everything?" I asked when we got there.

"We have some complaints."

"About what?"

"It's so hot, and the bosses don't want to put new units in."

"We'll put new units in. Why weren't we informed about this?"

"The boss didn't think it was important to you and your wife."

"Anything that deals with the people working here is important. What else?"

"The workers need a raise. They haven't had one in three years."

"How much? Who receives the least?"

"The lowest paying job is fifteen and the highest is twenty-five fifty."

"We'll give everyone a three-dollar raise. No, make it a five-dollar raise. Except the ones making twenty-five fifty. Bring their pay to thirty. Anything else?"

"One more thing, sir, about lunch. They would like catering for lunch, like a buffet."

"Okay, make that happen. Anything else?"

"No, sir, that's all."

"You have two days to get everything done. Understand?"

"We understand."

"I want to talk to everyone in management."

All the supervisors and bosses came into the conference room.

"Dear, do what you think?" I asked.

"Well, honey, I think you might want to fire some people."

"You think we should do that?"

"Yes, I think so."

"I'm giving them two days to get things organized."

We returned to the office.

"We better see progress," I said. "Is everyone here?"

"Yes, we're all here. What's the problem?"

"What's wrong with this picture? Some parts of the plant don't have air, and I want y'all to give them air. Next, I want to give everyone a raise. Some of them are making twenty-five fifty. They will now make thirty, and the one making the lowest will make twenty. Everyone else goes up by five dollars. Next, we're going get a food place to cater to our people at lunchtime. I'm giving you guys two days to make everything happen or some of y'all will be gone. Do you understand?"

"You're giving us two days to get everything done?"

"I'll tell you what: I'll give y'all a week, no more. That's what we want done. We'll come back in a week and it better be done, or we're going to fire some of you or lower your pay."

Jill and I got in the limousine and went to the other plant. We looked at everything. Jill asked all the plant management and supervisors to have a meeting, to check on things around the plant and to hear any complaints. Then we checked on other stuff, like what was going to be big on the market. We wanted the advertisement coordinator to show us some stuff that would put the company on the map.

"We can get the stuff in the stores around the globe, then we'll get that phone call."

"Where can I go and talk in private?"

"Follow me. I'll show you."

He showed me to an office and closed the door behind him.

I called headquarters and talked to our boss. "Jill with you?"

"No, ma'am."

"Okay, I don't want you to tell her anything, I need you to go undercover for three days."

"What am I supposed to tell her?"

"Her friend Brittney is coming down to Austin to stay with her, and I need you to leave tonight at 8:00 p.m. Take a flight to California and pick up Jenifer. Then you'll meet Drake in Washington at Renton. From there you'll drive about two miles down the road until you reach a hotel. Wait there until somebody comes to your room. He will ask if you want to buy, and you tell him yes. He's selling a chip that has important information on it and will save the world. If the wrong hand gets it, we will be in trouble, so we need to get that chip. Just be careful and don't let anybody get it. Actually, change of plans: it's only going to be you and Jenifer. Act like you're husband and wife. Drake will join Brittney and Jill at the ranch and help in case they need incoming stuff. They should already be on their way to Austin. You'll have to go and pick them up."

"Okay, over and out."

I opened the door and found a piece of paper addressed to Carrie Tate, whose office it was. The note said, "Quit or pay the consequences! I know your secret."

I went back to the conference room and said "Which of you is Carrie Tate?"

She raised her hand.

"Carrie, I don't know what's going on, but someone left you this note. It says 'Quit or pay the consequences. I know your secret.' Do you know why someone wrote this note to you? Do you want to tell us what's going on? What is the secret?"

"I was offered another job in the government, but I wasn't going to tell anyone until I knew for sure about this job."

"Jill, listen to see if you hear anybody talking about her."

She asked me what headquarters wanted. "I'll tell you when we leave."

"Okay."

Then she heard somebody say, "I can't believe she cheated on her husband with Willie Smocks in the copier room!"

"John, come here." I approached her and she told me what the secret was. "Carrie's been having sex with the supervisor, Willie Smocks, on third shift. She comes in two hours early. What do you think we should do?"

"I think we need to put a camera up in that room."

"I'll tell them to put the camera up when nobody's here. Let it be hidden."

"You ready to go home?"

"Yes."

We got back in the limousine. "Jamison, take us back to the ranch." I turned toward her. "Okay, headquarters called. They want two people to go on this case, me and Jenifer. I'm supposed to leave at 8:00 p.m. tonight to go to Los Angeles, then we'll get on another plane and land in Seattle. We'll rent a car and go to Renton to a hotel, then wait until a guy shows up at the room. He'll have a weapon and we'll arrest him. That should only take three days. When September gets here, we'll go to college in Hawaii. Sometime in August, we'll leave here and go to Hawaii for our classes. Drake and Brittney are coming here to help you until I get back. We've got to pick them up in four hours. When we get to the ranch, we'll ride the horses for a while, then spend more time with each other before we pick up Drake and Brittney."

We arrived at the ranch and went to change. "They should have the horses ready for us." I kissed her, and she told me she loved me. I told her I loved her. We walked outside, got on the horses, and rode for a couple of hours.

We found a little spot where we had a picnic and let the horses rest, then we fooled around. One thing led to another and we had sex right. Then we gathered everything up and got back on our horses. We had thirty minutes before Drake and Brittney landed, so we got in the limousine and went to the airport. When we got there, I told Jamison to stay with the limousine, that Jill and I would get Drake and Brittney.

"There they are," Jill said. "Hey, Drake, over here!"

They came over to us.

"Hey, John. I heard you're going on a case with Jenifer."

"Yeah, she's going to be with me on this case."

"Who else is on it?"

"Nobody but us two."

"Why you two?"

"I don't know. Ask the chief. She's the one who told me who's going. I leave tonight at 8:00 p.m. to go to the airport, then I'll fly to California to pick up Jenifer. Then one hour from Los Angeles to Seattle, then we'll pick a car from the rental place. We'll drive from Seattle to Renton and stay at a hotel on the outskirts of Renton. Then we'll wait until a guy knocks on our door. He'll try to sell us a chip for fifty million dollars."

"You'll have to get the money."

"Yes, we're going to rob a bank, but we'll put the money back after the arrest. What we plan to do once he gives us the guns and the chip is arrest him, then call the FBI to come get him. Welcome to the ranch. I hope y'all enjoy it."

Brittney said, "That's a big ranch."

"It's about a hundred and fifty acres of land."

Then Kevin said to me, "Your plane is ready. Jamison is driving you to the airport. You've got a private jet with a personal pilot. Your luggage is ready, sir." He whispered, "I know you're all double agents because I'm a double agent, too. I've been here for a long time and they told me everything. Come with me."

I kissed Jill and told Brittney goodbye, then went to the private jet. I had some wine. We landed in Los Angeles and the pilot fueled up the jet. I said I'd be back in a few minutes. I went inside the airport and found Jenifer. She told me that our plane wasn't there yet. I told her that we had our own plane and it was ready.

We went to the bar and I bought her a drink. It was an Alabama slammer, and I was drinking wine. Then I asked, "You ready to go?" and she said yes. We went to the plane and I said, "This is Jenifer, another agent. This is Jerry, our pilot when we have to go on a case. Jerry, take off." Jenifer and I drank wine together.

"We'll land in ten minutes," Jerry said.

"Okay."

Meanwhile back at the ranch, Drake and Brittney were in bed sleeping while Jill, Marie, Kevin, and Tracy played spades. It was Jill and Tracy against Marie and Kevin.

"If you lose a hand, you've got to take a piece of clothing off," Kevin said. "The winner gets to pick what they can do after." They were in the dining room with the door closed. Jill and Tracy lost the first hand.

They heard a noise from Drake and Brittney's room. Jill walked upstairs in just her bra and pants. She eased into the room. The sound came from the closet. She opened the door. Inside was a boy possum humping a girl possum. She closed the door back. The sound didn't wake Drake or Brittney. She eased out of the room and went back downstairs to the dining room.

Meanwhile, Jenifer and I landed in Seattle and got in the car that was waiting for us. I put everything in the trunk and we headed to the hotel on the outskirts of Renton. We parked the car and I got out and got the key to our room.

As I closed the door, Jenifer said, "I need to take a shower." She said she felt dirty.

"Okay."

She looked at me and said, "How about taking a shower with me?"

We both went to the bathroom and I turned the water on while she took her clothes off. Then I took off my clothes and got in the shower with her. I washed her body and she washed mine, then we had sex. Then we moved from the shower to the bed. We got up at 8:00 a.m. and took another shower.

Back at the ranch, Drake and Brittney went downstairs and found Marie on top of Tracy. They were buck naked, and Jill was fixing coffee in the kitchen. She had on a shirt. Drake and Brittney asked her what had happened, and she told them that they'd played spades. Drake said, "Y'all play buck naked? Where are your clothes? Go put some clothes on while we cook breakfast. Where is Kevin?"

"Right here."

"Dude, put some clothes on. Tracy, you and Marie need to get up before everybody else comes in. It's fixing to be late." Herod came in. He was ready for work. Then Jill came downstairs with her clothes on.

In Hawaii, Carolina and Daniel were on the beach, Daniel was getting ready to surf in a tournament. He was going up against the best there was. Carolina was on the phone with Jill. She asked how the house was, and Carolina said the house looked different. Carolina asked, "Where is John?"

"He and Jenifer are in Seattle on a case."

In Renton, we finished eating breakfast and were heading back to the hotel. We had the stuff we needed, so we lay in the bed watching TV. I fell asleep. When I woke up, Jenifer was kissing me. She just had a shirt on. Then she took off my shirt, and we didn't leave the room until we left for lunch.

Meanwhile, Kevin put something in Jill's drink. Drake and Brittney were having sex in their room. Jill said, "It's getting hot in here," as they were playing pool. She took off her shirt. She was drinking a screwdriver, and it was her shot. She didn't have a bra on.

Meanwhile, Ashley and Duck and their youngest daughter, Kim, were on the plane to go to Hawaii to see his parents. They'd just landed. As they got off the plane, Duck's parents were there waiting on them.

Back at the hotel, Jenifer and I were having sex. Then there was a knock on the door. Jenifer went to the bathroom and I put on my pants, then went to the door. "Who is it?"

"The man you've been waiting on. I've got some stuff you might want to buy."

I opened the door and he came in. He showed me the chip. I asked, "What about the weapons you said you have for sale?" We walked outside and he popped the trunk of his car. Inside were an AK-47, M247, M16, 9mm, and a .45 caliber gun. "How much is it going to cost me?"

"Ten million dollars."

"That's too much. I was thinking one million."

"What do you take me for? The chip is worth more than that."

Back at the ranch, Jill and Kevin were finishing their game. When Jill didn't have any clothes, they cleared the balls off the table. Kevin had his hand on her and kissed her. Then he laid her down on the pool table and they had sex.

He'd planned this. He'd volunteered me for the case because he wanted her. When she got up from the pool table, Kevin grabbed her and hit her. She grabbed him by his arm and slung him into the wall, then put her clothes back on and went upstairs. She shut the door behind her and locked it. Drake asked her what was wrong.

"Kevin planned all of this. He wanted John out of here so he could have his way with me. We were downstairs playing pool and I got hot. He must've put something in my drink. We had sex, but when I got off the pool table he started to hit me. I grabbed his arm and slung him into the wall, then put my clothes back on and came upstairs."

"Hard did you sling him?"

"Not hard."

Drake unlocked the door and went downstairs to check on him.

When he got down the stairs, Kevin was getting up. "What happened?" he said.

Drake went back upstairs and told Jill he was all right. Kevin followed.

"What's everybody staring at?" he asked.

"You're naked."

"I want all of y'all back to work, including you three."

"We don't work for you," Drake said. "You're not the boss, John and Jill are. You just help them out."

Back at the hotel, I said, "The chip is fake."

"No, it ain't. I got it from the United States defense computer. I used to work there until they found out what I was doing. Then they fired me and told me to pack all my stuff. While I was getting my things, I took the chip. Some of Mr. Yang's guys were transporting weapons. I caused a distraction and took their truck. They couldn't catch me. I tried to sell the chip to the Russians, but I saw five FBI agents with Mr. Yang's men. Some guys with them were Las Vegas mafia."

"What were you doing taking weapons from the mafia? Don't you know you're digging your own grave?"

I noticed some strange men watching us from the parking lot. He'd been followed. I ushered the guy inside and went to talk to Jenifer.

"We've got trouble, but I've got an idea," I said.

"Okay."

"I'll distract them while you get in the Cobra and take off."

"Okay, let's go through the window."

Jenifer and I kissed for good luck and we all went through the window. We went around the building and I shot at the men. They were shooting back, so I ran toward their trucks. I shot at their tires, then their radiator. I hit a few of them.

Back at the ranch, Kevin was still mad about what Jill had done. She said, "Anyone could have gone on this assignment, but you wanted John to go so you could have sex with me."

"Yes, I did. I wanted you for myself. You are one of the prettiest girls I've ever seen." Then he asked Drake if he could have sex with Brittney.

Drake said no, but Brittney said, "Why did you say no? I might be married to you, but I can have sex with anybody." She grabbed Kevin's hand. "Let's go to the bedroom." They went upstairs.

Drake asked Jill what she wanted to do. She said, "Let's go downstairs and play pool." They did, and while Jill was shooting, she had a hot flash.

In Hawaii, Ashley was getting a weird feeling. Her young daughter was in the store. She fainted and fell on the floor. They called 911, then Duck. Jacob saw the daughter and asked where Ashley was. They said she was in the ambulance, that she'd fainted. Duck picked Kim up from the hospital and took her to her grandpa.

Then Duck returned the hospital. He called his mom and told her what was going on, then he called the White House and told them to send his wife's medical chart, that she was in the hospital.

Meanwhile, Jenifer and I and the guy went to Burien, a little town that was about two miles away. We went to the sheriff and said, "Can you keep this guy in jail until the FBI picks him up? Here are the weapons. Guard this chip for your life. I called the FBI headquarters and they are supposed to send four agents to pick him up and take the chip from you." Jerry called me and said the plane was waiting in Seattle for us. We drove to Seattle and got on it.

Back at the ranch, Drake and Jill were downstairs. Jill tore her clothes off while playing pool. Kevin and Brittney were in the shower making passionate love. Drake kissed Jill everywhere. They knocked all the balls in the pockets and made passionate love on the table. Then Tracy and Marie came in looking for Kevin. They saw the light on downstairs and found them on the pool table buck naked.

Marie cleared her throat.

Jill and Drake stopped and said, "What are y'all doing down here?"

"Looking for Kevin."

"He went upstairs with Brittney."

Marie told Drake, "You've got a good-looking butt." Then she popped it. He told her to watch it. Tracy and Marie went back upstairs while Kevin and Brittney were coming downstairs to the kitchen.

Meanwhile in Hawaii, Ashley was missing. They found out she and two guys took a flight to Chicago. Daniel called the headquarters and asked permission to take a case to find Ashley. "She went to Chicago. Big Joe has to be behind this."

"Permission granted. I'll send some more agents to help you when they get back."

"Thank you," Daniel said. "Duck, we will find her and bring her back to you. But in case we are too late, don't say anything to your family. Tell them she had to go on a business trip. We will bring her back to you." They got two tickets to Chicago and got on the plane.

In the air over Los Angeles, we were fixing to land. We hugged goodbye and kissed before we landed. Billy was waiting for us to get off the plane. I told Jerry, the pilot, to make sure we fueled up. Billy, Jenifer, and I got something to eat and talked until Jerry came and got us. We got back on the plane and I called Jill.

"John, where are you?" she said.

"On our way back to Austin."

"Okay. I'll get Jamison to take us to the airport to wait on you."

"I'll see you when we land."

She called Jamison to get the limousine ready to pick us up at the airport.

Once there, they waited for about twenty minutes, then Jill got out of the limousine and saw John coming down the steps. They ran to each other and kissed, then held hands back to the limousine.

Back at the ranch, they said, "Welcome back, John! We just found out that any of us could have done this job. Kevin wanted to make sure that you went, and the only girl who could think like a criminal was Jenifer. Why not Billy? Kevin wanted you away from Jill so he could make his move on her. He asked the commander to get you and Jenifer to go on this case and nobody else."

"Where is Kevin now?"

"He got in his car as we were leaving."

"Who's taking care of everything while we're here?"

"Tracy and Marie."

"Okay. Let's go. Jill, follow me."

"Okay, dear." We went to our room and I shut the door. I grabbed her and turned her around and started to dance with her, then we kissed. I pushed her on the bed and made passionate love to her. We had sex for four hours, then took a shower together. When we put our clothes on, it was 4:00 p.m. We went back downstairs and the phone rang. It was the Commander, and she asked for me.

She said, "I've got another mission for you. Our agent, Ashley, is missing. Daniel and Carolina found out she went to Chicago. That's where they are, so I need you four to go to Chicago and meet up with them, then find out what's going on with Ashley. Bring her back. Then all of you will move to Hawaii and start college."

"What about the others?"

"I told them to go to Hawaii, that the rest of you will meet them there. I need you to leave today to go to Chicago, so pack enough for at least four days. Good luck. If you find her, make sure she's in her right mind. Actually, bring her here to headquarters. We can give her help that no one else can. When you get to Hawaii, sooner or later someone will find out who you are, so you need to be careful. Whatever you do, don't let Ashley get killed. Goodbye."

I hung up. "Jill, we need to get everybody here."

We gathered everyone inside. "Here is the news: us four have to go on a case. Tracy and Marie, you're in charge while we're gone. Make sure everything is taken care while we're gone. Make decisions together. We'll be gone at least four days. Marie, I want you to call Jerry and tell him to have the plane ready before we get there. When we get back, we'll pack our things and move to Hawaii to start college. Cynthia said when we get there to be careful because she thinks somebody knows who we are. Well, Jamison, is the limousine ready?"

"Yes, sir."

"How about our bags?"

"Yes, sir, they are in the trunk."

"Okay, let me make a phone call."

I called Billy and Jenifer and told them to go to Hawaii. We would start college soon.

"Be careful. People might know who we are, so just be careful." Then we hung up and I called Steven and Tiffney.

"Pack your bags and get ready to go to Hawaii. As soon as we get done with this case, we'll be on our way there. We'll get together and grill out. Y'all should see Billy and Jenifer. Also, be careful because people probably know who we are. Just enjoy the beach until we get there." I hung up. "Everyone ready to go?"

"Yes, let's go."

We went to the airport and Jerry took off. We sat back as we flew above Oklahoma, then Jerry said, "We will be landing in O'Hare Airport in twenty-five minutes. Please stay seated until we come to a stop."

Jerry put the wheels out as he landed the plane. "Thanks for flying with flight 7290."

We exited, then rented a solid black Ford Cobra and a solid black Dodge Charger.

Chapter 8

We left. I called Daniel and asked where they were. He told me they were on Maple Street near Hardee's. "Oh, we know where that is." We went to where they were and saw Ashley. She and two guys were at Joey's Bread Store. Two guys were holding Joey down while Ashley beat him up.

"John, she's got a sword."

She stabbed him four times. One of the guys grabbed him by his hair and bared his throat.

"Oh my god, she just cut his head off!"

"They're fixing to leave."

"Okay, Daniel, you and Carolina follow them, but not too close."

"Okay."

They followed Ashley and those two guys, then I had an idea. "I'm going to climb up on that pole and cut the wire for the telephone. Brittney, see if you can intercept their phone with this device. That way any number they dial comes to this number. Then give the device to Jill and show her how to use it. Drake, here's a jumpsuit. I'm going to cut the power. Hopefully we intercept their number and it comes to us. Then Jill can talk to them." I climbed the pole and cut the wire, then jumped down and went to the nearby telephone van. I put a jumpsuit on. The phone range and Jill answered.

In Hawaii, Steven, Tiffney, Billy, and Jenifer got off the plane. When they got off some girls put leis around their necks and said, "Aloha!" They grabbed a taxi and went to a real estate agency to buy their houses again. They'd been sold after everyone thought the Fabulous 8 died.

As they went in the building the deputy sheriff was watching them. "I don't know, but those four look familiar. They look like part of the Fabulous 8 group."

One local said, "You're crazy if you think they look like part of the Fabulous 8."

"Steven, we've got company. The Hawaiian police have been watching us ever since we got off the plane."

A female real estate agent said, "Sorry to keep you waiting."

"That all right. We've come to buy two houses. One used to be owned by Clay and Stacie of the Fabulous 8, and the other used to be owned by Shon and Jenny of the same group."

"Oh, those houses had famous celebrities in them." She mentioned that the Fabulous 8 had stayed on the pop charts at number one for ten weeks, and right now they were in the top fifty.

"How much for both houses?"

"A hundred and fifteen million dollars."

They paid it.

"Here are the receipts for what you gave me, and here are the keys."

"How far are the houses?"

"About three blocks from here."

"Thank you." They walked out and went around the corner. The deputy sheriff followed them, so they went in a store and asked to use the restroom. Billy and Steven went in the women's restroom. Then they sneaked out the back door, walked three blocks, and made it to their houses.

Billy and Jenifer walked across the road to their house. They unlocked their door and went in. As they were shutting the door, the deputy sheriff drove by. Then he said, "Wait a minute. There are lights on at those two houses?" He called it in and had twelve cops surround the two houses.

Back in Chicago, we cut the lights to Ashely and the two guys' hideout. I went inside and put video cameras everywhere. Then I went back outside, climbed the pole, and hooked the two wires together to restore the lights. They came on, and the video cameras came on, too. I climbed down and returned to the van.

"How did it go?"

"Worked like a charm."

"Drake, it's your turn. Put the taps on the phone and bug Big Joe's office."

"We've got company. Ashley and those two guys are back."

Daniel and Carolina climbed in the van. "What are y'all doing?"

"Well, while y'all were following Ashley, we rigged and bugged their hideout. See, we've got video. Drake is in there bugging the building so we can hear them." I called Drake. "How about it, Drake? Ashley and those two guys are coming in, so hurry out of there."

"One more place, then I can leave. Posing as a technician, Drake bumped into Ashley and stuck a bug on her. "Sorry, ma'am. I didn't mean to bump into you."

She pulled her sword out on. "Next time, I will slice your head off."

He told her he was sorry. Then he told us he was leaving. "Can you hear them real good?"

"Yes."

"Okay. I'm outside coming to the van."

"Good. Jill and I will stay here. The rest of you go to the hotel and relax. I'll watch the video and listen to them. Jill, you watch outside in case anyone comes out or comes toward us." We stayed there all night.

At the hotel, Drake, Brittney, Daniel, and Carolina took showers, then went to a nice restaurant. After that, they brought me and Jill food, then went back to the hotel.

"Why is there a van across from our hideout?" Big Joe said. "It's been there for a while. Bailey, I want you and three guys to find out why that van is there. If someone's in there, take care of them. Then I want you, Brantley, and Dusty to take care of Sarah Patterson tomorrow. She saw me kill the senator. I gave that senator a lot of money to win that election, and he was supposed to help me out. I got rid of him, so I want y'all to make sure she's dead."

"Okay, boss."

"Just get it done. This is her address."

Jill told John, "We have to save that woman."

"I know, but we don't have her address."

It was 6:00 a.m. I called Drake and told him to tell everybody that they needed to come now, that we had to rescue a woman before the hitmen killed her.

There were the two hitmen going in the building. They were talking to Big Joe, and he asked Ashley to go with them. The other two guys who were with her all the time were the other two double agents who were fired from the government. They were fixing to take over the headquarters. Big Joe wanted the double agents so he could take over them. He was really after the president and the United Nations because the president had killed his parents a long time ago, and if he could capture the commander, he could get her and her people to make bionics for him. Now they were preparing to move a ton of drugs and weapons to an island about twenty-five miles from Hawaii.

Jill called Billy, but he didn't answer his phone, so I told her to call Jenifer. Jenifer answered and Jill gave me the phone. I said, "Hello, Jenifer."

"John."

"Let me talk to Billy or Steven."

"Okay." Then she hollered, "Billy, telephone! It's John." Billy came to the phone.

"I need a favor. Can y'all leave on a sailboat and go to an island about twenty-five miles north to northeast of Honolulu? But don't do anything there. Some weapons and drugs are being shipped there. See if you can take pictures so you can bring it back to the authorities, but don't give it to them until we come to Hawaii. Be careful. Try not to use your powers unless your life is threatened or other people's."

"We've got a deputy sheriff who suspects who we are. We'll try to keep him from really finding out who we are until y'all get here."

"Try to leave without him knowing about it and borrow somebody's boat. Go to that island and try to get some pictures."

In Russia, Cameron, Becky, and Edie were in a dungeon. A Russian woman told Peyton and Meagan they were being held in a small city called Saratov, about one hundred miles from Moscow. The big mafia leader in Russia was Agraf Vasiliev. He had some KGB with him. They did what he said or they would die. He had two sons and one daughter. One of his sons was called Anekcahap, which in English was Alexander, and his other son was Bopuc, or Boris. His daughter's name was Ahha, which in English was Anna. His wife's name was Buktopua, or Victoria. The woman in New York was Duaha, and or Diana.

Peyton discovered her address and went to New York. She found her, but she didn't give Peyton the information she needed. She told her it was important, that if she heard or knew any more information to give her a call.

Meanwhile, back in Russia, the mafia kingpin called his two best experts to go to New York. One was Sergei, and the other was Maksim. In America, his name was Max, and Sergei was called Serg. Max and Serg left the next day to go to New York. Peyton went back to Washington, DC, and went to the headquarters of the FBI.

In Chicago, Jill and I found out where the woman was staying. We got there just before Big Joe's hitmen arrived. I knocked on the door and a little girl answered. She had to be about eight years old. I asked her, "Is your mommy home?"

"She's in the kitchen."

"Go get her."

The woman appeared and I asked if her name was Sarah Patterson.

"Yes, that's me."

"Grab your clothes and your little girl. You're coming with me."

"Who are you? I'm not going anywhere with you."

"Remember when you saw Big Joe kill a senator?"

"How do you know that?"

"He's sending his hitmen to kill you. We are here to protect you and your daughter. You don't want anybody kill your little girl, do you? So come on." I heard shouting. "Get back in the house! Get back in the house! They're already here. Jill will stay here with you until I get the car. Wait here. I will let you know when the coast is clear."

I sneaked around the hitmen's car and punched holes in their tires, then got in our car and took off toward the house.

"There they are!" one of the men shouted. "Let's get them! Oh, we've got flats."

I got back to the hosue and said, "Get in! They're coming." I told them to get down, then took off. I told Jill to call Drake. She did and asked if they could get Ashley. They said they couldn't.

"Tell them to get to the airport. We'll meet them there. Jill, let's trade places."

She grabbed the steering wheel and I slid over to the passenger seat.

"Get as close you can to her. She sees us coming. I'm going to to grab her and bring her in the car. Slow down a little. Okay, here it goes."

As I ducked, I grabbed her and took the sword out of her hand. "She can sit in the middle."

We made it to the airport and met up with the others.

"Daniel and Carolina, take Ashley to the headquarters and get Doc Adam to check her out. Then go back to Hawaii. Drake and Brittney, take Sarah and her daughter to California to Sarah's mom, then head back to Hawaii. Jill and I are heading to New York to talk to that Russian girl Diana about where Cameron, Becky, and Edie are. We'll see you guys in four days."

We got on the plane and went to New York. The first place we went was the police station. An officer said, "May I help you?"

We showed him our badges. "We are Agents John and Jill Warren. We're looking for a Russian girl named Diana. We'd like to ask her some question about three double agents in the Russia mafia. She might know where we can find them."

Meanwhile at the airport, the others got on the plane to go to Hawaii. It was delayed for a couple of hours. Daniel asked the pilot what was wrong. He told him the tower had had a bomb threat, and that any plane that took off would explode. No plane would land. They finally got word that they could fly and Drake sat with Brittney.

Back in New York, Jill and I were heading to Diana's apartment. "They were there," Jill said. We got out of the car and went to her apartment. We knocked, but no one answered, and one of her neighbors told us she hadn't been out of her apartment in two days. We pulled our guns out and I kicked the door in. Then we went in and hollered. We found her body on the floor. Two Russian guys came toward us. We fought and somebody came up behind me and hit me in my head.

They knocked me out and grabbed my wife, taking her with them. When I woke up, I was in the emergency room with stitches in my head. One of the detectives asked me questions about what had happened with Diana. I told him that when Jill and I got there, one of the neighbors said that usually Diana likes to run every day, but the last two days she'd been in that apartment and hadn't come out.

"She didn't answer when I knocked on the door, so we drew our weapons and I knock the door down. Then we went in and called her name, but no answered, so we walked around. We found her cut open with one bullet in her head and a second bullet in her heart. Then two Russians came at us. We fought them until somebody knocked me out. When I came to, I was here. I figure my wife brought me here. Where is she?"

"Someone named Rachel saw you come out the house. You were in a daze and she carried you to her car. She brought you to the emergency room. Is she your wife?"

"No, my wife's name is Jill. We are double agents looking for three agents who have been kidnapped. Those Russian must have her. Let me talk to Rachel."

She came in and asked me how I felt.

"I'll feel better when I find my wife and get the person who hit me in the head. Did you see anybody come out of the house before me?"

She said when she was going to her car, she saw me falling down the steps. "This happened before the cops arrived. I helped you up and carried you to my car. You passed out when I put your seat belt on. You were bleeding on the top of your head, so I held a rag to it and drove to the emergency room. You are the only person I saw."

"Okay, thank you."

"I'll take you to my apartment. You can stay there until you get better."

"I can't. I have to find my wife."

"But the doctor said you need to stay calm. I will help you. I've got friends everywhere. If I need something, I just ask my friends and they get it for me."

"Okay. My clothes are at the hotel."

We went to the hotel and I got all our stuff. She took me to her apartment and I grabbed everything and took it in. She told me I could sleep in the spare room.

Her ex-boyfriend Brian was in the apartment. He asked her why she'd brought me there and if we were dating. She told him she was through with him and demanded her key back. He wasn't going, so we talked. I told him I was her boyfriend and that he had to go and leave my girlfriend alone.

"Your girlfriend?" he said.

"Yes, she's mine. I want you out, or I will kick you out."

He was a big fellow, but he didn't know the strength I had, so he laughed at me and said, "Throw me out? I'd like to see that."

I grabbed his arm, opened the door, and threw him out, saying, "Don't come back." Back inside, I asked, "Where is the bathroom? I need to take a shower."

She showed me where the bathroom was, then showed me the room I would be sleeping in. I put my things in the room, then grabbed some clothes out of my bag, but I didn't take them to the bathroom. Rachel brought me a towel. I got in the shower and then felt a hand on me. Rachel joined me and washed my body as I washed her body. Then we had sex in the shower. We moved from the bathroom to the kitchen, then to her bedroom. We went to sleep around 4:00 a.m. and I got up at 8:00 a.m., got dressed, and returned to Diana's apartment. I looked for anything that would help me find Jill. Then I found a phone and tablet that no one else had found. I took them with me, then found some other stuff I could use. I returned to Rachel's apartment and cooked breakfast. She came in the kitchen in just her nightshirt.

I told her to sit down. "I figured out who hit me in the head. It was Diana's best friend, Amanda. She saw me fighting, so she hit me in the head with a vase. I'm going to talk to her after I eat breakfast."

I had the other items on the table and Rachel asked me about them.

"I found them in the apartment. I'm going get somebody to check them for clues that will help me find Jill and the other three agents. We've got one more month before we start college in Hawaii, so I need to find her."

I called headquarters and asked for a technician. Jerry came to the phone and said, "What do you need?"

"I'm fixing to send you some pictures. Use the zapper."

"Okay, go ahead."

I sent him the pictures. He used his device to zap the stuff to the lab.

"There you go," I said. "Let me know what you find. Anybody heard from Russia yet?"

"No. It's too dangerous."

"I'm leaving tomorrow night to go to Russia."

"What about everybody else?"

"No, don't let them know what's going on. They need to stay where they are."

"Okay."

"Thank you." I hung up. "Do you want to ride with me, Rachel?"

"Yes. Let me put some clothes on."

I followed her into the bedroom and popped her butt. I dressed her, then she put on deodorant and perfume and brushed her hair.

"Okay, I'm ready."

"Let's go then."

She locked the door and got on the motorcycle with me.

We returned to Diana's apartment building and knocked on the door of room 320. Amanda came to the door. She tried to slam it closed again, but I kept it from shutting. We went in. She grabbed something and was going to hit me with it, but I grabbed it from her and said I wanted to talk.

"Who's staying with you?" I asked.

"Nobody."

I asked her why she hit me in the head knowing the Russians were the ones trying to kill her. She said that if she hadn't hit me, they would've killed her.

"They've got my wife." She told me she was sorry. "Your best friend just got killed, and you attacked me instead of the killers. Now they're back in Russia with my wife, thanks to you. None of this had to happen."

"I'm sorry. I'll do anything you say, anything."

We left. Rachel said, "Let go back to my apartment."

"I wish Jill and I were on the beach in Hawaii with the rest. They are enjoying themselves before we go to college, but I'm searching for my wife and three other agents who were kidnapped a month ago."

We returned to Rachel's place, then I called Jerry at headquarters.

"So, John, what can I do for you?"

" Can you get me a silencer assault rifle with a scope, and a rope with a steel claw for climbing?"

"You'll get it when you get to Germany. Call me later and I'll tell you who your contact is."

I'd leave in the morning instead of that night, so we stayed in. Rachel cooked supper while I watched television. She was getting hot, so she started to take off some of her clothes. She changed into her nightshirt. I was still in the living room watching TV, then I got up and went in the kitchen. I said she must have been hot, and she said yes. I stood behind her while she cooked and massaged her back. She turned the stove off and

I turned her around. We kissed, then I made passionate love to her on the kitchen table. We ate at the same table, then went to the couch and cuddled.

In Russia, Jill was brought to Agraf. He looked at her, then tore off her clothes and made her spin around in a circle. Then he told one of his guys to take her to his room and to let the slaves wash her and get her ready to marry him as his third wife.

In New York, I got up the next morning at 8:00 a.m. I told Rachel, "Goodbye. I won't forget what you did."

Then I got on the motorcycle, went to the airport, and got on a plane. We had a delay between flights, then I got on the next plane that would stop in Germany. That was when I was supposed to call Jerry to find out who my contact was. We would land in Germany in ten minutes, so I was looking at a book.

Someone said "Please return everything to an upright position."

The wheels came out and we landed, then had a thirty minute delay, so I called Jerry.

"When you get to Russia, ask for a bread store. There's a man named Dave. He has a girl he wants us to take to the United States. Her name is Selena. She can speak some English, and he should have everything you want. Good luck."

"Thank you." I got on the next plane.

We landed in Moscow. I got off the plane and asked in Russian where the closest bread store was. They told me it was around the corner, so I went there and found it. When I went in a man asked, "Can I help you?" I told him I was looking for something sleek. He said in English, "Follow me." I followed him to the back. He asked, "Is this what you wanted?" He handed me an assault rifle and a rope with a gravity hook. I carried them in a bag, then a gorgeous woman came through the door. It was his daughter, Selena. She had a nine point six body.

"That your daughter?" I asked.

He told me yes.

"Okay. Can you get me close?"

"You go to the castle and I will do the rest."

"Then I'll be back to get her before we leave."

We left, and after a while he said, "This is the furthest I can go without them knowing."

I got out of the car and went toward the mountain.

I used the binoculars and saw how many guards there were. Then I attached the silencer to the assault rifle. I took out four guards, then threw the rope with the hook up to a ledge. I made sure it wasn't coming down, then climbed up and over the edge. Three more guards were coming. Two of them went another way, but the other stayed right in my way, I sneaked behind him and slit his throat, then went on and called Jill's name. Then there were three guys more coming my way. I grabbed my knife and rose to stab one guy, then the other guy. I hit his throat and crushed his windpipe. Then I threw my knife and it hit the guy in the throat. I grabbed my knife and ran.

Then there were two more guys. They came down with their swords. I ducked and punched one in the throat, then grabbed the other guy's sword and fought off the other guy. He looked up at his sword while it was in the air and I cut his head off. Then I heard Jill shouting at somebody. A guy had her against the wall and was trying to force himself on her. I hollered to distract him. When he turned, she punched him in the throat. Then she hit him in the stomach as he bent over. I came down with the sword and cut his head off. Then I gave her the assault rifle and we ran back to the ledge. Two guys were coming behind us. I punched one through the chest and ripped his heart out.

Jill jumped over the edge and landed on the ground. I threw my knife into a guy's head, then ran as they shot at us. I grabbed the assault rifle from Jill and shot at them while we ran.

Agraf was furious. "I want that girl! Kill the guy. Go after them now. I know where they're heading. Go to Saratov and wait on them. Take the helicopter to get there quickly. Don't stop."

We ran all the way there. We got there in thirty minutes, and as they were coming toward the castle, I shot the guards. Then we went in the castle and fought more guys. I hit a couple of them with blows to the head. I ripped another guy's heart out and turned a flip in the air, knocking a couple of them to the wall. Then I grabbed an AK-47 and shot any guy with a weapon. Jill opened the door to the prison. All three agents came out and I told them, "Grab any weapon you see and follow us." We went through and shot up the place. We killed lots of guys. Then I found four knifes and gave my AK-47 to Jill, using the knives as throwing knives and stabbing with them.

I fought several men as we came out of the castle. One fought with a sword, then Cameron threw me my own sword. blocked the guy's sword and came up, then turned around and cut his head off. We took a truck with weapons on board and three helicopters followed us flying low, shooting at us and knowing we could blow up. What they didn't know was there was a rocket launcher in the back. Cameron drove while I climbed in the back and grabbed the rocket launcher. It had three rockets with it, so I jumped off the back of the truck and shot at the helicopter.

The first hit one helicopter, and the explosion hit it into another helicopter. The third helicopter landed and we ran to it. We killed the three Russians inside, then got in the helicopter and I flew it. We flew to Moscow and landed at the airport. I told the pilot, Cowboy, to have the plane ready for us and to make sure Selena was on it. As we were getting on, another young woman came running with Agraf's men chasing her. I got off, ran, and picked her up, then ran back to the plane and told Cowboy to go. We were fixing to take off, but there was a truck at the end of the runway.

A guy was about to shoot a rocket launcher at us, but before he could shoot, we hit him with a wheel. Then we were up in the air heading to Germany. We walked about the cabin and then Jill sat in my lap. I said, "I missed you. When we get back to Los Angeles, we'll fly to Hawaii to meet the others."

No one else knew about any of this. Cowboy turned on the seat belt sign and said, "We're about to land in Germany." We landed and he said, "Thanks for flying with Cowboy's airline. Welcome back, Cameron, Becky, and Edie. Welcome home."

"Thank you. We're glad to be back."

We got off and went to the ticket line, then purchased our tickets to Los Angeles. There was a flight leaving in thirty minutes. Before we got on the plane, we went to a bar and got a drink. Cameron and I got Bud Lights. Then it was time to get on the plane.

Cameron sat with all the women, except for Jill. She and I sat in first class.

"They don't mind sitting with the average group even though they are rich," Cameron said.

We didn't want the two women to sit by themselves, so I asked Jill, "What do you want to do? We've got several hours before we land in Los Angeles. We can go and talk to the two women."

Jill told me she had to go to the bathroom, then motioned for me to follow her, so I did. She grabbed me by the hand and shut the door and locked it.

Then she took my clothes off and I ripped her clothes off and we had sex. After, we heard the captain call my name, so I put my clothes back on and went out the door. She locked it back and I went to the cockpit and asked what he wanted. He asked me if I was John Warren. I told him yes.

"Here is the radio."

I got on the radio and Agraf was on it. "So, you've got my niece. Well, guess who I have here?"

"I don't know."

"Your parents and your sister, Elizabeth."

"How do you know who our parents are?"

"I know who you really are, John. Your real name is Buddy. Jill, her name is Bella, and the rest of the Fabulous 8 are in Hawaii. They are under surveillance. If you don't return my niece, my guys will take out one of your family members at a time. I have guys at each of their houses. If you give me the two girls, I will release your families. You have three hours to comply once you land in Los Angeles."

The pilot asked, "Is that true?"

"Yes. We're part of Fabulous 8. How much longer before we get to Los Angeles?"

"Two hours and twelve minutes."

I left the cockpit and went to talk to the girls. I had Selena go with me and Bella got Katlin, Agraf's niece, to go with her. Before we said anything else, we announced that we were Bella and Buddy from the group Fabulous 8. One-on-one, I asked Selena, "Do you have something that Agraf wants? He's got our families. Tell the truth. After we land in Los Angeles we have to give him an answer."

"We have five double agents here," Cameron said. "We need to find out what they know. Maybe we can use it to our advantage. These girls can stay in the States. But they've got to tell us what they know or give us whatever Agraf wants. Do either of you have something that will help us out of this?"

"No, we don't know what we're supposed to get or have." I told Selena to stand up, then I searched her. I didn't find anything. Bella said she found a disk on Katlin and handed it to me.

"Why did he want both of you?"

"Agraf and my dad are cousin."

"So the prime minister is your dad's cousin, too?"

"Yes."

"That makes you two cousins, right?"

"That's why he wanted both of us. He killed my dad, so I took the disk. It shows who he's killed and how some people were treated. If the wrong hands get ahold of this, my uncle and her cousin will vanish forever."

We were about to land in Los Angeles.

"Okay, you guys just get back to your seats," I said. "We'll figure out what we're going to do when we land."

Everybody got back in their seats. Bella and I buckled up and held hands.

The captain came on the loudspeaker and said, "Welcome to Los Angeles, California, and thank you for flying with us on United Airlines."

We got off and waited by a pay phone. It rang and Cameron answered.

Agraf said, "Give the phone to Buddy."

Cameron said, "This is him."

Agraf was furious. "I know you're not Buddy. Give the phone to Buddy."

Cameron handed me the phone.

"What kind of joke are you playing?" he asked.

"I wasn't playing. All he did was answer the phone. Where are you?"

"About twenty miles from the airport, heading toward you. Got the merchandise?"

"Yes, we do. You have our parents?"

"You have the girls?"

"No."

"Why not?"

"I'm giving what you really want: the disk. I'll give you the disk and you give me our parents. Where do you want to meet?"

"How about the top of the garage?"

"Sounds good." I hung up. "Okay, girls, where do you want to go?"

"New York."

We bought them tickets for New York. "Here are your tickets. I'm going to call my friend Rachel and see if she can pick you up. She can help you get a job and a place to stay." I called her next and she answered. "This is John," I said. "No, wait a minute. My real name is Buddy Smithisom."

"You've got to be kidding me."

"No, I'm not kidding."

"I thought you guys were dead."

"No, we're alive. I was wondering if you can help a couple of girls for me. They are from Russia, and their names are Selena and Katlin."

"Yes, I'll help them all I can."

"Thank you. If you need more money, let me know and I'll send it to you." I hung up. "Cameron, Becky, Edie, you guys need to get back to headquarters. I think they need you. Bella and I will take care of this."

"Okay, Buddy. Good luck."

Bella and I walked to the top of the garage. When we got there, we sat and waited for about five minutes.

They showed up. Agraf got out of the car and told us that he wanted to see the disk. I told him we wanted to see our parents. He told his guys to let them out, so they did. I asked if they were all right.

"Do not make that exchange," they said. "We will willingly sacrifice our lives to help you."

But we told them no.

"I'll bring you the disk," I told Agraf. "You let them go."

Two guys waited as I moved closer, then one shot hit me in the arm. Then they shot our parents. I shot at them and they got back in their car. Bella took the two hitmen out with two shots.

The big guy got away. We called 911. I told our parents to be calm and quiet, not to say a word as the ambulance came and picked them up. Someone told me I was bleeding. I told him to just worry about our parents and get them to the hospital "I'm sorry," he said.

I asked him what had happened.

"They all are bleeding too much from the gunshot wounds. Most of them won't make it to the hospital. The rest might last about a day. We'll try to get them to the hospital. Maybe they'll make it."

Bella ran towards her parents. I grabbed her and held her tight and told her they'd risked their lives for us all the time. She cried in my arms. I called everyone else and told them they need to go to Chicago. I was going to have the bodies flown there. We invited a lot of people to the funeral.

We flew back to Chicago for the funeral. Some cried, but some were mad and wanted to kill the Russian mafia.

"How did he know who we were? Someone must have told him," James said.

A man approached us and said, "I'm sorry about your parents. It was my fault. I told him you were still alive and who your parents were."

Clay pulled his gun out and put the barrel against the man's head. I told Clay to put his gun away.

"That's not going to bring our parents back. If they were still here, they would say this: 'You're going to college. Don't worry about us. We already did our time.' He didn't know he was going to kill our parents. Give the guy a break."

"But I *did* know. I heard him say he was going to kill them."

"You better run, dude, because I won't be able to hold everyone back."

He ran for his life. Clay jumped over my head and grabbed the guy. Before I could get over there, he'd already broken his neck, I told Clay to run. Someone called the police. I told the others, "We'll get Clay and leave tonight to go back to Hawaii. Go to the hotel and get your things, then meet me and Bella at the airport. She and I are going stay here and finish up, then we'll go to Hawaii. Just find Clay, then get to the airport. Your tickets will be ready. James, you're in charge. Go now before the cops get here. Make sure you get Clay. Go."

They left. Bella and I started to go back inside when the dead man stood up. He was still alive after all. Then the cops showed up. They came in and asked what was going on.

We told them, "Nothing. Somebody called and said there had been a murder. There's no murder here."

Two men approached. "Did you see the dead body?"

"Where?"

"It was right here."

"You mean this guy behind me?" I asked.

"We saw your friend break his neck. Everybody said he was dead, then you told your friend to run."

"Well, if the guy were dead, would he be standing here? Ask him."

The cops asked him what happened.

"I really don't know. I must've passed out. I don't remember anything."

Bella and I went to the airport and got all the tickets. The others found Clay and met us at the airport.

Jenny asked, "What about Elizabeth?"

I told her she was staying with me and Bella. "She's coming with us when we leave. When you get to Hawaii, enroll her in school."

We hugged each other, and I kissed Tammy, Stacie, and Angie goodbye. Bella and I left the airport. First we stopped at the Demiro mansion. That was where my sister was at. Her friend's dad was a millionaire. I knocked on the door and Mr. Demiro answered. I asked him if was Elizabeth still there.

"I'm sorry about your parents," he said.

"Tell Elizabeth that we'll be back sometime tomorrow to pick her up. That is, if you don't mind for her to stay here until tomorrow."

"No, I don't mind."

They asked me and Bella to come in. The first thing Elizabeth asked was where Jenny and the others were. I told her they'd left to go to Hawaii. "She's going to enroll you in school. You're going into ninth grade."

My sister was six foot two inches tall and weighed a hundred and twenty-nine pounds. She was a pitcher and a first baseman in softball, and a forward in basketball. She also played tennis. She had blonde hair and blue eyes.

Mr. Demiro went in the study and I asked Elizabeth, "Have any men with weird accents been here?" I asked Bella to follow me to the study. "Can you hear him?" She told me yes. I asked, "What is he saying?"

"He said, 'Just send the stuff and I'll have my guys distribute it. I'll bring the money next week. We might have a problem. The girl is leaving tomorrow to go with her brother to live in Hawaii. I'll ask him to let her stay with us. You might have heard their parents got killed. Her name is Elizabeth and her brother and sister are Buddy and Jenny Smithisom.

Wait a minute. All the mafia want them dead! I'm not killing anybody.' Now someone else—wait, it's Big Joe!—he's saying, 'You either get rid of them or you and your family will join them.' 'Can I keep Elizabeth?' Mr. Demiro asks. 'I'll get rid of Buddy and Bella. My guys will take them to the junkyard. We'll tied them up and put them in a car, then put the car in the smasher.' "

We grabbed Elizabeth and went out the door. Elizabeth's friend Annie Marie hollered for her dad. She told him we'd grabbed Elizabeth and ran out the door.

He told his guys, "Get the girl back. It doesn't matter what you do to the other two, but do not harm the girl. Whatever you do, do not harm the girl."

drove all night and were tired. We stopped in Louisiana and rested there, then left at about 3:00 p.m. and went to Texas. Then we caught a flight to Hawaii. "We had to get you out of there, Elizabeth," I said.

We made it to the airport and took off. Hours later, we landed in Hawaii. After we touched the ground, we got off and walked to Jacob's store and asked him to take us to our house. He did and we went in.

I showed Elizabeth her room. She liked it. Then I showed her the bathroom and the pool. The first thing she asked was if she could go swimming. I told her to go ahead, so she put on her bathing suit. As I put our stuff up, Bella told me she was going to call everybody over and that we were home for good.

Meanwhile in Florida, Brent and Chance were on their last cruise together. They'd made enough money to go to college. Brent was going to UCLA for therapy after he came back from this last cruise. He was leaving the next day, and Chance was going to New York to study dancing. She'd gotten a scholarship to go to New York. She stuck with what she liked to do the best. During the summer they went on tours of ballroom dancing.

Back in Hawaii, everybody came over to our house for a welcome home party for Fabulous 8. All the locals asked us to sing some songs. We sang four songs and the party went on until 2:00 a.m.

We wanted to enjoy our last three days before we started our college classes and Elizabeth started school. She would be in the ninth grade. We partied for the last three days before going to college. Then one day I heard the doorbell ring. It was Fritz and his sister Donna. They'd already had two years of college in Florida.

They'd transferred to Hawaii for four more years. That would give them six years total. Fritz was going for a doctorate, and Donna was going to be a forensics specialist. She was in my classes. I told them everybody was home except my sister and Bella. "How's life treating y'all?"

"Good. We've finished two years of college."

"We're having a party. It'll start at eight and probably last until two. Ah, that sounds like Bella and Elizabeth now."

I looked out the window and didn't see anyone. That meant it was Bella and Elizabeth, then. They came in the door then and put the groceries on the table.

"Buddy, come and help!"

Donna approached her. She was scared of Bella, but she hugged her.

"When did you guys get here?" Bella asked.

"We arrived here a few minutes ago, right before you showed up."

"So you've come to visit?"

"No, we're going to school here!"

"Did you register for classes?"

"Yes, we did that this morning," Fritz said.

"I thought you just got here," Bella said.

"We just got to your house. We came in last night and got a hotel. We registered for our classes and looked for a place to live, then came here."

"Did you find somewhere to live?"

"No."

"Well, you guys can stay with us until you find a place of your own. We've got plenty of room."

"We were hoping you would say that. We've got our bags in the rental car."

Meanwhile in Chicago, Big Joe called Brantley for a job. He gave Brantley a picture of a young girl, about twenty-four years old, with a baby girl. He told Brantley, "I want you to kill her and bring me the little girl. That is my daughter and I want her. I don't care how you kill her mother; just bring me Rebecca. This is her address. Her mother's name is Joyce."

"When do you want this done?"

"As soon as possible. Do not harm my daughter."

Brantley retrieved his weapon 'and got in his car, went to that addresses, then sat there and waited.

He finally saw Joyce and had her in his sight. As he was about to pull the trigger, something stopped him. He said to himself that he couldn't do it. Then he saw Big Joe's car across from his and another of his guys sitting there, waiting on Joyce to come to the window. Brantley aimed at him and took him out. Then he took Big Joe's driver out. After that, he ran across the street and went into the building. He ran upstairs and busted Joyce's door down. She attacked him with a broom. He told her to stop or he would kill her.

"I'm trying to save you and your little girl. I was sent to kill you and bring Rebecca to Big Joe. Instead, I'm saving your life. When I tell you to run, you run with all your strength and stay low and close to me."

They ran, then he stopped at the door and saw his car blow up. They went back upstairs and went to the top of the apartment building. He made her lie down and be quiet. Then he took his rifle and scope and killed five guys.

"Stay here with your little girl until I get back," he said.

He climbed down and went to where the guys were.

Chapter 9

Brantley grabbed their weapons and went to a car, then hot-wired it. It was a Ferrari red. He went back to the building and asked Joyce if she knew how to drive. She told him yes and she drove.

Back in Hawaii, Donna was in her room unpacking her suitcase when Bella went and talked to her about her brother Fritz. She asked if he had a girlfriend.

"No. I thought you and Buddy were together."

"We're on and off."

Sudden they heard James and Tammy having some words with each other. James left and went to a hotel. Then Stacie was arguing with Clay. She slammed the door, got in her car, then joined Tammy.

Donna asked, "Is it all right if Buddy goes out with me?"

"Yes, you can go out with him."

Bella asked Fritz if he wanted to date her.

"Yes, I do."

"I was just asking your sister if you were dating somebody. We start college tomorrow."

Back in Chicago, at Big Joe called Bailey and told him he had a job for him. He wanted him to go to the mansion the next day and bring all his weapons with him. He'd heard news about Dusty, that somebody had planted a bomb under his car. When Dusty had gotten out of the car and shut the door, it had activated it and blown up. Lots of fragments had hit Dusty. He'd been taken him to the morgue, but the government had sent some guys to take his body to Alaska, to a little place call Valdez. There were doctors and scientists there who could erase his memory and fix his body.

Back in Hawaii, I went in my room with Donna. I shut the door and grabbed her. We kissed and couldn't stop touching each other. Soon our clothes were off and twe made passionate love to each other. Then the phone rang and it was the guys. They asked me to come to the hotel where James was. I put my clothes back on and went to Bella. She was in the kitchen getting stuff ready for our last party.

I called Shon and asked him if he'd written another song. He told me he was working on it. I asked him if it would be finished by tonight. He told me he would try, but couldn't guarantee it would be finished.

"Try. If you don't finish before tonight, we'll sang it later. See you tonight."

"Okay, bye."

I got in the Ferrari and went to the hotel where James was. I went up to room 324, and somebody was already in there, a maid who worked late. He opened the door and she was naked in his bed. He had his shorts on and was drunk.

"What happened?" I asked.

He told me Tammy wanted to date other people.

"What's wrong with that?"

He wanted to marry her, but she wasn't ready to get married yet, so he got mad and went out the door, then came to this hotel. He grabbed a bottle of scotch whiskey and drank it dry. I told him to sober up.

"We've got a party to go to, and we've got to play."

Meanwhile in Chicago, Bailey went to the mansion and Big Joe told him he'd sent Brantley to do a job, but he hadn't done it.

"I want both him and Joyce dead and I want my daughter back. I don't care how you do it. Just bring me his head. He has killed ten of my guys. I want you to find them and bring my daughter back. On second thought, don't kill them. Just bring all three back."

"Have you heard about how Dusty's doing?"

"Oh, you haven't heard. He's dead. His body was at the morgue, but I heard some government guys took it and disappeared. None of my guys know where he is. I want you bring me Brantley, Joyce, and my daughter. I'm going to kill those two slowly and cut them up and feed them to my sharks and crocodiles."

Back in Hawaii, Duck came to the house and brought his daughter. They were on vacation. I asked him if he'd heard from Ashley.

"No, I haven't heard from her since y'all brought her back. Her mother and sister ask about her every night."

"Are you staying for the surfing tournament next week?"

"No, we're leaving tomorrow so I can get her in school."

"Okay, good luck."

I called headquarters and talked to Becky. She was the acting commander until Cynthia got back, so I asked her how Ashley was. Becky told me she was getting better and they would find what had made her behave that way so they could send her home with her family.

At the military base in Alaksa, Dusty woke up and his voice was different. The scientists had programmed his memory to fight crime and to protect the good. They did tests on him to see how strong he was. He could bend iron rods.

Meanwhile, Brantley took Joyce and her little girl to the airport. He got three tickets to the Bahamas and they got on the plane. It took them to Nassau. Then they got off the plane and took a cab and went to Bimini, where he bought a house. Then he got a job to support them.

Back in Oahu, we lived in Nanakuli. We were getting ready for our party. I went upstairs and took a shower. I heard one of the girls come to the bathroom and the door shut behind her. I couldn't open my eyes. Then I felt one of the girls washing my back. I put my hands on her body and she kissed me. Our bodies touched each other, then she got out of the shower and dried off. She sneaked out of the bathroom before I could see her. I grabbed a towel and got out. Bella, Stacie, and Tammy were in the bathroom.

I asked, "Did one of y'all come in the shower with me?" They told me no. I said, "Somebody came in the shower with me. They washed my back."

I got ready and went downstairs. There was a girl there, about twenty-five years old. I asked what her name was. She told me Carolina. I noticed she looked a little wet, and she said she had just arrived in Hawaii. She'd been told everybody comes to our house to have fun before school starts.

Then James and Clay arrived. "Hey, Buddy, guess who we saw? Remember Zorn, the guy who owns that bar in Florida?"

"Yes, I remember."

"Well, he just opened a casino and is hosting a strip poker tournament. I heard the four sisters are going to be there."

"When is it?"

"About three weeks from today." Then Clay noticed Carolina. "Well, hello there. I haven't seen you here before."

"I just arrived in Hawaii. I'm going to be one of the teachers. I just graduated from Yale last year, so this is my first teaching job."

"Well, welcome to Hawaii. We're all students."

"Wait a minute. Aren't you guys Fabulous 8?"

"We are. I'm Buddy, the leader of the group. These are my two cousins, James and Clay. The three coming downstairs are Bella, Tammy, and Stacie."

"Do all of you live together?"

"No, only Bella and I live here, and my sister Elizabeth. Oh, I forgot, guys, look who's going to college with us. Fritz and Donna!"

I still wondered who had come in the shower with me so I could thank them. Carolina confessed it was her. One of the guys had let her in and she'd asked where the bathroom was. She'd gone upstairs, opened the door, and saw me in there, then she'd gotten in the shower with me. I told James and Clay what had happened.

They asked me how she looked.

"I couldn't see her. I had soap in my eyes and was trying to wash it out. She washed my back and had her boobs all over me. Then she got out and was gone by the time I was able to see. They were a pretty good size. They weren't small or huge."

Then there was another girl there. She looked about six foot one and had blue eyes and auburn red hair. I went over and asked her name. She said it was Beth. She was also a new teacher, but of high school. As a matter of fact, she was one of Elizabeth's teachers.

Everybody was about to leave the party at 11:00 p.m. because the teachers and others had to get up early in the morning. Beth asked which one of us was taking Elizabeth to school. I told her I would. I had to be at the college by 8:00 a.m.

"She's got homeroom and her first class with me. Just bring her in my class and we will get along just fine. I'll see you in the morning. Bye."

Then Carolina said, "You've got a nice butt."

"Thank you. I wish I could say the same, but you didn't let me see. I know you have perfect boobs."

"Thank you."

"I felt them on my back."

"Well, maybe if you're nice during my class I might give you a surprise."

" I don't have any of your classes, but James and Clay do."

"Tell them if they behave in my class, they'll get to see the surprise."

"I'll tell them, but I still want to have a chance."

"Are you dating Bella or Donna? Both of them are in my class. I wonder why you aren't."

"I see everybody every day. Bella and I have been dating on and off for the last two years. I figured we'd have different classes because everybody thinks I'm the leader. Before we started this band, we didn't have a boss or leader, but somehow they all picked me. Instead of deciding things together, they always pointed at me."

Meanwhile in Alaska, Cynthia had returned and noticed something was different. She went to sick bay where Ashley was. Ashley wasn't there. Cynthia sounded the alarm. Then Ashley jumped on her. Ashley dismantled her leg so she couldn't use it, then used a technique to knock her out. Then she picked her up and towed her out of the headquarters. Then she went back in and flipped the self-destruct button. She cut off communication to all double agents and killed twenty of them, then grabbed the commander. There was a ship waiting on her. It was Big Joe himself.

He asked her, "Is everything done?"

"If we don't leave, we'll be caught in the explosion. Where do you want me to put her?"

"Take her below and have the guys chain her up."

Meanwhile in another part of Alaska, the military was about to send their biggest project to guard the biggest missile. He would ride in the truck with the missile. First, they would fly from Alaska to Maine, then take the route from New York to Florida. From there, they would go to Texas. Then they would leave Texas and hit Las Vegas, Nevada, then head straight to Long Beach at the naval base.

Meanwhile, back in Hawaii, the last person had just gone home when Jimmy knocked on the door, so I let him in. He told me he had a partner in the club he owned. I asked him where the club was. He told me he and a friend of his decided to go into business together and that they wanted us to play four nights a week, Thursday to Sunday nights.

After he left, I told the guys, "We've got a little job and will go to school. I met a girl named Amy Wesson the other day. She was fine. James, she asked about you."

Meanwhile in the Bahamas, Lynn, Tammy, Missy, and Shannon were in a tournament for strip poker that was worth a hundred and twenty million dollars. It cost fifty thousand dollars to compete in the tournament. They made a hundred and fifty million apiece, and the tournament would start the next night. Brantley was asked to be a security guard at the club, which was called Zanerity. They had dancers and waitresses. He got Joyce a job there as a waitress.

Their babysitter left the house without Joyce's little girl. She'd been paid half a million dollars to leave. Bailey grabbed Rebecca and put a bomb in the house, then shot the babysitter's tires out. She flipped four times. Then he shot her between the eyes and went to the airport. A private jet was waiting for them.

Back in Hawaii, I asked a girl to go to the beach with me. Her name was Kaitlyn. She was six foot three inches tall, and weighed about a hundred and twenty-one pounds. She had dark blonde hair and green eyes. This was her second year in college, and she was a model. I got a blanket and some wine, but before I went outside, I noticed my phone wasn't glowing. When I picked it up, it didn't do anything. There was no sound at all. I told James and the rest of the group when they get home to call me, then Kaitlyn came in and asked if I was coming.

"No, we'll have to do this another time."

"Okay. I'll call you in the morning and will ride with you to school."

"Okay."

I called headquarters and got no answer, only a busy signal.

Then I saw it on the news. It was no accident. Somebody knew what they were doing. It had to be an inside job. So many people had been killed. Only few people were authorized to use the self-destruct button sequence: the commander, Becky, Ashley, and Cameron. There was only one person who could've done this. Then we got a call from Big Joe. I answered the phone. He laughed.

"Okay, double agent. I've got your commander. If you want to see her alive, you'll give me that code. If you don't, I will send you her head."

Back in the Bahamas, Brantley and Joyce arrived home. She got out of the car and was walking to the house when Brantley got out and ran to stop her.

"They've found us. Now they've got your little girl. Stand back. If you'd opened the door, we would've been blown up." Brantley checked the door and found the string. "I'm going to cut the string. Get back." She walked back toward the car. While she was standing there, two guys grabbed her and took her to Bailey.

Brantley went in the house. He heard something and then jumped through the window. The house blew up. Then the men went to Bailey and told him Brantley was dead, that he was in the house when it blew up.

Meanwhile in Las Vegas, some hitmen were in position to take the missile.

Back in Hawaii, we were trying to find a way to reach Cameron, Becky, and Edie. I called Kevin in Texas to get in touch with them and he told me Peyton and Megan were in Texas with him. He said, "Our headquarters was blown up and a lot of agents were killed in that frenzy by Ashley. She killed twenty agents and kidnapped the commander. Big Joe told me if we don't give him the code, he will send us her head."

"Well, what should we do?"

"Just give it to me and I will take care of it. You guys start your classes today."

We needed to get some sleep, so I gave Kevin the number and told him to call us if anything changed. Then I told him goodbye, and we hung up.

I went upstairs to bed and went to sleep with Bella. I got under the covers put my arm around her. I woke up at 5:30 a.m. I put my shorts on and my running shoes, then went downstairs and walked to the beach. I ran eight miles, four miles down the beach and four miles back to the house. Donna was up fixing breakfast. I sat down at the table and she fixed me a plate, so I ate and drank my coffee, then went upstairs and woke Elizabeth. I told her to go downstairs and eat, then get ready for school. I walked in the bedroom and tried to be quiet because Bella didn't have to go until 10:00 a.m. I was getting my clothes and she woke up and said she was going to take a shower with me. I told her to come on, that she could ride with Donna and Fritz.

At James and Tammy's house, they were still sleeping. When they woke up, Tammy went downstairs and cooked breakfast while James went outside to get the paper. Then he waited at the table. There was a knock on the door, so she opened it. It was Clay and Stacie.

"What time are we leaving to go to our class?"

"About 8:00 a.m."

It was 6:00 a.m. and we were all up. Bella called Tammy. They were leaving at 7:00 a.m. Our class was at 10:00 a.m.

In the Bahamas, the contestants for the strip poker tournament had just woken up and were eating breakfast. Brantley went to the Zanerity club and talked to the manager. He asked, "Has anybody come up here and asked for me or Joyce?"

"Yes, why?"

"I was a hitman for Big Joe. I was supposed to kill her, but I couldn't do it. I brought her and her little girl here to have a fresh start, away from Big Joe. Only you and two others knew about us here. Now they're both gone. I'm going to find out who did this."

Bella and I were in the shower together. We washed each other, then dried each other off. While she put her makeup on and fixed her hair, I put on deodorant, got dressed, brushed my hair and teeth, then put my shoes on and went outside to crank the Cobra up. Then I went back in to find out if Elizabeth was ready.

"Is everyone going?"

"I know Donna needs to be there at 8:00 a.m. because her first class is at eight just like mine."

"Well, Donna can ride with me."

"Oh, when you were in the shower Kaitlyn called and said she would see you in class."

"Okay. So how about it, Donna?"

"Okay, let me tell Bella that she and Fritz will be riding together."

Fritz's first class was at 9:00 a.m. Donna and Elizabeth got in the car. Then I got a phone call from Kevin. He said, "I got Peyton and Megan to go to Chicago. I wanted to let you know I might need a couple of you to go on a job in case they can't get her back."

"What about a couple of CIA or FBI agents?"

"I would like to use our own people."

"Well, we'd like to stay in school, but I know some are willing to go on a mission. Call me if you need us and I will talk to the rest to find out who is willing to go. Who do you need, a man and a woman?"

"How are Bella and Tammy? Tell them I asked about them, and that I'd like for them to come back to Texas. I enjoyed their company."

"How is everything in the business?"

"Okay. I'll call back at 3:00 p.m. and you can tell me who wants to go on the mission, if I need them."

"Okay. Bye."

I got in the car and everybody was buckled up. Then I smoked my tires as I left. First we took Elizabeth to school, then we went to the college. We had fifteen minutes before our class started, so Kaitlyn and I were in the corner kissing until the phone rang. It was Kevin again. He said he might need two people.

"I'll need one guy and one girl. They can volunteer, but if no one volunteers, you'll have to go, and you can pick a girl to go with you. When I call again, you must let me know who's taking the mission."

"Okay."

We hung up. We had five minutes to get to class. Kaitlyn asked, "What did you mean, a 'mission' when you were talking to that person on the phone? Why did you walk away from me when you get that call? You spoke privately with that person, but I've noticed certain people can be there when you get calls like that."

"Like who?"

"Bella, Tammy, Donna, Stacie, and some others."

"There are certain phone calls I might get that you don't need to hear."

Meanwhile in Florida, Dusty rode with the military with the biggest missile that anyone had ever seen. As they approached Texas, Dusty told the driver to keep on driving, that he was going to check on everything in the back. He climbed out the window and jumped onto the trailer, then made a phone call to Big Joe. Bailey answered.

"Hello? Who is this?"

"Is Big Joe around?"

"Yes. May I tell him who's calling?"

"It's Dusty."

Bailey dropped the phone. When he retrieved it, he said, "This is Bailey. I thought you were dead."

Big Joe grabbed the phone from Bailey.

"Who is this?"

Dusty told him what had happened. "They said I was dead. The government got two guys to go to the morgue and get my body, then they took me to Alaska and some scientists put steel where my arms and legs were. Then they tried to take all my memories away, so I would fight for good. They succeeded. I lost my memory and had a machine for a brain."

Back in Hawaii, we went in to class. We got done at 8:45 a.m. and had an hour and fifteen minutes before our next class, so we all walked to the library and sat there for thirty minutes. I grabbed Kaitlyn and held her in my lap. We were kicked out, so we went to the coffee shop. Kaitlyn left to get us something to drink.

"Okay," I said, "Kevin needs some volunteers to go on a mission. He needs one guy and one girl. Who wants to volunteer?"

Shon said he'd do it.

"What about a girl? I think Tammy would be the best for this job, but if another girl volunteers, she can go. Or, Shon, you can pick a girl to go with you." He picked Stacie.

Meanwhile in the Bahamas, Brantley was getting some guys to go with him to Chicago to get Joyce and her daughter from Big Joe. What he didn't know was Joyce was going to set Brantley up for Big Joe. She had it rigged. She'd known Brantley would help her instead of killing her.

Brantley met two girls at the bar. Their names were Jenifer and Abby, and they were ordering hurricanes. He asked if he could sit down with them and they said yes. They were a decoy to keep him from leaving. They were to take him to their room, get him drunk, and put some stuff in his drink to knock him out. Some of the guys were supposed to kill him, and the rest were supposed to catch the building on fire.

Brantley saw what they were doing, so he said, "Close your eyes and I will show you something." He swapped their glasses and told them to drink up. Then he got up to go to the airport as the girls drank their hurricanes.

They both passed out. He carried them both to the room and left a note on one of the girls before closing the door. He rigged it up that when the last guy came in, it would explode. Then he went back to the bar and heard gunshots. They were shooting at him.

Back in Hawaii, we were about to go to our next class. Our first day of college was just about over, and it was 2:00 p.m. Some of us were alread done for the day. I drove to Elizabeth's school and saw some girls outside smoking pot. I stopped, then saw my sister come out to join those girls. She was smoking, too, so I waited until somebody caught them before I went in. The principal ended up catching them. I went inside to his office and sat down, waiting on her to come in. The principal, Mrs. Hauli, noticed me and said, "Buddy, what are you doing here?"

"Waiting on my little sister."

"Who is your sister?"

"One of the girls you caught smoking pot. The one wearing a blue shirt and blue jeans shorts."

"Oh, her. I've already had her in my office twice today for disturbing class, then slashing one of the teacher's tires. What are you going to do for punishment?"

"I'll tell you what, Mrs. Hauli. let me do the punishment for you." I turned to the girls. "Okay, girls, this is your punishment: every day after school, you will help the janitor clean the bathrooms. You'll also have detention, where you will study. You'll also clean the school grounds for a month."

"Buddy, I wasn't going to give them all that."

"Well, they need to do something."

Meanwhile at Harvard, Brent had just transferred from UCLA. He was studying to be a therapist. He had four more years to go. He was studying hard in Massachusetts, so he got a good-paying job that helped him pay for his college. He called Chance to see how she was doing. She told him she was doing fine and asked him if, when summer arrived, he wanted to go on another cruise to dance.

"Sure, why not? That way we can make extra money."

Back in Hawaii, Wendy had learned everything at the lawyer's office, then she continued working while she went to college. They had a party and they asked us to sing there. Between us going to college and football practice, we sang at a club called the Hurricane four nights a week. It was new. It had only been open about a week, and they already were booked for the next month. Wendy's first day at her new job was Monday, and her parents had a party for her. Both of her brothers were coming. I saw Kaitlyn and tried to talk to her. James asked Bella out on a date since she and I had decided to date others for a while. Tammy asked Victor out. He was our fullback, and he told her yes. She changed her hair to a red-blonde. It was down to the middle of her back.

We were asked to be part of a couples' calendar, and we all said yes. We had to decide who was going to be on what month, and what we wanted to wear. We also had to decide who was going to be with who, since some of us were dating other people. I'd call them the next day and find out.

Back at Harvard, Brent called Chance and said, "There's a ballroom dance competition in Florida this weekend. We can meet in Miami and sign up for it. The winner gets a beautiful trophy and twenty-five million dollars."

"Okay, just let me know where the ballroom is."

On the beach, Cam and the gang were surfing, except the girls. We were having fun, but I made Elizabeth go home and do her homework. Bella went with her. She was getting ready for her date tonight with Jerry. She and Tammy were double dating.

We were supposed to play that night, but I told the owner, "Only some of us can play. We won't have a lead guitar, unless I play, but then we won't have a keyboards. Wait a minute, I forgot Jenny can play the keys. Okay, we can play tonight. I'll play lead guitar."

Meanwhile in Chicago, Ashley had killed five people for Big Joe. She was his big hitwoman. He'd just put a hit out on the leader of Germany, so he called in his best assassins to steal the disk of their weaponry. That way he could give it to the highest bidder and put the United States on its knees. He would be in control. He wanted to be the strongest, to have every country scared of him. He called Ashley and told her to kill the leader of Germany and steal the disk.

Back in Hawaii, I went home before the performance. Bella was in the shower when I got home, and Elizabeth was in her room. She asked me if she could go out with her friends. I asked her if she'd done all her homework and she told me yes.

"Okay, I'm going to ask Bella."

I went upstairs and she was just getting out of the shower.

"Did Elizabeth do all her homework?"

I dried her off while I was talking to her. We had sex right there in the bathroom, then moved into the bedroom. Then we got back in the shower together and washed each other off. The phone rang and it was Amy Warren. She wanted me to call her. I put on a tuxedo and played some tunes.

"You still going to play at that new club?" Bella asked.

"Yes, though some of you decided to go on dates. Amy is going to be at that new club. I heard they've got dancers who strip."

The waitresses were going to be topless. I told Elizabeth, "You can go with us, but I better not catch you like that."

"A couple of my friends are going to be there. They're going to be topless."

"Then you're not going. Mom and Dad would not approve of it. You can ask Jenny all you want, but you are staying with me and Bella, and you are going to do what I say until you move out."

<h1 style="text-align:center">Chapter 10</h1>

"I was going to move with my friends," Elizabeth said.

I told her she wasn't moving anywhere until she was old enough to move out.

"I don't care who your friends is. When Mom and Dad died, you became our responsibility, mine and Jenny's. You either stay with me or Jenny. Get ready. You are singing tonight."

Then she told me she was staying home.

"No, you're not."

Meanwhile in Chicago, there was a scientist at Big Joe's mansion. His name was Jack Hoaas, and he was married and had three daughters. Their names were Jessica, Jenifer, and Jeanie. His wife was Marie. Jack was the scientist who'd invented the implant that controlled Ashley. Big Joe told him he wanted him and his family to move to Hawaii, that he'd just bought a house with a lab in the basement. "I want you to get close to the Fabulous 8. Your older daughter, Jenny, she's about their age and can go to Hawaii for college. Ask her to get close to Buddy Smithisom, then wait a few days and capture them. I want all eight of them. When you have them, call me now and go home. Tell your family you're moving to Hawaii. Pack your bags. You're leaving tomorrow."

He left and went home.

Marie asked, "Why are you home so early? Did you get fired?"

"No, I've got some good news. Pack your bags. We are moving to Hawaii."

Meanwhile back in Hawaii, I was getting ready to go to the club to play music. Bella and her date went there as well because he wanted to go as part of Fabulous 8. We played until 10:00 p.m. Then Amy and I danced. I asked Jenny if Elizabeth could stay with her. Then Amy and I went to my house. We kissed as we went in. We were on the couch and I tried to make a move. I thought she wanted to have sex, but she told me she was waiting on getting married before having sex. I looked at the time and she asked me to take her home. We got in the Lamborghini and I drove toward her house. Then I saw Bella fighting some guys. Her date was on the ground crying.

He'd used the bathroom in his clothes. I told Amy to stay in the car and lock the doors until I got back, then went to where Bella was and helped her fight the guys until they left. I asked why her date wasn't helping her fight them.

"When they came over, he dropped down and start to cry."

I asked him why he was crying and how he could let Bella fight these battles by herself. Some of the guys came back, but they were laughing at the guy. I started to laugh at him, too. Then I told Bella she might have to take him home and I would pick her up at the guy's house. As I was walking back to the car, someone shot at me. I told Amy to get out, but as she opened the door the car blew up and she was killed instantly. One of the fragments went into the back of her head. I called 911 and told the chief of police everything I knew about what happened.

In the Bahamas, Tori and Cleve were trying to get everything at their club done. They asked Brantley to join them, but he kept turning them down. Then one day he decided to join them. He left and went to the bad side again, only now he was with the mafia in the Bahamas. He told Tori he would join with them. They'd heard that Big Joe had a scientist and his family going to Hawaii to trap the Fabulous 8, so he told Brantley to follow the Hoaas family to Hawaii. He wanted him to snatch Bella, Tammy, and Stacie.

Back in Hawaii, the chief of police arrested me because the only fingerprint they found was mine, so that was all they had to go by. They took me downtown and put me in the interrogation room. I told them the whole story. Amy's mom and dad were the ones who wanted me arrested, but I told them that I would never have killed Amy. They believed until they found fingerprints

"It looks like you were the one who did it."

"I didn't shoot the car. I have witnesses. Ask Bella and Luke."

"Wait a minute. Luke was there? My son?"

"Yes. He was on the ground crying. Amy and I came by. I was taking her home when I saw Bella fighting some guys by herself. Your son was on the ground crying and one of the guys kicked him. I stopped and helped her. I told Amy to keep the doors locked. Some of the guys came back to laugh at your son because he'd wet his clothes. I told them that they'd better run. Then I scared them by grabbing some metal and bending it. They ran, so I told Bella she'd better drive. Luke looked like he couldn't drive. While I was walking back to the car, I heard gunshots. I ducked, then hollered at Amy to get out. She got out, but the car blew up and some of the fragments hit her in the back of the head. That's when I called 911. If I'd killed her, would I have stayed? No."

One of the officers entered the room and told him Amy's dad, Jack, was dead and that Claire, her mother, had gone to the airport.

" Buddy, you are free to go. It looks like Claire is the one who did it."

"Wait a minute. You said she's gone, Chief?"

"They spoted her at the airport. She's leaving the island."

"There's no way you make it before they take off."

"But you can."

"No. That would reveal my powers to people. Let me call my sister. She can bring the plane down."

I called Jenny and told her to come there. Next minute, she arrived up at the police station. I asked, "Can you transport me from here to the plane?"

Meanwhile at the airport, the Hoaas family made it to Hawaii. A limousine picked them up and took them to the house Big Joe had bought. The driver told them he would be back later and to try to get comfortable. Everything that he'd asked for was there. The driver gave Jack the keys to the house and told him he could drive any of the cars. Big Joe had good taste in cars. He had a Lamborghini, a red Ferrari, a black GT, and a yellow Corvette. Jack unlocked the door to the house as Cam and Angie went over and welcomed them to the neighborhood.

Jack and his wife didn't know they were talking to some of Fabulous 8. The only ones who knew were Jeanie, Jenifer, and Jessica, but they were in their room getting everything settled in. The youngest one saw who was at the door and went back upstairs and told the other two.

Meanwhile on the plane, I appeared in the lavatory. One of the stewardesses was in there. She was doing her makeup and I scared her. Then she asked me where I'd come from. I told her I'd just walked in there.

"There was nobody in here when I came in."

" I was hiding. Nobody knew I was in here. Look out there and tell me if there's a woman who looks like she's on drugs. She should be about fifty years old."

She opened the door and looked out, seeing a woman who appeared to be shaken. I looked and there she was. I told her to ask the woman to come into the lavatory.

"Tell her you've got some drugs and you can't let people know about it."

She did, and asked the woman to follow her to the lavatory. When she opened the door, she was not expecting me to be there. I grabbed her and she closed the door. Then I handcuffed her and called Jenny, saying, "Now."

Claire and I appeared at the police department.

"Here she is."

They took her to the interrogation room while I stood at the glass listening to the questions they asked her. Her mother-in-law had been giving her the drugs. Later, when she was on trial, we asked the judge if we could sit in the court to help the DA prosecute Claire. The judge asked the lawyer who represented Claire. It was Big Joe's lawyer. His name was Bobby Freemen, and he was Big Joe's little brother. He'd just graduated from Harvard the previous year, so he had one year of experience. The judge asked him and he said, "Let me talk to my client." Then he talked to Claire about letting me help the DA.

Meanwhile at the Hoaas house, Jack was getting the lab ready so he could make plenty of implants. Brantley was watching their house, hoping he could catch Bella, Tammy, and Stacie. He asked a boy where Bella lived. The boy said, "I'll take you to there for ten dollars."

"Okay."

He gave the boy ten dollars and the boy took him to the house. She was home, so the boy left and Brantley sneaked inside the house through the window upstairs. Bella was in the shower and Brantley went in the bedroom. He waited behind the door when she came in and put a chloroform rag over her face. It knocked her out and Brantley put her in the van he'd rented and went back to his hotel. He carried her upstairs to the roof and tied her up.

There, he handcuffed her to the pipe. Then he gave her a shot to knock her out for a couple of hours. After that, he went downstairs and got in the van, then drove for a while until he saw Tammy and Stacie walking down the street. He stopped the van and used a blowgun with knockout darts, shooting each of them. Then he picked them up and took them to the hotel roof, where he tied both up. Then he called Tori and told him he had all three girls.

"I'm sending the helicopter to pick the girls up. You stay and find out all the information at Hoaas house from Big Joe. We know he has the information we want."

Meanwhile in Los Angeles, a child actress named Kendra Smitty had just found out that her mom—who'd died two days before with cancer—was not her birth mom. For the last two days she'd been searching to find out who her birth mom was. Then she heard about a woman with three sisters. Her name was Lynn. No one knew where she was. The last time she'd been seen, she'd been stranded with her three sisters at a nude beach in Florida.

At the courthouse in Hawaii, the judge asked the jury for their verdict. One stood up and said, "We've found the defendant not guilty on all counts."

"Mrs. Clarie Fette, you are free to go."

I approached the juror. "You say she's not guilty, so I'm telling you this.: you are all guilty, just like her." Then I walked away from them and went to the judge's office. He told me to enter in and I came in. He asked me what I wanted.

"You don't believe she's innocent, do you, Judge?"

"Whatever the jurors decided will stand unless you've found some information that will allow me to overturn the verdict."

"I will find the information I need."

Then I turned and walked out his office. James came to the courthouse. He and Clay told me they couldn't find Bella, Tammy, or Stacie.

"Are you sure you can't find them? Did you look everywhere?"

"Yes, we looked everywhere. Bella was supposed to meet me at Sparrow Café for lunch and she didn't show up. You know she always shows up. You've been with her a long time."

"I do know her, and yes, that is weird. Maybe she texted you?"

"No, she didn't. That was the first thing I checked. The last I heard from her was that she was taking a shower, and that was at 10:45 a.m. We were all supposed to meet at the café, all five of us. The only ones there were me and Clay. We waited for an hour. I think something happened to them, and we looked everywhere. Your sister and Angie said Tammy and Stacie were supposed to meet them for tennis, but they didn't show up."

"Something's wrong. You might be right, we need to find them. There's another club that's about to open. It's owned by a guy from New York."

"Who is the guy?"

"Some well-known guy in New York. His name is Daniel Hogan. He is a new mafia leader. He must have bought out the Stregha restaurant because that's where the new club is. It's not a restaurant anymore."

"Maybe we can go to the restaurant tonight and check to see anybody knows where Bella, Tammy, and Stacie are."

Meanwhile at the beach, Cam was getting ready to surf. He had a tournament in three days. Angie, Shon, and Jenny were there to support him and watch him practice.

I had some of the cops watching the hotel where Big Joe was. I told them to keep an eye on anybody walking in or out of the hotel. I told James and Clay to get the camera from the corner. Then I went to the house to check for things that could lead us to who took Bella, Tammy, and Stacie. We departed and went in different directions. I went to the house, and James and Clay went to the corner from their house.

I got to the house and received a phone call. It was the DA. She said that Big Joe had my sister, Jenny, and Angie, and that if I didn't back off Claire's case, his men would blow them into bits.

"I'm not giving up on this case. You know me better than that. I will not stop until I find out why the jury said she was innocent. All the evidence convicted her. We know she killed her husband, but we need to find out how she got Amy killed. There had to be hitmen. They had to have followed us and waited until I was coming back before they started shooting. She was trying to get out when they fired on my car."

Meanwhile in the Bahamas, the strip poker tournament was happening at The Strip Club. Lynn, Missy, and Tammy were at the tournament. Their other sister, Shannon, was at home sick. They were playing for her, and they all went to different tables.

There were a couple of PIs looking for Lynn. They asked around, then asked Tammy, "Can you tell us who Lynn is?"

"Why?"

They told her she had a daughter who'd been looking for her.

"Did you say she has a daughter?"

"That's correct. I've got her records."

"I know my sister had a baby, but they told her that her baby died, that she had a boy."

"I've got the records of Lynn Grant. Is not that her name?"

"Yes, but like I said, they told us she had a boy and he died."

"According to these records, she had a little girl and she gave the baby up for adoption. She was adopted by a rich couple. Her name is Kendra Smitty. She is a movie star. Her adopted mother recently died and she found out she was adopted, so she asked her friends how she could find out about her birth mother. They told her about us."

Back in Hawaii, I was trying to take care of the two kidnappings. Dina, the DA, told me to give up the case on Claire, but I wouldn't. I would put it on hold until I got the girls safe at home. I called all the guys and told them to meet me in one hour at Papa's Strip Club. Then I called the FBI and talked to their superior officer. Her name was Sheila. I asked her if could she spare a couple of her agents.

"There is a case I want them to take over that you will be interested in." So got two of her best agents on the case.

"Can they be in Hawaii tomorrow morning? I can pick them up."

She told me they'd be there tomorrow afternoon at 3:00 p.m. After we hung up, I left the courthouse and went to Papa's Strip Club. I was the first one there. A girl called to me as I walked toward the door. She was my sister's best friend, Heather Wright. She was a gorgeous girl in her late twenties. She lured me from the door and had me in a corner. We were behind a big SUV.

I asked her why she was doing this, then I saw the guys. They were laughing at me. I said, "Let's go in." We got a table in the corner. I saw

Kim. All the waitresses were topless. James asked Kathy where her kids were.

"They're with their grandparents in California. Zane's got a concert in San Francisco. My dad is taking Zane to the concert while Madison, Chloe, and Emery stay with their grandma."

"When is Roy coming home?"

"In two weeks."

"Are you with somebody, like a friend, or are you by yourself?"

"By myself."

I told her to sit with us. Then I told the guys, "We've got to decide what we're going to do. We've got two kidnappings. We know who did one kidnapping: Big Joe. I'm the one who caused that kidnapping. But the other one… I don't know who'd want to kidnap the girls."

We talked about what we were going to do. I told them we needed to figure out where we were going to stay and who was going to go. Then Heather walk in. I asked her if she'd seen my sister. She said no.

"Is that your sister dancing?"

"Where?"

"Turn around."

I did, and there was Elizabeth half naked. I grabbed my jacket, went up the stage, and put it around her.

She got mad at me and walked off the stage. The owner of the club said, "What's the big ideal? You just lost me a lot of money. Everybody wants to see her."

"She's not working here. I don't care what you say."

Then I walked out the door and caught up with Elizabeth. She told me to let her go.

"No. Jenny has been kidnapped."

"What did you say?"

"She's been kidnapped and we're trying to find her. That's why I don't want you to work here. It only takes one person to know who you are, so you must be careful because I don't want another sister to be kidnapped, hurt, or killed."

Kendra was only six years old when her mom died of a heart attack. They'd been planning to move to Los Angeles. She had a part in a movie as a little girl in New York named Sophia. She'd looked in her mother's files and found out she was adopted, so she'd asked questions about her birth mother. Her aunt, Louise, couldn't tell her about her adoption because she didn't know who her birth mother was. So she asked the person who would know who she was: the doctor who'd birthed her. His name was Dr. Leroy Spraine, and he worked at the hospital in New York.

"Can we take a trip to New York?" she asked.

"Where are we going to get the money?" her aunt asked.

"I've got some, but I was keeping it for a special day." She gathered her money, then they left and went to New York.

Back in Hawaii, I was still talking to Elizabeth when James came out.

"Are we going to do something?" he asked.

"Yes, I'm about to come back in and we'll discuss what to do. Liz, I want you go to Kathy's and stay there until we get back. If you want to you guys can stay at the house. When we get back we will have all the girls with us."

I kissed her on her cheek and hugged her neck, then she got in the Lamborghini and drove off. I went back in the club and asked Kim if she could bring us a pitcher of Bud Light. As we sat and watched Amy, Anne, and Britney strip down to nothing, I told James, "I'm leaving to go to the Bahamas. I want you to watch Liz. Make sure that she doesn't do anything around these clubs. Clay's going with me. We'll leave in one hour. If you want to stay at the house with them, you can. It's up to you."

I went to the house to get everything in order before Clay and I left. Kathy and Elizabeth were there. I went upstairs to the bedroom and got some clothes for Bella. Clay was supposed to get some clothes for Tammy and Stacie. Then I went downstairs. James was there with some stuff we needed. I called Leroy and told him to get the plane ready for me and Clay. Then I was got some weapons we might need and put them in a bag by themselves.

In Los Angeles, Kendra and Aunt Louise were getting ready to go to New York to talk to the doctor. The plane was stopping in Chicago. While they were up in the air, they had a hostage situation. Some guys from Turkey took over the plane. Our government had their people in prison. The president heard about the situation and was on top of it. She contacted the double agents and talked to Kevin. They asked for some assistance on the situation. He told the president, "I'll try to find some." Then he called me and told me that the president needed our help.

"I'm taking you off the case you're on now and putting you on this one. It's got priority over the kidnapping."

"Wait a minute. How can that have priority over our loved ones?"

"Well, I can get someone else to help the FBI out."

"What is Agent Will doing? I can send him in. It's about time for Elizabeth to take her spot in the double agents. She can be Will's partner."

"Has everybody got to your house?"

I told him no, then told Will to call Cam and Shon and have them to come to my house. I hung up and called James. By the time I dialed the phone, James came in the house.

"Buddy, what's the deal? We need to leave now."

Meanwhile, in the Bahamas, nobody could leave the island. Lynn asked how long until the hostage situation would be under control. They told them they would let them know, so they needed to go back to their hotel and stay there. The private investigator told Lynn that her daughter was on the flight with the hostage situation. It was supposed to go to Chicago, but instead it was heading to Atlanta.

Then Missy said to Lynn and Tammy, "Is that Bella, Tammy, and Stacie with those guys? It looks like there are chains around their neck and hands."

"Yes, it is," Lynn said. "They hardly have any clothes on. I wonder if Buddy and the guys are somewhere around here. Let's follow them and see where they are taking them."

They followed them, staying as far back as they could without them knowing.

Meanwhile, in Hawaii, I was waiting on Cam and Shon to get to the house. We heard a car pull up and car doors slamming. Elizabeth looked out of the window. It was Cam and Shon coming to the door.

"Okay, everybody's here. Now, here is the news: Elizabeth, you are now officially a double agent. You will be Will's partner on this job. You'll go to the Bahamas and will bring the girls back."

"I thought that's what you guys were supposed to do," James said.

"No. The president wants us to take care of the hostages situation. All five of us."

"Who's going to Chicago to get the other girls?" Cam asked.

"Edie and Becky. They've already gone to Chicago. Will, you'll fly to Key West, then rent a boat and sail to the Bahamas. We're flying to Atlanta. Our job is to get on the plane and take out the threat. Everybody knows what they're supposed to do, right? Cam, call Leroy and tell him to get our plane ready. Elizabeth, here is your badge and your gun."

"How long have you had this?"

"Three months. Kevin, our temporary boss, said you're ready."

We went outside. I put a bullet in the gun and showed her how to shoot it. Then I put up ten targets and told her to shoot them. She hit nine out of ten, then she threw two knives at an apple she'd thrown in the air. When the apple fell to the ground, there was a hole where the bullet had gone through it, and the knives split the apple in two. I asked her where she'd learned to do that with the knives and to shoot like that.

"Mom and Dad."

"She's good," James said. "We don't have to worry about her. She's in better shape than we are."

Back in Chicago, Big Joe called a meeting with all mafia bosses in New York, Miami, the Bahamas, Las Vegas, California, and Hawaii. The meeting was in Washington, DC.

The FBI and secret agents said to the president, "There's some more bad news. All the mafia bosses are in our state, and we don't have enough agents to take care of the problem. We have to get the state patrolmen and city cops to do more than what they're supposed to do."

In the Bahamas, Tori and Cleve were at their house. They had kidnapped Bella, Tammy, and Stacie, and the three sisters had followed the two guys, trying to get close enough without being caught.

In Hawaii, we were at the airport getting ready to fly. We loaded all the equipment and asked the tower permission for takeoff. "This is flight 179. Permission to take off!"

"Permission granted."

I told Shon, "When we get close to Georgia, call the tower and ask permission to land."

"Okay."

"Our job is to get inside flight 2345 and neutralize the threat on the plane. That is our job. We are to rescue the hostages."

"What about our loved ones! Do they have somebody to rescue them?" James asked.

"We have four double agents heading to the Bahamas and six going to Chicago. They should have that under control."

Back in Washington, DC, all the mafia leaders were talking amongst themselves about the hostage situation. We were getting closer Georgia. I told Shon to go call the tower. The mafia had a plan while we were taking care of the hostage situation. They decided to steal the biggest missile in the United States and *sell* it to Russia for four million dollars. We didn't have enough double agents to take care of them, but we were going to try.

In the Bahamas, Lynn, Missy, and Tammy were two blocks from the mansion of Tori Polanski, who had the girls in chains. They knew they shouldn't get the cops involved with this. The Bahamas police would not take them seriously, so they tried to get in the mansion to rescue the three girls, but they got caught. Instead of three girls, Tori got six girls. He told his men to take them to his room and tie their hands and feet, then watch them until he got there.

Back in Chicago, Becky and Edie had just arrived and tried to find out where Big Joe had gone. He'd gone into a nightclub. They saw strippers and asked around. They were looking for Jenny and Angie. Then they saw Big Joe's men come in.

"We know they're here, so tell us where they are, or you're going to have a problem. We are looking for two girls. We know Big Joe has them."

While they sat at the table, four guys appeared and surrounded it. "We heard you're looking for us."

"If you're a Big Joe's men, yes, we're looking for you."

"Well, here we are. What are you going to do about it?"

"If you give us the right answer, nothing. But if you give us the wrong answer, trouble. Where are the girls?"

"We don't know anything about them."

"Then why did you run?"

Back in the Bahamas, Will and Elizabeth had arrived. First they went to the hotel. They asked the manager if he had seen the people they were looking for. They showed him pictures of the three double agents.

"No, I have not seen them."

They told the manager that if he saw them, he should call and ask for Will Garrison.

"We'll be at the hotel called Mermaids."

Will and Elizabeth hailed a cab and went to the hotel. They gave the cab driver fifty dollars, then took their luggage inside.

The desk clerk asked, "May I help you?"

They said yes, they had reservations.

"Name?"

"It's under Will Foxtrot."

"Oh, there it is. Rooms 27 and 28. Bellboy, carry Mr. Foxtrot's their luggage to Rooms 27 and 28." The bellboy picked up their luggage and took them to their rooms. Will gave the bellboy five dollars. Then they left their rooms and went out of the hotel.

They asked everybody they met if they had seen these three girls. A lot of people shook their heads and said no, but most of them were lying.

Back on the plane, Shon called the tower in Atlanta, Georgia. At first he got no response, but then they heard a racket. Shon tried it again and somebody called back to them, "Flight 179, we've been taken over by the Turkish militia. The airport is closed due to an emergency flight."

Shon called back and said, "Tower, this is flight 179 Requesting permission to land."

The head of the tower said, "No, you have to land at the next airport."

Shon said to me, "The tower said no, that we have to go to another airport."

"Call the tower and ask them for the head of security," I said.

Shon did. The head of the tower told Shon to get off this frequency. Shon gave me the radio. I told the tower, "Let me speak to the head of security, *now*." He finally gave the radio to security. I said, "The president sent us here. You listen to what I have to say. You will give us permission to land. Do you understand? We need to get on board that plane."

"We understand, but I don't think the Turkish men understand."

"Where are they?"

"They've got us as hostages. There are about thirty of them."

"Can you distract them?"

"We can try."

"Let us know so we can land."

Back in Washington, DC, the FBI had some men keeping an eye on the mafia. The leader of the mafia, Mr. Yang, sat down with the other leaders and discussed what they wanted to do. Mr. Yang talked about stealing the missile and selling it to the highest bidder. Derek talked to Mr. Yang, saying he knew somebody in The Pentagon who could steal the plans and knew all the names of the Secret Service, the FBI, the CIA, the double agents, and all the military. They could make the USA vulnerable to other parts of the world.

In the Bahamas, Will and Elizabeth were still trying to find Jenny and Angie, but the bosses were in Washington, DC. He'd left his right-hand man to keep an eye on the two girls. They went to another strip club where all the waitress were topless. He asked the girl named Kim if she had seen Jerry. He was Big Joe's right-hand man, and was the leader when Big Joe was gone on business.

Back in Hawaii, the Hoaas family was still working on their project. Jeanie was at school, but she didn't know we weren't there. She'd been out sick the last three days. She asked the teachers if they had seen us. The teachers told her we had to go out of town on business. She asked the teacher if she could go to the bathroom, that she was not feeling good. The teacher let her go. She went to the bathroom, called her dad, and told him that I, James, Clay, Shon, and Cam were gone, that we'd left the state.

"The teacher told me they would be back next week, but she could not tell me my friends were being kidnapped. What are we going to do?"

"There's nothing we can do that isn't part of our job," he said. "Our job is to make sure that when it's time we have all eight of them in the lab. Big Joe will do the rest. Don't fall in love with Buddy. He will break your heart."

Meanwhile, at the Atlanta airport, Cam landed the plane. Part of the Turkish militia in the tower started shooting. We came out the plane and fired on them as we ran for cover. We were trying to get in the tower, but they had it blocked. We had ten minutes to get it under our control before the plane landed. We ran for cover. There were fireworks. We got inside the building and took control. Flight 2345 called the tower and asked permission to land. The tower gave them permission. The five of us found a way to get on board the flight. We sneaked into the landing gear area.

The security let the Turkish leader go on the plane. Flight 2345 asked permission to take off. The tower granted that permission. The next destination was Washington, DC. They commanded the pilot to fly into The White House, making themselves suicide bombers. One by one we climbed out of the hole.

In Washington, DC, the president heard about flight 2345. She asked who was in charge. The vice president told her it was the Turkish militia. The president asked the secretary if we had anybody aboard the flight. The secretary said, "Yes, we've got five guys. They should be on the plane now."

"Can you get me in touch with flight 2345?"

"We can try."

"Well, let's get on with it."

Mr. Torrey called flight 2345. "Flight 2345, this is Homeland Security. Identify yourself."

One of the Turkish militiamen told the copilot to rip the radio out. He told the pilot to stay on course.

The pilot said, "We cannot land on The White House."

He pointed the at the pilot. "I want you to fly into The White House."

The pilot said, "That's suicide."

"We're doing this for our country."

"Mayday, mayday, this is flight 2345! It's an emergency. The Turkish militia wants us to fly into The White House!"

"Mrs. President, we need to evacuate. Flight 2345 is heading straight for us."

On the plane, we took care of half of the Turkish militia. I said to James, "You and Clay take the stairs to the pilot. We need to turn this plane around. What was that? I heard a gunshot. I think it came from the pilot's room, James, go upstairs and find out what's going on."

Back in the Bahamas, Will and Elizabeth found out where Tori's hideout was. They tried to get closer. Will climbed up higher and used binoculars to see if he could spot Tammy, Stacie, and Bella in the mansion. They were spotted and pretended they were birdwatching.

Tori's men saw what they were looking at. They tried to get them, but Will and Elizabeth escaped and ran through the woods. They hid there for six hours. Then they waited another thirty minutes before they came out of the woods. They walked back to their hotel and went to their rooms.

After that, they took a shower and got dressed, then went out to eat. They went to the most expensive restaurant and met some people there. The people asked if they could sit at their table.

"We don't mind," Will said.

The woman said to Will and Elizabeth, "What is your name?"

"Will and Elizabeth. What are your names?"

The man was tall, with black hair and blue eyes. His name was Terry. The lady was gorgeous, with blonde hair and green eyes. "We are siblings and are on vacation. I play for the San Francisco 49ers. Where are y'all from?"

"Hawaii. We came to the Bahamas to find our friends."

"Oh, the ones who were kidnapped in Hawaii! They're part of Fabulous 8."

"The pop group, yes."

Back on the plane, James told me that he couldn't get the door open, so I went upstairs and picked the lock. We got it open and took over the plane. I moved the pilot out of the chair and Cam took the controls. I told Clay to get on the radio, but he said the radio was damaged. I told James to go downstairs with the prisoners and have someone come upstairs with the phone. There were two jets pursuing us. We needed to send a message to the president and ask her to call off the jets. We also needed to call JFK Airport for an emergency landing. Clay told me he got the radio working. I told him to call the tower in JFK to have all the emergency vehicles ready.

Back in Chicago, Becky and Edie found out some stuff about Big Joe, and discovered that all the mafia leaders were in Washington, DC. That sounded like trouble, having all the mafia leaders in one building. Becky saw Big Joe's right-hand man going into the strip club called Playboy Paradise. She told Edie, "Stay here." Becky walked into the strip club and walked around. She found two thugs, but she couldn't find the four guys.

In Washington, DC, we were flying Flight 2345 to JFK Airport, where we landed the plane safely. The passengers were safe. We'd done our job. We'd taken out the bad guys and saved the passengers.

Back in Chicago, two girls told Becky everything about the situation. They told her about some guys who were part of Big Joe's guys. They'd left the mansion in a hurry and gone to the airport to look for somebody. They'd stayed there for thirty minutes. Then they'd gotten in the car and gone to the strip club. Edie was standing outside until Becky was ready. Becky returned and told Edie what she'd discovered. "Edie, you go in with me to find the four guys. It costs fifty dollars apiece." Becky gave the guy a hundred dollars, so they got in. It was 5:00 p.m. in the afternoon. At 6:00 p.m. it was happy hour. Becky and Edie left and went back to the hotel.

When they got there, they asked the desk clerk if they had any mail. The desk clerk said no. Then they asked if they had any messages. The desk clerk said, "You have one message." It was from me. I'd asked if Shon and Cam had made it there. Then I'd asked for Becky to call me. Becky and Edie went to their room and Becky called me. I was at the airport.

"Who is this?"

"Becky."

"Oh. Did Shon and Cam find you guys?" They'd left ahead of us.

"No, they didn't."

"Okay. They haven't called me yet."

On the plane over the Bahamas, our goal was to find Will and Elizabeth, get their information, and bust out Bella, Tammy, and Stacie. Three days had passed since they'd been kidnapped. We were missing school because of this. We wanted to bring them back. They were part of our lives.

We landed at the airport. Will and Elizabeth were there waiting for us. They gave us all the information that we needed. We told them they could go home, that their work was done, or they could stay. They chose to stay with us. There were five of us. They took us to the hotel and we got rooms. They said we would go tomorrow and figure out how to get in the mansion. Each one of us got a room by ourselves. We took showers and got dressed to go out and met at a restaurant. The food was good and expensive, but we didn't mind. We walked on the beach. In some areas people stripped down and walked on the beach. There were good-looking women on the beach. Some were nude, and some had bikinis on.

I met a girl. She was twenty-one years old. She had long blonde hair, green eyes, and was about six foot one. She had to weigh about a hundred and thirty pounds. She was wearing a hot pink bikini. I was walking down the beach and stopped her and asked her name. She was Italian, but spoke a little English. Her name was Rebecca. I told her my name. We started talking and I walked her back to her hotel to her room. She asked me to come in. It was 1:30 a.m. I told her I could come in for a little while, but I had to get back to my room soon. We got to talking, then started kissing. I put my hand under her shirt and unsnapped her bra. Then I slowly unbuttoned her blouse. She took my shirt off and I pulled her shirt and bra off. I played with her boobs, then slowly kissed her stomach down to her belly button.

Then I unbuttoned her pants and pulled them off. All she had on was her thong. Then she sat up and got between my legs. She unbuttoned my pants and pulled them off. She lay on the couch and I was on top of her. I slowly grabbed her thong and brought it down to her knees, then pulled it off her leg. I got between her legs and felt her hot body. She grabbed my boxers and pulled them off, then put her naked body against mine. We went to her bed and had sex until and 8:00 a.m.

Then we got up and took a shower together. I got dressed and went back to the hotel where I found James and Clay. They were at the restaurant eating breakfast when I caught up with them. They asked me where I had been. I told them, "I met a girl. We walked on the beach, then I took her back to her hotel and she asked me up to her room. I went in."

"You have sex with her?"

"Yes, it was good. How was your night?"

"It was good. We played cards all night until 4:00 a.m. and then went to the bed. We got up at seven and came down for breakfast."

"Have y'all seen Will and Elizabeth?" I asked.

They told me no.

"Weren't they with y'all?"

"Yes, but that was last night. They went to their rooms."

We went to their rooms, but they were not there. We tried to open the doors, but they were locked. We went downstairs to the desk clerk and asked if he could unlock Rooms 27 and 28. He gave us the keys and we went back upstairs and unlocked the doors. Clay and I went inside, but no one was there. We looked everywhere, but we couldn't find them, so we went to the restaurant and ate breakfast. Then we saw Will and Elizabeth in a police car. They were in the back seat with handcuffs on.

We finished our food and paid for it, then rushed out the door. We called a cab and told him, "Take us to the police station." He did. We got out the cab and went inside. Will and Elizabeth were still in handcuffs. We asked the police officer what had happened.

"They were harassing Tori's and Cleve's men, accusing them of kidnapping those missing girls, Bella, Tammy, and Stacie. He called us and we arrested them."

"Well, officer, we are double agents looking for our friends. They were following them and saw three girls who looked like our friends. You need to look for our friends instead of arresting our agents. Our friends are in trouble. Do you have something on them? Is that why you arrested them? If you aren't charging them, let them go. We are all on a mission, and we're wasting precious time. Our friends have been missing for three days already. Will, Elizabeth, let's go. You can take us to Tori's mansion."

We freed them and started to walk out the door.

The sheriff said, "Wait a minute. Y'all can't go anywhere."

" Who says we can't go?" I asked.

"The judge."

He grabbed Will and Elizabeth and put them back in jail. I pulled my gun out and told him to let them out. He unlocked the door and they came out. We told the sheriff to get in the cell. He told us we weren't getting away with this.

"Yes, we are."

All four of us went to the door. I went first and the coast was clear. We ran around the building and hear sirens. Cops were everywhere. We went to the hotel and there were cops there, too. I told Will and Elizabeth to catch the plane back to Hawaii.

I told Clay that he had to go with them, that James and I would rescue the girls. When they got to the airport, there were cops everywhere. They shot at them, and our agents shot back. A bullet hit Clay in the leg. He told them to run to the airplane. As Will was getting on board a bullet hit him in the leg as well. Elizabeth helped him inside and the plane took off. The cops looked for Clay, but they couldn't find him. They searched high and low. The sheriff called and spoke to the leader and was told that Clay has been shot, that they'd hit one of them. The Sheriff told one of his men, "Do not shoot the girl. Find Clay and kill him. Let them go." The cops left.

At the hotel, James and I called a guy about some weapons.

The guy called back and said, "I'll meet you at Serino in ten minutes. Do you have the money?"

"Yes, we've got it."

"I'll see you then."

Meanwhile, on the plane, Elizabeth asked, "Is there a doctor on board?"

"Yes, I'm a doctor."

"This man has been shot in the leg. Can you treat him?"

"Yes, I can."

While they were in the air, he treated Will.

Where are we going?" Elizabeth asked.

"Hawaii," Will said. "When we get there, we'll called headquarters and tell them where we are." They landed in Hawaii and went to Kilos's house. He asked them what they were doing here.

"Do you have the keys to Buddy's and Bella's house?" they asked.

"Sure."

"Can you take us there?"

"Yes, I can. Silos."

"Yes, Pops?"

"I'll be back in ten minutes. Just keep an eye out for customers."

"Okay, Father."

Will and Elizabeth got in the car and Kilos took them to the house. When they got there, Elizabeth took the key and unlocked the door. They helped Will in. Kilos asked Will where he wanted to go. Elizabeth called headquarters. Kevin answered the phone.

"Can I speak to our boss?" she asked.

"This is he."

"Will told me to call you and tell you that we are in Hawaii, and if you need us, call us at Buddy's and Bella's house."

"Okay. Are y'all all right?"

"I'm doing fine, but Will got shot in the leg. The doctor told him to stay off it."

Back in New York City, Aunt Louise and Kendra were at the doctor's office. The nurses took them to Dr. Willoughby Jones.

"Dr. Jones, you might know my sister," Louise said. "She and her husband George came about six years ago and adopted a baby. You gave her a baby girl. Do you remember that woman who signed the adoption papers? They paid four million dollars."

"Oh, yeah, cute couple. They came to me about adopting a baby. There was a young lady who'd had a baby that day. She had a baby girl, but her mother had other plans for her. She asked me if anybody wanted to adopt a child. I told her I had a couple who would pay four million dollars for a baby. She said to take the baby and give it to that couple. When the mother asked where her baby was, she was told she'd had a baby boy and he'd died. The girl's got to be six years old now. What was her name?"

"Kendra. Can you give me her adoption papers?"

"Sorry, can't do that."

"Why not?"

"You are not the mother."

"I'm her aunt, and I'm also a lawyer. I know a lot of judges."

"Maria?"

"Yes, Doctor?"

"Give me the paperwork and adoption papers on Kendra Smitty."

"Here they are, Doctor."

"That should be everything. The mother's name is on the paperwork."

"Where?"

"On the left-hand corner."

"It says Lynn. Do you have the last name?"

"No, the mother never gave it to us."

"Any idea where she is?"

"I heard she was in Bahamas with her sisters. They were in a strip poker tournament. She won a jackpot worth four million dollars."

Meanwhile, in Washington, DC, Big Joe called his lawyer, Chad. "I want you to do me a favor: I want you set up a fall for Fabulous 8. Is Claire with you?"

"Yes, she's with me."

"I want her to kill my wife. Strangle her with a wire. I'm going to send Bailey to you. He's going to kill Claire. Then I want you to send two men to the hotel where Shon and Cam are. I want you to pretend to take them where the girls are. Do not take them to the girls. I want you to knock them out with chloroform and take them to our old warehouse. Then take my wife's body to the warehouse. Bailey will slit Claire's throat. Then you'll put the guns in Shon's and Cam's hands and help them pull the triggers. Do one shot in the head and the other in the heart. Take the blood and put it on the knife. Then I want Bailey to come to Washington, DC. Then I want you, Chad, to call 911 and report a murder. I want you to tell the cops you saw it all. You got it?"

"Yes, Big Joe, I've got it. When do you want this to happen?"

"Tomorrow night at midnight. I want you, Bailey, and Claire to go to that warehouse and get everything ready."

Back in the Bahamas, James and I were talking to a guy about different weapons. He said he could get us an AK-47, an M-50, and some hand grenades. He could also get us grenade launchers. We told him we needed a couple of night vision goggles and that we'd give him five million dollars. He asked me where I wanted to meet. I told him the Razor Back Restaurant in two hours and not to be late.

Chapter 11

We arrived at Razor Back Restaurant and asked the driver, "How is the food here?"

"It's good, but I can take you to a better restaurant."

"That's all right. We're supposed to meet some people here."

James and I got out, went in the restaurant, and went to the bar. Then we asked the bartender if he knew Mr. Sparaquse.

"Yes, I know him. His table is upstairs. Last table in the corner."

We left the bar and went upstairs. Two guys were sitting at a table. We walked over and asked, "Do you have the merchandise?"

They took us back downstairs and into a room. After closing the door, one asked, "You have the cash?"

We put two briefcases full of money on the table. "Do you have the weapons?"

They took us out the back door and opened a van door.

James and I looked at the weapons and checked them out, then made the trade and called a cab. We went back to the hotel and went to our room. James put all the weapons in his room. He was the weapons expert. I went to my room and took a shower.

Back in Los Angeles, Aunt Louise and Kendra had just gotten to Los Angeles and Louise's husband Henry was waiting for them at the airport. Louise gave Henry a hug and a kiss. He picked up Kendra and hugged her, too. "Welcome home," he said.

"It's good to be home. We found out who her mother is. She's in the Bahamas. No one can find her. She and two of her sisters went for a walk and never returned to their hotel. They've been missing for three days. We found her grandfather. He lives in Washington, DC. He stays in a home for the elderly, so we went to see him before we came home. Let me call Kendra's agent."

Louise called her agent, who said Kendra needed to be at the studio by 9:00 a.m. to do a movie.

Kendra and her aunt and uncle made it home. Louise said, "Another thing we found out: she's got a brother. Her mother had another child. She and her brother have the same father."

"Who is the father?"

"Do you remember about three years ago when you heard about the leader of the mafia in Las Vegas?"

"No, I don't."

"You don't remember him getting killed? A lot of people think his right-hand man had him killed. He wanted the business for himself. That's who her father is."

Back in Chicago, in Big Joe's warehouse, Chad, Bailey, and Claire were taking care of things. Chad sent two men to kidnap Shon and Cam. The two men went to their room and told them they knew where the girls were. Shon and Cam agreed to go with them and they put blindfolds over their eyes. They arrived at a warehouse and their abductors helped them out of the car. While walking toward the warehouse, one guy drugged them and they passed out. The men carried them inside the warehouse and chained them up. It was 11:00 p.m. and Claire was at Big Joe's house. She was in the bushes waiting for midnight. Later she looked at her watch. It was 11:59 p.m. Thirty-five seconds before midnight. She put her ski mask on, then knocked on the door. Big Joe's wife, Sheila, came to the door. She opened it, then tried to close it again, but Claire put her foot in the doorway. Sheila ran to the kitchen as Claire took a rope out of her pocket. Sheila grabbed a knife and tried to protect herself. She stabbed Claire's arm and Claire slapped her. Sheila fell and hit her head on the table.

Claire got down on the floor. Then she put the rope around Sheila's neck and strangled her. After that, she called Chad and told him it was done. Chad told Bailey to pick up Claire and Sheila at Big Joe's house. Bailey went there and picked up Sheila's body. He asked Claire to get in the van, then went to the warehouse. Once there, Claire got out and walked in the warehouse. Bailey already put Sheila's body inside. As he was coming back from the van, he pulled out his knife and slit Claire's throat. Chad grabbed Shon, then put a gun in his hand and helped him pull the trigger. Bailey did the same with Cam.

Bailey left, went to a bar, and called Big Joe. "The job is done."

"Enjoy your time off. Can I speak to Chad?"

"He's still at the warehouse."

Big Joe hung up and called Chad. "Is it done? Is my plan working?"

"Yes, it's working. I just called 911 and reported a murder in the old warehouse. They are sending cops now."

"Okay, you stay there and let me know when everything is done. Make sure you don't touch any of the evidence."

Meanwhile, in the Bahamas, James and I went to our rooms. I took a shower. The desk clerk and some lady came to my room. I was still in the shower when the desk clerk unlocked the door. When I came out all I had on was a towel. The lady was sitting on the couch.

"May I help you?" I asked. "Who are you?"

"My name is Maria Duncan. You know, the leader of the mafia in Greece, the Duncan family? We've come to the Bahamas for our anniversary. We were wondering if Fabulous 8 can sing at our fifth anniversary party."

"There are only two of us at the moment. The four girls were kidnapped, two in the Bahamas and two in Chicago. Let me talk to James."

I put on some clothes on, then called James and asked him to come to my room.

James arrived and asked, "Who is this fine woman?"

"James, this is Mrs. Duncan. You know the mafia leader from Greece?"

"Oh, yeah."

"She wants us to sing at their fifth anniversary."

"But it's just me and you."

"I know, that's what I tried to tell her. I told her the girls have been kidnapped. We've also got one guy missing in the Bahamas. He's been shot. We don't know where he is and have got people looking for him now."

"Let me talk to my husband and see if we can get your friends back," Marie said. "Can you sing tonight? The party will start at 9:00 p.m."

"Yes, we'll be there."

"Come at 8:45 p.m. You know Heintz restaurant? It's two blocks from here. Wear a tuxedo and we'll talk there. Do well enough and we'll talk about getting the girls back. You say you're missing three in the Bahamas and two in Chicago?"

"Yes. The girls are being held in a mansion. So, Marie, how old are you?"

"Why do you want to know how old I am?"

"You look familiar. What school did you go to in tenth grade?"

"Drysdale High."

"Yeah, you don't remember us. That's the school we went to."

"Oh, yeah, now I remember."

"You and I used to date. Then you dated Clay, but you stayed there only one year. What happened? I thought you liked it there."

"My dad got a job offer in New Orleans, so my last two years of high school were there. I went to Greece in my last year of school. That's where I met Kenneth Duncan and fell in love with him. We got married five years ago. He is the head of a corporation in New York and is worth millions. We came to the Bahamas for our anniversary."

She got up and kissed James and me on the cheek, then walked out the door.

James and I looked at each other. "I reckon we're going to have some fun tonight," I said.

"Yep! We're going to have more fun than we've ever had."

It's 7:30 p.m. Only an hour and forty-five minutes before we had to be there.

I went to the closet and grabbed my tuxedo and put it on. James went to his room and put his tuxedo on. I told him I would meet him in the hall. Then we went to the party. A limousine picked us up.

Back in Chicago, Shon and Cam opened their eyes and saw cops everywhere. They asked why they were tied up.

Detective Carson said, "You should be ashamed of yourselves."

"What are you talking about?" Shon asked.

The two police officers lifted them up, untied them, and handcuffed them, then brought them to the two bodies.

"That woman looks familiar," Shon said.

"She should. Her name is Claire."

"Not the same Claire who was on trial for the murder of her daughter and husband?"

"Yes, the same one. Y'all got lucky and cut her throat with this knife. Your fingerprints are all over the knife. Do you know who this other lady is?"

"No."

"You both should know her. She's Big Joe's wife. You strangled her with this rope. All the evidence leads to both of you. We'll read you your rights."

Chad approached and told the detective he'd seen it all. The detective told the rookie to get Chad's description of what had happened in the warehouse.

"All right, boys, take them downtown and book them." Shon and Cam were arrested and charged with double murder. The DA sat down with them and asked what had happened.

"We don't know," Shon said. "All we know is two guys appeared and said they wanted to take us to the girls. He said we had to be blindfolded. When we got to our destination, we felt needles hit our arms and we passed out. When we came to, the cops were here. That's when they arrested us."

"Do you know any lawyers that can help you?"

"Yes, we have a lawyer."

"No, you cannot use her. She can only help if Fabulous 8 as a group is in trouble."

"Are you sure about that?"

"Do you know any other lawyer?"

"We'll need to get in touch with Buddy. Here is his number. Try to get in touch with him."

"Okay, don't say anything."

In the Bahamas, James and I were at the party. We played and sang for Maria and her husband's fifth anniversary, and they paid for our drinks. We played until midnight, but the whole time we were there they never said anything about helping us rescue the girls.

I looked at my phone. I had a missed call from Chicago, so I called the number back. It was our lawyer. I called her back.

"Beth?"

"Buddy, Cam and Shon are in trouble. We are at the police station. They have been arrested for murder."

"What you mean, they've been arrested for murder? All they were supposed to do was find Jenny and Angie. How can they get in this mess?" She explained what had happened.

"That sounds like Big Joe's doing. Beth, take care of it right now. We're still trying to take care of things over here. We're at a party right now."

"Wait a minute. You're are at a party? Aren't you supposed to be looking for Bella, Tammy, and Stacie?"

"Do you remember Kenneth Duncan, the mafia leader from Greece, and his wife, Maria?"

"Yes, I remember them."

I explained that they were supposed to help us find the girls.

Kenneth had both of his hitmen with him for protection. He was the only mafia leader who wasn't in Washington, DC. Mr. Yang was angry because he wasn't there.

Kendra's aunt Louise heard her brother was in jail, but she didn't tell Kendra. They told her they couldn't find him. They still didn't know where her mom was. Kendra and Aunt Louise got tickets to Wyoming to see her aunt, Shannon. They flew.

Back in the Bahamas, James and I were getting ready to ask Kenneth if he was going to help us get the girls from the notorious Tori mansion. Kenneth looked at us and laughed. "I don't know who told you we would help you."

"Wait a minute. You mean my cousin and I came here and played for your anniversary, and you're not going to help us?"

"No. Torri and I are best friends. I will not do that to him."

"We are out of here."

We left and went back to the hotel. I went to my room and James went to his room and checked all the weapons. Everything was accounted for. I met James in the hall.

"Cobra operation," I said.

I told him to get two binoculars and two pairs of night vision goggles. James went back into the room and got the equipment, then we took the car and went toward the mansion. We stopped about twenty yards from it and investigated different ways to get in.

There was a guard at every entrance. I walked around one side and James walked the other side. We met in the back and walked twenty-five yards straight into the woods.

Cleve walked by the window and told Tori, "I saw two guys pass by the window."

Tori told his guys, "Go out there and search for two guys. They are deadly. Shoot to kill every man. Hear or see anything, call on the radio for backup."

James and I ran through the woods. We heard footsteps behind us and saw five guys coming our way, so we hid behind the trees. Two went one way and three went the other way. We followed the ones who went back in the woods. I sneaked up behind one of them and cut his throat. James hid by a tree with 9mm and a silencer. He shot two of the men. Two others came back toward us. One came by the tree I was hiding behind. I snapped his neck. The other guy ran. James threw his knife and hit him in the back, then snapped his neck.

Tori called on the radio. "Eric, Bobby, answer me. Where are you?"

We grabbed one of the radios and went back toward the house. More guards were standing there, so we went toward the side door. One of the guards came out of the house when we reached the door.

James grabbed him and broke his neck, then we both went in house. I went upstairs and he went downstairs. We searched everywhere. The girls were in the basement. Cleve and Tori got away. There was a lock on the basement door. I broke it, then opened the door. All six of the girls came out of the room. They all were in handcuffs, so I picked all the handcuffs and we got out of the house, then ran toward the car. James was in front. He got in the driver's seat and I got in the passenger seat. Two of the girls were in the front seat with us, and other four were in the back. He stepped on the gas and we took off and got back to the hotel. Tori and Cleve's men were looking for us, so we went to another hotel. We got four rooms, James and Tammy in one room, Stacie and the other Tammy in a different room, Lynn and Missy in another room, and Bella and me in the other room.

Meanwhile, in Chicago, Beth had just landed at the airport. She called a cab and asked the driver to take her to the police department. When they got there, she walked inside and asked for Shon and Cam's cell.

"Who are you?" the sergeant asked.

"I am Fabulous 8's lawyer. I've come to represent Shon and Cam. Take me to their cell."

The officer led her to them and said, "You've got a visitor."

"We don't want any visitors," Shon said.

"So you don't want my help?" Beth asked.

"They told us you couldn't take our case because it doesn't deal with Fabulous 8 business," Cam said.

"Who told you that?"

"The new DA. He's getting us a different lawyer."

"Who is the lawyer?"

"His brother. He just finished college."

Back in the Bahamas, Bella and I were in our room. We took a shower together and got ready to go out for supper. We asked the other girls about going out to eat with us, but they told us they were going to take showers and go to bed. I asked Stacie if she was going with us to eat and she said yes. Soon everybody wanted to go. Then I got a phone call.

It was Beth. She told me the new DA said she couldn't represent Shon and Cam because she was Fabulous 8's lawyer as a band, and that the only person she could represent was me because I was the leader of the band.

"How did I become the leader over all eight of us?" I asked. "All of us are leaders, so you can represent any one of us. Give that DA my number and tell him to call me. I will send him our contract with the clause in it."

Meanwhile, in Washington, DC, Mr. Yang talked to his three hitmen and told them to go to Hawaii, kidnap Big Joe's scientist and his family, then take them to his underground laboratory in his Los Angeles mansion.

Hitmen Dewayne, Larry, and Andy sneaked out of the room and went to the airport. Derek noticed Mr. Yang was by himself. Four of them had gone out, but he was the only one who had come back in. He got Michael to follow the hitmen.

"Let me know where they are going."

Daniel saw Derek send one of his guys out to follow Mr. Yang's guys.

Back in the Bahamas, Clay was found and was rushed to the hospital. His leg was wrapped and was still bleeding. He had passed out. If it weren't for a young guy who had found him, he would've been dead.

"Does anyone know who he is?" the doctor asked.

"No. This young man found him."

"We need to figure who he is so we can find his family."

One of the nurses said, "I think I know who he is. Do any of you have a poster of Fabulous 8?"

"I do," one said. She retrieved out a big poster from her locker.

"There he is. His name is Clay Smithisom. He's part of Fabulous 8. We need to find Buddy and James Smithisom."

The young man who'd found Clay told the doctor, "Fix him and I will pay his bill. Do not tell Buddy and James where he is."

Then he pulled out a 9mm out and pointed it at the nurse.

"I want you fix him up and let me know how much his bill is." He grabbed the poster of the Fabulous 8 and tore it up in front of the nurse and scared her away.

"Sir, we don't know your name."

"My name is John Rooster. I'm the mafia leader of New Orleans. I've been watching every mafia group, and they all have the same enemy: Fabulous 8. If I can get them to work for me, I can take control. All I've got to do is send them out and I know I can take over all the mafia groups."

At the restaurant, Bella and I had just arrived. James, Tammy, and Stacie were already there. We still didn't know where Clay was.

Shon and Cam were in jail in Chicago for a double murder, and they had the best lawyer, Beth Spree.

"I thought she only dealt with if we were singing."

"No, y'all didn't read the clause. It says if we get in trouble, just like Shon and Cam are, she can be our lawyer."

"It also said it has to be the leader of the group, and that's you."

"No, it's all of us. You guys need to read the contract."

Meanwhile, in Chicago, it was the first day of the trial. The DA called their first witness. It was a young lady in her twenties. She came to the stand and the DA asked her, "Have you seen these two guys before?"

"Yes, last night at that woman's house."

"Are you talking about Claire?"

"No, I'm talking about Big Joe wife, Sheila."

"I've never heard of her," Shon said.

"Claire saw them together," the young woman continued, "then I saw the other guy grab Claire and take her to their room. I didn't hear anything else until it was on television that the two guys were arrested for the murder of Claire and Sheila, and that they were part of a group called Fabulous 8. I knew they were no good."

"Why are you saying that?" Shon asked.

"Boys, what is she talking about?" Beth asked.

"Our friends are missing. That's why we're here."

"Are you sure that's why you're here? Did Buddy send you to kill Claire because she got off free? Is that why?"

"No. We were sent here to find Jenny and Angie. They were kidnapped by Big Joe because Buddy wanted to put Claire in prison. Big Joe had some of his guys kidnap Jenny and Angie. He wants to keep Buddy from putting Claire in prison for killing her daughter and husband."

"It looks to me like you wanted same thing Buddy wanted, except you killed her and were caught by Big Joe's lawyer."

"Wait a minute. Your Honor, can I talk to my clients?"

"Sure. We'll recess for five minutes."

"Okay, guys, tell me everything, including what Buddy's got to do with this."

"Claire's daughter was dating Buddy. One night he was trying to help Bella and her boyfriend get out of trouble. She was fighting some guys by herself. We think they were some of Big Joe's guys. We think he and Claire were seeing each other, so she asked him if she could use some of his guys to set her family up."

Meanwhile, in the Bahamas, Bella and I went to the beach and talked.

"Are you going out with anybody right now?" she asked.

I told her no.

"You know I will always love you, even if we're not together."

"What do you mean?"

"If we decide not to date each other, I will always love you, and we need to say that to each other every time we see each other."

We were holding hands. We stopped and I kissed her.

"Why did you kiss me?" she asked.

"I thought that's what you wanted. I thought you wanted to date me."

"No, I just wanted you to know that when we decide to date again, it's for real and for good. No more dating anybody else."

"Who are you dating?"

"Nobody right now. I just want to finish college and work for a while before I get serious with anyone, whether dating or getting married."

"I understand, but that's not what I want in the future. I want to be able to date or marry somebody before I get out of college. We're all in the band, and we're also double agents. I came close to getting married to Claire's daughter, Amy, but she got killed by Big Joe's men. Claire was trying to set us up, but it didn't work. Now they have Shon and Cam for a double murder in Chicago."

"Who did they kill?"

"Supposedly Claire and Big Joe's wife. Her name was Sheila. I know Shon and Cam. They would not kill anyone unless they were being shot at or a person they were protecting was threatened. They were set up, and I think we should leave here and go to Chicago. Help their case. How about it, Bella? That way we all can go back to college. I talked to the dean and he said we can come back next year since we'll miss the rest of this year."

I kissed her again, then she asked me why I did that.

"Anytime I see you and we are by ourselves, I'm going to do that. When you were kidnapped, I sometimes thought I might not see you again, so every opportunity I get, I'm going to kiss you."

"If you get a girlfriend, are you still going to kiss me?"

"Yes. I will still kiss you even if you have a boyfriend."

She kissed me, then said she liked that, and we turned around and walked back to the hotel.

Stacie met us and said, "Have you heard from Clay or why he didn't show up?"

"Oh, I didn't want to say until we heard from him, but we still haven't. This is what happened: Elizabeth, Will, and Clay were supposed to be on a plane to go back to Hawaii, but they were ambushed by Tori and Cleve's men. Clay got shot in the leg, so he told them to run while he distracted them. Will and Elizabeth made a run for it to the plane. As Will was going up the steps, he got shot in the leg, but they made it on the plane. They are at our house, but we think Tori and Cleve's men got Clay because we haven't heard from him. If he were still hiding, he would've called by now. Until we find out more information, our job is to help Shon and Cam."

We went up to our room and Stacie stayed there because Lynn, Tammy, and Missy had left to go to the airport. They'd changed their flight to so they could leave now. We told Stacie she could stay with us, then I called James and told them to come to our room.

"Okay, we'll be there in fifteen minutes."

Suddenly there was a knock at the door. It was the Bahamas police, the chief and his two deputies. "What's wrong?" I asked.

"You are all under arrest."

"For what?"

"For breaking into Mr. King's mansion. We have witnesses. They say you stole six of Tori's girls. Do you see any girls here?"

"Yes, those two women right there."

"They're our girlfriends. He kidnapped them."

"All he knows is you're dangerous and you're trying to ruin his business. He told me to bring the lovely girls back to his mansion. They're his girls now. When he tells them they can leave, then they can leave. Until then, they belong to him."

Bella hollered, "Forget about us! You two needs to escape so you can help Shon and Cam!"

"No, we're getting you out of here! That way we all can save Shon and Cam!"

"No!" Then she sucker punched me in the gut, drop-kicked me, and shut the door.

We couldn't follow them. James helped me up and said, "Why are they doing this?"

"I don't know."

James saw something through the window. There were three men on the roof. They were aiming at the cops, so I used a mirror to blind them. James did the same, but we didn't get the third guy and he shot me in the arm and James in the leg. I saw where the bullet came from and had only one hand to use my weapon. I set it on something to steady it, then looked through the scope, found the guy, and shot him. The other two ran back to their car.

Meanwhile, Lynn, Tammy, and Missy were heading back home to New York. They were at an airport and had a two-hour delay, so they sat in a restaurant and had some red wine with their lunch. There were three guys watching them. The guys saw Tammy had a ring on her finger. She had been married the longest, but she'd had six affairs already.

The three guys went to their table. The ladies had an hour and thirty minutes before their flight left, so they went to the bathrooms. Two of the guys went to the ladies' restroom with Lynn. Tammy and Missy went to the men's restroom with the other guy. Lynn and one of the guys went in a stall and had sex. The third man was having sex with Tammy. Another man came in and watched. Then Missy took all her clothes off and had sex with him. They had sex for a couple of hours and missed their flight.

The next flight was at 11:00 a.m., so the three guys asked if they wanted to stay with them at their apartment. They told them yes.

Back in the Bahamas, James and I were trying to tend to our wounds. I fixed James's leg, then helped him to the car and drove him to the hospital. When we got there, James was going into shock. I told somebody to get me a doctor. They grabbed a wheelchair and brought it out to James, then rolled him to the operating room, leaving my contact information with the nurse.

Then I left the hospital and went back to the hotel.

I was thinking about what I was going to do, if I was going to stay here and wait on James to get out of the hospital, or leave tomorrow and go to Chicago. Maybe I'd go to Hawaii and stay there for a couple of days, then go to Chicago. I took a shower, got dressed, and went to a restaurant. I had steak and shrimp for supper, then went to a club. I went inside and sat a table where all the waitresses were topless. There was one waitress there that I'd met in Hawaii. Her name was Heather. She was one of my sister Elizabeth's friends. I asked her how long she'd been here.

"About two years now. I left that club in Hawaii about a year ago. How is Elizabeth doing?"

"She's doing good. She was trying to do what you're doing."

"Oh, stripping."

"Yes, but I stopped that. She's too young to do that. I see you are a waitress."

"Yes, but I still strip now and then."

"I see you've still got good-looking boobs. They look bigger than when you were in Hawaii."

"Thank you."

"You're close to my age, aren't you?"

"Yes, you're one year older than me."

"What time you get off?"

"Actually, I get off in ten minutes."

"Do you want to do something?"

"Where are Bella, Tammy, Stacie, Angie, and Jenny? Usually if you're around, they are, too."

"Bella, Tammy, and Stacie were kidnapped. James and I got shot trying to rescue them. I got shot in the arm and James got shot in the leg. Then I rushed him to the hospital because he went into shock. Angie and Jenny were kidnapped by Big Joe's men. Shon and Cam went to Chicago to find and bring them back, but now they're in jail for a double murder. Clay, well, I think he got kidnapped by Tori's men. He was supposed to be home with Will and Elizabeth, but he got shot in the leg and told them to run to the plane. One guy shot Will in the leg. So that leaves me trying to figure out what I'm going to do."

"Oh, okay. That means I've got you to myself."

"Yep. Are we leaving here?"

Heather and I left the club and walked on the beach. She grabbed my hand and held it. We turned toward each other. She kissed me and said we should go to her place.

"Okay. I'm not with anybody right now. I've had two girlfriends I really loved, and they all ended up dead."

"How do you feel about Bella?"

"I will always love her, but we're not dating."

"Who was your first?"

"Lauren. She was a maniac. She didn't want me talk to any girls at all."

"What happened to her?"

"She tried to blow us up, but I took care of that. Then she was jealous of Bella. I could talk to her cousin, Brittney. There were a few girls I couldn't talk to. Then she tried to kill Angie, but our high school kicker stepped in front of her and she stabbed him. After she kidnapped Bella, we went after them. She just shot me in the leg and was about to pull the trigger again when Tammy took her gun and shot her in the head. The second girl I was in love with was Amy. She was Claire's daughter."

"Are you talking about the same Claire who was killed the other day by Shon and Cam?"

"Yes, but Shon and Cam didn't kill her. Amy and I were going to her house when I saw Bella fighting a lot of guys by herself. Her boyfriend was on the ground crying, so I told Amy to stay in the car. I went and helped Bella out. As I was walking back toward the car, some guys started shooting at me. Amy opened the door and was about to get out when an RPG came roaring by my head and hit my car. She died. The guys were Big Joe's men. Her mother, Claire, ordered the RPG to hit my car."

Back at the hospital, James had just gotten out of surgery when a guy came in and grabbed him. The doctor called me while Heather and I were going to her place.

"Your friend James has been kidnapped," he said.

"My cousin has been kidnapped?"

"Yes. We just got out of surgery and put him in a room for recovery when this guy came out of nowhere and took him."

"Have you called the cops?"

"No."

"I'll take care of it. What did the guy look like?"

"Black hair, medium build, green eyes, He was wearing an orange shirt with brown pants, a black belt, and Air Jordan sneakers. He drove a dark blue Silverado with the license plate SVD 332, Nevada tags."

"Okay, thank you." I hung up and asked Heather, "Do you want to go with me? I just got a phone call from the hospital. Somebody kidnapped James."

She said yes, she'd go with me, so we went downtown looking for a blue Silverado with Nevada tags. We drove up and down the town, then stopped at a restaurant to eat. Then we saw the truck parked at a hotel, so we moved closer. I checked the plates. SVD 332, Nevada.

We went to the office and asked the desk clerk, "Do you know whose truck that is?"

"Which one?"

"The dark blue Silverado."

"Oh, I don't know. He paid me cash. Put James as the name."

"What room is he in?"

"Thirty-two."

"Thank you."

We left the office and went to room 32. I told Heather to dress like she was going out with some of the guys.

"Ask him if he knows where Turkey Trots Academy is."

Heather pulled her shirt down so it hung off her shoulder. She wasn't wearing a bra, so her boobs could be seen, and her skirt was short. I asked if she had any panties on.

"No, see?"

She lifted her skirt up to show me. Then she went to room 32 and knocked on the door. Some guy opened it. He had blond hair.

While we were at the hotel, the guy and my cousins were on their way to Nevada.

At the hotel, there was a guy and a girl in bed. The girl looked like she was doped up, and the boy was having sex with her. Heather walked in the room and I saw him look around, then close the door.

I went running to the room and banged on the door. Then I kicked it open, pulled my 9mm on them, and showed my badge. I grabbed Heather and told her to wait in the car for me. Then I grabbed the guy and clotheslined him. After that, I pulled the boy off the girl and threw him down. I grabbed him and tied his hands together, then hung him up by his hands. I pulled the girl up, threw her clothes to her, and gave her some money. Then I found the keys to the truck and gave them to her.

"Can you drive?" I asked. She told me yes. "Just take this truck and leave. Get away from here."

The other guy got up and tried to run out. I hit him with a right hook and knocked him out, then dragged him back in and tied his hands together. Then I lifted him up by the other guy and stripped their clothes off, threw them on the bed, and left the door wide open for people to see them.

I left the room and got in the car, then we went to the new club. The guy at the door told us we couldn't go in. I showed him the badge and my gun.

"You can go in, but she can't," he said.

I asked him why she couldn't come in.

"Because she works at the other club. She might tell the other owner our secrets."

"Why would she want to do that?"

"We've got things the other club doesn't have."

"Well, I'll tell Fabulous 8 not to come here. How's that?"

"You know the Fabulous 8?"

"Yes, I do. They are personal friends of mine. If you let her in, I'll ask them to sing at your club."

"Let me talk to the owner."

The guy left the door and locked it. After a minute, the door opened again. The guy returned with the owner. It was Bobby.

"Well, well. How are you, Buddy?" he asked.

"How you doing, Bobby?"

"I'm doing fine. The door guy… I forgot his name."

"It's Sammie, sir," the door guy said.

"You don't know who you're talking to, do you?" Bobby asked.

"No. He's got a badge."

"He's part of Fabulous 8. If he comes here and has somebody with him, you let them in. Oh, hi, Heather. How are you doing? Are you ready to work for me?"

She told him no.

"The club you work at is owned by the mafia. They own most of the clubs, then there's mine and Steve's. Well, come on in."

Heather and I went in and sat at Bobby's table.

"So, where is the rest of Fabulous 8?" Bobby asked.

"They're spread out everywhere."

"When can you get them here?"

"I don't know. I'll have to call you when I talk to them."

"How about you sing a song for us? I know Heather can sing. How about it?"

"Okay."

Bobby got up on the stage. "Ladies and gentlemen, we've got a special treat tonight. One of the Fabulous 8 is here, along with a friend. Buddy Smithisom and his lovely friend, Miss Heather Tarus, are going to sing one of Fabulous 8's song."

"Thank you. Glad to be here. This is a song I usually do with Stacie, but she's not here, so I'm going to sing it with Heather."

We started to sing. There was an agent named Jerry sitting in the crowd. "Wow, they sing real good together," he said to himself. "I'd like to get them together. I can take them places. Fabulous 8 will be no more."

Bobby overheard and had that laugh, the bad person laugh. Then Heather approached them. "Here's the plan," Bobby said. "I'm going get Buddy drunk. You talk to him. Heather, ask him how much money he has in the bank, then tell him you've got to go to the bathroom. Tell us how much he's got. Then we'll come over and say we can make you both stars. All we need is a certain amount of money. I'll send him some drinks. My plan is to ruin Fabulous 8. My daughter loves Fabulous 8, but she has her own group, Gorgeous 5. With Fabulous 8 out of the way, they'll have a chance. After I get him drunk, Jerry, you come over and say you think he and Heather can be a hit in the business of music. It'll cost him some money, though. When he agrees, Heather, you sign his name on the contract, then get on his phone and transfer the money into this account. We'll help you put Buddy in the car. Take him back to your house and do what you can to get pregnant."

Heather walked back to my table and asked, "How much money do you have in the bank?"

I got on my phone to check and she watched everything I did.

"Sixty million dollars," I said.

She said she had to go to the bathroom and got up. On her way back, she told Jerry and Bobby what they wanted to hear, then returned to the table and gave me a Bud Light. She had a screwdriver. Then Bobby had his waitress bring me shot after shot. I had a twelve-pack. Heather grabbed my phone. They brought me one more shot and a screwdriver. Then she motioned Jerry and Bobby over.

" I'm Jerry," the agent said. "I could be your next agent. I think you and Heather, could be the next big thing in pop music."

"You think so?"

"I know so. All I need from you is some money to go in an account for you guys."

"How much?"

"Sixty million dollars."

"I've got that. Where do I sign?"

Heather grabbed my hand and signed my name to the contract, then got on my phone, logged into my back account, and punched in the transfer. It didn't work. Then she grabbed my finger and pushed transfer again. It sent.

"It's done."

"I'll get my bouncer to put Buddy in your car. Heather, we'll meet tomorrow at 8:00 a.m. at the hotel. Then we'll finish our business."

Heather got in the car and drove to her apartment. Once there, she took all my clothes off and put me on the bed. Then she stripped and got on top of me. We had sex all night, until 7:00 a.m. in the morning. She made sure she got pregnant with my child. I woke up around 12:00 p.m.

I couldn't find my clothes. I walked out of the apartment with no clothes on, then checked my account on my phone. I was broke. I went back in the apartment and called the bank. They told me I'd transferred all my money to another account.

"Are you sure?"

"Yes. It was your finger that sent the money from your account to another one."

I called Elizabeth. "Can you get fifty thousand dollars out of my safe? It's behind the picture of Bella and me from school. Deposit it and transfer it to my account."

I fell asleep. About six hours later, I woke up with Elizabeth in my face. I asked her how long she'd been there.

"For a while. I even dressed you. What happened?"

"How much money did you get for me?"

"Thirty thousand dollars."

"You remember a guy named Bobby, don't you, Liz?"

"Yes, I know him well."

"I really don't know what happened. I have a feeling he's behind this. They ripped me off somehow. I had sixty million dollars in the bank and now I'm broke. I remember Heather wanted to know how much money I had, and I told her. I think there was an agent there as well. Some years ago Bobby managed his daughter's group, Gorgeous 5. We beat them out of a music contract and Clay heard Bobby wanted revenge. I'd forgotten about it, but I think this is part of his revenge, though I can't prove it. We need to get out of here. I need to get to Chicago to help Shon and Cam. Can you call a cab?"

The cab dropped us off at the airport and we took off to Chicago. After we landed, we rented a black Ferrari. I called Beth and asked her which courthouse they were at. She told me it was in the middle of town.

We got to the courthouse and found Beth. "I don't think there's any hope of keeping Shon and Cam out of jail," she said.

I asked her why she said that. We paid her good money to keep us out of trouble.

"I know, but every time we think we've got a breakthrough, some more evidence turns up, or more people come forward and say they saw them at the crime scene."

"More people said they saw them at the warehouse? How many more said that?"

"About four."

"Let me talk to them."

They were the DA's witnesses for this case, so Beth asked the DA if she could examine them.

"No, wait a minute," he said.

"That tells me you're lying. I bet you paid four people to lie. You either let Beth talk to your witnesses or we go to the judge about it."

"Well, Buddy, you're in hot water yourself. I heard you got Fabulous 8 in trouble."

"What do you mean?"

"You signed a contract for you and Heather as a duo. You gave up sixty million dollars."

"What contract? I didn't sign anything. It was forged."

"That's not what the news reported."

"I'm not the one on trial. I'm trying to get my friends out of jail."

Shon and Cam heard what I'd supposedly done, so I told them, "I was framed. I don't remember any of this." I remembered having sex with Heather and that I hadn't used a condom. I knew she'd wanted to get pregnant. Then I got a phone call from Will.

"Hey, Will. How is everything at the house?"

"What house?"

"Mine and Bella's house."

"I'm in jail. All of you lost your houses in Hawaii."

"What?"

"Some people from the Bahamas took over the houses."

"Why are you in jail?"

"Cops kicked in the door. Someone reported drugs in the house and they found some cocaine."

"Somebody is out to hurt us." I turned to Elizabeth. "Liz, I want you to stay here and help Beth. Take care of this. Help keep Shon and Cam out of jail."

"Where are you going?"

"Back to Hawaii to get Will out of jail and get our houses back. I'm going to take care of this problem, but keep me informed about what's going on here."

I went to talk to Shon and Cam.

"Guys, Beth and Liz are going to help you. I've got to get Will out of jail in Hawaii. I know you guys didn't kill Big Joe's wife and Claire, so be patient. Beth is going to take care of this. Liz, I want you to go back to the warehouse and see if anybody else has been there. Then talk to the DA's four witnesses. I'll call you when I get to Hawaii. Once you get them out, come back to Hawaii so we can figure out where the rest of our gang is."

I left the courthouse and went back to the airport.

Meanwhile, in Los Angeles, Tammy and Lynn got off the plane. Lynn met her fiancé at the Los Angeles airport and told him they were supposed to meet a little girl. Tammy's husband picked them up and took them to studio 26. They approached a shack where a security guard was sitting. Lynn asked the guard for Kendra.

"Who wants to see her?"

"Her mother, Lynn."

He called and said, "There's a woman saying she's Kendra mother. Her name is Lynn."

They called Kendra's aunt, Louise. "There's a woman here saying she's Kendra's mother. Her name is Lynn."

"Tell the guard to let her in."

The guard said, "What about the two guys and woman with her?"

"Let them all come in. The woman must be her sister."

The guard took them to studio 26.

"Where is Kendra?" Lynn asked.

"Over there, the little girl on the swing set in the purple dress."

Louise approached them. "Hello, my name is Louise. I'm Kendra's aunt. You must be Lynn."

"Yes, I am."

"Wait here. Kendra, can you come here?"

"Yes, Aunt Louise. Who are these people?"

"This is your mother, Lynn."

"Hi, Kendra," Lynn said. "It's nice to meet you. I wish somebody had told me you were alive. This is my fiancé and my sister, Tammy. This her husband."

"Nice to meet you, Kendra."

"It's up to you to decide if you want to stay with us or your Aunt Louise. I travel to different places for my job."

"May I ask what you do?"

"I play poker. Sometimes I can win half of million dollars, but you have to pay five thousand dollars to play."

Meanwhile, in Hawaii, I got off the plane and caught a cab to my house.

"Buddy? When did you get in?" the driver asked.

"Just now. Take me to my house."

"I heard somebody is fixing to buy your house if you don't pay the taxes on it."

"How much are the taxes?"

"Fifteen thousand dollars."

"Take me to the courthouse, then. I can pay it. How about the other houses?"

"Same situation."

I went to the bank and George was waiting for me. Some guy moved in front of me. "What do you think you are doing?" he said. "I was here first."

"Yeah, right. Everybody knows I was here first."

"No, Buddy, he was there first." George said.

"Do you know who I am?" I asked.

"Yes. You are Buddy Smithisom. You used to have a house here, but the Fabulous 8 is over."

"I don't think so. George, take the money out of my special account and pay all the taxes for our five houses."

"Okay, it's done, Buddy."

"Thank you."

I asked the cab driver, Jock, if he could take me to the house.

"Sure."

He drove me there.

"Thanks. I'll see you later," I said.

"You go, dude!"

"Rock on."

Then I opened the door. There was tape everywhere. I took it all down and threw it in the trash. Then I changed clothes. Luckily they hadn't thrown our clothes out. I put everything back like it should be, then heard a car door slam. It was the cops with some guy.

I opened the door and asked, "May I help y'all?"

"Wait a minute. We've got papers saying you forfeited all yours houses for not paying taxes."

I showed them the paper that showed the house and anything that belonged to Fabulous 8 had been paid for.

Chapter 12

The guy, whose name was Mr. Sarge, tore up my papers and said, "What papers? Arrest him!"

The cop told him no. "We are not arresting him."

"I said arrest him, or you're going to lose your job."

"Well, I reckon I'll lose my job, then."

Mr. Sarge called the chief of police and told him that none of his guys would arrest me.

"My officers do not work for you. I've got paperwork that shows you cannot touch any of the Fabulous 8's houses. If you don't leave his land, he can have you arrested for trespassing."

"I'll be back."

"Mr. Sarge, I think you should leave Hawaii. Sergeant, escort Mr. Sarge off the premises and take him to the airport."

"Yes, sir."

"You haven't heard the last of me," Mr. Sarge said. "You'll pay for this."

"Yeah, yeah. I hear that all the time. By the way, who do you work for? Big Joe?"

"Your two friends are going to pay for what they did."

"You listen to me. Anything happens to any of my family and you will pay the price. Do you understand?"

"Yes, but I'm not worried about you."

I got in the Hummer and went to the police department and asked to talk to the Chief Jack Worthy. Sergeant Frank Smilly said, "You can go right in, Buddy."

"Thanks, Frank. So, Jack, how is your family?"

"They're doing good. You come to get Will? I would like to bring him here, but we've got a new judge, and he won't let him out. He said he will pay the consequence for his actions. He said they found drugs in the house."

"Who found the drugs?"

"That guy, Mr. Sarge."

"Okay, that explains everything. He planned it all. He was sent to ruin Fabulous 8 and our reputation."

Back at the warehouse in Alaska, where most of the Fabulous 8 had been taken, Bella, Tammy, and Stacie were trying to find a way to get out, but they hadn't succeeded. In another room across from the girls was Clay. In another room a scientist had invented a device that would wipe people's memories. They had already taken the memory of the previous president. He was in a corner going backward and forward. His mind was gone. The scientist's next victims were Jenny and Angie.

Bobby's brother Jimmy was living in Hawaii, and he was the coach for the Hawaii Warriors. He was also one of the best surfing champions. He'd won the last two years. Before that, Russell was the champion. Cam had come in third two times and second four times. Jimmy liked Russell and Duck's sister, Wendy. She was a model and a beauty queen who performed in pageants. She was in college in Hawaii. She came by the house while I was there. I tried to tell her that Ashley was in Chicago on personal business, but she said, "I come to see you."

"Oh. Okay."

"Where is everybody? Where is my sister-in-law?"

"I just told you."

"Oh, I didn't hear you. I was looking at you, Buddy."

"Oh, okay. I'm glad you're not married."

"Why?"

"So we can fool around."

"Why do you say that? Do you want to go out with me?"

"Yes."

"We'll go out this Friday."

"Our homecoming is this Friday."

Then I remembered.

"Oh, my goodness! We were supposed to sing this Friday at the homecoming dance. Most of my group is either in jail, in Chicago, or missing."

"Well, that means you can take me to the dance Friday night."

"I will. Who did they get to sing?"

"A group called Gorgeous 5."

"What?"

"They're called Gorgeous 5."

"No, it can't be. Can you come over later?"

"Yes, I can. We can go out."

"I'll try not keep you out late. What time is your class?"

"11:00 a.m."

"Well, you can spend the night here when you come back later. Bring some clothes for tomorrow and I'll take you to school."

We kissed and she left. I got in the Hummer and went to the courthouse to talk to the judge. Then I heard a voice that I'd thought I'd never hear again. It was Angel Wesson. I used to date her about four years ago. She was working for the judge. I turned around and there she was, blonde hair and green eyes. She was about six foot three inches tall. With high heels, she was six foot six inches, and was gorgeous.

I asked her how she'd been. She told me that when she found out we were in Hawaii, she'd moved here to go to college. I asked her if the judge was in the office. She told me that he'd just left for the day. Then I asked her if she knew his number. She told me she knew where he lived and would take me to him.

"Let's go then," I said.

I walked to the Hummer and she got in her car, then I followed her to her house. She stayed in an uptown penthouse. I sat in the Hummer until she left the car, then she got in the Hummer with me.

"Go two blocks from here then, turn left at the stoplight by the steak house," she said. "There are the apartments. He stays in apartment 23B."

We went up the driveway and parked in front of the apartment. She got out with me and knocked on his door. A little girl opened it.

"Who is it?" the judge called.

"A man and a woman," she said.

He came to the door.

"Whose little girl is she?" Angel asked.

"Mine. It's just me and her. My wife, her mother, died about a year ago with cancer."

"Why didn't you tell me?" Angel asked.

"Oh, where are my manners? Come on in. May I help you, sir?"

"This is Buddy Smithisom," Angels said. "He's come to talk to you about his friend Will."

"Oh, the one in jail for drugs."

"Yes, sir," I said. "Those drugs were planted by Mr. Sarge. He wants to hurt the Fabulous 8. I need my friend. My sister is missing, and we don't know who's got her. I'm thinking it could be Big Joe, but I don't have any evidence. Before I left the Bahamas there was a guy we knew who was the manager of his daughter's band, back when the Fabulous 8 first come out. We had a competition called Battle of the Bands.

Whoever won got a recording contract. We won, but the other band manager told one of my guys he'd get revenge. He stole all my money, and our contract will be over in five days. That's why I need my friend out of jail, sir."

"I'll tell you what. Come to the courthouse tomorrow and I will look at the paperwork. If it checks out, I'll release him."

"What time do you want me be there?"

"Come around 11:00 a.m."

"Thank you, sir. Angel, do you want me to take you home?"

"No. If the judge doesn't mind, I'll stay here for a little while."

"No, I don't mind at all."

"Buddy, I'll see you tomorrow."

"Okay."

I got in the Hummer and left.

Meanwhile, in Los Angeles, Lynn and her fiancé were watching other stars while Kendra was finishing up. Dusty was sitting there waiting for a chance to kidnap Kendra for Big Joe. What Lynn didn't know was that her fiancé was going to help Dusty kidnap Kendra, and Tammy didn't know that her husband was working for Big Joe. Lynn's fiancé and Tammy's husband were working together. They were planning to take over Mr. Yang's business. Big Joe was about to become more powerful. He would get all the businesses.

Lynn's fiancé told her to go ahead, that he would bring Kendra with him. He waited a few minutes, then Dusty hit him in the head and grabbed Kendra. They went out the back door. Kendra hollered, but nobody was around.

Lynn came back in and found her fiancé on the floor out cold. She asked if anyone had seen Kendra. They told her no. Then she called Aunt Louise and asked, "Do you know where Kendra is?"

"No. Why?"

"We can't find her. We've looked everywhere and she's not here. Someone knocked my fiancé out." He finally got up. "What happened to you, and where is my daughter?" Lynn asked.

"I don't know. We were leaving when somebody hit me in the head."

"We need to call the cops, dear."

"No, we don't need the cops."

"Why not? That doesn't make any sense. Why don't you want me to call the cops? This is my daughter we're talking about."

He called Jocko, Tammy's husband. "We need to clear this up. If we don't, they'll find out who we work for and that we're brothers."

Back in Hawaii, I was on my way back to the house and had just driven up when Wendy pulled up. She asked if I could pick her up at her house.

"Yes, I'm going now," I said.

I followed to her house. She went in and put her keys on the bar as her parents were not there. Then she left them a note and grabbed some clothes. After locking the door, she climbed in the Hummer and we went to my house.

Inside, she asked, "Where do you want me sleep?"

I told her to put her clothes in the empty room. I was in the kitchen finding us something to eat. She cooked for us and I went in the living room and turned on the TV.

"The food is ready," she called.

"Okay."

Then I heard on the news that Kendra had been kidnapped. Wendy brought me my food and sat on the couch with me.

"When are we going to get ready to go out?" she asked.

"We'll leave in about four hours."

We finished eating. As we watched television, she moved closer to me. I put my arm around her and whispered sweet nothings in her ear. Then she turned toward me and we kissed. I put my hands under her shirt and unsnapped her bra. I played with her boobs, then pulled her shirt off. Her bra followed. She took off my shirt and kissed my chest.

Then something caught my eye on the news. A warehouse in Chicago had burned down, the same one where they'd found the bodies of Claire and Big Joe's wife.

I told Wendy I thought someone was trying to get rid of the evidence.

Then we kissed again. I got on top of her body and was getting hot. She put her hand down my pants. She got on top of me, unbuttoned my pants, and zipped them down. She pulled me out of my boxers played with me. We kissed some more. Then I slid her down under me and got back on top of her. We kissed some more and I put my hand down her pants. Then I unzipped them and pulled them off. Her thong was still on. That was the only thing left as my hot body rubbed against her. I went down, licking and kissing her body. Then we were buck naked on the couch having sex.

She got on top of me. We slowly worked ourselves to the bedroom. It was 3:00 a.m. when we finally went to sleep, and we got up at 9:00 a.m. We took a shower together. I went downstairs to the kitchen to fix us breakfast before I got ready. She was getting her clothes on when I called her to eat. I still wore my bathrobe with nothing on under it. Wendy came down wearing a short dress, solid black. She bent over in front of me. She wasn't wearing panties.

"Wear that black thong I bought for you yesterday," I said.

It was silk. She was wearing her boots. I told her to sit down and eat.

"I'll go get your thong for you."

I went upstairs and got it, then returned downstairs. Wendy was sitting at the table. I sat down and drank my coffee, then ate my grits and eggs with toast. She was just about finished. I gave her the thong and she put it on as I finished eating. Then we went back upstairs and she went to the bathroom. I went to my bedroom to put my clothes on. I put a T-shirt on that had Hawaii Warriors on it. She brushed her teeth and put some perfume on, then brushed her hair while I put my socks and shoes on. After that I brushed my teeth and put my cologne on. It was 10:00 a.m.

We went downstairs and I grabbed the keys to the Lamborghini. I locked the door to the house and we got in the Lamborghini. When I dropped Wendy off at college, we kissed and she got out. A lot of people looked at her.

"Wait a minute," said her best friend. "I wondered where you were. Now I know."

"I spent the night with Buddy."

"Where is everybody else. How was it?"

"Great. Nothing big."

"Anytime you get with any of those five guys, it's a big deal. That means the five girls aren't with them and you've got a chance with them. Did y'all have sex?"

"Yes. It was wonderful."

I made it to the courthouse and went to the judge's office. No one answered when I knocked. The door opened and my friend Angel was in there having sex with the judge.

"Could you knock?" she said, putting her clothes on quickly.

"I did, but no one answered, so I came in. I thought something had happened to y'all." After the judge put his clothes on again, I said, "Well, Judge Dolson, have you gotten my friend out yet?"

"No, son, I'm still working on it. Give me thirty minutes and he should be out."

"Okay. Where do you want me to wait?"

"Go to the police station. You'll have to sign some papers to get him out."

"I'll let you guys get back to what you were doing."

"Okay. Goodbye, Buddy," Angel said.

"Goodbye, Angel."

I got back in the elevator and went down to the first floor.

I was getting in the car when somebody shot at me. They just missed my head and hit a pole. I got in the car and took off chasing them, but they got away. They were in a blue F-150 with tanned windows. I went to the police department. When I got there some of the officers were leaving.

"What's going on?" I asked.

"There's some guys riding around in a blue F-150 with tanned windows."

"I know. He just shot at me a minute ago."

"Now we can go after him. The chief didn't want us to pursue him if he wasn't doing anything wrong."

"Well, just be careful. He's dangerous. Where is the Sergeant Hines?"

"In the station."

"Okay, thank you."

I turned and was walking toward the station when the truck returned and shot up the police station.

Four of the cops were hit. One was already dead. I grabbed my gun and shot at him. Most of the cops were wounded. I went inside the police station and some of them were hurt, too. I asked for Sergeant Hines.

"He's over there. He's dead. His prisoner, too, the girl."

"What girl?"

"I think it's your friend, the one he was bringing up to get released."

It was somebody's little girl. I went down to the jail cell and Will was still there and alive. I opened the door and hugged him. Then we went up and I found his paperwork, signed it, gave it to one of the officers, and said, "I'm taking my friend with me."

"Go ahead. He was supposed be released anyway."

"Thank you. Will, let's go."

As we were getting in, that truck came by again and shot Will. We shut the doors and I asked him where he'd been shot. He told me his arm, so I told him to sit up and put a cloth on his wound. Then I spun my tires and went to the emergency room. When we got there, I got a wheelchair and put him in it, then told a nurse he'd been shot. They grabbed him from me and took him to the operating room.

The doctor told me he would take care of him.

"Thank you. I will be back in thirty minutes. I've got to pick up somebody at the college."

I drove to the college and Wendy was waiting on me. She opened the door and saw blood everywhere. "What happened here?"

"Someone shot Will and I took him to the hospital. We're heading back now."

She got in and shut the door. When I saw the truck again, I took off fast after it. I told her to get down. As I rammed them, they backed up and came at my side. One of the guys in the back rolled down the back window and pull out an AK-47, shooting some rounds into my Hummer. I turned around and got behind them. I told Wendy to take the wheel while I shot at the truck.

Meanwhile, in Alaska, Bella, Tammy, and Stacie were still trying to find a way to get out. The only clothes they had on were their bras and thongs. They picked the door to their room at last. Tammy put a choke hold on one of the guards, then two more appeared. Bella picked up a knife and threw it at one of them. Stacie did a roundhouse kick and felled him. Then Bella ran toward the other guy and wrapped his head in her legs, breaking his neck. Then they went to another room and she knocked on the door.

"Anybody there?" Stacie called.

"That sounds like Jenny and Angie," Tammy said. "Hey, Jenny, is that you?"

"Yes. Is that you, Tammy?"

"Yes. We'll have y'all out in a minute."

Stacie grabbed a hairpin and picked the lock. The door opened and they all hugged one another. Then they went two ways. Jenny and Angie went upstairs, and Bella, Tammy, and Stacie went downstairs. As Jenny and Angie were going upstairs, two guys were coming down. They went into a room until they passed by. They waited until they were halfway down, then came out of the room and went up the stairs. They looked through the peephole of a door and saw Clay, so Angie pulled out a hairpin and picked the lock.

They hugged him. "Let's get out of here."

"Wait, somebody's coming."

A guard had seen the door open and came to investigate. As he went in, Clay broke his neck. He took the guy's gun and they went downstairs. They looked down the hall and then through another peephole. Clay heard James and Angie speaking.

"Hey," Jenny said, "that sound like James. Hey, where are you?"

"I'm in the room behind you."

"Oh, okay."

Angie picked the lock.

Clay opened the door and they all hugged one another. "Let's get out of here."

They went downstairs and Jenny said, "We need to find Bella, Tammy, and Stacie."

"What do you mean?"

"They're down here somewhere. They found us. What they're wearing might make your mouth water, Clay."

"Why do you say that?"

"They're in their bras and thongs, and that's all, unless they've found some clothes."

They walked a little further until they found Bella, Tammy, and Stacie. They had killed eight guys with their bare hands. They turned around and saw James and Clay. They hugged them. James and Clay were glad to see everybody there.

"One person is missing."

"Yeah, it's Buddy."

"You don't think he set this up so he can go big, do you?"

"No, he wouldn't do that to us," Jenny said. "He's probably trying get Shon and Cam out of jail."

"What do you mean, he's getting Shon and Cam out of jail? What did they do?"

"Big Joe's lawyer found them in a warehouse and with two bodies. They were covered in blood. Then I heard on the news that Buddy and a girl named Heather sign a recording contract together. When he was asked about Fabulous 8, he said our band is finish. Bella, you know that sixty million dollars you guys had in your account? It's gone. I know you were saving it for your wedding. Then I heard he got Heather pregnant and she left with the money."

Meanwhile, at the Los Angeles airport, Dusty held Kendra and took her on a plane. "You'll like Big Joe. He's a good guy. He'll buy you anything."

"What about my mom and my aunts?"

"You have a new family now, with brothers and sister. You'll have anything you want and a big room."

At Harvard, Brent was doing really well in his studies. He was a straight A student. He was going to medical school for two years. He was smart and didn't have parties like everybody else did, but that was going to change. He made a new friend who partied all the time. His name was Michael. Brent started to go everywhere Michael went, but then his grades started dropping.

Michael's plan was to get Brent's grades down. His best friend from school wanted him to fail so he could be smarter than him. Brent was averaging a D in all of his classes now, which was unusual. He had always been an honor student. But Michael hooked him up with a gorgeous girl.

Her name was Rachel and she was a model for Victoria's Secret. One night, Brent had a party for passing his exam. He'd made a 91 on it. That was when he met Rachel and got into trouble. What he didn't do was drugs. Michael got some beer keg and all kinds of liquor, then invited a guy who sold all kinds of drugs. Michael put some drugs in Brent's drink and told him to drink all of it. After the third one, Brent started feeling weird and started to take his clothes off. He still had his pants on. That was the farthest he got before Chance came to the party.

"What's wrong with you?" she asked.

He said he didn't know.

Then Rachel went over to Brent and whispered some words in his ear. She grabbed his hand and they went to his room. He shut the door and locked it. She undressed him and they had sex. She was hottest girl. Chance was looking for him, then heard him talking in his room with Rachel.

Back on the plane going to Chicago, Dusty called Big Joe and told him they were on their way. Big Joe told Dusty to take Kendra to his mansion. "Okay, sir. We'll land in twenty minutes."

"My limousine is waiting to pick you up."

"We will be there. Kendra is sleep."

The pilot announced, "We will land in Chicago in two minutes. Everybody get back to your seat and fasten your seat belt."

Back in Hawaii, we arrived back at the hospital and asked the nurse for Will. She told us to go to room 32 on the third floor. We got in the elevator and got off on the third floor, then went to the room 32. Will was awake.

"What happened to you and Stacie?" I asked.

"She broke up with me to date Clay."

"What about Tammy?"

"She was dating a guy named Henry White. He was twenty-five years old. He was called up to the White House for an interview, but she didn't know about it. Then she was kidnapped. James is still dating Bella as far as I know."

"They are okay, then. Russell's bringing his family and Duck's kids. Liz is trying to help Beth get Shon and Cam out of the jail. I will call and find out when they're coming home. I'm trying to get Fabulous 8 back on track."

"You better hope they didn't see what you said on television about Fabulous 8," Wendy said.

"Why?"

"Did you watch the news?"

"No."

"It came on as a special bulletin during the news. It made you look bad, so you need to go back on the air. I can get you on WKRAD Channel 5. A friend owes me a favor."

"Okay, call her while I find out when Will can come home."

Back in Alaska, the other seven were together in a room, but they still couldn't get out because more guys showed up.

"I don't believe Buddy said that. He wanted us to make this group for all ages. We are well-known in every country. If we break up, we'll all go our separate ways, and I don't think we're ready for that. What are we going to do?"

"I say let's try to message Buddy to tell him where we are," Bella said.

"That sounds like a good idea. I don't want to believe it, but what if it's true? Bella, what are you going to do or say to him?" James asked.

"I don't know. I'm not dating Buddy, I'm dating you. Well, if you still want to."

"I do, but I don't know what will happen when Buddy rescues us. You guys always end up dating each other."

"He might be dating someone else now."

"Well, try to get a message to him."

"How?"

"Anybody got a rod or hairpin?"

Angie said that she did, so she gave it to James and he put it in his cell phone. "That way any phone number I dial will go to their cell phone as a text message. Hope this works."

Meanwhile, in Hawaii, I got a text message. "Wait a minute. That sounds like James's music, the one I set up for his texts." I looked at my phone and found a message from James. They were all in Alaska in a warehouse.

"Come and rescue us. Also, are you dating anyone? That's what Bella wants to know."

"Ask her why she wants to know."

"Bella, he wants to know why you're asking."

"Tell him I was hoping we could get back together after he comes to get us."

"She said she was hoping you guys could get back together when you get us out."

"Tell her it won't last longer than a week, that she'll find somebody else. I'm surprised you guys aren't mad at me for what I supposedly said on the news bulletin. I'm trying to get everything back to how it used to be. But first, I'm coming to get you guys. I will be there in four hours."

"Okay, good luck. See you when you get here."

"Well, James, is he coming?"

"Yes, he said he'll be here in four hours."

"Yes!"

"He also said he did say those things about the band being over, but he's trying to get everything back on track after he comes to get us."

"I can't believe my own brother would do that to his family," Jenny said.

"You right. That can't be Buddy. We're too important to him. Somebody must have done this to hurt us. I wonder who wants us out of the picture?"

Meanwhile, in Hawaii, I told Wendy to buy me a ticket to Alaska while I talked to the doctor about Will going home.

"He can leave tomorrow at 1:00 p.m. All you need to do is come and get him."

"Can Wendy get him for me? I have to leave for Alaska tonight."

"That's fine. Just tell her go to the desk and sign in. She'll tell the nurse who she's there to pick up. Make sure she says she's Will's sister because our policy is that only family members can pick up patients."

"Okay, I'll tell her."

I went back to Will's room.

"Good news. Will, you can go home tomorrow. Wendy will pick you up. All you've got to do is go to the front desk and sign in. Tell the nurse you are Will's sister. That's the only way you can pick him up."

"Okay."

"How about it, Will?"

"What the doctor say?"

"That's what he told me to tell Wendy."

"Well, okay, since you're going to get your sister."

"Yes, I'm bringing them all back."

"Okay."

"Wendy, what time do I need to be at the airport?"

"7:00 p.m."

"It's 3:30 p.m. now, so I'd like to get my stuff ready."

"How about if I come back and stay with you, Will?" Wendy asked.

"Okay."

"I'll see you after I take Buddy to the airport."

"Okay."

We left and returned to the house. As I drove up to the driveway I heard bikers coming.

We went into the garage and I turned off the car. We went inside the house. The first thing we did was take our shoes and socks off. Then I grabbed Wendy and pulled her close to me and kissed her. I unzipped her dress and it fell to the floor. She took off my shirt and we went up the stairs to the bedroom. I picked her up and put her on the bed. We kissed as I undid her bra and took it off, then she unzipped my pants and pulled them off. Our hot bodies were on top of each other and we made passionate love.

We got ready and left about 6:25 p.m. She dropped me off and I told her she could go back to the hospital. We kissed and she left as I got on the plane. Hours later we were about to land when there was a problem.

The captain come on the speaker system and said, "We're about to land without landing gear, so everybody put your head between your knees."

We did what the captain told us.

We hit the runway and the wings were torn all to pieces, but no one was hurt. A fire truck and ambulance arrived.

We got out of our seats and went to the door, sliding out of the plane, which was on fire. I went to the car rental and got a Suburban, then found a hotel and booked a room for a couple of days.

"You'll be in room 33."

He gave me the key and I went to my room. After putting my things down, I called the desk clerk and asked him if he knew of any restaurants close by.

"There are a couple nearby. You have to wear nice clothes."

"Okay, thank you."

I took a shower and got ready to go out to eat.

When I got downstairs, I asked the clerk which restaurant was better. He told me the Trout.

Meanwhile, in Chicago, Dusty and Kendra got in the limousine and went to Big Joe's mansion. They arrived and Big Joe's kids came and met Kendra.

"Welcome to our home," they said. "You will enjoy here."

"Thank you, but I'm not staying here long," Kendra answered.

"That's what Shiela said about two years ago, and she's still here."

"All right, take her to her room."

"I'll show you where your room is."

She followed Jackson and he showed her to her room.

Back in Los Angeles, Lynn was crying because no one knew where her daughter was. They'd called the cops and told them what had happened.

"Did you see the person who took her?" the officer asked.

"They hit me in the head from behind," Lynn's fiancé said. "I was out cold for an hour."

"We will look into this."

Aunt Louise arrived. "What have you done? I was willing to let you take her home with you so she can get to know you, and you let somebody take her! Have you heard from the kidnapper?"

"No, we haven't."

"Do you think you will?"

"I don't know."

Chief of Police Sandy Verum approached them. "What's going on?" she asked.

"We have a Code 17."

"Who's been kidnapped?"

"My niece, Kendra," Aunt Louise said.

"No, not Kendra!"

"Yes."

"And who are you?" She turned to Lynn.

"I am her mother."

"I thought her mom died."

"She was adopted. This is her birth mother, Lynn. They were taking her home so she can get to know them."

"Has the kidnapper left a note or called you?" the chief asked. "When they do, we'll come and take care of it."

Aunt Louise looked at Lynn. "It's your fault. I never should've let you take her with you."

Lynn's fiancé went outside and called Big Joe's mansion. "Is Dusty there with Kendra?"

"Yes, he is."

"Let me talk to him."

Meanwhile, in Alaska, I was on my way to the Trout. I found it and he parked, then some guy stopped me on my way inside.

"Mister, you got a light?"

"No, I don't."

His eyes widened as if somebody was coming up behind me. I turned around and saw three guys with chains. One tried to hit me, so I grabbed a knife out of my socks and threw it, hitting him in the chest. Then another guy ran toward me. I grabbed his arm and put a hold on him and he passed out. One guy was left. He took off running. I grabbed the guy who'd asked for a light and took him into the restaurant. As we approached the door, a man stopped us.

He told me my friend couldn't go in because of the way he was dressed. I pulled out my gun and pointed it at the man.

"He's going to stay with me and you're going to feed us."

"Call the cops and tell them we've got a guy here with a gun, that he's scaring off the customers!"

I slapped the guy and asked the man with me what he wanted to eat. He said I was in trouble and that more of his guys would be coming for me.

"Are you sure? One of your guys is dead. I don't think anybody is coming here."

Then the cops arrived. The deputy told me to drop my gun.

I dropped it and he told me I was under arrest. He let the other guy get away. While the officer was putting handcuffs on me, I fixed it so that he handcuffed the chair. Then I ran through the kitchen, out the back, and sneaked around to the front until I caught up with the guy. He saw me and ran faster. I ran after him and jumped on him, then put a hold on him and carried him to a hotel. I paid for a room, sat him in a chair, and tied him up. Then I slapped him.

He woke up and asked, "Do you know who I am?"

"No. I don't care who you are. You're going to give me the information I want, or I'll leave you here with the rats. You're going to cooperate, or I'll let the rats start nibbling on you. First question: do you know where Big Joe's warehouse is?"

"No. I don't who Big Joe is."

"You're a liar."

I grabbed his finger and bent it back until it snapped. He screamed.

"Now, I'm going to ask you again. Where is Big Joe's warehouse?"

"Okay, okay! It's about six miles from the outskirts of town. It's heavily guarded by ex-military men."

"I'm wanted by the cops, so thank you and goodbye."

"Wait! You're going to leave me here with the rats?"

"What rats? There no rats here in this room."

I left him there and went downstairs, telling the clerk to go upstairs and untie him. I left and walked about two miles, then pushed a button on my phone. The hotel exploded. Fire trucks, ambulances, and cops arrived at the scene.

I arrived back at my hotel. There were a lot of cops there, so I went around the back and went up the stairs. I heard some coming down the hall.

I found an unlocked room and stayed there until they left the third floor. Then I went to my room, grabbed my suitcase, and put a couple of my weapons together. I grabbed some clips and went out the window, down the ladder, and around the building. I saw a black Porsche 911. I hot-wired it, then took. I went toward the outskirts of town and went about six miles, but I didn't see the warehouse, so I went another quarter mile and found it in the woods. It was a big warehouse. I went further into the woods, parked, grabbed both of my weapons, and headed out on foot. I walked miles before I got to the back of the warehouse. When I got closer I jumped over the fence.

Meanwhile, back in Chicago, Beth was at a restaurant waiting on Elizabeth. She was supposed to be there at noon, and it was already 1:00 p.m. She was still getting ready. She'd just gotten out of the shower and was about to put her clothes on when she heard a noise. She put her house coat on and walked in the living room, where she saw a guy sitting on the couch.

"Who are you?" she asked.

He snapped his finger and three guys surrounded her.

"Don't fight us. Come peacefully or we'll take you by force."

She tried to run, but one guy grabbed her and another put something over her mouth.

She was knocked out, so one of the guys put her over his shoulder. They went to the airport and put her on a private jet with Big Joe. She had no clothes on except for her house coat. Her hands and legs were tied together. She woke up while they were in the air, headed to Alaska.

As Big Joe turned around in his chair, she said, "You're not getting away with this."

"I already have. Nobody knows where you are and this time you will not escape me."

"You're forgetting about Buddy."

"No, I'm not. Two guys are about go to jail for something they didn't, do and the lawyer is about to go to jail herself."

"What do you mean, she's going to jail?!"

It was time, so he called his men. "You know what you're supposed to do."

"Yes, sir."

They called the chief of police and told him what restaurant to go to and who had the drugs on them.

At the restaurant, the cops surrounded the place. The staff asked the police what was going on. The dogs sniffed the place, then two of them approached Beth barking and growling. The police asked her to stand up slowly. When she got up, a bag of some white substance fell out her coat pocket. The police picked the bag up and arrested Beth. Big Joe got a phone call. Elizabeth heard him say, "It's done."

Meanwhile, back in Alaska, I was at the window and heard some guys coming. I climbed a tree to hide. Putting a silencer on my weapon, I sat in the tree and saw four guys come out. I shot one guy in the head, but they don't know where I was, so they ran as I took each one out. Then I jumped out of the tree and went inside. I saw Bella through a window and knocked on the door. Then they saw me. I shot the doorknob and opened the door. They all hugged me, and Bella kissed me.

"I'm glad you came to get us."

"We've missed school, but we've got another chance next year."

"Let me ask you a question, Buddy."

"I know what you want to ask me, but you can ask it later. Right now, we're trying to get out of here. These guys have a military background, so they know how to shoot and fight. Let's get out of here. Stay close to me. James and Clay, y'all stay behind us. Here's a weapon for both of you. All the girls stay between me and Clay."

They did. We got closer to the fence and told them each to follow me over. We ran as close to the woods as we could. An alarm sounded. One of the guys called Big Joe.

"Sir?"

"Yes?"

"Some of the prisoners escaped."

"How?"

"One guy infiltrated our defenses. Some of the guys were killed."

"Don't worry about them, just make way for me. When we arrive in Alaska, come and pick us up in the limousine. Have a room ready for Miss Liz. Have everything done by the time we get there. We're going to have a feast. Make sure the scientist has the machine ready."

"Yes, sir. I'll tell them to get it ready."

"We should land in ten minutes. Call Chicago and tell Dusty to get Kendra. Then take the private jet and come to Alaska with her. I don't want anybody to follow them, so call him now." As they were getting ready to land at the airport, he got on the phone and called his warehouse. "Is the limousine at the airport?"

"They just left."

"We're about to land. I told you to tell them to have the limousine there before we arrived."

In Chicago, Beth asked for her phone call and called me.

"Hello?"

"Where are you?" she asked.

"Who is this?"

"It's Beth."

"Oh! How is everything?"

"I'm in jail, and Liz is missing. She was supposed to meet me at the restaurant, but she didn't show up."

"Why are you in jail?"

"Someone planted drugs on me. It must've been the guy who helped me with my coat. He must work for Big Joe. Big Joe must think we're getting closer to the truth and getting Shon and Cam free, so he had to throw a monkey wrench into my progress. I bet he's behind Liz going missing, too."

"As soon as we get back to the city we'll go to the airport. Most of us will go back to Hawaii and a couple of us will go to Chicago to help you get out of jail."

We got to the Porsche. Some of them got in and I told James, "Go to the airport and drop them off, then come back and pick up the rest of us."

"Okay."

James, Clay, Tammy, Jenny, and Stacie went first. That left me, Bella, and Angie in the woods until they got back. We sat in a little hut we found. When they got to the airport, the guy whose Porsche I'd stolen was there. He saw his car and ran over. James saw the guy running toward them and he took off.

As we waited for James to get back, Bella asked, "Are we going to date now?"

I told her I was dating somebody else.

"Who are you dating?"

"You know Duck's sister?"

"You mean you're dating Wendy?"

"Yes. I know she's two years younger than me. We started to date about a week ago. Didn't you say you wanted to date James?"

"Yes, but he told me he's still with Tammy."

"We can still have sex anytime you want."

"How about now? That's what we're going to do anyway."

"Have you heard anything about Shon and Cam?" Angie asked.

"They're still in jail, and now our lawyer is in jail. We have to go to Chicago to help them out."

"I'll go with you to Chicago," Bella said.

"Okay."

Then I heard a horn. I told them to stay put until I got back.

Angie asked Bella, "Why are you doing this? You're not giving us a chance to date Buddy."

"Why, do you want to date him?"

"Well, I was thinking about asking him to go out with me, but there's always something in the way. You and Stacie date Buddy more than me and Tammy, and we'd like to get a chance."

"Do you want to go with Buddy to Chicago?"

She said no.

"Well, you act like you're mad at me and Stacie."

"You don't understand. We're going to get Shon and Cam out of jail, then I want to be with Cam. It's all right, you can go."

"Okay."

"But when you get back, us girls are going to talk about who wants to be with who."

I hollered and said, "Come on!" James had arrived. I opened the car door and let the girls get in the back, then I got in the front seat with James. "Let's go!"

He took off before I could shut the door.

We got there in ten minutes, and the guy whose car I'd stolen was there with a gun pointed at my sister. I told James to get closer to him. James said, "No, he might shoot Jenny!"

"Well, do something!"

"I am doing something!"

"Just get closer without him shooting at Jenny."

I rolled the window down enough to shoot the gun out of his hand, then jumped out of the car. I jumped on him before he retrieved the gun, then pushed him down and grabbed his gun. I told him to stand up and get in his car. I left him some money for gas, then we went into the airport.

"Okay, this is what's going to happen," I said. "Bella and I are going to Chicago. The rest of y'all are going back to Hawaii."

"Okay."

"We meet y'all in Hawaii in a couple days."

As we headed inside, I saw Big Joe and Elizabeth. "Do y'all see who I see there? Big Joe. He's got Liz. I can't get to her without them seeing all of us, so just let them go by for now. There's Big Joe other's plane. You guys go on. Bella and I are going to take one of Big Joe's planes."

We waved goodbye to them, then sneaked outside and ran to the plane. I told Bella to stay put and I would return for her. Then I waited for my chance and snatched Elizabeth when Big Joe wasn't looking. I sent her to join the others in Hawaii. Then I went toward the cockpit. I pulled my gun and told the pilot to go or I would shoot him.

"You wouldn't shoot me," he said.

"Do you want to find out? Take us to the airport in Chicago."

"Tower, this is flight 3345, requesting permission to take off."

"That's a negative. Big Joe did not give me permission to let you take off."

"Sorry, I can't let you leave unless Big Joe gives the go ahead," the pilot said.

"That's okay. Get up."

I told him to get in a chair, then retrieved Bella and she tied the pilot up.

"I can fly, and I don't care what they said," I said. "Let me check everything. Okay, it's good. Now crank. Everything is good. Let's take off."

"Buddy, look!"

"Yes, I see what they're doing."

They were trying to block the runway.

I kept on going, then I got it up and we were up in the air.

"Chicago, here we come."

Big Joe told the tower, "Call the Chicago tower and tell them to let the plane land, but send some guys out there to get Buddy and Bella. Take them to the mansion."

"Okay."

When we got to Chicago, the tower said, "Flight 3345, you have permission to land."

"Roger that."

I landed, but saw some guys coming with guns, so I told Bella to go down the hatch. We climbed toward the landing gear, then I helped her get down.

"See that truck?" I said. "Let's get on it."

We rode until we got closer to the fence, then jumped off and climbed the fence. We heard dogs coming as I helped her down, then we ran to a car. We were lucky that one was unlocked. I hot-wired it and told her to get in. She buckled up and we took off to the police station. One inside, I asked the desk clerk, "Where do we go to visit prisoners?"

"What is their name?"

"Beth. She's a lawyer who was framed for drugs."

"Oh, you're talk about the lady we picked up from the restaurant."

"Yes, she's the one."

"Okay, follow me."

We followed him and he took us to her cell. A couple of girls had tried to stab her. I wanted to kill them. Then we approached the cell I told them, "If you touch her, you will pay. Just think about how somebody can slit your throat at night." They backed off and I asked the officer, "Is there any way I can get her out?"

"Let me talk to the judge."

He called the courthouse and asked for Judge Springfield.

"This is his assistant. May I help you?"

"This is Sergeant Henry Collion. Let me talk to Judge Springfield."

"Sir, you've got a phone call from the police department."

"Hello?" the judge said.

"Judge Springfield, this is Sergeant Collion. There's a guy here wondering if he can get the young lawyer out of jail."

"Why is she in jail?"

"She was caught with cocaine, a bag of it."

"Bring her here to the courthouse so I can talk to them."

"Okay, thanks."

"Goodbye."

"Okay, sir. The judge said to take her to the courthouse. You can go with her. He wants to talk to her."

"We'll meet you over there. How is the case going for those two guys with murder charges?"

"Those boys are going to fry."

We needed to get Shon and Cam out of jail. "Okay, let's go to the courthouse."

We went to the courthouse and up to Judge Springfield's office. He was on the third floor.

As we got off the elevator, we found Judge Springfield's office, opened the door, and sat down. The sergeant and Beth arrived, so the judge told us to come in his office. Bella and I went in and sat down. He asked us who we were.

"Have you ever heard of Fabulous 8?"

"Yes, my daughter loves their music."

"Bella and I are part of the group. Some of our friends are in jail for the murders of Claire and Sheila. They are part of the Fabulous 8 as well. How much is Beth's bond?"

"Half a million dollars."

"Wow, that's a lot for her. Give me two hours and I'll have the money."

I called the house in Hawaii and Wendy answered the phone.

"Hello?"

I told Wendy to check behind the horse in the picture in the kitchen. She went in the kitchen and said, "I see the picture."

"Look behind it. There's a safe."

"Yes."

"Okay, three to the right three times, then five to the left twice, then two to the right once. How much money is in there?"

"One hundred billion dollars."

"Get half a million out and deposit it in my account."

"Okay."

She hung up and got the money, got in the car, and drove to the bank to deposit it. Then she called me and said she'd done it.

I went to the bank and withdrew the money. Then I went to the courthouse and paid the bond. Beth got out of jail.

"Tell me where Liz went," I said. "Did she have some information?"

"Yes, she'd gone to the warehouse where the murders happened."

"We'll go there tomorrow. Go back to your hotel. I'm going back to the police department to talk to Shon and Cam. Let's go, Bella."

We returned to the police department. "Thanks for your help, Sergeant Collion. Can you take us to Shon and Cam's cell? We'd like to talk to them."

"Okay."

He took us to their cell. They were just sitting there.

"How is everything?" I asked.

"It would be nice if we could get out of here."

"We're trying to get y'all out of here. Just be patient."

"We haven't seen Beth in a while."

"She was put in jail. We think Liz found something to help y'all out of jail, but she was kidnapped before she could give the information to Beth. Big Joe took her. We'll go to the warehouse tomorrow with Beth. Now we've got to get a hotel room before there aren't any left."

Bella and I found a room at the hotel where Beth was staying. Once inside, we turned on the television and sat on the couch. Bella asked if I wanted something to drink.

"Why not? I wonder what we have here!"

She got off the couch and looked in the kitchen. "Well, I found some vodka."

"Okay, what else?"

"Hey, there's some orange juice."

"Good. Make us some screwdriver."

She did and brought me a glass.

"Is everybody jealous of you?" I asked. "If so, why?"

"Well, Angie said Stacie and I have dated you more than any of them. Of course, not your sister. But Angie and Tammy are jealous."

"I'm not the only guy here. There's James, Clay, Shon, and Cam."

"I've dated most of them, but they claim that every time you rescue me, we end up dating each other."

"Is that true?"

"Yes, it is. Every time you rescue me, we end up dating for a while. Except this time. You said you're dating Ashley's sister-in-law."

"Well, right now I'm here with you trying to get our friends out of jail for something they didn't do. We're friends right now, and I like that."

"We are always going to be friends."

After she brought me a screwdriver, I grabbed her by the hand and pulled her down beside me. "Why did you do that?" she asked.

"Let's talk."

We talked for a while, then she asked, "What about our future?"

I asked if she thought we'd get married in the future. She told me she didn't know.

"Okay. I think we will."

We drank our screwdrivers. We both had four and sat together on the couch watching a scary movie. I put my arms around her and during the movie she fell asleep, so I picked her up and put her in bed. I took off her clothes, wrapped her up, turned off the television, and went to bed.

Meanwhile, in California, Lynn and the others had not heard from the kidnapper. The chief of police, Sandy asked Lynn her how it happened.

"My fiancé was bringing her out while I brought the car to the front. When I was came back in, he was out cold on the floor and my daughter was gone. I asked him what happened and he told me somebody hit him on the head and took Kendra. She was gone. We looked everywhere for her. But he did get a phone call afterwards. I asked him who was it and he said nobody important. He went outside, and when he came back in he said he had to leave for Chicago for business. He didn't know when he'd be back. Something is fishy about this. I think he's got something to do with is."

"I think it's odd that he told you to get the car while he got Kendra," Aunt Louise said. "Your sister's husband was behaving oddly, too. I think they're both involved with this kidnapping."

"I think so, too, but we need more evidence on this," Sandy said. "Try to get more information so we can make an arrest. Right now we've got nothing. I can't help you if nobody knows who kidnapped her. I'm out of here, so if you get more information for me, I'll get my guys on it."

Lynn was crying, so Aunt Louise hugged her. "It'll be all right," she said.

"I can't believe my fiancé and brother-in-law could be responsible for this. Are you sure it was them?"

"I think so."

"When he comes back, I'll confront him and talk to my sister. Can you take me to Hollywood Boulevard? She lives on Lane Street."

"I know where that is. I lived a block from there."

"Okay, thanks."

They left the studio and went to Tammy's home.

Meanwhile, in Hawaii, Tammy and Stacie were heading to the beach. They asked everybody else if they wanted to go, but the others said they had things to do before going to the beach. Tammy said she'd heard of a Battle of the Bands competition in one month.

"Do you think I should sign us up, to show our fans we are still playing music?"

"What are y'all talking about?" Clay asked.

"We're talking about playing in the Battle of the Bands to see if we can beat some of these young people, since we're going to be the oldest group."

"That sounds like fun. Let's do it. What you think Buddy will say about it?"

"Let's ask him."

Clay called me. We were still sleeping. Bella said, "Buddy, your phone is ringing!"

I grabbed it and said, "Hello?"

"It's Clay. Did I wake you?"

"Yes. I was sleeping."

"Good."

"What's the matter?"

"Nothing. Tammy said she's going to enter us in the Battle of the Bands. It's one month from today."

"Okay, tell her to sign us up."

"We'll do it today. Good night."

I hung up and went back to bed. I snuggled up to Bella and put my arm around her. We woke up around 10:00 a.m. and took showers, then put our clothes on and left the hotel.

Clay and Tammy signed us up for Battle of the Bands. The guy in charge of the contest asked his workers who had written Fabulous 8 down.

"Two people showed up and put them down. I think they were in the band."

Meanwhile, in Chicago, we stopped at a restaurant and ate breakfast, meeting Beth there.

"The judge is giving us three days to clear Shon and Cam," Beth said.

"Where do you want us start?"

"Go to the warehouse and check for things the forensics team might've missed. Check everywhere and everything. Do you know what you'll need?"

"Yes, we've got it with us."

Bella and I headed towards Big Joe's warehouse. I noticed that we were being followed, but I didn't know who they were. They weren't Big Joe's men. I turned down a street and lost it, then we followed it. They knew we were following them, so they pulled over and we went on before they had a chance to follow us again.

We arrived at the warehouse and parked on the side. Nobody knew we were there. We went inside and checked for fingerprints, then checked everything else we needed to. It took us four hours to go over everything, but we got it done. Then we took it to get processed, gathering all the stuff and putting it in the car. As we were getting in, we saw somebody coming around the corner. It was the car that had followed us. We sat there. The car came up to us and the driver got out and walked toward us. I got my gun out of my holster and had it cocked.

The guy pulled his own gun out and said, "Let me see your hands!"

"Who are you?" I asked.

"FBI. We were sent here on a case. Big Joe's wife was helping us to get information on Big Joe. She had a lot of stuff on him. Until those two guys killed her, anyway."

"Those two guys were framed. We are here to prove it."

"Who are y'all?"

"My name is Buddy Smithisom, and this is Bella. We are part of Fabulous 8. We're also double agents. Why were you following us?"

"We were hoping you would lead us to some evidence that these two guys killed our informant. It would make our job easier."

"There's going to be no evidence on them."

"Why do you say that?"

"Those two guys are our friends, and they're part of Fabulous 8. They were here to find my sister and our other friend. They were framed because they were getting close. I can tell you who killed Sheila; it had to be her husband, Big Joe. So why don't you ask his men about the murder instead talking to us?"

I got out of the car and he patted me down and took my wallet. "Okay, you are who you say you are, but how about your friend in the car?"

I told Bella to get out of the car and come over beside me. "You can't touch her if your partner isn't a woman. You can't search her or pat her down. We know the rules. It has to be another female."

Bella went back toward the front of the car and the FBI agent told her to stop. I told Bella to get in the car and turn it on. He pulled out his gun and was going to shoot her. I struggled with him and he dropped it. Then I punched him in the stomach, pushed him, and jumped in the car. I hit the gas. He picked up his gun and shot me in the arm as we took off. He returned to his own car and they followed behind us. I took another road and we turned left into a yard. I got out of the car and wiped the road where we'd turned off.

We closed the fence and locked it. then waited until they passed through. We sat there quietly, and then for a few minutes after they were gone. We eased onto the road, then got on the highway. We went to the police station where the forensics team was to process the evidence. I asked the sergeant where the team was.

He pointed down the hall and said, "It's on your right. Today we only have one person in the office, and she is booked. Nobody else is coming to help her. You can ask her, though."

We went down the hall and knocked on the door. A woman was inside working. I cleared my throat and she looked up and recognized us. It was Jade. "Why did you leave me here?" she asked.

"We couldn't take you with us. We didn't even know we were going to Hawaii to finish school. All we were going to do was have a good Christmas holiday."

"Well, how can I help you?"

"We've got some evidence for you to process so we can give it to our lawyer to get out Shon and Cam out of jail."

"Oh, I've already got that done. They are innocent. How is Elizabeth?"

"She was kidnapped by Big Joe, but she's all right now. Whatever information she had never got to our lawyer."

Jade asked Bella to come and help her. Then she asked, "How about you and Buddy?"

"What do you mean?"

"Are you married?"

"No, none of us are married. We got too busy to get married."

"You mean James is available to date? I thought you and Buddy would already be married with kids."

"Nope. But Buddy might have a baby with another girl."

"Is he the only one like that?"

"As far as I know he is."

"Is it all right if I date him?"

"He can date any girl he wants."

"Thank you. Can you tell him that I'd like to see him?"

"How about I go get him and you can tell him yourself?"

"Okay."

Bella found me down the hall and said, "Come on."

We returned to the room and Bella went and sat down in the office. Jade my hand and asked, "Are you dating anyone?"

"I've got a girlfriend in Hawaii."

"Oh, Bella told me you weren't dating anyone right now."

"Well, we haven't been dating for about a week now."

"Oh. I was hoping we could go out."

"I can take you out tonight. What time do you want me to pick you up?"

"How about 7:00 p.m.?"

"That'll work all right. Here's the stuff you need."

We went in her office where Bella was. "I'll take you and Bella out, then after we do that, I'll take Bella back to the room and then I'll take you home."

"Okay. Sounds great."

Bella and I walked out of the office. "I think there's a position in forensics at home. I'm going to call Michael."

I called the college and asked Jenifer if she had Michael's number. Then Bella said, "I've got Michael's number! He's been trying to give me that job so we can be closer, but I turned him down."

"Okay then, give me the number."

"Here it is."

I dialed that number and Michael's wife answered the phone and said, "Who is this?"

"Buddy. Is Michael home?"

She told me yes, then I heard her say, "Hey, Michael, there's a guy on the phone! His name is Buddy."

"Okay, dear, I've got the phone." She hung up on her end.

"Michael, this Buddy Smithisom," I said.

"May I help you?"

"Do you still have a position open in forensics at the police department?"

"Yes. Why?"

"I know a woman who just started college and she's working at the police department in Chicago in forensics. She might be interested."

"It's third shift."

"Okay, that should work for her. I'll get back to you." Then I called Jackson and asked him about an apartment. "Hello, Jackson, is that you?"

"Who is this?"

"It's Buddy."

"Oh. What do you want?"

"I was wonder if you still had that apartment left?"

"Yes, I've got one."

"How much?"

"Two thousand dollars."

"Okay, we'll get it to you."

"It will be ready for you when you get here."

"Thank you. Goodbye."

Then I called Tammy. "Who is this?" she asked.

"It's Buddy."

"Oh. What do you need?"

"I need you or Clay to go to the safe at the house and get two thousand dollars. Go to Jackson and give it to him for an apartment. Make sure everything is done well."

Tammy hung up and I put my phone away, then Bella said we'd forgotten something. We got back out and went into the police station again. As we went through the door, our car blew up.

"What was that?" I looked out the door; our car was on fire.

The sergeant asked, "What happened? Did your car just blow up? What caused that?"

"I don't know."

Then returned to forensics and I called Jade. She came out and I asked if she had any more evidence.

"Yes, I'll go and get it." A few minutes later, she came back with the evidence. We didn't have a car any longer, so she gave me the keys to her car. "It's the red Ferrari," she said.

"Okay." I grabbed Bella by the hand and said, "Let's go. We can give this stuff to Beth to get Shon and Cam out of jail."

We walked outside and went to where all the employees parked. We found Jade's car when I pressed the key remote to unlock the door. I opened the door for Bella, then got in on the driver's side. We went to the courthouse on the other side of town. While we drove Bella called Beth and told her to meet us at the courthouse. We had the evidence. Beth said she was at the restaurant next to the courthouse. As we approached she said, "I think I see you. No, that's not you, unless you're in a red Ferrari."

"That's us. We see you."

"What happened to the other car?"

"It blew up. We'll tell you when we get there."

We parked and I helped Bella out of the car. We joined Beth and I told the ladies to link their arms with mine, with me in the middle. We went up to the third floor and went to the judge's chambers. His secretary was by the doorway. We told her we'd like to see the judge. She disappeared inside for a moment, then reappeared and said, "He will see you now."

We went in his chamber and gave him the evidence. "Here's the proof that they are innocent."

He looked at the evidence. "You're right. Okay, let me call the chief of police and have his guys bring Shon and Cam to my chambers."

"Thank you."

We waited until they brought them a few minutes later. I waited at the elevator until the door opened. Then I said, "It's good to be free. I know some people will be glad to see you two."

We walked into the judge's chambers and the judge said, "You two are free to go. Just sign this paperwork and get your things out of evidence."

Then they signed the paper and we left the courthouse. The guys were free men. We got in the Ferrari and I asked them where they wanted to go.

Meanwhile, in California, Lynn was talking to Tammy about her husband, Jason Ward, and Lynn's fiancé, Stephen Riggs. Lynn asked Tammy, "Did Jason say anything about having to go to Chicago?"

"No. He said we were going home, so we did. Oh, here he is now."

Jason entered the room.

"Jason, let me ask you a question," Lynn said. "Do you know what happened?"

"We left before he told you to go and get the car," Tammy said. "We heard him say he would get Kendra as we were heading out the door. You were behind us."

"Oh, that's right. I saw you two leaving in the car. Right after she was kidnapped and Stephen woke up, his phone rang. He went outside to answer it. Then five minutes later he came in and said he had to go to Chicago."

Lynn sat down on the couch. "I can't go home now. Can I stay with you guys?"

Tammy looked at Jason.

"Yes, you can," he said. "I think you need some protection."

"Wait a minute," Tammy said. "Don't you have Buddy Smithisom's number?"

"Yes."

"Call him tomorrow. Maybe you can stay with him for a while."

Then Shannon called. and Jason answered the phone.

"Hello?" Shannon said.

"Shannon, is that you?"

"Yes."

"How do you feel?"

"I'm doing fine. Bill took me to the doctor."

"How is Bill doing, and your daughters, Jessica and Pamela?"

"They are doing well. Doing good in school with their grades. Have you heard about that strip poker tournament in France? The pot is twenty-five million dollars. It only costs a thousand dollars to sign up it. Next week the big wheels are going to be there."

"Shannon said there's a strip poker tournament in France," Jason said. "The jackpot is twenty-five million dollars, and it only cost a thousand dollars to get in. All the big wheels will be there. She wants to know if y'all want to go."

"Tell her we'll let her know."

"Why don't you guys go and I'll stay here and watch for news about Kendra? I'll look for her myself."

"How about it, Lynn?"

"I don't know. I think I should stay here and wait on any information about my daughter."

"I'll tell you what," Jason said. "Once I hear anything, I'll call you and you can come back. By the time you come back, I'll have her for you. How about that?"

"Call Buddy," Lynn said. "He might be able to find some way to get her back. Once you get her, call me. I will be on the next plane back here."

"So you're going?"

"Yes, we're going. Tell Shannon that she and Missy should meet us in Los Angeles. Then we'll go to France."

Jason relayed the message and Shannon said, "Okay, Missy will come to my house. Then we can get on the plane to Los Angeles."

Back in Chicago, Bella, Shon, Cam, and I were heading back to the hotel. When we got there I opened the door for Bella and we went inside holding hands. I asked the clerk about another room. "We need it for two more days. Do you have a room on the fourth floor?

"Yes, we've got one."

"Okay, I'll take it."

I gave the key to Shon and Cam and told them it was their responsibility to bring it back when we left to go home. We all went to our rooms.

Bella and I sat on our couch and she put her tired legs on my lap. I rubbed them as she lay back. Then I rubbed her stomach and pulled her shirt off. I massaged her body while she was lying there, then I took off her bra and massaged her boobs. I massaged the rest of her body and she fell asleep. I watched television until it was time to pick Jade up from work. Bella was still buck naked on the couch from when I'd given her a massage, so I picked her up and put her in the bed. I kissed her sweet lips, then left and locked the door. I got on the elevator and there was a gorgeous girl there. She was by herself and wore a short dress. She didn't notice I was watching her. She had her hands all over herself and I realized she was playing with herself. Then the elevator stopped. We tried to get it going again, but it wouldn't budge. I told her my name. She said she knew what my name was.

I asked her name and she said it was Lauren. She even looked like my ex-girlfriend from school, but she was dead. I moved closer to her and we started kissing. My hands were all over body. I squeezed her boobs, then she unzipped my pants and we had sex in the elevator before it started working again. She was a hot chick. I made her holler as we had sex. I was still kissing her when the elevator finally came down. When the door opened we were still kissing. Her thong was on the floor. We didn't see it at first. It was hot pink.

The clerk told me, "Jade called and said she will be at the police department, that you were supposed to pick her up two hours ago."

"Okay." I went to the police department and Jade hollered at me for being late picking her up.

"I was stuck in an elevator for three hours. That's why I didn't make it. Plus my phone didn't have service. I was out of luck, but I'm here."

"Fine."

I took her home and we went upstairs to her apartment. Inside, she took her shoes off, then her shirt, then pulled down her skirt till it hit the floor. She looked at me, knowing it was making me hot.

"What's making you hot?" she asked.

"Just you taking your clothes off."

"What about if I do this?"

She unhooked her bra and moved to stand in front of me, pulled her thong off slowly. Her butt was in my face.

"Do that make you hot?" she asked.

I told her yes, then she went in her room.

"I'm leaving," I said. "I'll be back later to pick you up to go out."

"Okay, just lock the door. I'm getting in the shower."

I headed back to the hotel.

As I was leaving, two detectives went to the apartments. They wanted something from Jade. They left their badges in the car and put on ski masks so nobody could recognize them. One picked the lock on her door and they went in. They were looking for evidence on Big Joe. They ransacked her apartment, then heard her coming out of the shower. They hid and one watched her drying off. Then he ambushed her and threw her on the bed. The other held her down while the first got on top of her. They took turns on her, disguising their voices so she couldn't recognize them. One told her if she told anyone about it, she would die.

"That information you have on Big Joe, he wants you to get rid of it. If you give it to the cops, you will die. Wherever you go, he will know."

They tied her up and sneaked out again. When they reached their car, they took off their ski masks. One of Jade's next-door neighbors came into her apartment. She hollered for Jade, then went into her bedroom. She was tied to the bed. She untied her and hugged her. "It's all right."

Then Jade's best friend Jacqueline arrived and asked what had happened. Jade grabbed her house coat and put it around herself, then said, "Call Buddy and tell him not to pick me up. Tell him anything other than of the truth."

"Who's Buddy?" Jacqueline asked.

"You know, Buddy Smithisom."

"He's here and you didn't tell me?"

"This is the first time that I've seen you this week. If you would come over like you used to, you would have seen them."

"What you mean, 'them'?"

"Shon, Bella, and Cam."

"Oh, they're here, too?"

"Yes. I want you to call him now."

"What's his number?"

"Get my phone. The number's under Bella's name."

Jacqueline found Bella's name and dialed. I was getting off the elevator when Jade's name came up on my phone.

"Hey, girl, what do you need?"

"Buddy, this isn't Jade," a different voice said. "Do you know who I am?"

"No. Am I supposed to know you?"

"Who was Jade's best friend in school who loved to hang with Fabulous 8?"

"Jacqueline."

"Yep."

"I haven't seen you since we were in twelfth grade. You were in my class right before school let out for Christmas holiday. What's going on? How is Jade doing? Is she ready for our date tonight?"

"That what I'm calling you about. She said she won't be able to go on the date."

"What's going on? If she's canceling, why isn't she calling me herself? Something has to be wrong. I'll be there in thirty minutes with Bella."

I went in the room and told Bella to put on her shoes. "We're going over to Jade apartment. Something is wrong. Guess who I was just talking to?"

"Who?"

"Jacqueline."

We left and went to Jade's apartment. When we got there, there were cops everywhere. As we headed for the apartment, we asked some people standing outside what had happened.

"Jade's apartment got broken into."

"When?"

"Just now. She was in the shower. When she got out two guys ambushed her and threw her on the bed. She only had a towel around her."

We ran up the stairs to the apartment. I told Bella to go in and check on Jade. I spoke to one of the officers.

"What a mess," I said. "Looks like they were looking for something and couldn't find it."

Then we heard Jade coming out of the bathroom. I heard my name being called. I walked in the room and found Jade sitting on the bed. I asked her if she was all right.

"Yes, I'm all right."

I went over and put my arm around her.

She got up and moved.

"What happened? I want the truth," I said.

"When I got here she was buck naked on the bed," Jacqueline said. "I think she was raped. Go get Foxy Lutheran. She has the most experience on this kind of case."

"Okay."

I went outside and asked for Foxy.

"I'm here behind you."

I turned around and there was a woman with long legs, standing about six foot six inches, with long blonde hair and green eyes.

"Can you come in and check on Jade? I think she was raped."

"Then she needs to go to the hospital."

I went back inside.

"Bella, take her to hospital to get her checked out. I'm going to find out more information."

Bella and Jacqueline helped Jade down the stairs to the car.

Meanwhile, back in Hawaii, Clay and Tammy went to a club called Palanaki Nightlife. That was where the Battle of the Bands was going to take place. Clay and Tammy went inside. It was big. They walked over to the owner of the club, Mr. Pila Hailana, and asked about the lineup for the Battle of the Bands.

"Who's your group?" he asked.

"Fabulous 8!" Clay said.

"Wait a minute. Fabulous 8 signed up for this?"

"Yes, we did."

"Most of the battles are way younger than y'all, but if that's what you want, you're on the list. You'll be the last ones to sing. The group going before you guys will probably end up winning. I've heard they're good."

"What's the name of the group?"

"Gorgeous 5."

"I know them. What do you think will make them the winners? You have a beautiful club here. Is it named after someone? I've got a sister with that name."

"It was my wife's name. After she died of cancer, I bought this club and named it after her to represent what it means to my daughter. With this club, she's hoping she can get a shot at her dream."

"She can sing?" Tammy asked.

"Yes, she can sing really well. Do you guys want to hear her?"

"Sure. What's her name?"

"Kila. In English it's Jill."

He called Kila over. When Clay saw her, he fell in love. She had blonde hair and blue eyes and had a nine point five body. Then she got onstage. Clay and Tammy got on the stage with her. Tammy played the piano while Clay played the guitar. Kila told them what song she was going to sing. It was one of their songs. She started to sing and she was doing really well. A man sat down and listened to her, then he asked Mr. Hailana about her.

Mr. Hailana told the guy she was his daughter. Then the man asked about the couple playing with her.

"Oh, that's Kami and Kimo. They sure know the Fabulous 8 songs really well."

"I'll tell you who I am. My name is Steve Wright, and I'm a producer at Wright's Recording in New York. I find talent. I heard Fabulous 8 is going to be here to sing in the Battle of the Bands, as well as another group called Gorgeous 5. Wait a minute. Those two are part of Fabulous 8! That's Tammy and Clay! Well, I still want her."

"You still want my daughter?"

"Yes, sir, if she has any songs she can call her own."

"No, sir."

"How many songs does she need for you to sign her?" Clay asked.

"Just one."

"She will have it by the time you come back for the Battle of the Bands, which is next month. Unless you come back before that time."

Back in Chicago, Buddy was talking to the police about how the two guys had come in.

"Your fingerprints are the only ones we've found," Foxy said.

"You didn't find any on anything else?"

"No, but the door is the only place we found your fingerprints. They must've worn gloves…or you could've planned this."

"Why would I plan this?"

"Because she wouldn't sleep with you."

"That's wrong! She would've slept with me anytime, actually. I got her a job in Hawaii. I'll show you. I bet you I can get in your pants right now. If I win, you have to go out with me. If I lose, I'll give you fifty thousand dollars. That a deal?"

I started to sing to her. As I moved closer to her I put my hand under her shirt, then felt her boobs. Then I slowly put my hand down her pants. The next minute, we were on Jade's bed having sex.

She told me what time to pick her up.

I got off her and she finished her job. Then she took me to the hospital. We kissed when I got out. The nurse told me where to find Jade's room.

"The only fingerprints they found were mine, but they were on the door," I told them when I arrived. "These guys left no fingerprints anywhere."

"I want you to go to my home and look behind the picture of the cat," Jade said. "There's a safe. The combination is twenty-five right, six left, and thirty-two right. There's a tape. Get it and take it to the cops."

There was a guy outside of Jade's room who left when he heard me coming out to talk to the doctor. The guy called Big Joe and told him he knew where the tape was. Big Joe told the guy to destroy the tape.

"Actually, put a different tape in its place."

"Okay."

The guy left the hospital and went to Jade's apartment. He put on a police jacket and went in inside. After shutting the door, he found the picture of the cat and the safe behind it. He opened it and there was the tape. He took it and left a fake in its place, then closed the safe back and put the picture back like it was. Back in his car, he drove toward the lake and stopped on a bridge. He looked around to make sure no one was there, then tore up the tape and threw it in the lake. Then he got back in the car and went to the mansion.

I asked Bella to stay with Jade at the hospital. "I'm going to take care of stuff at Jade's apartment. Jacqueline, why don't you go back with us to Hawaii? You've got to tell us now because tomorrow we're leaving early in the morning. If you decide to go, let Bella know."

"Okay."

"I'll come back in a little while and tell you what time we're leaving."

I kissed Bella, then left and drove back to Jade's apartment. When I got there, one of the residents said, "There was a policeman here, but he didn't stay long. Maybe thirty minutes. He must have been checking on something."

"I've got to go in and get something for Jade."

"Okay. Tell her we miss her and we hope she gets better."

"I will. We're leaving tomorrow and she's going with us."

"Oh, you're going home?"

"Yes."

I went inside and found the picture of the cat with the safe behind it. Then I opened the safe and found the tape. I grabbed it and closed the safe back, put the picture of the cat back on the wall, then went to the door. Two guys were watching me when I came out. I had seen them before. They saw me come down the stairs, then we started fighting. They pulled their knives on me and one ran at me. I ducked under him, then came behind him and put him in a hold as I rammed the knife through his throat. The other guy ran, so I got in the car and went to the police station. I saw Sergeant Gibson and handed him the tape, saying, "It shows everything Big Joe has done."

He put it in the laptop and played it, but it showed nothing that dealt with the deaths. It was everything good Big Joe had done for the good city of Chicago.

"This doesn't have anything to do with the deaths. This just shows what he's done for our city. I'm sorry, but we can't arrest him."

"Jade told me she had some stuff on him. I've got to tell her what I found."

I left and returned to the hospital.

As I was turning in the parking lot, I saw Big Joe's limousine. I parked and hurried inside. Jade was the only person in the room.

"Where are Bella and Jacqueline?"

"They walked out."

"That tape was a fake. Well, not quite a fake. It had all of Big Joe's good deeds on it."

"What do you mean?"

"I watched it. It showed nothing but good deeds."

"I know what I had. Somebody must have taken it. It had to be Big Joe's men."

"When I got there your next-door neighbor told me that an officer was there. She said he stayed about thirty minutes, then left before I pulled up."

Bella and Jacqueline came back to the room, then I left and walked down the hall. I saw Ashley in somebody's room. She grabbed her sword and I ran in the room while she was chopping someone up. Then she swung at me. I ducked and she threw a smoke bomb. When the smoke cleared, she was gone.

I tried to find Ashley. I looked out the window, but didn't spot her anywhere. One of the nurses was screaming as I ran back to the room where Ashely had been. Bella and Jacqueline joined me.

"Who is this?" I asked, meaning the body on the bed. They told me it was Senator Kathy Regin from Illinois. "Why would anybody kill her?"

"I don't know. She was supposed to have surgery on her heart."

"I need to find out any information."

"Buddy, be careful."

"I will. We're leaving tomorrow. Do you have an answer, Jacqueline?"

"Yes, I'm going."

"Okay, I've already got everything. All we've got to do is go to the airport. Our personal pilot will be there at 12:00 p.m. They've got everything ready at our house. Bella, you call Tammy and tell her what we need. I'm going back to the hotel. I need you to stay here, Bella. Do you want me to take you home, Jacqueline?"

"Yes, if you don't mind."

"I don't. That way, I can see your family, who I haven't seen in a long time."

"Okay."

We went out to the parking lot and I noticed a car had two guys in it. They'd just gotten there. I called Bella and said, "Watch out for any suspicious guys in the hospital. They might come after you two. If you see them, call me."

"Okay."

We hung up and I left the parking lot.

I asked Jacqueline if she lived at the same house she had in high school. She told me yes, so I took her home. She told me to come in, so I got out the car. Her two sisters asked her who I was.

"You guys were little babies when he was here in Chicago. You remember my brother, Sammie? He was in eighth grade when you were in twelfth grade. Now he's in eleventh grade, and he broke James's records as a quarterback. He's the best pitcher we've got. Come on in."

I walked in and her mother said, "What did we tell you about bringing boys in the house?"

"Mrs. Titus, you don't remember me," I said.

"No. Was I supposed to?"

"Your son should, too."

"I don't remember you at all."

"Mom, this is Buddy Smithisom. You remember, part of Fabulous 8? Their parents got killed two years ago."

"Wait a minute. Not the linebacker who hurt that quarterback in the state championship?" Sammie said.

"Yes, the same."

"Oh, wow. It's been a long time."

"You know, Mom, he's the one who dated Emily."

"Well, I'll be. It's been a long time. How are your mom and dad?"

"They've been dead for about two years now."

"Oh! Jacqueline just said that. I'm so sorry."

"Where is Emily?"

"She married a doctor in Texas and has two boys."

"Where is your dad?"

"Still working at the radio station. He's in charge of the station now."

"Mrs. Titus, your daughter has an opportunity to go to college and make something of her life. I asked her if she wanted to go with us to Hawaii and she told me yes. I'll come pick her up tomorrow morning around 10:00 a.m."

I left after that and returned to the hotel. Once there, I went to room 423. As I knocked on the door, a young lady came out her room and said, "They're not there."

"Where are they?"

"Room 419. They're with three girls from a modeling agency."

"Thank you."

I went to the room 419 and knocked. One of the girls opened the door. She was a redhead with blue eyes.

"Are there two guys here?" I asked.

"Yes. Come on in."

I went in and saw the other two girls. One was black haired with green eyes, and the other had blonde hair and blue eyes. One girl's name was Rhonda, and the blonde was Becky. The redhead was Jessica. Shon and Cam were inside as well.

"Shon, we're leaving tomorrow morning for Hawaii," I said.

Jessica said she was born and raised in Hawaii.

"So you're Hawaiian?"

"Yes, I am."

"Where were you born?"

"Honolulu. My name in Hawaiian is Iekika Onakea. My father is the chief of the police in Honolulu. We've been traveling for a while."

We sat at their table and I sat between Jessica and Rhonda. Shon sat between Rhonda and Becky and Cam sat between Becky and Jessica.

"Do y'all want to play strip poker?" I asked.

"I don't know if they want to play strip poker," Shon and Cam said.

I asked the girls and they told me yes, so the first thing we did was take our shoes off. I took the cards and dealt out five-card stud, and Cam won the first hand. I took off my shirt. Shon did, too. The three girls took off their pants. Then it was Rhonda's turn to deal. Cam won again, so Shon and I took our pants off and the girls took off their shirts. We were all half naked except for Cam. Then it was Shon's turn to deal. He won that hand. I took off my boxers and Cam took off his shirt. Two of the girls took off their bras and the other took off her thong. I dealt the cards since I was out of the game, and Shon won again. Cam took off his pants and the two girls who'd taken off their bras took off their thongs. The other girl took off her bra. I grabbed Jessica and we went in her room and had a lot of sex. Then I put my clothes back on and went to my room. I told Jessica to come room to 321 at about 11:00 p.m.

"Okay," she said.

I returned to my room and noticed the door had been broken into. I slowly opened the door and rolled in the room, but I didn't see anybody, so I checked the whole room and found nothing missing. I still wondered why somebody had broken into our room, but hadn't taken anything. I looked around one more time to make sure, then found wire going toward the cabinets. It looked like explosives attached at the end and inside the cabinet door, so I followed the wire till it reached the door to the bathroom. It was attached to some C-4. I left the room and went downstairs to the lobby.

When I got there I told the desk clerk, "Call 911. There's a bomb. I'm going back up to the sixth floor to evacuate people. When they come down, make sure they leave the building."

The desk clerk called 911 and told them about the C-4. I went back upstairs and went from room to room, telling everybody, "There's a bomb! Go downstairs now! Do not stop. Take the stairs if you can. Those who are old or crippled, take the elevator, but do not rush. Take your time so nobody falls and get hurts."

I repeated the message on every floor, then heard the siren.

I went back in one more time to make sure nobody was in there, then came back out and saw the chief of police, Sergeant Richard Reins. He was the one in charge of the bomb squad. He asked what was going on.

"Come with me," I said.

"Just tell me what room it's in and I'll send my guys up there. Have to be careful."

"It's in room 321. Go to the bathroom. You'll see where the C-4 is. Then follow the wire to the cabinets. The door was shut."

"Okay, John, Kevin, and Steve, I want y'all three go to the room 321 and check it out, then report to me what you need."

They went up to the third floor. Once inside, Steve went to the bathroom and saw the wire. He snipped it, defusing the C-4, and then they followed the wire to the kitchen up to the cabinet door. They slowly opened it. There was a timer on it.

"Can you get what's his name?" he asked.

"Who?" Richard asked.

"Buddy. Tell him to come up."

"You know we can't let him go up here."

"If he doesn't come up, the three of us will die."

They came down to get me.

"Okay, Buddy, put this vest on. Now go up to your room."

I returned to the room and found Steve. "Look at the bomb. Do you know those girls?"

It had a film of Bella and Jade at the hospital on it.

"They're my friends. I need some patrol at the hospital now."

Steve called his sergeant. "We need some cops at Wayme hospital."

Richard got one of his sergeants to get four patrol cars to the hospital. "Which one, Richard?"

"Wayme."

"Who are the people?"

"It's two women. Y'all know one, Jade, and Buddy's wife, Bella."

"She's not my wife yet. We just live together."

"Oh, okay. What do you think about this bomb?"

"I say cut the red wire and let it come off the door now."

Steve snipped the red wire. It turned off, then when they took it off the door another timer started. We had twenty minutes to get it to the disposal can, which was in the truck. Steve told Richard to get the disposal can. We headed out of the room and took the elevator to the lobby. As we were getting ready to get out of the elevator we saw a guy in the corner balled up. Steve went outside while I approached the guy. When I got closer to him, he jumped up and had a gun pointed at me. He told me to move upstairs and put the gun at my back.

"Where's Buddy?" Shon asked Steve.

"He was coming out with us. There was a guy balled up on the floor and I think he went to check on him. That was the last time I saw him."

As I went upstairs, I tried to think of a way I could get the guy before he shot me. We made it to the sixth floor and he told me to go to the roof. He opened the door and told me to go first. We walked toward the edge of the roof and he told me, "Now take off your shoes and socks, then your shirt and pants."

Then he told me to get on the edge, so I did. When I looked down, I saw Ashley. "I'm sorry." As the guy pulled the trigger, I turned a flip and kicked the gun out his hand. Then we started fighting. We were pretty evenly matched, but I subdued him at last.

"Now tell me who you're working for."

"You should know."

"I suspect it's Big Joe."

"I know you saw your friend, but you will never get her back."

"We *will* get her back."

We were fighting again, then he threw some smoke bombs and disappeared, so I grabbed my clothes and went inside.

I returned to the third floor and when the elevator door opened I checked to make sure no little kids were in the hall. The only person there was the pretty girl I'd met in the elevator before. She saw me and said, "Wait a minute. I know you."

"Yes."

I grabbed her by hand and unlocked the door to my room, then we went in. I kissed her and grabbed her boobs, then put my hand down her panties. I was making her hot. I pulled her panties off and we had sex on the couch for about three hours. Then we got up and took a shower together. While we were in the shower we had sex again, then she got out and got ready. I asked her where she was going. She told me she had to go back to her room with her husband. Then somebody knocked on my door. I told her to answer it while I put my clothes on.

"Who is it?" she called through the door.

"I'm a close friend of Buddy's. Is he here?"

"Yes. May I ask who's speaking?"

"Tell him it's John Fargo."

"Okay, I'll tell him." She returned to the bathroom and said, "It's a guy named John Fargo."

"Oh, let him in."

She went to the door and let him in. Her husband saw her in my room. She quickly closed the door before he made it, but he knocked and called her name.

"Lauren! Lauren, I know you're in there. You better open this door before I break it down."

I grabbed my gun and went to the door. When I opened it, I pulled my gun on her husband.

"You better get that gun out of my face," he said.

He tried to take my gun, but I grabbed him by the arm and had him in an arm bar against the door. "Get out of here or I will do more than that," I said. Then I turned him loose and told him to leave.

"I came to get my wife."

I kissed her in front of her husband, then she left with him.

And now back to business. "Okay, have you found out who broke into Jade's apartment?"

"No. They must've worn gloves."

"Yes, I think so, too."

"We need to find out why they tried to hurt Jade. She must know a lot of things that are making her attackers nervous."

"Okay, keep going. If you find any more information, just fax it to me or call me. If you get a chance to come to Hawaii, let me know."

"When are you supposed to go back to Hawaii?"

"Tomorrow morning."

"Goodbye, then. Until next time."

I looked at the clock. It was getting close to 6:00 p.m. I had to pick up Foxy at 6:30 p.m., so I grabbed my stuff, brushed my teeth, and combed my hair, then put on my socks and shoes. As I got done tying my shoes the phone rang. It was Foxy. She sounded scared. I asked her what was wrong.

"Nothing. I can take care of it. You don't have to come."

"Are you sure?"

"Yes, I'm sure."

"Okay. If you need me for anything just call me and I will be there."

I turned on the television and watched for a while until Jessica got there.

"How was your date?" she asked.

"It was canceled at the last minute. I think she's in trouble. That person might be at her house."

"What are you going to do about it?"

"She told me not to come, so what can I do?"

"I can go with you to her house to check on her if you want me to."

"All right. We'll go see if she's all right, then come back to the room."

She asked if I knew where she lived.

"Near the hospital."

Bella was watching television when there were gunshots in the hospital. Some nurses were shot. They told Bella, "There are four guys coming for you. They called you two by your names. You two need to hide."

"I'll call Buddy."

She called me as Jessica and I left the room and headed to the elevator. I answered and Bella was crying. I told her to calm down and tell me what was going on.

"There four guys coming after us. They've already killed a lot of people."

"I will be there in fifteen minutes."

I got in the elevator, but I noticed that while I was on the phone, Jessica was also on the phone. Then she took the stairs while I took the elevator. The elevator stopped and started going back up, so I opened the little trap door and climbed up by using my bionic arms. I went to the floor and took the stairs to the lobby, then ran to the parking lot. I figured they must have put a bomb on my car, so I ran until I found a Lamborghini. I hot-wired it drove it to the hospital.

When I arrived, I ran through the emergency room and saw a lot of dead bodies. Then Jessica called me and asked where I was.

"Why do you want to know? You're working for Big Joe or one of the big guns from the Bahamas."

"We will find you, and we are going to get rid of the Fabulous 8. You killed my brother and father."

"Wait a minute. Fabulous 8 hasn't killed anybody, unless they threatened us or our families."

"Do you remember when six of you were in Miami and you put a vest with a bomb strapped on it onto one of the guards as they climbed the wall? My brother and father were the guards up there when the bomb blew up. It killed both of them. After that, I made a vow that I would get my revenge on Fabulous 8, starting with the leader then on down. All I had to do was get you one-on-one, and I would have had you, too. I sent some men to Hawaii to take care of James, Tammy, Stacie, Clay, your sisters, and Angie."

"I'm sorry about your family. You can blame Derek for that. All he had to do was turn them loose. None of this would have happened. I'm sorry of your loss, but that doesn't give you the right to destroy people."

I hung up on her and went to the elevator, but there were dead bodies in it, so I took the stairs and went up to the third floor. Then I heard gunshots.

I saw two of the guys going toward the last room down the hall, so I ran down another hall and circled back to the first room. I threw something down the hall as a distraction. They heard it and came back. I saw them coming. As one went by me, I grabbed him. The other turned around and shot at me. I used the first guy as a shield, then returned fire and killed the second guy. The first was dead, so I dropped him.

"Bella!" I yelled.

She heard me, but didn't answer. I went behind the next two guys, sneaking up on one and cutting his throat. There was only one guy left.

I went to another room and found Bella standing there. I grabbed her and held her. She told me she was too scared to do anything. "We've got to get out of here. We'll leave tonight and go back home. Remember that girl, Jessica?"

"No, I don't remember a Jessica."

"Do you remember when you were trying to escape from Derek's place? When Shon put that vest on one of his guards and you guys climbed that wall and knocked those two guards out? By the time you got to the boat the wall blew up. Well, I met this girl named Jessica and those two guards were her father and brother. She wants to make sure we all pay for it. That's why those four guys are here. She's working with one of the big bosses. You know they all want us dead. Big Joe still has that big missile that any country would like to get their hands on, and he will give it to the highest bidder. We'll need to get on soon, but right now we need to get out of here. There's one more guy somewhere out there, so stay here."

I went out first and heard a noise, so I went to investigate. The guy came up behind and stabbed me in the back, so I turned around and hit him. We fought. He pushed the knife deeper into my back. I flipped him over my back, then grabbed him and broke his neck. Then I hollered to Bella and told her to come out with Jade. She came out alone. I asked her where Jade was and she told me she was dead. She'd been shot three times. I called James and Tammy answered the phone.

"Get Larry to get the plane ready now and come and pick us up tonight," I said.

"I thought you guys were coming home tomorrow."

"No, we're coming home tonight. Have the limousine pick us up."

"Okay, I'll tell him. About what time are you expecting to be here?"

"Tell him to be at the Chicago airport at 7:00 p.m. We'll be there around that time, so he needs to be there."

"Okay, I'll tell him and the others. Where do you want to meet?"

"How about at my house?"

"Okay. That way we can all stay there tonight."

Then she asked about her sister.

"She's doing good. She's right behind me. We were bringing a surprise, but now our plan has changed. We'll tell you all about it when we get home."

"Okay. See when all you get home."

"Bye. Love y'all."

I hung up the phone and we ran downstairs. "Stay here and let me check everything, all right?" I said. I looked outside and it looked like the coast was clear, so I motioned Bella to come on, telling her to stay low.

"What car are we going to?" she asked.

"I took a Lamborghini, that red one. When I tell you to go, I want you to run as fast as you can. When I say three, you run. Okay. One, two, three!"

She ran as fast as she could and I ran behind her. We made it to the car. I turned it on and drove off.

"Where are we going?" she asked.

"To Jacqueline's house to pick her up. Then we're going back to the hotel to get Shon and Cam. We'll grab our things and head to the airport. We're leaving tonight. There should be a plane here by 7:00 p.m."

"You mean, we should be home tonight in our own bed?"

"Yes, that's what I'm saying. Are you ready to go home?"

"We were supposed to go home tomorrow. What makes you want to go home tonight?"

"It's getting too dangerous for us here, as you saw in the hospital."

"Okay."

We arrived at Jacqueline's house and I parked and we went to the door.

"Hey, it's Buddy!" I called as I knocked.

Jacqueline opened the door and asked, "Where is Jade?"

"She's dead."

"No, she's not."

"Yes. Four guys shot up the hospital. A lot of people were killed, and she got shot three times."

Jade ran at Bella, but I caught her. "It's not Bella's fault. She did the best she could. I couldn't even find the guys at first. Somehow three bullets hit her. Bella was in front of her and didn't find out she was hit until after I came in. I killed all four of the guys."

"Why did you come here?"

"To see if you're still going with us."

"No, I've changed my mind. I'm going to stay here and fight for Jade. She died fighting for justice, so I'm going to stay and fight for justice, too. Plus, my family needs me."

Bella and I got back in the car and drove to the hotel to pick up Shon and Cam.

In the lobby, Bella heard the clerk calling Jessica on the phone. She grabbed the knife out of my pocket and threw it at him. The knife hit him in the throat, killing him instantly, so we took the stairs and went to the fourth floor. We knocked on the door, but nobody answered, so I busted down the door. Shon and Cam were tied up with a bomb hooked to them. I checked the bomb out. "It looks like the bomb you had on you, Shon."

"It's similar."

"Okay, there's the red wire." I cut it, then unhooked the bomb and Bella untied them. I set the timer to explode in ten minutes so we had time to leave by going to the roof and jumping to the other building. I looked out the door. "The coast is clear. I want Shon to go first, then Bella, then you, Cam. I'll go last. I've got to do things. From the roof, jump to the other building. I'll be right behind you. Now go."

I went to the next room over and turned on the gas to the stove, then ran up the stairs to the roof. They were jumping to the other building and I was right behind them. One of Big Joe's men shot me while I was in the air. I bell between the two buildings, but Cam jumped off the roof and caught me. We were waited for Bella and Shon to come down. Cam put me over his shoulder and we went to the front and found them. All of us ran to the car. Bella and I got in the back.

Meanwhile, Tammy called Larry and asked him if he was ready to go to the airport.

"You've got to be there at 7:00 p.m. I will get James to take you to the airport so you can get the plane ready. The rest of us will go to Buddy and Bella's house and have it ready for them to be there."

"Okay."

"Let's do this. Our friends will be home soon."

James took Larry to the airport and told him to be careful. Larry went to the hangar and saw somebody messing with the plane. A guy appeared behind Larry and cut his throat. Then they replaced him with one of their guys.

"Do not do anything until you come back. You'll meet up with some of the other guys, then you'll follow the limousine to Buddy and Bella's house. There, you'll kill all of the guys. When it's done, bring all of the women to me. Then I want you to send all the guys' heads to Big Joe to let him know there is going to be a new head man around here. Our names are Eric and Philip. Our family is from Spain, and our father's family name is Baez. We are coming to America to take over all the mafias and to rule over Spain and America. We will be the biggest bosses and everybody will look to us. We will rule over all of them when we get the Fabulous 8 out of the way. We can take over the whole world."

"Okay."

"You and the rest can stay at the airport. I want you to kill Jarez when everything is done."

"Okay."

"I want you to bring the girls to my house in Spain after you send the Fabulous 8 guys' heads to Big Joe."

"Okay, I will do it."

"When he gets back, wait until you get to their house. Then kill him along with the others."

"Okay, sir."

Eric and Philip got in the limousine and went to their private jet.

Back in Chicago, Shon drove us to the airport.

"There's Larry!"

We got out of the car and they helped me to the plane. Then I saw the pilot's face.

"This is our plane, but that's not Larry," I told Cam. "We need to take over the plane. Tell him you'll be his copilot and distract him while I call James and get him to meet us on one of the other islands."

I called James and Tammy answered the phone. I told her to tell James to meet us at one of the islands, then to tell Clay to go up to the roof and keep a look out until we got there.

"Okay, I'll tell them."

"Something is wrong. Larry didn't pick us up, some other guy did. I'm going to get Cam to fly us home. Tell James I will call him when I want him to pick us up in the Hummer. Tell him to wear some protective armor, and I want you to put the bulletproof walls up around the house."

"Okay."

"Bella, tell Tammy the other part of the code so that she can put it in."

"Okay, sis, here it is." She gave her the code.

Tammy repeated it back.

"Yes, that's it. When James leaves and Clay goes to the roof, put that in and push the green button."

"Okay, got it."

We hung up with each other and I told Shon, "Grab him and bring him to us. Tie his hands and take everything out of his pockets."

After he'd done that, I asked the guy, "Who are you, and what did you do with our pilot?"

"You will all die. We're the people you don't want to mess with. We are dangerous."

"*We* are the people you don't want to mess with," I responded. "Why do you think a lot of the mafia want us dead? Because we cause problems for them. Now tell us who are you and who your boss is. Where is our pilot?" He was silent. "Well, since you don't want to tell us, okay. Bella, enter all his information in the police station computer and work your magic."

She worked on the computer and found out that he worked for the mafia in Spain. The heads of the group were Eric and Philip. They were cousins. They'd taken over when their dads died. They were trying to take over the world. They'd come to America and had just left today to go back to Spain. They had people in America who would do anything to destroy the Fabulous 8.

"We need to be careful who we let to do things with us," Bella said. "That's all the information we've got."

"Okay."

"Let me do some things to him."

"Okay. He's all yours, dear."

She grabbed him and was about to break his arm when I stopped her. "Are you going to talk to us, or do you want me let her finish what she was about to start?" I asked him.

"No, I'll talk now."

"Tell me what you were supposed to do when we get home."

"I was supposed to meet up with the other guys and follow the limousine to your house. Then we were going to kill all the guys and take the girls back to Spain. We'd take the guys' heads to Big Joe."

"Cam, how far are we from Hawaii?"

"About ten minutes out."

"I'm going to call James and tell him to meet us at the airport."

I called James and asked him where he was. He told me he was at the other island.

"Change of plans. Leave from there and meet us at the airport. Be ready for anything."

"Okay."

"There are people out to kill us, so be careful."

"Okay."

We hung up with each other.

"Keep him tied up until we land. Then let him go and move quickly toward James. We need to lose them so we can get to the house and fight."

"Okay."

"You know what to do?"

"Yes. Once we land, us three will go and get James to come closer, then you'll untie his ropes and leave the plane. You'll run and jump in the window."

"It doesn't matter who sits in front. As long as I've got a window, I can jump in."

"Okay."

"Everybody in your seats. We are about to land, and I see James. He is in the helicopter. If he can get close, we can pull you in."

"Okay."

"Hold on. Here we go."

Cam landed the plane with no issue.

"Good landing, Cam. Let's go, let's go!"

Bella, Shon, and Cam ran out of the plane toward James. They told James to go. Bella got up front and they took off while I untied the guy and ran out. As I left I shot the gas tank. The plane exploded as I ran. I jumped and caught the bar, then Shon and Cam helped me get inside.

"Let's get out of here, James."

"Okay, hang on."

"How is everything at our house?

"The shield is up. The limousine should be there by now."

"There's a new mafia that wants us gone. They want to take over America, so they are worse than Big Joe. They want to make him look bad. Watch out for anybody suspicious. They are all bad. Home sweet home! There she is down below. Bella, you're the only one who can open a hole for a helicopter to fit through. This will be the first time we try this, so here we go. Bella, say the words."

"Okay, here it goes. Lima, lima, look out!" Slowly, the shield made a hole big enough for a helicopter to fit through.

"Easy, James. Steady. Okay, we're through now. You can close it, Bella."

"Close," she said, and it closed.

We got out of the helicopter and walked into the house.

We hugged everybody. "We've got everybody here! No one goes home until I say you can. We are in danger. So long as we are all together, we are safe. Everybody, go to the living room."

"Okay."

"Get Clay down from the lookout while we take a shower. The rest of y'all get the sleeping arrangements ready."

Bella and I went to our bedroom and got in the shower. As she got out, I got in. Then she went to the bedroom and got my clothes out and set them on the bed. She came back in the bathroom when I got out of the shower and gave me a towel, then put her stuff on as I blow-dried my hair and dried the rest of my body. Then I put on deodorant, brushed my teeth, and combed my hair while Bella brushed her long, beautiful hair. Then I went to the bedroom and put on my clothes. We went down the stairs to the living room.

"Everyone here? There's Cam. Okay, our names are going to change to our Hawaiian name."

"Okay."

"Bella, your name is Palanaki."

"Okay."

"Tammy, yours is Kami. Stacie, yours is Kaki. Angie, yours is Anie. And, Jenny, your name is Kimi."

"Okay."

"Everybody, learn your names. Now the rest of us. My name will be Puki. James, yours is Kimo. Clay, your name is Kalai. Cam's name is Kama. Shon's name is Kana. Those are our names while we're here. Elizabeth's will be Elikapeka, and some of us will need to change our hair color."

"Okay."

"Palanaki, your hair color will stay the same. I want both my sisters' hair colors to change, and I want Kana's to change as well. If any of you need to go somewhere, at least three people will go. I don't want to take a chance on anybody getting kidnapped or killed. Y'all need to be careful. Tomorrow we'll all go to the beach. We're going to have fun. We'll put on a concert tomorrow night. I'm going to get our own bodyguards for the concert. That way, we can forget about all these mafia people trying to kill us, because *we* are their biggest threat. We stay together. We can beat this, and we can do other things like we normally do. We might need to take a trip to Paris, France. That way we can enjoy ourselves."

"Okay."

"And we are grilling out. I want you to call Wendy and tell her I'm going to break up with her."

"Why are you going do that?"

"Because I don't want her to get into this mess."

"What, she loves you and still wants to be with you, and you're going to turn her down?"

"Yes. Plus, we've got to go to France. I got a phone call from the agency. They want me to meet with a French double agent about a matter dealing with several missiles that we have. That's why I said we're all going to France. The girl has a photo shoot, and you guys are going to be the escort. They will tell us when we're leaving. After the photo shoot is done, you guys will come back to Hawaii. I will stay in France to finish the mission. I'm going to bed. See y'all tomorrow."

I called Wendy and told her what I was going to do.

"Are you trying to break up with me?" she asked.

"That would be the best thing."

"I understand. I'll call my brothers and tell them what you did. I'll tell them you broke my heart. Are you willing to go through that?"

"Yes, I'm willing. Let me talk to Duck to see what he will say."

"Come on, Buddy, don't do that."

"Well, they might still get mad at me."

"Anyway, he's supposed to come home. His wife, Ashley, has been missing for a month."

"I know where she is, but there's no way anybody will ever get her back. That mind helmet has destroyed her mind."

"There might be a way. I can ask my mom and dad about a potion. After she drinks that, her youngest child can say something."

"I can get in touch with your brother to bring her back. We leave in three days. I've got couple of agents who can bring her home, and they are among the best in the FBI and CIA. I'll give them a call after I get off the phone with you."

"Okay. I love you. Come over to the house in the morning."

"Okay, I'll be there. Goodbye."

I hung up and called our friends in the FBI and CIA: Carl and Michael in the FBI, and Fritz and his sister, Donna, in the CIA. I called the FBI first and talked to Sheila. I asked her if Carl and Michael were free to go on a mission to Chicago to bring Ashley back to Hawaii. They would be working with the CIA.

"Yes, they will be free once they arrive here in in the office. They just got back from Florida."

"Okay, thank you."

We hung up and I called CIA office. I got the secretary and asked her, "Is the chief in?"

She told me he was gone for the day. "May I help you?"

"I was wondering if Fritz and Donna are free. There's a mission that the FBI might need them for. Not all the double agents are free and we need some CIA help."

"I'll call the chief and call you back tomorrow."

"Okay, bye."

We hung up and I climbed in bed with Palanaki. She was already asleep. I put my arm around her and went to sleep. At about 5:00 a.m. she kicked the covers off and she slept in her nightshirt. I moved closer to her and watched her sleep, then got up and went down to the kitchen. My sister was up and I asked her why she wasn't asleep. She asked me same thing.

"There are bad people who want us dead, and I broke up with Wendy because of you-know-who upstairs in bed."

"You're telling me you want Palanaki?"

"Yes, but I don't think she wants to date me. Also, I want to date Kami. That's why I want y'all back in Hawaii after the photo shoot. I'm risking all of our lives. It's part our job descriptions that it's going to be dangerous."

"Yes, I know it's part our job."

"But I really don't like it. All of us guys think the same, though everybody says I'm the boss. This is what we're going to do. We're going to make it official. We're going have a meeting after everybody gets up and eats. I am expecting a phone call from the CIA, so I'm going back upstairs to sleep. I'll see you when I come back down, sis."

I went upstairs and back to bed.

It was 5:45 a.m. when I crawled back in bed with Palanaki. She woke up when I jumped in bed. She asked why I was in bed, and I told her, "You were asleep when I came to bed. Then around 5:00 a.m. you kicked off the covers. I lay there and watched you sleep, then got up and went down to the kitchen. Kimi was fixing some coffee. I told her to fix me some, then she asked why I was down here. I told her I was worried about the people trying to kill us."

"What time is it?"

"It's 6:00 a.m."

"I'm getting up. Unless you have something in mind?"

"I've got plenty of reasons for you to stay in bed with me. That is, if you want to do it."

"I want to do it anytime and anywhere you want to."

We had sex for three hours.

We decided to get in the shower together. We were the only ones who had not dressed or eaten breakfast. I went downstairs with no clothes on and everyone was in the living room and saw me.

My sister hollered, "Puki, you need to put some clothes on before you come down here!"

"Okay, I'm going upstairs."

Palanaki was in the shower when I got to the bathroom and we washed each other. She got out before I did. She went to the bedroom and put our clothes out on the bed, then came back in the bathroom and gave me a towel. I dried off and combed my hair while she put her makeup on, then we brushed our teeth and put on deodorant. We went in the bedroom and put our clothes on, then we went downstairs and ate breakfast while the rest waited in the living room. We took our food to the living room, then Kimo asked me, "Why are you calling a meeting?"

"We are going to get stuff straight. Seems like everybody is putting me in charge, and I don't know why, so I'm going get us to vote on a top person. You all have paper and a pen in front of you. Everyone write who you want to be the boss. Take control. Okay?"

We voted and I put Kami down. She was better in a lot of situations than I was.

"Okay, start with Elikapeka. Who did you put?"

She said she put Puki.

"Okay, next is Palanaki. Who did you put?"

She told me she put Puki.

"Okay, that's two for Puki. Next is Kimo. Who did you put down?"

"I put down Kami."

"Okay, that means it's two to two, because I put her as well. Next is Kaki. Who did you put down?"

She told me she put Puki.

"Now it's Puki three, Kami two. Kama?"

He told me he put Kami. It was three to three.

"Well, we know what's going to happen. I'm going to win by one. I think it should be Kami, but she doesn't want it."

"Puki, you've got to do it. You are in charge because you know what has to be done."

"Now that that's over, I'll think about what we're going to do." I thought a moment, then said, "We'll all go to France for that photo shoot, then when that's over all of you are coming back here. At some point some of us should go to Chicago and help Kendra get back to her mother and aunts. Make sure when y'all get back here that you help as much as you can. Then I want Kami to sign us up for a cruise line to play for a couple nights. That way we can enjoy a cruise. Let's go to the beach! Then I'll come home later and start to grill out. Let's invite all our friends. I'm leave that to Kami."

"Okay."

"Everybody can go home tonight. I think everything will be all right. If you see anybody out of the ordinary, report it to me. That way I can consider our options. We've got two more days before we go to France."

"Okay."

After the others left, I spoke to Kami alone.

"You will be the only one knows this. If I'm not back in four days, take that trip without me. That means you will be in charge. If they ask you why, tell them I told you to do this and that I trust you to keep everybody safe. That's why I've decided you'll go back with them instead of staying with me. I don't need somebody else to get in trouble if there's trouble. We need somebody who can make stuff happen."

"Okay."

"Let's go to the beach."

As we were leaving, Wendy knocked on the door. I went over and let her in, but I noticed Palanaki was outside when I let her in. I was the last one to leave. Then Palanaki came back in and asked why Wendy was here.

"I told her to come over."

"I thought that you were going to break up with her."

"I tried to, but she was going to tell her brothers that I broke her heart."

"Well, what are you going to do?"

"What do you want me to do?"

"I want you to break up with her, and I want you to do it now."

"Why? Are you still in love with me, or do you not want anybody to date me? I thought you were dating Kimo. That's who you wanted to date. What happened there?"

"I decided not to date Kimo, so right now, I'm not dating anybody."

"Kimo and I are dating again," Kami said.

"Oh, okay. That's why you're not dating him. I'm not breaking up with Wendy. She will meet us in France, but she will go back with you guys."

"Okay."

"At the cookout, I will tell you guys some more things. Now y'all go have a good time."

Us guys were out there surfing and the girls had their bikinis on in the sun, just lying there as we all got dark like the natives. They were the gorgeous women. We stayed on the beach for about six hours, Kimo and I went back to the house to start the cookout. As we were going back, we talked. I asked him who was he dating. He told me he had planned to date Palanaki, but wasn't going to now. I asked him what had happened.

"I saw how she acted with you with Wendy," he said. "That what made me change my mind. She did ask me to go out with her."

"What did Kami say when you asked her out?"

"She told me yes. You know, I liked Wendy before you did, Puki."

"Well, do you want to date her? I can ask her if you want me to," I offered.

"No, I will."

"Okay."

"How about Kami?" I asked.

"Well, I can stay and date Kami, or I can move with Wendy."

"Wait a minute. You will leave Fabulous 8 just to be with Wendy?"

"If she wants me."

"Why do you want to do this?"

"Well, I want something different, actually," he confessed. "I like when we break into banks and houses and run away from the law."

"You like that better than what we're doing now?"

"Yes. I'm not the only person who wants to do that. I like it when we all travel and flee from the cops. We like stealing from the mafia and putting the money in the bank for us and our kids that we might decide to have one day. That way, they can enjoy their lives."

"Okay, we will talk about this during our cookout, but we have to exclude Wendy. Actually, why don't we talk about it after the cookout?"

"This is boring, this life we've got now. We are not people who sit on the beach. We are people who take from the mafia and run from the cops. That's who we are, Puki."

We got the grill going as the rest of Fabulous 8 came back from the beach with Elikapeka and Wendy.

"Puki, what are you going to tell Elikapeka?"

"I don't know. I guess we'll see what she wants to do, if see wants to go to school and remain a double agent."

"What are y'all talking about?" Palanaki asked.

"You will find out after we all eat."

"No, I want you to tell me now. What are y'all talking about?"

"Like I said, everybody will find out after we all eat."

"Okay, but I think you could tell me what you were talk about when we were coming up."

"Well, you're fixing to hear about it now. I've got everyone's attention. I'm leaving tomorrow to go to France. I'll leave a day ahead of you guys, and after you're done with the photo shoot, you'll leave to come back to Hawaii. If I'm not back in four days, you'll go on the cruise without me. I already told Kami that she's in charge when I'm gone."

"But that's not what you were talking about when we came up."

"Kimo and I were talking about the life we had before, when we used to steal things from the mafia. We were talking about going back to doing that. Why do we want to do that when we've got a good life here? Why do we want to go back to a life of crime, having the cops chasing us? We've been kidnapped before. That's not enough excitement. What does everybody think? Go back to how we used to be, or stay like we are? Show me hands for going back to the old days."

Nobody raised their hand. "Okay, it's official. We'll just keeping doing what we're doing."

I walked to Kimo alone and asked him why he didn't raise his hand. He told me Kami and Palanaki weren't going to raise their hands, but everybody else was going to.

"I heard them talk about it. We'll stay like we are in the life we've got now, which isn't bad. There is some excitement in what we do."

"Why do y'all want to go back to the old days?"

"We like when we run from the cops and drive different cars. But we won't force anybody to do what we want. We actually didn't want that kind of life starting off, but we had no choice in the matter."

"Let's just have fun for now and worry about the future later. Let's just enjoy it. I have to leave around 6:00 a.m., so all I want us to do is get ready to sing on the beach and for everybody to get their food."

I turned off the grill and we sat down and ate our food. We had one hour before we'd go down to the beach for our concert, which started at 8:00 p.m.

"How is everybody's food?"

Then I get a phone call from the CIA.

"Let me get this."

I walked toward the house and talked to the CIA boss, asking for Fritz and Donna for the case with Carl and Michael. They needed to be in Chicago tomorrow morning to meet them.

"They should be back from Iran tonight. I'll ask them to get on the plane first thing in the morning to Chicago."

"Thank you."

They would go there to bring Ashley back and locate Kendra. I knew Lynn, so if they knew where the girl was, I wanted them to tell our boss at the double agents' headquarters.

I hung up and put the phone in the house.

Then I returned to the beach and we got on the stage. I got on the keyboard, making sure the sound was good as the rest of the group was getting everything ready.

"Well, it's time, you guys."

Caleb announced us. "They need no introduction here. Here's the Fabulous 8." I spoke for a moment, then we started singing. Our concert raised over $5.5 million for the children's hospital in Waikiki. We sang twelve songs, then signed autographs. After that, we had a party and drank. At some point I walked off and headed to the house because I had to get up early in the morning. I told Palanaki that she could stay, then told her to wake me up when she came in the room.

I fell asleep around 1:00 a.m. Palanaki crawled in bed and put her arm around me, but she did not wake me up. I was really close to her. Then my alarm woke me and I got up. She was still sleeping. I took a shower. As I was getting ready in the bathroom, she woke up and said, "You weren't going to wake me up, were you?"

"No, not before I finished getting ready."

We had sex, then I put on my clothes.

She went downstairs and fixed my breakfast as I finished getting ready, then I came downstairs. She gave me my food and a cup of coffee. After I finished, I got up and kissed Palanaki and told her I'd see them when they got to Paris, which would be two days from now.

"Come later and pick up the Hummer. I will leave the keys in the locker. You have the key to it in your pocketbook."

"What do you mean, it's in my pocketbook?"

"I put it in there last night before I went to bed."

I kissed her again and drove to the airport.

I left the key in the locker, then got on a private plane. We took off at 6:00 a.m. It was about 5:00 p.m. when we landed in Paris, France, so I got out of the plane and told Jim to go back to Hawaii to pick up the rest.

"Yes, sir. As soon as I fuel up."

I got a taxi, left the airport, and got a hotel. I spoke in French to the desk clerk, then he told me I had a message to go to the big church down the street. I asked for directions to the church.

I walked about two miles down the street and I was followed by a terrorist group. I made it to the church and went in, hollering for the person I was supposed to meet. I looked everywhere, then heard a sound I didn't want to hear. It was a missile, and it was coming towards the church. I ran toward the window. As I was getting ready to jump through it, the missile exploded against the church and threw me out of the window. I landed against the opposite building and was knocked out cold. When I woke, I got up and saw a girl, then collapsed against her. She got her brother to carry me to their home. She, her father, and brother took care of me. I had amnesia and didn't know who I was. Her name was Celine.

I worked in France for nine months until my memory returned. Everybody was looking for me. Celine asked me to marry her and I told her yes. She wanted to go back to America.

"I can't let people know I'm alive."

We got married in Paris, France, and had our honeymoon there. I learned their culture and their ways. Even the double agent agency could not know about me being alive until I figured out who was behind the attack. When we got to America I could contact my leader and find out who knew where I was going. Hopefully, we could get back to Hawaii. That was where my friends still lived, but now that we'd gotten married, we'd have to live in some other place in Hawaii.

About the Author

Bennie Atkinson was born on January 29, 1967 in Lee County, a little town in Bishopville, South Carolina. His parents are Bennie and Diane Atkinson, and he has one brother and two sisters. He's the oldest. He went to Bishopville High School. He graduated in June of 1986 and joined the Navy in 1987. He was in Japan for two years and got to see other countries while he was in the Navy. He also got to go to Hawaii. During the other two years he was stationed in Long Beach, California. They gave him a choice, to resign or get out, so he chose to get out, but he joined the National Guard and did eighteen more years. He met his wife in 1991. They dated for a year and a half before they got married. They had some bad years and a lot of good years. This July they will be married for twenty-six years, and he loved every year. His wife's name is Tammy Gardner Atkinson. He worked at Roller Bearing in Hartsville, South Carolina for fourteen years. He worked in a lot of other places, but Roller Bearing was the job he worked the longest. The rest were only three to five years. He goes to church on Sunday morning and Sunday night. When he was little he went to a Holiness Church, but when his brother-in-law got killed, they started going to Gum Branch Baptist Church.

www.ingramcontent.com/pod-product-compliance
Lightning Source LLC
Chambersburg PA
CBHW032028310726
48972CB00002B/578

9 798889 389477